MAGIC IN BLOOD

MAYTÉ LOSADA

KWE PUBLISHING, LLC

Losada, Mayté. *Magic in Blood.*

Copyright © 2020 by Mayté Losada

All rights reserved.

ISBN (hardback): 978-1-950306-13-8 (ebook): 978-1-950306-14-5

Library of Congress Catalog Number: 2020903350

You can find Mayté at: **maytelosada.com** or on instagram @maytelosada_

Jacket art © 2020 Billelis

Jacket design © 2020 Liona Design Co.

Photo by Misfit Moon Photography.

Published by KWE Publishing: www.kwepub.com

To those courageous enough to wonder...

"To live in the light for far too long is to forget that the world is mostly made of darkness. To live in darkness for far too long is to remember that the world has barely any light."

Luthyn Solavon Thaegan
Patron King of the Kingdom of Lysmir

Sunsier and Moonsier
The Twin Cities

1. Entry Gate
2. Outer City Square
3. Clock Tower
4. The Rising Sun of All
5. Stone's End Inn
6. Khadir's House
7. Nivrashmo Street
8. Golden Crow
9. Palace Iishraq
10. Inner City Gate
11. Library Grand Splendid
12. Scholar Museum of Rodessian History
13. Academy of Magical Studies and Art
14. Academy of Historical Studies
15. Academy of Politics and Foreign Affairs
16. Academy of Literature
17. 5th Academy
18. Head and Hand Housing
19. Student Housing
20. Port Market
21. King's Port Bar

Minanich
Pyator
Volkova
Pyatovan Sea
Lin Ha
Han wei
Shao Yun Islands
Northern Ocean
Sarajova
Vhir
Vylara
The Sourielian Forest
Ferreow
Sunsier Moonsier
Rodessian Sea
Risno
Meris
Lorys
Jysmir
Haeh
Mias
The Raven Mountains
Rinelle
ashmoor
Rodessa
Naiama
Azaneh
Olongua
Sun Spire Sea
Akelan Sea
Soteros
Southern Ocean
Navias

PROLOGUE

She laid in her bed, pretty, perfect, surrounded in red.

He laid in his, cracked, ice-cold, decayed, and just as dead.

I : SIVREHYA RITHLOREN

Kingdom of Meris
Royal Palace, City of Maeh

The scroll remained unopened, untouched on the table. We had been staring at it, perhaps hoping it would burst into flames as a conjured joke from my sister, but no such luck. The ivory-colored scroll remained innocent, lying peacefully.

It was my brother who spoke first. "I don't suppose we open it?"

"We should, I guess. Might as well know what *they* have to say," I responded after some silence.

He picked up the small thing, ripped off the wax seal, sending it falling to the ground. He unraveled it, looked at me, sighing before he cleared his throat.

"I, King Alaeric of Lysmir, along with some close court members, am on my way to you and shall be arriving within the hour of when this raven is received by you. We require an audience with your Majesties. I have rather horrid news to share, news I am very sure you are already aware of. I, and my entourage, am not here on peaceful terms. A war is coming, your Majesties."

No sooner had my brother finished saying the second 'Majesties' did he slam his hand, and the letter, on the stone slab table. His face contorted with anger. It mirrored the emotions swirling inside me.

But still, he laughed. A harsh, feigned laugh. "They can't possibly be serious. They *can't* possibly be *serious*." His voice filled with poison, dripping from his words.

He raised his hand to his temples, squeezing them, his eyes shut, body tense. The small scroll once in his now clenched hand fell to the table in a swaying motion before settling down. The little black raven squawked, fluttering its inky wings.

"They're near, then. I'm assuming past the border, close to the castle." My voice was calm, opposite of everything I was feeling.

"I say we curse that bird to explode into blood above them while they're still making their way here." Daemon fell back into his seat, slouching a bit. His pristine dark scarlet garb scrunched a bit.

I eyed the raven, watching it cock its head, waiting for us to tie another scroll to its leg. "It's an innocent bird."

"It works for the Thaegans. Anyone, or anything involved with them, for that matter," he said, motioning towards the bird, "is far from innocent."

"Perhaps. Though I don't doubt if it had the choice of working for the Lysmiran royals or freedom, it would have chosen freedom." My brother looked at me, then the raven, then back at me. He sighed, running a pale fair-skinned hand through his jet-black hair. The contrast of the stark difference was a common Rithloren trait. Paper-colored skin, black hair darker than the night, and red eyes the color of blood. The eyes weren't ours though; they belonged to every blood mage. Everyone who could will the magic in their blood and do terrible things with it.

"Alright Siv, you win. But I do suggest sending them back something."

"Agreed. And I have to admit, I like the idea of there being a red shower."

"And how will we do that?" Daemon crossed his legs, looking at me expectedly.

"We'll still conjure up a curse, but we'll just add a little charm to it. One that takes the shape of a black raven. And once it's flying above all their pretty little heads, it'll burst. Showering them in scarlet, staining their pristine ivory and silver clothes. It'll be quite the show."

My brother smiled wickedly, an evil glint shimmering in his dark eyes. "I like the way you think sister." But his features darkened quickly. "What do you suppose the news is? As far as I'm concerned, we haven't done anything terrible to them in years. The letter said we are aware of whatever this splendid news is."

"I wish I knew. The king even mentioned a war is coming. And to be honest, we all knew one day soon that war would come. The Kingdoms are buried far too deep in this endless pit of hate to have any hope of crawling out."

"They threaten us with war. They said we did something unforgivable and they're coming here to demand an audience. As much as I loathe every single Lysmiran and every single filthy Thaegan with a passion, we might as well hear them out. They want a war; we can give them one. But only after we know why. I am not deploying our soldiers on the battlefield unless this is worthy of war. Their sacrifices must be worth it."

I felt fury bubbling inside, churning inside me. "Can I meet them at the door and kill them all?" I offered, only half-joking. I would be daft to kill the king and high officials of another kingdom, as much as I might loathe each and every one of them.

"That'd be a dream," Daemon huffed in response. "I'd come with some snacks to watch, perhaps some biscuits, or our kitchen's amazing blackberry pie." My brother's voice held disappointment but I couldn't help the laugh that erupted. A smile tugged on his face at my response, to my delight.

I stopped laughing as quickly as I could, suppressing the image of my brother spilling food all over him as he cheered me on as he usually did, and cleared my throat. "They're coming whether we'd like them to or not. The next question is, what the hell are we going to do? We have to tell Mother and Father. They'll refuse to let them stay the night; hell, they'll probably refuse to even *see* them!" I stood up from the chair, and flattened my skirt. "They're coming here uninvited, demanding an audience with the threat of war. If they stay past sunset I'll personally slash on their cheeks and use their own worthless blood to portal them back to their filthy kingdom."

"A great idea. Keep that in mind, because you might just have to." Daemon nodded in approval, smiling. "The king mentioned close court members, meaning he's not alone. He'll have his usual ten to twenty guards, his heir no doubt, and then the court's most loyal members. I can't imagine how many he'd bring, but they're all nobility, which means they're all strong in their magic." Daemon squeezed his temple, no doubt thinking hard and angry. He was right.

"We have to tell them. We have to tell everyone they're coming." I whispered. He looked up at me, painfully nodding.

Silence settled between us once again, but my brother broke it with a heavy sigh, "You're strong-headed and can handle an enemy king without exploding his body." What a compliment! I laughed. "You go to the throne room and meet them; I'll get Mother. If they happen to make it here before I have a chance of finding her and explaining everything, do your best to entertain their filthy souls."

"Gladly. I have a few clever insults running through my head right now I'd love to shower them with." I began to walk out the door when my brother eyed me warningly.

"Nothing too much. We don't want blood to be spilled."

"Blood will already be spilled, on their lovely ivory capes, brother, but I assure you no other blood will be spilled unless *absolutely* necessary."

"Ah!" He raised his hands, plucking the raven gently from the air. "How could I forget the welcoming gift? I'll take care of this one. Could you get our parents instead?"

"Yes, but what about Rhiannyn?"

At the mention of our hot-headed, unafraid-to-murder-all-the-enemies-in-the-room-without-a-second-thought sister, Daemon's face fell. His body shifted uncomfortably.

"She'll go mad. She'll rain hell on them. Not that we don't want that secretly. But," he sighed, elongating 'but,' "try not to tell her. She should be reading at the gazebo by the lake at this hour. As she usually does. So hopefully, praise Darkness, she's not here when they are. Because unlike us, I don't think she'll hold back trying to bleed them all dry."

I nodded, making my way to the black double doors leading to a long winding hallway. "Do you think our parents will be mad about the raven?"

"Oh, no doubt. But we both know they'd secretly love to do that too." My brother's voice rang from inside the room. I turned to face him, smiling mischievously. He mirrored me and winked. With that, I spun on the heel of my shoe and made my way to my parents' chamber, bad news at hand, but a wicked surprise in mind.

I made my way down the winding hall, the red one. Where the walls seemed to bleed, for they were all the color of blood. The floor was slate grey, the tapestries all shades of red. This hall had always been my favorite, perhaps because it led to the library and the grand balcony, and was also my favorite color.

Usually, I walked throughout the hall, admiring the paintings, the handcrafted tapestries of spectacular sceneries that no doubt took years to finish. But today I sped past all of them, ignoring them, not giving them a single thought. And part of me felt guilty for it. I loved these works of art; I loved the way they seemed to teem with life and magic. When I was younger, I would talk to the people in the paintings, when Daemon and Rhiannyn were off doing royal duties. One of the perks of being the youngest, I guess, is that you don't have to sit through hours-long lessons on how to rule a kingdom, how to orchestrate a demonstration, and how to kill rumors with words. All that itching monarch stuff. I found it rather boring. My childhood was spent, when not with my siblings, with the people in the paintings and the people in the millions of books in which I had stuck my nose.

But as I hurried down the hall, keeping my eyes straight at the end of it, where a pair of opened double doors led to the stairs, I felt a pang in my chest. A guilty pang, that I was neglecting something important. I shoved the thought into the void in my mind.

No thinking of that now, Siv. You'll apologize to them later.

"Your Highness!" A deep voice bellowed behind me, ricocheting off the walls. I stopped mid-track, stumbling on the layers of my long dress.

I steadied myself just as two of the royal guards came to me, panting, their arms out.

"Are you alright, your Highness?" One guard, Ivanov, a half-Pyatovan soldier asked, his thick accent nearly masking all the words.

"Yes, we're so sorry we startled you, miss." The other, Killain, nodded, worried.

I waved a hand dismissively through the air.

"No need to worry, gentlemen, I have been through much worse than a simple stumble." I flashed a smile and they seemed to relax. I couldn't blame them for being worried. After all, they were the royal guard. It was in their extremely detailed job description to not let us die. And that included not getting us hurt. But perhaps it was also some sort of platonic affection. After all, I had known these two since I was little, and sometimes, I'd sneak them chocolate after dinner.

"Good then," they unanimously responded. I nodded, flattening my skirt from the tumble.

Ivanov paled. "Your Highness, our border scouts have spotted a small caravan of Lysmirans. The King appears to be among them."

"Yes," continued Killian, "we couldn't find their Highnesses Daemon or Rhiannyn. And we sent others to get the Queen and King." They both bowed their heads respectively.

I closed my eyes, and took in a deep breath, letting it out loudly. "Don't worry, Daemon and I were so graciously advised of their arrival just moments ago by a letter of raven from the King himself. He wishes to speak with us, and have an audience, the bastard." I smile faintly, "Thank you, Ivanov, Killian," I bowed my head at each as I said their names. "For the warning, tell the others they are expected. And tell my mother to meet me in the throne room." I watched them nod and I turned around, this time making my way to the throne room and not my parent's chambers. I needed all the time I would get to prepare myself mentally for Lysmirans.

～

The bells ringing sounded their arrival. The large double doors opened and the light poured through, their bodies dark in the contrast. No one announced their names formally. They wouldn't be treated as valued guests. My mother almost murdered someone after my brother had gone to her with the news. But as the queen she was, she put on her crown, fixed her hair in a few short minutes and walked down the stairs, eyes speckled with a raging storm of anger and hatred.

.   As they approached, I lowered my head to hide my smile. They looked ridiculous. The blood was splattered all over their pristine silver-grey capes, lined with stark white fur. The red was turning into an ugly brown color, seeping into the fabric, drying in their white golden hair, on their pale faces. The glistening metal of the soldier's garb was also stained, and neither were their white stallions spared from the blood, the bright red mottled on their white hair. My mother turned to look at me, her face remained without a sliver of emotion until her hair covered her facial features from the view of the Lysmirans. She motioned with her eyes towards them, a silent way to ask if I had known or had something to do with it. I smirked. She mirrored my expression, perhaps to quietly voice her approval and turned back to face the front, where the king and his entourage were quickly approaching us.

Looks of *absolute* disgust and anger rested on their handsome and delicate faces. Their silver eyes held glares sharper than daggers. I could see the king of Lysmir trembling with rage. His hair was tainted scarlet, as were his face and his clothing. He slid off his horse, followed by whom I'm assuming was his son, whose face was covered by a hood. Two other figures along with half of their guards slid off their mounts. The king of Lysmir stomped past the door, past our guards and straight towards my mother, who sat on the throne. Her face fell into a calm gaze. But a deadly calm, like a wolf in the shadows, watching its prey before it pounces and kills. She always had a lethally still demeanor. She said I get mine from her, and I couldn't disagree. When my father and siblings were mad, you could see it. You could see them shake with anger, their temples hardening, their bodies tensing, their hands clutched tight. The emotion radiated from them like piercing rays from the sun. My mother and I were different. If we were mad, you wouldn't know. A blank stare with empty eyes might mean we're bored, or it might mean we're plotting your murder. We didn't tense; we didn't shake. We remained calm and relaxed, yet lethal all the same.

The king's entourage followed him into the throne room, yet the king didn't stop. He was about to set his filthy foot on the first step up to the platform where the thrones sat in their full glory, but I cleared my throat and eyed him warningly.

"*That*, Your Majesty, is close enough." My voice was laced with poison, though I said it as sweetly as I could. I didn't know why, maybe it was restraint. If I didn't sound nice, I'd be screaming curses at him, and my mother wouldn't have any of that. The king stepped back; I could tell he didn't want to. If I didn't know better, he wanted to climb those few steps and stab my mother in the heart with that pearl hilted sword in his sheath and then take her soul and rip it to shreds. But then again, my mother probably wouldn't want anything more than to bleed him dry, or maybe even take some of his blood and make a makeshift noose to strangle him with, or, of course, cast an old-fashioned curse of endless torture, boiling blood—the possibilities were endless.

"I must admit that our messenger raven exploding into blood, showering upon us, covering us in this filth was very unexpected, incredibly rude and intolerable." The king of Lysmir chided, his chin held high. Little did he know it wasn't the real raven he had sent bearing the message of his disclosed arrival but a lovely charm my brother fashioned out of his own blood. The real raven was probably in our Raven Keep, where my brother was writing down a message to send back to Lysmir for King Alaeric and his entire wretched family to see. But I wouldn't be the one to tell him that; he'd find out himself, when he arrived back home.

"You barging in here unannounced, crossing our borders without even giving us a notice was very unexpected, incredibly rude and *intolerable*."

The king eyed me, poison dripping from his gaze. "I didn't appreciate your discourtesy."

"Do not expect courtesy from us when you show no courtesy yourself." I clapped back while keeping my voice plain and level. Everyone else behind the king remained silent. The man beside him hadn't yet taken off his hood; he seemed like some royal assassin with an oath of chastisement and silence in service to the king's bidding.

Before the irked king could mutter another word or insult my mother cleared her throat and spoke. "King Alaeric," her cold voice rang throughout the large room, echoing, filling all the empty spaces, "why are you here?"

"To declare *war* on your filthy country." He spat. And at that, that one word, 'war,' the room shifted. And I felt something change in the air. My mother tensed, I tensed, our soldiers, who wore enchanted armor, tensed. And the Lysmirans, with all their hatred, *tensed*. The king himself seemed to know the weight of the word. And yet he had still said it.

War. So, he had been serious.

He declared it on us. Knowing very well he was bargaining his own kingdom in the process. But he had done it anyway, and now, now the threat of destruction loomed over us all. Seven bloody hells how I loathed him. I swore to the Dark Mother there was a threat of war between our two kingdoms bloody every week, but it never happened. It never happened because we all knew what war would mean. And now, it was happening, and the world that was already flipped upside down, flipped again.

My mother looked at him in disgust. "That much I know." She responded in a flat, emotionless voice. She almost sounded bored. But I knew, we all knew she was just hiding the fear that crept in us all.

"What I don't know is why. If you declare war on us, it's only proper you inform us on the reason why."

"You monsters—"

I cut him off. "No vile language, Your Majesty." My voice was warning, as my eyes had been when he came in. While he glared at me, I blankly bored into his eyes, unafraid of the hatred that so obviously laid there.

"Of course, your Highness, my deepest apologies," he feigned a smile, flashing his white teeth, before returning his gaze towards my mother, "as I was saying. One of you did something unspeakable. One of you committed a horrendous crime, one worth a lifetime of punishment and torture, and of course war." What the bloody hell was this lunatic talking about? We had done nothing. The last time we had spoken face-to-face was years ago when a Merisan envoy was killed, and punishment to the Lysmirans was served in this very room.

"I must apologize, Your Majesty, but I haven't the slightest clue of what you're speaking about." My mother batted her lashes, bored.

The king however, was not emotionless as my mother; he was taken aback. He was almost laughing out of the sheer shock and anger flowing out of him, but he managed to say, "I'm sorry?"

"You heard me. I haven't a clue what you're talking about." She repeated, shifting her position in the throne.

"How dare you act innocent!" His voice raised, his hands in the air. "How dare you? You *monsters* murdered my daughter, my heir, my Verena, in cold blood using one of your sick unnatural blood curses. She had fifty cuts on her; she was bathing in her own blood! On her bed, in the morning her chambermaid found her. Bleeding from so many different places, lying dead underneath a symbol drawn in blood on the wall above her head. Drawn no doubt by a filthy blood mage like one of you!" He cursed and screamed. But my mother and I heard none of it. We were both shocked, still and subconsciously tuning out the curses the king was throwing our way. We looked at each other, alarmed. We knew, we *knew* none of us had cast a symbol to kill the heir of Lysmir. But if a symbol was truly drawn, one of our kinds used, then we had a problem. One worthy of war.

"King Alaeric, Your Majesty, I'm sorry for your loss, but I can assure you my family had nothing to do with the death of your daughter." My mother calmly said. She was hiding her confusion and panic as much as I was. If none of us did it, who did? Who was able to make it seem as if one of us killed the heir to the Lysmiran throne?

But the king was having none of it, his face becoming redder and redder with anger by the second. "One of your filthy blood demons killed my daughter in cold blood with your unnatural magic! Murderers! I am not here on friendly terms; I will not negotiate my daughter's death. I declare war on your kingdom. You have stepped too far, Rithlorens, and I will give you a war and by the end of it—"

"Silence from you!" My mother stood up abruptly, yelling, "How dare you storm into my kingdom, demanding an audience, only to disrespect us in our own castle and accuse us of murdering your daughter! I can assure you none of us murdered your heir. Her death, her blood is *not* on us."

The king didn't believe her. "I refuse to believe you monsters had nothing to do with it. Are you so cold-hearted as to not even admit to the terror you committed?" He questioned, his tone calmer, but no less hateful. I eyed the young man beside him as his eyes bored into mine. Anyone could have flinched by the mere power they held in their glare. But I bored into his silver eyes straight back, unbothered by the curses he was mentally throwing at me.

"Show us the symbol," I demanded. The king's gaze shifted from my mother to me.

"Pardon?"

"You said there was a symbol drawn on her wall. Show us that symbol. Surely one of your people drew it down somewhere. Show us then."

"We have it, yes, drawn on a piece of parchment. But why would I want to give you a symbol that led to my daughter's death? You could conjure it on us, especially since Rithlorens are known to be able to bend blood." I almost laughed. Who did he think he was to think so lowly of us? Did he really think we, Rithlorens, blood mages, would not know the symbol of cutting someone open so they bled to death? Ha. Imbecile.

"I assure you the symbol is part of our vast knowledge of curses. It is not an unknown curse, so believe me, do not fear that showing us the symbol will cause us to use it against you. If we wanted to, we would have already."

The king retained his posture under the pounds of armor he was wearing. I watched him as he pulled the parchment out of his pocket, his hands gripping it into a crumbled ball as they turned into white knuckle fists.

"If I give this to you, do not think you can curse us out of existence and be relieved of your crime." His pale face contorted, the muscles shifting angrily.

At that moment I wished we could curse them out of existence, that there was some complicated symbol we could fashion from blood to do just that. But we couldn't, because even with our wide range of abilities, there were still some things we weren't able to do. And cursing someone out of existence was one of them.

"We won't." My mother said in her voice like cold death. It was meant to reassure them, but it had felt more like a threat. Like a promise that she'd do something so much worse.

II : SIVREHYA RITHLOREN

Kingdom of Meris
Royal Palace, City of Maeh

I watched in carefully hidden amusement as the king tried to spit out another insult, another string of colorful words of which I'd already heard a million times over as a guard handed my mother the piece of ivory-colored parchment, folded. As she made her way to the throne and sat down, I leaned over to see the symbol as she opened the folded piece of paper. The moment my mother laid eyes on the symbol drawn, she gasped quietly. I looked up and eyed the king. "This is the exact copy?"

"You doubt *me*? I drew every cursed line of that bloody sign." Oh, forgive me Your Majesty, but I hate you, it would be no surprise I'd doubt you for literally anything.

"Seven bloody hells. This is the symbol. Sivrehya this..." My mother trailed off; her voice had been barely a whisper.

My eyes narrowed. I had studied this design to death, and my eyes caught something off. "No. It's not. If this is exactly the symbol drawn on the wall, there's a mistake. The lines on the third circle should be straight up and down, with the symbols of the curse in between. But the symbols of the curse are not in between; they're on the lines, like the other two circles. Those are right, but not the third. This symbol doesn't exist. Any of us would have known that." My mother looked at the small circle, her finger tracing it, her eyes widening.

"Holy Darkness. You're right." She gasped. I looked up from the paper and looked at the king, his entourage.

"This symbol, though similar to the real one, is not true. This one is fake. There's a design that isn't correct. Without that design done right, the curse wouldn't work." Blood curses are very complex and every line, every symbol, every little detail must be exact, or else the magic won't oblige.

Again, the king looked unimpressed. "I don't believe you for one second your Highness. Not for one filthy second. Lies leave your mouth, no truth."

"King Alaeric," my mother protested, "this symbol is not drawn accurately. It should be enough proof that we have nothing to do with Crown Princess Verena's death."

"Don't dare speak her name, witch!"

"Do not call my mother a witch!" I countered immediately. Seldom did I raise my voice. Seldom did I let anger show. But this time my voice rose and my anger could be seen. That bastard had no right to call my mother a witch. So badly did I want to bleed him dry, to turn him into a dry husk of a mage, or to curse him with some eternal torture, whether that be pain of some sort or being stuck in the deepest, darkest limbo on this land.

"Silence please, please!" My mother's voice rang out. Both of us turned to look at my mother who sat down again. She sighed, exasperated, tired and yet bubbling with hateful emotions. "Listen, Your Majesty, all we can say is that this symbol is wrong. The curse would not have worked if this was drawn on her wall."

"Perhaps you are lying. You are saying it is drawn wrong but I can assure you, it is drawn right." The king rebuffed, seemingly proud of having found a hole in our argument. Darkness help him.

"But you drew this line by line, every detail copied perfectly. If indeed that is true, and we were indeed lying that this symbol was drawn incorrectly, then you would know. You would know for a fact that we are lying. You saw the symbol on the wall; we did not. You drew it; we did not. If you know you drew this perfectly, you would have known that when we said it was wrong it was a lie. But you didn't. You didn't scream lies; your facial expression didn't change. So, we're not lying." I couldn't help but smile. Did he truly believe he found a crack in our proof? No one spoke. We were all silent, feeling the tension still floating around freely between each of us.

But the short silence was shattered by the echoing sound of a door being pushed open and slamming shut. We all looked at the source of sound. There in the hallway to our left stood my sister. Eyes glowering, full of what everyone else's eyes were full of: rage, burning hatred. Her hands were clenched, her eyes on us and then in horror, our guests.

"Rhiannyn, what is the meaning of this? I'm in the middle of a meeting." Our mother scolded, standing up, making her way towards her other daughter. I looked at my sister quizzically.

"What in the name of the seven bloody hells are these despicable bastardous monsters doing in our kingdom, let alone our castle!" She shrieked as her hand was raised and all of a sudden all of the Lysmirans were screaming in pain, thrashing on the ground, begging for their anguish to end. I could see the steam coming out of the armor of one guard, and slowly a second. She was boiling their blood, cooking them alive, killing them slowly in agonizing pain.

"Rhiannyn enough, stop!" My mother yelled, ending my sister's torture on our "guests." "What in bleeding skies are you doing?"

"Why don't you answer why they're here first?" My sister spat back in her anger. She hadn't meant to disrespect our mother, but instead did it out of her emotion. Her voice was full of poison. The gears of death churning in her head could be seen by all in the room. I watched as the Lysmirans slowly stood up, taking off their caps, burning up from the short moment where their blood was turning into a steaming torture. The king was beyond vexed. Every single one of them was. My eyes remained on the two guards still on the floor; their thrashing stopped, and they simply laid there motionless. She had killed them. Their armor accelerated what she had done to them.

"Your daughter is more of a monster than any of us!" A Lysmiran girl with golden hair screamed out. Her hair was rather unkempt; her skin red and flushed from the heat. Her cape had been thrown on the ground. My gaze shifted to her.

"I beg to differ, you royal soul-sucking beast!" My sister was about to run towards her but two strong arms belonging to my mother wrapped themselves around her.

"Rhiannyn, enough please!" Our mother begged as the king of Lysmir walked over to Rhiannyn, his eyes glowing. I turned my head to the noble lady who had spoken; she was smirking. Our guards turned to face each other, unsure of what to do. Suddenly my sister stopped struggling, but with the end of her tantrum came ear-splitting screams of agony. My mother and sister fell to the floor, and our guards suddenly as well. I heard laughing, but not from us.

"Enough!" My voice was a deafening screech. Slowly everyone stopped what they were doing. The screams stopped. The devious laughing stopped. But not because of my voice. Slowly standing up I made my way down the steps, my red eyes glowing, and my mind concentrating on holding everyone in the room hostage. It was slowly draining, I could feel it, but I didn't let it show.

"Let. Me. Go." The king of Lysmir seethed. I ignored him, instead making my way through everyone in the room, like a maze. I met the eyes of enemies and our guards, landing on a pair of silver eyes. Confusion and resentment swirled inside them. The silvery hood that covered his face before was on the floor. His pale face still held a pinkish tint. Drops of sweat were trickling down his face. He looked like his father, only younger, and to my disgust, *a lot* more handsome. His features were sharp; his body towered over me. I wagered this was Ivar Thaegan, Prince of Lysmir. "Let me g–"

I whipped my head to face the king, sighing and cutting him off, "I heard you the first time."

"You didn't let me go." Was he bloody serious? Praise Darkness.

"Forgive me. I wasn't aware we were in Lysmir where your commands are higher than mine." I scolded. No shame. I didn't care; he attacked my sister and mother. Sure, Rhiannyn attacked them, out of anger. But that anger came from somewhere deeper than her hatred for them. I knew that. Whatever her reason, it was worth boiling their blood because of it. He was about to spit out some more nonsense but I waved my hand, letting go of everyone. They all huffed, slowly moving their bodies after being unable to move. "Rhiannyn. What happened?"

"She attacked us yo—"

"King Alaeric, Your Majesty, I am speaking to my sister, not you. For the love of Darkness be *quiet*. You and *all* your people." I had enough of his childlike wails and complaining. With that, he shut up. Thank Darkness. Once again, I turned to my sister. She was huffing, fixing her hair and dress. She looked at me. "Rhiannyn, what happened?"

"Father—" Her voice whimpered; my heart started racing. "He —he's dead."

Everyone stopped. My world stopped. It froze. Any noise was drowned out. The screams from our mother were drowned out. The laughs of that annoying noble Lysmiran girl were drowned out. The pain was a throbbing in my head, a heart that was begging to be released.

"No." The sound that came out of my mouth was so soft, so quiet, I didn't think I even said anything. "*No.*"

"On the floor of his room, his skin ice cold and ashen white, crumbling and cracked. Eyes colorless. Almost as if his soul was ripped out and destroyed. Almost as if," she paused, her eyes moving from mine to the king of Lysmir, "one of them did it."

One hand raised to point to the king, the other clenched in a fist, trembling. "So, I'm asking, why the hell are they here? Father is dead! Dead! Murdered by one of them! Get them out of my sight or at least let me torture them to death to repay for his." She seethed.

This wasn't happening. It couldn't be. No. *No.* I refused.

"He's not. He can't be." Our mother pleaded to Rhiannyn. But my sister's silence was all it took to know what she had seen of our father was the truth. She rushed out of the throne room, wailing. I felt her pain, and it hurt far too much.

"Nonsense!" King Alaeric spoke in a brute voice, "Your Highnesses, I assure you we did not kill His Majesty; none of us had anything to do with his terrible demise."

"Lies!" My sister screeched, "lies!"

Before she could unleash her power and curse all the Lysmirans, I stood between her and the king. Though with every fiber of my being, I wanted my sister to unleash her worst curse. We couldn't do this here. "King Alaeric," I started, making sure every word I said was laced with hatred and poison that everyone could taste, "you came here to blame us for your daughter's death. We told you we did not kill her, we told you this symbol drawn on her wall is not real, and yet, you do not believe us. So, *enlighten* me, after hearing of my father's death, a death akin to a death caused by a destroyed soul, why should *we* believe *you*? You say that you had nothing to do with his murder, very well. Say what you may. But Your Majesty, we do not believe you. Now *leave*." How I wished simple words had the power to kill, because if they did, they'd all be dead now.

My sister was sobbing inconsolably, her body heaved on mine. I tried to balance her weight, as she slumped on me, in pain and grief.

Turning away from the king, I faced her and tightened my grip around her, my hand caressing her hair. "Leave sister, I'll take care of them." I whispered, walking her towards the door she came from, the same one my mother ran through, with tears flying behind her. She nodded, sobbing, sniffling, limping her way down the hall. I watched her with agony filling up inside me.

I twisted on my heel to once again face the monstrous monarch and his entourage. The king looked at me with an empty look on his face, yet he didn't budge. I wanted to yell at him to get the hell out; I wanted to tear him apart, all of them. I wanted them to hurt; I wanted to scream. I wanted to be pulled into oblivion and disappear.

"I'd rather not go and sort this out."

How—is he? He can't be serious. Mother of Darkness, praise Hell, bleeding skies and holy fucking shit that man cannot be serious.

"No," I deadpanned, my face straight and empty as I could make it. "You, *all of you,* are leaving, right now. If you do not pass the border within the hour, I will track each one of you down and have you stand trial for defying an order from a Merisan royal." He dared defy me. I wasn't kidding. I would slice my hand, raise my blood, cast a spell to track those filthy monsters down and make them answer. "And believe me, Your Majesty, it will not end well for you, your people, or anyone in this room that isn't Merisan for that matter."

"We are not le—"

My impatience for that man made me cut him off. "I'll escort you to the door." As I raised an arm to show them to the door, I started making my way past them, careful to keep all my instincts alert.

"Absolutely not!" He screamed. Like a *child*.

"*Now* Your Majesty, do not make me conjure up a portal back to your realm and make me push all of you through it." A smile started appearing on my face, slowly, deadly, holding within it all the terrible thoughts for them I could muster.

"As if I'd let you do that! You could have it open up to a pit of flames and spikes and have us falling towards that for all I know."

"Exactly, I could. So, it's either I escort you out of my castle *now*, or you risk the chance of all of you falling into a pit of flames and spikes." I cocked my head, "make your choice, but make it fast, my patience is running out."

The king, to his chagrin most likely, sighed, defeated. "Very well. We will leave. But know this, I *will* assemble my armies for war. I declare it upon Meris. On the night of the full moon, in two weeks' time, I *will* be ready at the fields. I will send assassins, I will fight you to the death, to the destruction of you, your family and all these unnatural mages like you. Mark my words, Sivrehya Rithloren, your kingdom *will* fall."

My, the king must have gotten so mad he forgot to use simple manners. Every part of me wanted to choke the life out of him, every part of me wanted me to turn his skin pale blue, not because his soul was destroyed, but because I stopped the air from helping him breath. But I couldn't, to my irritation. Instead I forced a smile. Painful as it was, I forced it and then cleared my throat. "Perhaps *Alaeric Thaegan*," emphasizing his name so he'd know his mistake of not addressing me as he should have, "perhaps. But if we fall, know, with absolute certainty that we will take you down with us."

My father was dead. My world was being shredded about. And now this king was declaring war on us and all I wanted to do was to raise Darkness to end everything once and for all. But again, I couldn't. The least I could do was threaten him as he had me. And when the time came, I would keep my word, and tear them to shreds. But that would have to wait. For now.

The guards opened the heavy double doors, exposing us to the cloudy grey outside. A slight breeze flowed through the room, tangling itself in my hair and dress. In front of us there were the many steps that led to the grassy area, flowers lined the pathway, guards were lined up as usual. Everything seemed the same but so terribly different at the same time. The last time our kingdoms fought it was several years ago. It was a short battle, barely two days long. Almost zero casualties, over a stupid thing that none of us could even remember anymore. I sighed. War. An actual war loomed in the distance, in front of all of us, plagued with death and chaos and Darkness. I stopped, letting the Lysmirans walk in front of me, down the steps and onto the ground. The guards mounted their horses, the nobles preparing their once pristine garbs for the journey home. A little boy sprinted from the king's side and readied an ornate silver carriage, no doubt for his majesty and his highness. None of us spoke, none of us wanted to.

But the peaceful silence that had settled over us was broken by a high-pitched voice. "You filthy princess!" I rolled my eyes. I guess someone did want to talk after all. Not a single moment of goddamn peace with these fools around.

"You'll pay, you'll all pay! How dare you blame us for something we never did and then deny what you did to us! You killed our beloved Princess Verena and for that we will never forgive! You are all monsters, each and every one! Demons! Beasts!" The girl shrieked, throwing her arms around. Good Darkness, she was acting like a child. Who did she think she was to call us those words? Highborn or not, she was in Meris, not Lysmir. The bitch.

"Forgive me, you are?"

"Oh! You don't know who I am. How dare you not know who I am?" She screamed; her neck veins stuck out with her anger. Good Darkness, bleeding skies, torching nights, who the hell was she? Like her asking that would suddenly spark a once unknown piece of useless information into my head. Like poof!

"As I said, forgive me, *you are*?" I pressed. Was she going to say her name or keep screaming?

"I'm Maeghalin Salvaen! *The* Maeghalin Salvaen, of the Lysmiran Royal Court!" Her voice lowered in volume, but poison still dripped from it. I walked towards them, slowly, still not knowing who the absolute hell she was.

"Oh!" I feigned fear, placing hand to my heart, "Miss Maeghalin Salvaen of the royal court of Lysmir, my apologies, I honestly hope you can forgive me," my face contorted quickly, into a frown, "because I still don't know who you are."

Shock was written all over her sharp features. Disgust and shock. Her dull grey eyes narrowed, blond eyebrows furrowing together, no doubt from displeasure. "Ah." She placed a hand on her chest, in offense from my response. Praise Darkness, I couldn't care less. "You heartless, horrible bit—"

I closed my eyes, breathing in and out, fisting my hands at my sides, trying very hard not to just—

"Miss Maeghalin, you're irrelevant."

"How dare you disrespect me! M—"

"Do *not* talk about me disrespecting you. You are in *my* kingdom. You have *no* place here, no voice here, and you are the one disrespecting me." I silenced her, my stare was like daggers, boring down on her with hatred and loath. The glare I gave her for a few seconds too long for her liking seemed to have shut her up for good, so I turned to the others, batting my lashes and feigning yet again, another smile. "Enjoy your travels back, if only we never have to see each other again." Then I turned and looked at his royal pain in the ass and his son, "Farewell Your Majesty, Your Highness, members of the royal court." I curtsied, "it hasn't been a pleasure." My right heel twisted and I walked through the large double doors, quickly pricked myself with the sharp tip of my dagger, and with a flick of my wrist bid my blood to form a noose around the handles of the door, to slam it in their faces.

III : SIVREHYA RITHLOREN

Kingdom of Meris
Royal Palace, City of Maeh

The noise shook the walls. And the silence that came after hurt. So, I ran. I ran past the guards, past the doors, through the throne room, up the stairs, through the curving halls and down and up various staircases before I reached my room. And the moment I was in isolation, in the safe seclusion of my room, I leaned against the closed door, as my own tears fought their way through, finally falling, like me. How I managed to keep a front of emotionless apathy during all of that chaos surprised even me. The moment she had said the word "dead," I felt pain and anger and confusion and fear and, above all, heart-wrenching sadness. The sadness that doesn't make you stronger, or teach you some legendary lesson. It was the kind of sadness that simply hurt. All over, I felt my body ache. My chest heaved, trying to grasp onto some air as I cried. My throat hurt. My stomach hurt. My dress was a mess, damp from the tears, my hair was plastered to my face, my eyes were puffy, my face red. And still, I hurt. I wanted it to end, the pain; in that moment, it was too much.

A soft knock stilled me. I sniffled, quickly wiping the tears across my face in order to dry them. Instantly my face felt dry. I pushed aside the discomfort and fixed my dress.

"Sis?" My brother's voice was soothing but filled with worry. I reached for the handle and twisted it, opening the door and facing my brother, who always stood tall and proud even in moments filled with despair.

"He's dead, Sivrehya." His voice was broken, cracked and

stained with heartache. I leaned over and wrapped my arms around him, tightly. Neither of us liked affection: it was Rhiannyn who enjoyed hugs and the comfort of our mother stroking her hair in times of grief. But this time was different and for that Daemon hugged me back.

"Is it true?" My voice cracked, "Is what Rhiannyn said true?"

"What did she say?" He asked, still holding me tightly.

"His skin, ice-cold to the touch, ashen-white and crumpling. Eyes like colorless voids." I repeated what she had screamed out with such anger, with pain. It hurt even imagining it. We slowly pulled apart, looking at each other. His dark red eyes lost their usual glimmer. He was breaking apart inside, slowly like an old building, losing a part of itself every day. And I knew the answer before he even had to say it. The emotions swirling in his eyes were enough to tell me that what my sister saw, he saw too.

My brother's voice held a stoic calm. Almost eerie. "What did they say?" No anger, no venom, no hatred. The grief overpowered every emotion he felt towards the Lysmirans.

"They denied it." At that, his features contoured with anger now, his pale face, hinted with just a touch of red. Sprouted no doubt from rage.

"Of course they did. Why in the name of Darkness would those bastards confess?" Poisonous, every single word he said. I shook my head.

"Daemon. They said *we* killed their heir, Princess Verena Thaegan. The declaration of war was for her murder. They blame us." He stilled. I searched his darkened eyes as our gazes met once again.

"Why the bloody hell did they blame us?"

"Because a symbol was drawn in blood on her wall. It was the symbol of a thousand cuts. She was found bled dry, lying in a pool of her own scarlet."

The anger faded, changing into fear. "Darkness save us, are you serious?"

"Yes but, the symbol was drawn wrong. It was a small, almost unnoticeable mistake."

He looked at me, his ears perked, interested. "How do you know?"

"The king drew a picture, I asked that he would show it to us, and he did, saying he drew it line by line. Blood mages who know that symbol, who've studied it, would have known it was drawn incorrectly."

"Meaning we're in the clear?" He was hopeful, as was I. But something was nagging at me. This inexplicable feeling that something was off.

"Meaning the symbol he drew was wrong. The truth is, I don't know if a blood mage killed her. I know it wasn't one of us. But we have a whole population of ruthless blood mages under our reign. One of them might have done it, or perhaps none. Nevertheless, the king said he didn't believe us, he said he's given us two weeks' time before he's in the fields and waging a war whether we're ready or not."

"He said that? Bloody bastard."

"He did. We can't just not do anything. I tried reasoning with him, saying this was fake, but he didn't buy it—"

"Did you believe him?" He cut me off. I looked at him, confused, and then the realization hit me.

"Well no. But, Daemon, what if a blood mage really did kill Verena? Without seeing the real symbol, none of us can be sure. What they described is an awful lot like something we've all done. And the mistake was tiny, which means, he might have simply just drawn something wrong."

"But you said he drew it line by line. And if he did, then this symbol wouldn't have worked, it would be a null drawing decorating a wall. It couldn't have killed her. And if all this is true, I have to believe he's telling the truth on this one thing. Because if one of us did kill Verena, then one of us broke a cardinal law, and one of us will have to pay for starting a war."

"War was inevitable Daemon, even if it means both of our falls. It was always going to happen, someday," I reminded him.

"I know Siv, but a war over something trivial, a war over simple anger and rage will be messy. It will be fought in a hurry, without much thought. It would be fought with the sole idea of destroying our kingdom. But a war fought on the death of someone, someone like the heir, *that* war will be calculated to the last breath. Its objective will be to destroy everything, to *obliterate* us."

I couldn't help but see his reason. It made perfect sense, and I hated it. I hated having to rely on the king of our sworn enemy telling the truth. I hated having to believe him in order to make sure we and all our blood mages were in the clear.

"We have just as much of a reason to fight them. They killed Father."

Silence. He looked at me, boring his red eyes into mine. "And if they didn't."

What?

Anger bubbled inside me. How could he think of defending them in the slightest way? "Daemon you can't possibly be taking their side."

"I'm not. Trust me, I would never think nor dream about such a thing. But think about it. Verena dies, in a way in which it seems one of us did it. But none of us did it, assuming, of course, the symbol is wrong. Father dies in a way that a soul mage would kill, and they denied it. So, what if they didn't kill him?"

"Well, what if they *did*?" I countered my hands in fists. Daemon was always the rational one, always the one who thought about everything for too long. He got that from our mother. "What Rhiannyn described is akin to a soul mages' terrible work. But he didn't defend himself like I tried to do. He just screamed like a child," I rebuffed.

"I know. I heard, and I saw." My brother chuckled, fake of course. When the faintest sign of smile flashed on his face, just for a split second, I wondered if I had imagined it. "But that doesn't change anything. They're going to war for Verena, whether we killed her or not." I didn't respond, I didn't know how, so I let silence take over. We simply just stood there, my back leaning against a wall, his body was firm and brooding.

"Will we go to war for Father?"

"I don't know, Sivrehya. As much as I want to prove they did it, I don't know how." He sighed, running a hand through his tousled hair. "I think in this war, we just fight for survival. We fight to protect ourselves. You know I refuse to wage war on lies."

I closed my eyes, the tears brimming them falling down. Rolling quickly down my cheeks and onto the floor, on the skirt of my dress, or anywhere. "I know. Wars fought on lies are dishonorable things. And above all, we believe in honor and justice."

Daemon smiled, a distant, sad smile. But a smile nonetheless. "You and Rhiannyn value vengeance too."

"As if you didn't either." I flashed a smile, my face twisting in pain as I did. How terrible that it hurt to smile after crying endlessly. One would think a display of happiness wouldn't hurt so damn much.

"I do. It's quite fun. And when the time comes, we will avenge Father, whether from a total stranger or from the king of Lysmir."

I leaned into him, pressing my head on his chest. He enveloped me, his warmth making me feel just a little better. "I *hate* him," I managed, bitterly after silence began to settle.

Silence once again, but then he kissed my hair and spoke, "Me too sis, me too."

~

My brother left to meet our general and his son. War was close, too close. Too near to create intricate ways to slowly destroy the Lysmirans and their damned royal family. My sister was probably off comforting my mother. The guards were trading whispers with everyone in the castle and no doubt so were the royal court members, who had found out about what happened in their own ways, preparing the speech my mother would give to our army and our people.

And I was lying in my bed, sinking into the crimson-colored sheets staring blankly at the grey ceiling, thinking of how simple the day had started, and how hellish it became. I had woken up early to take a ride on my horse. I drank the same pomegranate tea, ate the same biscuits and then, as always, retreated to the training room and then to the west room for some peaceful reading time. And that was when the hell-storm began.

I had been sitting, peacefully, minding my own business, sticking my nose and my focus into an ancient piece of text written by our Matron Queen, Maehra Solavon Rithloren, when the bird came in through the window, squawking and flapping its wings in a manner as if to show its life flashing before its eyes.

The moment it came tumbling in, I thought nothing of it. Why would I? It was a messenger raven, sent by someone in the kingdom to someone specific here. So, I raised the book once again to eye level, and crossed my legs at the ankle, stretching just a bit to relax a little more. The chaise lounge I had been on was the color of scarlet, but darker, a hint of black entwined evenly throughout the velvet fabric. It was only when the bird remained in the room, circling like someone desperately lost, that I realized this bird had a general message, not one meant for a single person. I groaned. The book was so incredibly interesting, and the particular passage I was reading was on the famous curse symbol that could trap the Darkness itself and more. And of course, I was in the middle of reading about Maehra's famous curse on the assassin that tried to kill her when this bloody bird had come in. I cursed it mentally, before forcing myself off the chaise lounge. Gently putting down the book, I picked up the glass next to it that was filled a little bit with a bright cherry-colored drink and downed it.

"You better be bringing me some bloody important message or else I swear to Mother Darkness I will–," my voice left me. My body, my blood froze. The infuriating cries from the raven might as well have stopped because the world was silent. My eyes narrowed, my mind twisting, hoping the wave of panic was a simple misunderstanding. I was hoping it

was a mean trick of the light. But as I walked closer to the lost creature, as I gingerly took the small scroll from its robe cage on the bird's right leg, my chest heaved. The scroll fell to the floor, the wax seal it was closed with was facing me. Staring at me, judging and laughing at me with its evil design. A silver circle, with a dagger printed on it, surrounded by a misty cloud of sorts. The seal of the Thaegans, the royal family of the Kingdom of Lysmir.

Well fuck.

I had called for my brother Daemon, who was most likely going to take the news the least worst of all of my family. Our father, who was in bed with a fever, was in no mood to be stressed by the contents of this letter. Rhiannyn would have burned the entire castle down out of spite. Our mother, well, my mother, would have had Daemon read it to her, out of fear of opening it herself.

The moment he had heard the words "Lysmir" and "letter" and "Thaegan" spoken by me in the same sentence, he was running down to the west room before I even had the chance to finish. And then there we were. Staring at the small ivory-colored scroll, hoping it would burn, hoping that it would simply disappear.

It hadn't. Not that it would have. But then we read the contents, and the Lysmirans dumped their news on us, declared war and then in the midst of all the chaos, someone had crept in and snuffed the life out of my father. And now I was here, lying in bed, my face itchy from the drying tears, my head throbbing with the pain that came from crying far too long and my chest heaving from trying to breathe through it all. I hated this pain. The pain that wasn't from being stabbed in the stomach with a dagger, or three arrows being shot in your back, or even anything close to physical pain. It stemmed from within, this invisible thing that gnawed at you, and slowly tore you apart from grief. I silently prayed my mom was strong enough to deal with the pain again. She lost my oldest brother, Laidon, years before to a wicked curse, and when she heard that he died, she retreated into her chambers and cried the days and nights out. She wasn't herself after that. She was a hollowed-out version, who became stronger as time went by. She had loved Laidon with all her heart; she always would. But Father, he was her one true love. And the romance they shared was something I aspired to have one day. But Father was dead, and my mother, who never fully regained her strength after Laidon's passing, would be a shell of what and who she once was.

I twisted on the bed, turning so I lay on my right side and my eyes found the window. The sky cleared, the grey clouds that once shrouded over and made everything look dull had taken their leave. In their wake was a light blue sunny day, feigning that good things were happening. I moved onto my back again and raised my hand in front of me, taking the dagger that was hidden in the folds of my dress with the other. I dug the tip of the blade into my palm and drew a line down my hand. Blood slowly welled from the shallow wound, trailing down my arm. What spell, what curse or charm could fix this? I knew of only one. It brought the dead back. But it was expressly forbidden under any and all circumstances. It was dark magic, darker than the kind we used. It was time-consuming, extremely intricate and it ate up your energy, unlike any other spell or charm or curse. And then, of course, there was the sacrifice it demanded. A life for a life. It wouldn't work unless you had someone else's life to trade for the life of the deceased. Messy business. That's why no one dared do it. That and those who walked past the line that separated the living from the dead didn't belong in the realm of those who were alive. The dead stayed dead. But I would be lying if seeing the blood slowly draw itself a path from the cut down my pale arm didn't make me think of bringing him back. It would be hopeless and stupid. I would have to kill someone, and perform quite possibly the hardest and most enduring spell in all of blood magic history. And the man that would come back, in the end, presuming the whole ordeal didn't kill me, wouldn't be my father. It would be a hollowed-out shell of the shell that was the late king of Meris.

I sighed, using the blood that had fallen to design the symbol of healing. The shallow cut withered and faded, turning into nothing as if it had not even existed in the first place.

What Daemon told me, his fear that maybe the Thaegans hadn't dealt a hand in our father's death, rolled in my mind. They had to have been part of it or at least have some common knowledge of it. But then, they had blamed us for Verena's death, and if one of our people had done it, we didn't have the slightest clue. Part of me deep down craved the truth. The idea of never knowing what truly happened would eat away at me, and I knew it. For our sakes, for our sanity, for this goddamn war, I needed to know the truth. The truth of Verena's death and the truth of my father's.

And that gave me a dangerous idea.

Perhaps that was the first time I had smiled a real smile this entire day. I flipped off the bed, not caring to fix my dress. The books, the few I had in my room, were sitting on a black bookshelf. I reached above me for the thick grey book on magical and mythical creatures. We didn't have many, but those we had were usually ferocious, dark and made of something else entirely. I flipped through the thick pages, passing all the elegantly drawn pictures, the detailed descriptions of what the creatures could do, where to find them, what they ate, basically anything about them. This book covered almost, if not all, of the magical beasts in our land. From the fire-breathing deer and hawk hybrid monster that was the peryton, to the lethal sea dragons that roamed the seas and sunk ships. But I didn't care for any of those; I had one particular monster in mind. One that would be a death wish if crossed. One with too many heads and too many eyes, each closed, each if opened, would unleash a powerful force of magic. The Neithisis. The monster that lived eternally and knew everything. Everything about the past and everything about the present. All one had to do was simply ask it a question and be especially wary of its eleven closed eyes that hid magical properties. Should one get on its wrong side, the result was death. Not only that, but the beast was more than mysterious. No one knows where to find it exactly; it seemed to shift and disappear, and reappear and then poof, it was gone. The truth is, that even for all its knowledge, this book could only guess at where the Neithisis lived and how to find it. And on any regular day, the lack of information would have annoyed me to pieces, as it did in the past. But this was no ordinary day. Before I had no pressing questions for such a creature, no real intention for scouting it out, of traveling the lands to find it and ask it something I desperately needed the answer to. But now I did. I needed the truth of what happened. And I was completely mad for thinking this, for even starting to plan my trip to where this book could best direct me in the direction of the Neithisis.

The Twin Cities, Sunsier and Moonsier, was the last place, and perhaps the only place with those who know how to find the elusive creature that is the Neithisis.

~

"Are you mad?" My sister dropped her teacup, sending it shattering in a million pieces in equally different directions.

No. Well...maybe just a little.

"Rhiannyn, I have to know. We all have to know the truth. Of not only what really happened to Father, but also what happened to Verena. The Thaegans might be declaring war on us on a lie."

She huffed, "They are, Siv! They claimed we killed their precious princess and we didn't."

"We didn't. But maybe someone in our kingdom did."

At this she laughed, looking at me as if I were even more mad. "You really think one of our people would do something that fucking *stupid*?"

"No. But I can't be completely sure. None of us can. And instead of questioning and accusing them all one by one, I want to go to the Twin Cities and find this mythical beast and ask it what the hell actually happened. The Neithisis, for all its power, cannot tell a lie. So, whatever its answer, good or bad, will be the truth."

Rhiannyn looked down, sighing. My brother combed a hand through his hair, his eyes finding mine. He shifted in his chair, clasping his hands together, his elbows on the table.

"No one knows the entire truth on the Neithisis. Probably not even the people of the Twin Cities. If you do this—"

Our sister interjected, "Daemon, you can't possibly mean for her to actually go through with this!"

Daemon turned to face her, "Rhi, we're at war with a kingdom who is waging it in the name of their dead princess. They will be worse than ruthless. That aside, I think we both know we want to know the truth. With a deadly battle ahead of us we can't exhaust resources in order to uncover the truth. Asking a simple question to something that for sure knows what happened is the best we can do."

"And what if the Neithisis cannot be found? We need all the power we can get. Sivrehya is strong, probably stronger than any of us. We'll need her on the battlefield."

"Then I'll come back in time for the war." I cut the silence that was beginning to settle between us. At this, Rhiannyn turned to face me. "It's in two weeks' time. If I don't have the answer by then I'll come home. I'll fight. But please sister, I'm not asking for permission. If there's even a small chance that I can find out the truth behind all this chaos, then I'll take it."

"Siv," she paused, sighing, leaning her head against the back of the seat. "Mother is worse than ever, she is no state to rule a kingdom, especially one at war. Someone needs to take care of her and the kingdom in her name. And I'll be happy to do it, but I'll need help. Daemon will no doubt be on the frontlines with General Silian and Jace and all of our soldiers."

"You have the members of the royal court, those that won't be fighting. You'll have the small council; you'll have the people who have been there by Mother and Father's side for their reign and longer. But, should you need my help just conjure a portal and come get me. We will be miles away, but we have our magic, and with that, we can do anything."

She seemed only slightly more convinced of my slightly brilliant idea. "Daemon, what do you think?"

My brother looked from her to me, then back to her. "I think it needs to be done. If anyone is going to do this, it's her. But Siv," his eyes on me now, "one week is preferable, but two weeks at most. No more. And please send letters, or signs, anything to tell us how you're doing and how your search is going. Clear?"

"Crystal, brother." I smiled triumphantly; a small sliver of hope began to weave inside me. He nodded his head at me, sparing only a small smile for my sake before standing up and pushing the chair back.

"Alright then, Rhiannyn will rule the kingdom in Mother's name. I will handle the war and Sivrehya will travel to the Twin Cities to find out what the hell happened to Verena and our father. Good." With that, he downed the last of his wine, and left the glass on the table.

Rhiannyn mirrored his actions, having dropped her tea, grabbed a glass and poured herself some wine before taking my arm. "Siv, be safe out there. Don't hesitate to use your magic in that city. It has its fair share of secrets."

"I won't," I offered her a reassuring wink. It was worth it, for she shot a small yet grateful smile back.

"When will you leave then?" She asked, pouring herself more wine, before once again downing it, perhaps in an attempt to forget all the terrible things she had just gone through.

"Tomorrow."

She shook her head, "not tomorrow Siv. Tomorrow we need to tell the people. We need you there. Mother is in no shape to go. They need to see as many of us as they can, to know for sure that we aren't going to let them get hurt. If they see their ever-powerful princess, they'll feel safer."

I wanted to protest, to tell her it was time-sensitive and that I needed to go to the Twin Cities as soon as possible. But I knew she was right, as per usual. The kingdom needed to know we were at war, but they also needed to know not to panic, to stay calm, because the Rithloren siblings would make sure that no damn soul mage would even think about doing anything cruel to them. And for that, Daemon and Rhiannyn, for all their power, all the love they got from the people, needed me too. Because the people knew I was particularly powerful, and they knew I would protect them, because that is what a princess does. And I was, after all, a princess. So, I nodded, and Rhiannyn nodded back, setting down her glass.

"I'll leave the day after tomorrow then." I offered her a weak smile and nodded, pulling her in for a hug. "Stay strong Rhi, for mom, for everyone."

"I will." She cupped my cheek, wiping a tear that began its descent down my face and smiled. "You stay strong too."

"Always." I watched her slice a cut into her palm and fix the broken tea cup before setting it on the table and walking out. Silence filled the room; silence was something I had heard of all too much of in these past few hours.

My brother still stood, his hands in tight fists. Our sister was now gone, and in his eyes, I saw something that was left unspoken.

My insides curled, knowing whatever he left unsaid was nothing particularly good. "What is it?"

My brother shifted uncomfortably. His eyes avoiding mine, looking all over, as if searching for the right words to say.

"Daemon, you're worrying me."

"I," he started, before sitting back down, letting out a long sigh. "Do not above all things, tell Rhiannyn this." He looked at me, warningly.

"You have my word." I responded, my body tensing. Whatever he was about to say, I knew would have set Rhiannyn off. As much as we both loved our sister, we looked at each other in silent words that neither of us would speak about it with her.

"With the raven we decided not to kill, I sent back a scroll, with a symbol on it. A portal symbol that would bring the king and the new crown prince to Father's bed chamber should an act of hate be brought onto the scroll."

I stood there, dumbfounded and frozen. My brother was logical. He didn't allow his emotions to control him; he was the one who thought of every possibility, the one who thought things thoroughly through before enacting them. And yet, he had done this.

"At least tell me you made an anti-magic symbol for them once they got there." Anger bubbled inside me, not at him, but rather at the thought of two of our worst enemies seeing Father when even I hadn't. Part of it was because I couldn't bring myself to, the other was because Daemon had said Mother wasn't allowing anyone in the room.

He looked at me as if I were stupid, but in a brotherly way, in the way of pure sarcasm.

"You dare doubt me?" He said mockingly, pretending to be hurt. I almost laughed, almost. I would have, should everything about the situation not have been so terrible.

Instead I just flashed a smile, one we both knew was fake and said, "Never."

"I made sure Mother was gone, I made sure Rhiannyn was with her, and yes, I put a symbol on the ceiling. I wanted them to see what they had done, to see if perhaps they'd break or offer some sort of information after seeing him in that state." My brother drew a ragged breath, pain laced within it.

"I'm assuming they didn't."

"No, they didn't. But I had to try." His eyes met mine. He looked defeated almost, but I knew he was not the one to give up. "But Siv, they said, or rather the prince said, that Father's eyes weren't black."

I looked at him, confusion swirling around in my head. Why would that even matter? "His eyes were colorless white, faded, or at least that's what Rhiannyn said."

"And they were. But the prince said, insisted, that when a soul was destroyed, the eyes turn black."

And like the clasp of a box, clicking into place with perfection, the realization dawned on me. The soul mages had proof that they didn't kill our father. Just as we had proof that we didn't kill their princess. But of course, neither one of us believed each other, and yet...

"I didn't believe them." He continued, but I heard the unspoken words clearly as the moon on a cloudless night; *if they didn't kill Father, we have someone masquerading as one of them.* In other words, we had a problem. A terrible and rather strange but horrible problem.

Silence settled once again before I shattered it. "Then I need to find that Neithisis." All he did was nod, and all I could do was nod back before walking out of the room.

I approached my parent's bedchamber, holding my breath, feeling my heart beat inside me with the will to escape its bone cage. I gulped. Never had I been this afraid to see her, to see her weak and crumbled. The love of her life died. Stripped from her in a heinous way. Broken and cracked like her. Fighting back the tears, the one act my mother trained me to never let show, I raised my hand, brought it to the frame of the door and knocked. The guards around me, if they wanted to offer condolences, didn't. Maybe it was better that way. I hated receiving pity, having people feel sorry for me. It made me feel weak, something I couldn't afford, especially not now. They had simply nodded when I made my appearance and I nodded back. They never had to take an oath of silence, but many times it seemed like they did.

The door handle shifted and then the door opened slowly as my mother's maid poked her head out. Paler than usual. Her brown eyes held fear. Her fingertips were covered in blood. I grimaced. My father laid somewhere in there, dead. I could feel myself feeling faint, the darkness threatening to envelop me whole. I swayed, blinking and shaking my head, trying to regain my composure.

"Ophelia." My voice whimpered. "I need to see her."

The maid simply nodded, opened the door more and let me in, walking out and closing the door. Leaving me standing, my mother on the floor damp with tears, and my father, dead on their bed. I walked in, carefully, almost afraid, as if I was walking into this scene made of glass and one wrong step would make it shatter into countless pieces.

"M—mother?" The word wobbled from my lips into the cold

air. My eyes, betraying all my senses traveled slowly towards the bed. There was a crisp red sheet covering my father's decaying body. I shut my eyes, squeezing out the tears that threatened to fall. Inside, I was glad for the sheet that hid my father's corpse. He was a proud, strong and powerful man. He would have hated people seeing him in such a state. Even in death, I could imagine him bellowing at some poor servant to cover his corpse and bury him immediately.

"Sivrehya darling," she said, breaking her rule about tears herself. I opened my eyes, batting away the incoming tears, sniffling. My mother, broken and frail but still undeniably strong, stood where just seconds before she was half sitting on the floor. Her hair was a mess, with strands sticking out at random spots. The black kohl around her eyes was rubbed off, streaking down her face. Her eyes red and puffy, her face flushed. She seemed the living embodiment of a broken heart. It pained me to see her suffer this way.

"I—I just wanted to let you know that I'm leaving." The moment the words left my mouth she whimpered. Like the regal queen she was though, she straightened her back and slowly made her way to the nearest chair. Once there, she fell on its seat. She brought her once stark white but now black- and grey-stained handkerchief up to her face. "I'm so sorry, Mother, I promise I'll be back soon. See, I'm going to the Twin Cities to find the Neithisis and ask it what happened and–"

My mother sighed, facing me, offering me a weak smile. "Everyone is leaving me. Laidon, your father, Daemon soon for war, and now you." My feet carried to her, and I enveloped her in a tight hug.

"Oh Mom," I fought back tears, I wouldn't allow myself to cry. "I'll be back and Rhi will be here. But I need to know. And then I'll come back and then we'll fight those damned Lysmirans with everything we have."

Her sobs showed on my damp dress; her shudders shook me. "Oh Sivrehya, I'm so tired of war, I want it all to just end. All this fighting, all this tension. I'm sick of it, I need it to end."

"Me too, Mom, me too." I wanted to cry with her. I wanted to show her she wasn't alone. But I didn't, I wiped the tears instead and willed them to stop.

No more crying Sivrehya. No more crying. You need to be strong, for her, for Rhi and Daemon. For Meris, for you.

"Once you find out the truth, tell me." My mother's voice did not quiver; the pain her other words held was gone, her eyes dark. She separated herself from me and stood up, pushing my hair out of my face and behind my ears. "Tell me who did it so I can make them hurt worse than Hell." Danger flickered in her dark red eyes. It matched the dark thing swirling inside me. I nodded.

"I will."

"Farewell then my darling, be safe." She kissed my hair and gave me a small smile. I hugged her once more, for luck, for strength, for something. And then I walked away, wiping the last tear off my face. I closed the doors of her room once again, facing the darkened hallway alone, save for the guards.

"If she gets worse," I looked one in the eye, but they all knew I was speaking to all of them, "get me. Daemon and Jace will be on the battlefields, Rhiannyn is going to have to rule the kingdom in Mother's stead. I know she said she's taking care of her, and I trust with all my life that my sister will, but running a kingdom is no simple feat, especially if it happens to be at war, so if something is wrong tell her, get her and then get *me*. I'll be in the Twin Cities, somewhere in the Merchants' Quarter."

The guard cocked his head, "Very well, of course, Your Highness, but how?"

"Find a way, any way you can think of, but one that's inconspicuous." He nodded his head and I nodded mine back.

IV: IVAR THAEGAN

Kingdom of Lysmir
Royal Palace, City of Lorys

I looked outside the window. My father had been pacing for the past hour, so fast and steady I was sure he was going to dig a track in the floor from the amount of walking. He was angry. No, beyond that. The moment we had reached the castle, walked inside and the doors closed, he *killed* two maids. Their bodies were probably being cremated at the moment. Yet, in all his rage, which caused him to lose control for a split second, and from that loss of control two souls were ripped apart, he hadn't shed a tear. I wagered they both had families, both of which would never see them again. I was already plagued with hatred and anger, but that just piled up on top. I idolized my father, I did; he taught me everything I knew. He allowed me to use my power, which many Scholars in the kingdom said was uncannily strong when my mother optioned for me to stop using it. He showed me the truth of what the blood mages are, ruthless monsters. But I knew, deep down, I'd be lying if I didn't think my father was a monster. He was. So was I. We all were. Monsters against monsters. I've always been told it takes a monster to defeat one, and that monsters come in many kinds. Some were better than others...and some far worse than others. Father repeated the same words before we departed for Meris. It had been my first time seeing the woman who my father called the Bloody Queen in years. It had been just as long since we had seen the princess whose power and beauty was renowned and feared, for good reason. She had rendered us immobile with a flash of her glowing red eyes. I felt the blood inside me freeze in place, *solidify*. The girl...she hadn't even *faltered*. I remembered being taught only particularly strong mages of that kind can solidify blood. It was no surprise she could, she was a Rithloren after all, and that cursed family was known to have the strongest blood mages this world knew. But she was able to solidify blood in thirty people at once, with her mind, for a long amount of time and without even breaking a sweat. I shook my head in disbelief. Father told me the princess was strong. But this, what she had done, wasn't supposed to be possible. Maybe she had help. She had to have had help.

My rambling thoughts broke with the sudden boom of the army commander's deep voice as it rang across the room. "Perhaps we should start waging war on them much earlier. We've been preparing for two weeks, they zero. We'll be ready in one. If we want to win, have the best chance of winning this, we need to take them by surprise, Your Majesty." General Dorian Salvaen stood up from his seat, downing the last of the pale red wine he had poured himself. My father stopped pacing, leaning now on the table and eyeing the silver swirls made of wood. Each one representing a tenth of our army. The blood-red pyramids represented the army of the Rithlorens. But in truth, we hadn't seen their army in ages, or in any of our lifetimes. It was a secret how many soldiers they had on their side.

Father was beyond vexed, crimson-faced from his anger. The blood mages killed Verena, his only surviving daughter and heir, in cold blood for whatever sinister reason floating in their heads, and now they had the audacity to deny it. It was enough to boil his blood, my blood; that cursed princess who screamed at us like a lunatic didn't even have to do it for us.

"With all due respect, General, I must be honest, I don't think that accelerating the date of the fighting will change anything. While the logistics of a fight can take a while, Meris is known to be heavily guarded. They'll have reinforcements we can't see, reinforcements that can wipe us out in seconds." The king's voice hinted at something as if he was trying his hardest not to outwardly say the blood mages could possibly curse us out of existence if vexed enough. But I figured, if they could, they would have already.

"You're right." The general sounded tired and utterly done. Like my father, like me, like all of us.

The king had endured a lot today; we all had. I remembered the moment the castle doors were closed, Maeghalin and her ladies-in-waiting had screamed and whined, practically dressing down, tearing their clothes off in the middle of the hallway. Maeghalin claimed too many people saw her in the blood-stained clothing and she was "utterly embarrassed" that people saw their future queen in *such a state*. I rolled my eyes. The girl couldn't stand blood, she was fearful of and appalled by it, so much so that I was shocked she didn't faint in the middle of the Merisan throne room, or even when the raven had exploded above us.

Her high-pitched wails were annoying if I was to be honest, and despite my secret efforts with my father, she remained my betrothed. Though she was upset and angry at Verena's death by the hand of a monstrous blood mage, I sensed she was a little happy. A small part of her, I knew, was relishing in the fact that just mere hours ago my sister left the queen's throne empty, and she would be the one to fill it when I, by default, became my father's heir. The thought first crossed my mind when she had decided to come with us on the trip. The second time was when she started commanding our servants with more brutality and demand in her voice than before. She was bolder, and I knew I couldn't be the only one who saw it. My mind flashed back to the youngest princess of Meris, to the way her scarlet eyes threw daggers at Maeghalin with her stare. The way her voice, colder than ice, sliced through Maeghalin's confidence like a sharp knife cutting through softened butter. Avran, my best friend and Maeghalin's twin, caught me smiling, asked why, and when I realized it was because my enemy was the only one able to stand up to the snob that Maeghalin was, I cursed myself. I hate that wretched blood princess. While I appreciated, deep down, that someone finally put that girl in her rightful place, it didn't warrant a smile. At least, not from me. Avran also told me that Maeghalin had been staring at me the entire time she had disrobed in the hall. I hadn't noticed it. Pity.

"But we should touch on the unexpected issue that arose today." My voice stilled the room. Both the general and my father turned to face me. The guards as well. "Someone murdered the king of Meris." Silence instantly prevailed. So much so that I could almost hear the beat of my heart. My father turned away from the carved table and sighed. Avran looked down at his feet uncomfortably, and the general just looked at me, with a look on his face that words couldn't describe. Was it disappointment, anger, agreement?

"Gentlemen, I need to speak alone with Ivar for a moment." The king's voice rang throughout the room, bouncing off the armor, off the walls and windows. The general and Avran nodded, and made their way out the door, closing it lightly behind them. It was then that my father turned to face me, his face contorting with raw emotion.

"Father–"

"They lied." He cut me off; his voice held this desperateness to it, a sliver of fear and hopelessness.

"Did they though?"

"Yes." Shakiness. "I have to believe that they did."

"That princess almost *killed* you, Father, almost killed us all. They might be monsters, but they aren't dumb, they know how badly things would end if they decided to suddenly kill half of the Lysmiran royal court." I countered. I wanted them to have lied, I wanted that wretched princess to have lied only to spite her family into trying to kill us. It'd be more of a reason to end their worthless lives. But the truth couldn't be put aside and ignored. Rithlorens were smart. They, like us, were not the ones to make mistakes. Which makes this entire ordeal so much more infuriating.

"They killed Verena, they killed her. Then like the bastards they are, they denied it and decided to frame us for the supposed murder of their king." My father tried to sound reassuring, he tried to take away all fear from his words, but the crack was audible. The thoughts swirling in my mind, about to leave my mouth, died when a sudden series of frantic knocks sounded at the door. Both of us turned our heads slowly to the door, my father sighing before telling the person to come in. I watched intently as the door handle twisted and the door opened, revealing a pale-faced Avran.

"Avran?" I eyed him curiously, "what happened?"

My friend didn't speak. Instead he held out our messenger raven, the very raven that exploded into blood above us out of nowhere. I almost laughed. The raven wasn't dead, it wasn't splattered scarlet all over the ground, in our hair and on our clothes. It was unharmed, in Avran's hand, a small ivory scroll with a very familiar red seal attached to its leg with a rope.

"I haven't opened it. But I found him flying in circles in the main hall," Avran explained as my father walked past me in a hurry I rarely see in him. He was anxious to see what the scroll held. My father ripped the scroll so ferociously, the poor bird yelped in pain. He threw it aside, and it struggled for a bit before regaining its ability to fly. Avran caught it with both hands and looked at me, then my father, then back at me. "I'll bring it back to the Raven Keep." His gaze lingered on the scroll for a split second then turned to me. An unspoken message, telling me to tell him the contents of that parchment. I gave him a subtle nod, and with that he left, closing the door in his wake.

I turned back to my father, and without even thinking about it, I took a small step back. If he was outraged and full of hatred before, what was he now? He looked at me, his silver eyes darkened, with a feral look, darker than hatred, than anger and all the other emotions alike to those. I gulped.

"Father?" I made sure to make my voice sound strong, rid of fear. He said no words; he simply threw the paper on the ground and spat on it. I expected it was done as an act of repulsiveness for whatever was written on the paper, but when the paper started glowing red, the color drained from my face, and the thought left my head. My eyes widened as they settled on the contents on the parchment. A small, detailed and intricate symbol was drawn on the paper with a reddish-brown liquid. Blood no doubt. I watched as the glowing light connected all the lines, and the little ornate designs, until it glowed together as one, as a unit. And from that, the light poured in until the room we stood in disappeared and in its wake, once the light slowly faded, was a very different room.

Kingdom of Meris
Royal Palace, City of Maeh

My muscles responded before my mind did, as my fingers curled around the hilt of my sword and pulled it out with alarming speed. I turned around, surveying the room and its contents, as fast as I could. The more I knew of the place, the better chance my father and I had to get out of this sick prison those bloody bastards put us in. But as soon as I turned to look behind me, after seeing what was in front of me and behind my father was only a stone wall, I froze. My soul could have left my body.

Because now, in front of me was not another stone wall as I would have thought, no. It was the crown prince of Meris himself, Daemon Rithloren, the one who once cursed everyone who had conspired to kill his family with eternal damnation. And beside him, a large four-poster bed, with a dead man lying in it. It didn't take much other than Daemon's death glare and the crown on the man's head to tell me who he was. He was the king of Meris. And he was indeed dead. But that wasn't what made the color drain from my face, what made me freeze in place. It was his ashen, broken, cracked skin. It was the dust around him. It was the fact that the king was dead, in a way only a soul mage would kill.

V : IVAR THAEGAN

Kingdom of Meris
Royal Palace, City of Maeh

The crown prince looked at us, his arms crossed, his facial features radiating a calm but feral glare that spelled out death in the worst way. It was directed at us. I heard my father come up next to me, his own sword unsheathed.

"I could, if I wanted to, rip your soul apart, young man. I don't know what sick illusion this is, but snap us out of it, or you and your family will pay." My father seethed, poison dripping from his words.

But the crown prince was unmoved, his expression now bored. It was clear my father's menacing voice was not menacing enough for Daemon Rithloren. Instead he stepped forward and looked up at the ceiling. I paled as my gaze went from the prince to a symbol painted in blood, (and whose blood it was I didn't care) but whatever it meant, it wasn't good for us.

"You could try, Your Majesty, but if you did, it would be a wasted effort. That is an anti-magic spell. So, your plans of ripping my soul apart are shattered, sorry." His voice lightened up a bit for the last word. "As for this being an illusion, it's not. I am appalled you think I have the ability to do that. I am after all a *blood* mage so chaos magic isn't really my forte," he snapped at my father. "This is very real. That symbol your darling messenger raven gave to you, the very one that should have exploded over your heads but didn't, was a portal symbol, one activated by any sign of hatred towards it."

"Come again?" My father spat.

"An act of hatred upon it. Whether crumbling it up, ripping it apart, stomping on it, throwing it in the fire, spitting on it, as I sense you did," he raised a brow as he said it. "Anything really, with emotions of hate twisted within would have worked. That's how it opened and brought you here." The prince's voice remained calm, a lethal calm. But I would be lying if beneath all that hatred and anger, I did not see sadness and pain. No doubt because of his father's death.

"The raven we sent you *exploded* above us, and yet you're telling me that the raven you sent back was ours? How did you manage this?" My father jutted an elbow into my side for asking such a stupid question. But I was curious by nature; I needed to know.

"My sister convinced me to conjure up a fake raven to explode into blood and instead use the real one you sent up to send a lovely little message back."

"Which sister?" I shot, not even knowing why. Again, my father shot me a disapproving look. I ignored him and based on the crown prince's bored features, so had he.

"Sivrehya." Cold and short. "Now to the reason why I brought you here." He turned to face his father, "You see him now; you see what my sister Rhiannyn said is not a lie but in fact the truth. A soul mage killed my father. Tell me why and *who*." He demanded, in such a way, that I weren't trained and angry and just as dangerous as he was, I would have answered him right away, begging for my life.

My father laughed. "You're insane, young man. Truly mad. We had nothing to do with your father's murder. That's the truth."

Daemon remained calm. "Sivrehya's words reign true. If you do not believe us when we say we have nothing to do with Verena's murder, why should we when you say you have nothing to do with our father's?"

At this my father was speechless. I pointed to the dead king, "Verena had a bloody symbol drawn on her wall. This king has nothing but—"

"Nothing but the signs of a soul destroyed. You cannot deny it, Thaegan. *Look* at him and tell me that his soul wasn't destroyed.

Tell me it wasn't the doing of your kind." He remained calm, threateningly calm.

I had to remain the same way, especially when he had taken my ability to crush his soul with a few delicate strokes on the ceiling. I cursed their abilities, the way they could easily bend things to their will. I looked at the dead king, trying my best to suppress my fear. The king's soul was destroyed, all the signs were there. And I would know, as I had destroyed my fair share of souls in the past. My mind raked for information, for the name of the person that would have been this inexplicably stupid to murder the king of an enemy kingdom in such an obvious way. I knew none of the royal court members would have been mad and plain stupid enough to do this, but someone did, one of our citizens. And it pained me having to track them down and make them pay.

The crown prince took my silence as defeat as he huffed. As he did, my eyes caught onto something, and hope, the smallest sliver of it, surfaced inside me. I looked at the king, this time taking in everything about his appearance. There was a little thing, something that was wrong, that should have been different.

His eyes. They were ashen and white. But that's not what happened when a soul was destroyed. The eyes became black voids. It was always said that eyes were the windows to the soul, and with no soul left to look at, a pit of darkness remained in its place. But not with the king. This strange sensation of relief washed over me. I looked at my father, but he simply remained in a silent staring contest of death with the crown prince. But when my gaze fell back on the king, I noticed it was a one-sided contest, since the prince's eyes were boring into me.

"The eyes, Your Highness. When a soul is destroyed the person's eyes become endless black pits. There's nothing there anymore. Your father, the king, his eyes are ashen and cracked as you can see. His soul was not destroyed. This is a trick of some sort. One of you probably covered his death due to natural causes with some cinders to fool us." My gaze bored into his, throwing daggers and silent curses his way. He was again unbothered. "His soul was *not* destroyed."

"Right of course, and the symbol drawn on Her Highness's wall does not exist." He replied. I blinked. What did the symbol drawn on my sister's wall have anything to do with this?

"I'm sorry?"

"Very well, Prince Ivar, let's say I believe you." He leaned forward. "My father's soul wasn't destroyed because his eyes are not an oblivion of blackness, but then, you must believe me when I say that the symbol drawn in blood on your sister's wall is fake."

I blinked again. This man was...I searched for a word that didn't come to me. "No," I breathed.

The prince stilled, looked at me and my father, then leaned back and shrugged. "Fine then. Your kind killed my father, in cold blood, as you see here. And the war you declared on us, we declare on you. Enjoy the last days of your life, because when we meet next, it will be as monsters against monsters, snuffing out the candle light that is our lives. I will enjoy ripping you apart, Thaegans. That I'm sure you believe, no?" He cocked his head and gave us a sinister smile. Bastard. But I'd be lying if I didn't believe he'd enjoy it as much as I would enjoy killing him.

"We will enjoy destr—" I didn't have time to finish. The crown prince lunged towards us and pushed us back against the wall.

No, not a wall. Because there wasn't a wall. There was a void, and a moment where I was falling in open space.

Kingdom of Lysmir,
Royal Palace, City of Lorys

A thud, and then pain. I groaned, turning my body slowly, my face against grass. I blinked the green blades from my face, coughing and spitting them from my mouth. I sat up, craning my neck and bending my back, shaking off the pain from hitting the ground. I spotted my father not too far away, in the same pain. I looked around me. Above me the sky was clear, the air was warm.

We were outside, in the grassland behind the castle. Standing up, I started walking, avoiding the pain that shot up from my thigh. Blasted prince and his blasted portal that he no doubt drew from bending blood from his mind behind us so we wouldn't be the wiser. Damn him for drawing a symbol that blocked us from our magic. I hated him. Father Darkness how much I hated him. Him and his bloody family.

We hadn't fallen far, so our tumble through open air was rather short. And the castle was close. I lifted my hand to shield my eyes from the blaring sun and looked up at the windows. I prayed, hoped, no one had seen that embarrassing fall. My father hurried to my side, brushing the grass blades from his ivory cloak. First stained with the dried blood from the conjured raven and now pale green from the grass. He cursed.

"I need a new cape now." He grumbled and sped up. Stomping.

"Father!" I called out. He stopped, huffed in anger and turned around.

"What! What is it?" He barked.

I sighed, frantically, "You saw the king. His eyes weren't black. He wasn't killed by a soul mage. While everything else is eerily close to what happens, if not exactly what happens, the eyes are different. Their claim against us is false!" I couldn't help but be a little relieved, and a little, Darkness be damned, happy.

My father, however, maintained a stoic expression. His expression was empty of all emotion, except in his eyes. They were clouded with anger. But it was scary, he was mad, so mad, incredibly beyond vexed that he was *calm*. I recognized his demeanor in someone else. The princess of Meris. She maintained a perfectly calm face despite probably wanting to rip all of our heads off. Both of them mirrored each other. Hate practically dripping off them. It was nerve-racking being near someone who could maintain such a tranquil face when within them a storm was raging.

I looked at him, my eyes boring into his, and they held a darkness I knew all too well, "Father?" My voice didn't quiver; I wouldn't let it.

"I do not *care*. I do not care in the slightest. Because I know they killed my heir, and I will not let them live another day because of it. This war will mean their *destruction*. It will mean the end of blood mages and the damned Rithlorens. I will assure that and the survival of Lysmir."

"But Father, don't you—"

"Ivar. Let it go!" This time his voice could shake mountains, and the anger in his eyes could fuel a battle. "We cannot do anything about their damned king."

Or maybe you just don't want to, the thought ringing in my head as he turned his back towards me and continued on.

I huffed in annoyance. He was being close-minded; he was being the soldier he was before he was crowned king. The emotionless one. "Father, I need to know what happened. I think you do, too. That's your daughter on the deathbed, my *sister*, swimming in her own blood. And that was the damn *king* of Meris we are being framed for killing!"

He stopped dead and turned, his face tight and red. "I know, goddammit! I fucking know!" He bellowed with such ferocity most anyone would cower and run. But I was not most anyone. I was Ivar Thaegan. I've had my fair share of him screaming in my face, yelling threats, insults, commands, and all while doing so much worse. The years, the time, that no longer held a certain number blurred my tears into nothing. Now, I stared at him as he stared at me. With anger.

"Then why don't you want to know what the hell happened!"

"I do want to know, trust me, I do." His voice, though still tense, lowered. "But I have to win a war. I can't go hunting for answers when I don't even know where the hell to start."

I knew he would say that. *I* would have said that, if I were him. But I wasn't him, was I? "I can." There was uncertainty in my voice, as if perhaps I was just uncertain as I sounded. And I was, the words spilled out before I had the chance to truly think about their weight.

"You know where to begin?" My father raised a brow, skeptically.

HA. Absolutely not.

"Well, no," I started, but my father already sighed and turned around, making his way to the castle. I hurried on to match his quick pace and tried to reason with him. "Father, listen. I don't know. But I will, I promise. I'll find something."

"This hunt can't take years or months, and preferably not even *weeks*; we would need the answers as soon as possible."

"Right, yes, I agree."

"I'm glad you do," He didn't sound glad, quite the opposite. His voice was thick with distrust. Not in me, but in my ability to actually find out the truth. His eyes scanned the horizon, filled with the familiar mountains that stood all around us. In his voice, brusque and cold, he asked, "now explain to me how the hell you plan on finding out the truth in such a little amount of time? There are no prophets out there, no one who can look into the past and conjure up the truth."

My mouth refused above all things to open. Not that I knew what I was going to say.

"Give it up." And with that, his voice lingering in the damp air, he marched off. Perhaps to retire to his office, to the map and to the general.

And I simply stood there, watching him, my head lowered. And with nowhere else to go, nothing else to do, I made my way to the library, the one place I could think of that might have some answers to the questions that burned inside my head.

The library in our castle was huge. So big one could easily get lost in the countless aisles that towered high, the swirling staircases, the dark corners and the balconies. It was a mess, but it was where I felt most at home, in an even bigger castle. I usually stuck my face in fictional books, because if it was one thing that fascinated me, it was the stories of different worlds, different magic, different histories that weren't like ours.

Because our history, the past of this kingdom, all the kingdoms, all the cities and this world even, is a particularly dark and dangerous one. Filled with magic and death at every turn of the years and months and weeks and even days. It was a nightmare story for the children; it seemed like one anyway. My mother, when I was younger, would sit next to me at night and read me a story. They were always happy stories, filled with whimsical tales of dashing princes and damsels in distress. Of slain dragons who kidnapped fair maidens, of fields with flowers and smiles on everyone's faces. At the end, every night I would ask if that was our world. And every time she would smile weakly, kiss my forehead and say the same thing, "there was once a world filled with awe and wonder. But that world was never ours."

When she was there, I never saw the world for what it was. Despite her often cold and distant demeanor, she gave me hope that the world was a little bit like the stories she always told my siblings and me. But then, one day, she died. And with it the hope died. Because from that day on, I saw the world for what it was. Dark, dangerous and deadly. Filled with monsters. And I was one of them.

But for now, that didn't matter. All that mattered was finding a particular book. One on magical and mythical beasts. And it wouldn't be in the fictional section, the only area of the library I could figure my way through.

"Ivar?" My name rang out from a deep voice, sounding off all the walls and books. I turned around.

"Avran?"

"Where the hell—" Avran started screaming out again but his words died off as he rounded the corner and saw me. His eyes widened. "Where the hell did you *go*? You just *vanished*. Your father threw that paper on the ground and the next thing I know is there's a flash of light and you're gone!" He huffed, catching his breath.

"Have you been running?"

He looked at me as if I were stupid, "Yes, I've been *running*. You fucking vanished into a flash of light. So naturally, I freak out. Next thing you know, the guards are running around and then this maid comes up to me and says she saw you and the king fall out of, you know, the fucking sky itself. So naturally, again, I freak out. Because what does she mean, you fell out of the sky? I thought, surely, she's going mad. But no, she's not, she's not mad. Because I see you and the king on the ground, limping and screaming your way back here. And then I tried to find you, but poof you ran off to the library for whatever purpose. So yes, Ivar, I have been *running*! Have you been running? Because I swear to—"

"Avran."

"Hm?" He stretched his arms behind him, panting, slowly regaining his steady breath.

"I'm fine. Really, I'm all good."

He laughed, actually *laughed,* "Well, that's wonderful and all. But Ivar, you vanished in a flash of light, and reappeared falling out of the sky. The *sky!* I need an explanation."

My eyes darkened, narrowed, at the thought of the crown prince and what he did. "We were magically whisked back to Meris, to the dead king's room with the crown prince staring daggers in our direction. And then he pushed us back through a bloody portal that conveniently was in the middle of the air."

"Holy shit. If I could do that, imagine the possibilities, they'd be great."

"Yes, I agree. We'd all be dead."

He smacked my arm, "Hey! Not true, I wouldn't kill everyone. Accidentally. Maybe." He looked off into space, maybe hoping for me to be wrong. I smiled.

"Right."

Avran shot me an annoyed look. "Anyway," he said, elongating the word. "Why exactly did you run off here first, of all places?"

"I need to find a book."

"A book. Ah, okay. Mind being more specific?"

I elbowed him, and immediately he swatted me away.

"Aye! Watch the clothes, I need to look good for later."

Now, *that* piqued my interest. I smirked and asked, "and now what could possibly be happening later that you need to be dressed extra nice for? Hmm?" I eyed his rather extravagant garb. He wore a long silver coat with black buttons and black details sewn on. His pants were a crisp black, matching his boots. His hair was even *styled*. His hair was never styled, save for those fancy balls and boring royal court meetings which happened once in never.

"Something..." Avran trailed off, ignoring my questioning eyes.

"I'd like to wager it's more like *someone*, over something?" I poked him in the shoulder, "am I wrong?" There was a grin that I didn't stop from appearing on my face.

"No." He replied after some time, still refusing to meet my gaze, perhaps to hide his blushed cheeks which I could very much see. "But enough about that, we need to find this very interesting book on what now?"

"The truth is..." I said as I made my way over to one of the chaise lounges in the library and collapsed onto it. Sighing. My head in my hands, I continued. "The truth is I don't know what book I'm looking for, I don't know what..." I trailed off, feeling my eyes slowly start to water.

"Hey, Iv, it's okay." Avran sat down next to me, wrapping an arm around me, holding me, as I fought to keep back the tears that so desperately wanted to come out.

"But it's *not* okay, Av." My voice trembled, I trembled. "It's not."

Avran said nothing, but in the silence I could feel him agreeing with me.

"Do you know what sucks?" I lifted my head up, meeting his worried gaze. He remained silent. "That my sister died, Avran. That Verena, who was always there for me, who held me when others couldn't, who stood by my side, who stood up to our father when I couldn't..." I trailed off, the wobbly words dying in my throat. I shut my eyes, squeezing out the tears, feeling them roll down my face, the itchy trail they left behind. My chest heaved. "She died Avran, she fucking died."

My friend, the only one I had left, held me again, this time tighter. "I know, I'm sorry, I'm so sorry." His words, though genuine, did nothing. And I knew the words couldn't heal me, the words couldn't reverse what had happened, but I so wish they could.

"Do you know what the worst part is?"

Silence.

"That she's dead, murdered, gone forever and *I'm* not allowed to cry, I'm not allowed to mourn because my father would do worse than kill me and now we're going to war with Meris and in the end I still don't know what the hell happened to their king and the world is crumbling down and I—I don't know what the hell to do..."

Avran let go of me, his hands around my arms. "I—I am genuinely sorry, and if there was a way to turn back time, to undo what happened, I would do it."

"I know you would be stupid enough to sell your soul for it."

He winked, "You know we both would."

I stifled a laugh. He wasn't wrong. I moved from Avran's hold and fell onto my back, my eyes glazing over the intricate ceiling designs of the library. Silence settled over us once again, like a blanket. I wiped the tears away from my face, breathing in and out and in and out until they were gone. Until I could see everything clearly.

"I have to do something Av, and I have no idea where to start, but something feels terribly off and it's eating away at me and I know the chances of finding out the truth are incredibly slim and I know what my father said is true but—but I need to know."

Silence, again.

"What did your father say?"

"Hm?" I opened my eyes, turning my head to face him. His pale silver eyes bored into mine.

"You said you know what your father said is true."

"Oh..." I trailed off, trying to remember what my father had said.

It had been something about a prophet?

Oh!

"He said that no one can look into the past and tell the truth or —I'm not sure, something along those lin—" Avran suddenly pulled at my arm, pulling me off the chaise, and I stumbled, doubling over, almost falling flat on my face.

I looked at him, raising a brow. "Explanation?"

But he didn't say a word, he just pulled, dragged me through the library, weaving us between the shelves of countless books. And then after what seemed like forever, he came to an abrupt stop and I slammed into him.

"Avran?" I said it warningly, threateningly. He turned beaming, mischief in his cloudy eyes.

"Look," he started, as his eyes went from my own to the books in front of us. He scanned them thoroughly, looking for something. "I might have an idea, a wild one, but there's a chance you'll be able to uncover the truth of what really happened to Verena and the king of Meris."

I looked at him, dumbfounded.

"You do?"

"Yes," his eyes still searching for whatever it was he had in mind as he continued, "it might not work, I might be wrong, but I remember learning about this magical creature, that probably is older than time itself. But if I remember correctly...aha!" He pulled a thick grey book off the shelf.

The Unabridged Encyclopedia of Mythical and Magical Creatures of Rodessa.

At that I just looked at him, confused but all the same curious.

"Mythical and magical creatures in Rodessa?" I questioned.

"Yes," he turned to me. "Because you know, there are such things as mythical and magical creatures that live on the continent of Rodessa, you know the continent we live on..." His smile, his ever-famous smile edged itself on his face. I lightly punched him.

"Yes, I know we live on the continent of Rodessa and that we have mythical and magical creatures, you smartass." I scowled, but he just laughed, proud of himself. I rolled my eyes.

"Well good, but anyway, there's this one creature, the really old one I was talking about," he flipped through the pages of the book. "And besides having nine eyes too many, and magical powers attached to each if it opens them, blah blah blah, it knows everything in the past and cannot lie..." He trailed off, elongating the word "lie" as he brought up a finger to scan the page he flipped to.

The Neithisis. I remembered learning about it when I was younger, as it was featured in a lot of those warning stories for little children.

"Aha!" Avran shoved the book into my chest. I huffed, grabbing it before it fell to the floor.

"There! See!" He pointed to a paragraph. I looked at him, still confused, and then read it, and as I did, my spirits fluttered just a bit.

And ever so slowly a smile appeared on my face, "Avran, you genius!" I would have hugged him if I weren't holding this gigantic book.

"But the problem is, no one really knows how or where to find them. They're very mysterious things." He sounded defeated, but I just smiled, my eyes on one sentence in particular. And as I read it, a dangerous idea formed in my head.

I looked at my friend, smiling wickedly. "Not to worry, I'll find it, Avran. I'm going to find it and get the truth."

This time he was confused, but all the same I slammed the book shut, put it back on the shelf and hugged my friend. I took his face with both my hands and shook it. His eyes wide.

"Thank you, thank you, thank you!" I placed a wet kiss on his forehead and ran off, his fading voice trailing after me. But I continued running, with the sentence from the book swimming in my head, shining like the sun.

VI : IVAR THAEGAN

Kingdom of Lysmir
Royal Palace, City of Lorys

I f someone thought the library was big, the Lysmiran palace was ten times, perhaps even more than ten times bigger than the room filled with books. It was enormous, and one could say, that one person being me, that it was far too big. As a child I would play hide-and-seek with my siblings and we could never find each other, not without using our magic. There were too many halls, too many rooms, too many secret passageways, with some covered in cobwebs which led to an entire channel of secret entrances to various rooms. I often thought of them as the veins inside a body, all tangled and leading to different places. The palace was so old, almost an entire millennium old, and I knew the passages had been built the moment this palace had been. They had been lost to history and I doubted anyone used them anymore. But I hadn't dared mention them to anyone, except of course, my sisters. It was a secret we all kept, should our father not know and then try to destroy them or perhaps ban us from using them. Which would then make us only want to escape into their darkness even more.

But despite the endless secret ways and countless rooms, the easiest person to find was my father, for he was usually in three places. His office, the training grounds where he trained every morning or well, actually, maybe it was only two places he could be found in. He was rarely in his chamber, which is where one would usually sleep. Unless you were the king of Lysmir, which meant then you'd probably sleep on the large couch that lay in his large office. But right now, of all times, my father wasn't in either his office or the training grounds. Or his chamber, or the stables where he sometimes frequented to feed his horse from childhood. One that he could no longer ride, but if he had a heart, still loved.

I had no idea where else to look for him. One would assume that I, his son, would be able to find him, to know the places he'd be when he wasn't in others. But I wasn't. Much to my discontent.

Avran had helped me find the book that looked more like a weight one lifted in training to grow stronger. That thing that was perhaps the largest book I had ever seen, and definitely the heaviest. It was the unabridged version of the entire encyclopedia of magical and mythical creatures in our world. Those that still existed and those that faded with time, mostly for the better. There had been monsters, Darkness made flesh, that fed on magic, that feasted on it. That despite their greatest fear of light, would run through it if magic was on the other side of it. They smelled it, thirsted for it. And they were ruthless, deadly creatures, the worst ones. They lived where the Darkness triumphed the most in its days, where it had perhaps originated. The Raven Mountains.

Many, if not all, believed that with the Darkness gone, that those creatures were also gone. But, some part of me knew, the Darkness was never truly gone. It had left terrible things that were forever in its wake, to perhaps remind the world of what it was, what it could be and what it would be, should it ever come back.

There were of course those that were gone, for certain. Those that died when the Siblings, better known as the Dark Crowns, shrouded the world in Darkness and destroyed everything. And there were those who had survived it all, and those who came after, that were still around. The Neithisis was one of those two. I liked to think it was the former. After all, I had read the books on the Dark Crowns. I had heard they encountered a creature who had nine too many eyes, should the norm be two and ten too many heads, should the norm be one.

While those books had only a mere couple sentences on the creature, this book, the one that Avran showed me, held *pages* on the mythical beast. In all their worth, they gave me one important line, a starting place. And for now, that was enough.

The Twin Cities, Sunsier and Moonsier, was the last place, and perhaps the only place, with those who know how to find the elusive creature that is the Neithisis.

The moment my eyes read that, I grabbed the nearest quill and copied down the sentence word for word. I wasn't looking for permission to go to the Twin Cities from my father, but I figured he'd better know where I was. And in my experience, it was better I told him where I'd be in person and not on a piece of parchment.

But I couldn't find him. Praise Darkness, the one singular time I needed him slightly urgently, he was gone. If only this palace wasn't so damn big, I'd have found him by now. The servants all bowed and apologized when they couldn't tell me where he was. Nor did the guards know where my father had escaped to. I racked my mind for something, anything, that could tell me where the absolute hell my father was.

There was only one place that came to mind. I was debating shrugging it off, considering the place was locked, and though my father had the key, he never stepped foot into the room.

My mother's room. The one that was once filled with Silver Root, her favorite flower. The one that smelled like them and also of raspberry tea. The one that was the most colorful of all the rooms in the castle, the one that was filled with light and warmth. The one she left behind when one day she retired to her bed to sleep and never woke.

My father had the room locked up the moment her body was placed into a silver casket and buried however many feet under the ground. I lost her so many years ago, it felt like an eternity. Perhaps because she wasn't the only one I had lost then. I always assumed that's why my mother left us too, because my youngest sister had always been her favorite child. Despite her loving Verena and me just as much, she and my younger sister had always had this special bond that back then filled me with the childish hope that other feelings, despite the anger and pain, existed. But of course, that hope had been smothered by their deaths.

My feet carried me, warily, to my mother's room. The double doors, tall and grey, were closed. But when I reached my trembling hand out, and turned the silver knob, it didn't stay stiff like all the times before. It moved, ever so slightly. It creaked; no doubt it was rusted after years of disuse. I peeked inside, craning my neck and squinting my eyes to see through the darkness. The curtains were drawn, blocking the fading light from outside. The air was thick and musty; it smelled old and locked off from everything. But despite all that I saw a figure, sitting, on my mother's favorite chair.

"Father," I crept into the room, shutting the door behind me.

"So, you found me." His voice was still strong, still cold and harsh. He hadn't been crying then, merely thinking.

"I did." My feet stayed glued in their place, perhaps because what I said was true. My father looked like a brooding shadow, an assassin with a target and a sharpened dagger that was ready to hit it. He looked anything but weak.

"Did you love her?" A stupid question really. I already knew the answer. I always had, though I doubt he knew I did.

"No. But just because I did not love her, does not mean I can't miss her. I respected her, as she did me. She was able to rule this great kingdom with an iron fist. She was there when I couldn't be. For that, I miss her." He paused and even through the darkness that swallowed up the room, I could feel his beady silver eyes on me. "Why are you here?"

I fought the urge to clap back with some kind of insult, but despite his question sounding less like curiosity and more like a disgusted demand, I cooled down the red emotions that immediately spiked inside me. Nothing good would come out of it.

"I found a starting place. For finding out what happened to Verena and the king." I heard him sigh, in no doubt, dismay. It was no secret that my father and I weren't close. We barely got along, and while the act of respecting each other was there and all, the love wasn't. I was sure it never had been there, for I had always doubted my father was capable of loving. If he was, it was something that he kept hidden. As a child I looked up to him, not as a father, but rather a leader. A king. And a soldier. Someone I wanted to be when I grew up. Well, more the soldier than king. Verena was always meant to be queen; I was never meant to be king. But Verena was dead, and now that meant I was his heir. There was no relief, no happiness in that. Because deep down the thought of ruling a kingdom, despite me having received training, scared me too much.

"Did I not tell you to give up?" Ah, he spoke in his ever-discouraging voice. I stopped letting that get to me. Part of me was glad, thankful that he had always been cruel, because from all his terror, he made me strong.

"You did, but you know that with this, I can't. I *won't*," I added for emphasis. "I'm not here to ask for permission. I'm here to tell you where I'm going."

At that he stood up and, like lightning, made his way towards me. Pure fury floated around him, filling the air. In the darkness, I could make out his pale face, now just slightly red. I could see his neck, a vein bulging. Emotions were not something my father usually kept hidden; the closest would be when he felt something so strongly that he seemed calm. But that wasn't really hiding emotions, that was just feeling too much of them.

"You are staying here!" My father didn't bother to keep his voice low. He yelled. Bellowed. Filling the entire room with his voice, sending it bouncing off the dusty walls.

"We are going to *war*. War. And I need all the soul mages I can get if I want to tear those damn blood mages to pieces." He didn't need to say them, but I heard his unspoken words; *you are powerful, very powerful and you need to be here to tear them apart.* Part of me resented him for seeing me more as a piece in his game of destruction and less like his actual child. We both knew I was strangely good with our magic. It showed early on, when I had done something not even he could do now as an adult. My mother was scared, perhaps another reason she and I never became as close as she was with my sisters as time passed. My father instead saw me as a weapon, a valuable asset. Not a child. Not anymore. I was thrown into training, harsh training that left me tired, aching and bleeding. He created a monster, worse than the one I would have become if I hadn't been so damn powerful. Being strong and good with magic was important, very important. But there was a point where being too good, too powerful, made you a threat, made you become something to use, control and fear.

"Make no mistake, Father, I want to tear them apart, and I *will*. But first, I have to find out what happened. Perhaps not for you. But for Verena."

My father trembled, his body shaking. "She is dead." His voice, like cold death. "Dead. Do not bother doing *anything* for her."

"Then for me!" I exploded. My power surging through me, begging to be used, to be unleashed to do all the terrible things it could do. "Because I am still alive, and forgive me for wanting to know what the hell happened to my sister!" I laced my voice with passion and outrage. For my father. The moment the last word left my mouth I was gone. I didn't bother to see my father's face, to witness his reaction, which no doubt would be more screaming.

But I heard footsteps behind me. Loud, calculated ones. Like my father's. I spun around, bracing myself for another round of screaming. It was nothing I wasn't used to. I swear to the Dark Father, something like this happened at least one a week. Over trivial things. Over important things. In the end it didn't matter. Usually we came to some agreement, some compromising between the two of us, and then we moved on. Coldly and distantly like before, like always.

"One week. That is all you get. We go to war after the second. I want you back and I want you to update me on everything." He said this rather bluntly, with a hint of tiredness. I blinked, knowing I hadn't been looking for his permission, but somewhat relieved he wouldn't be forever fuming at me.

"Very well." I replied tersely.

"And say goodbye to Lady Maeghalin. It's not good to leave without saying farewell to your betrothed."

Ah yes. My betrothed. Maeghalin Salvaen. Darkness save me.

I feigned a smile and nodded as I said, "Of course father, wouldn't dream of it."

My father nodded curtly, and turned around, walking away down the lengthy stone hallway to Darkness knows where. I, on the other hand, headed to the White Hall. The part of the palace where everything was sickly white and where Maeghalin was. I grimaced at the thought, as I sent silent daggers in my father's direction. He knew, he knew damn well I didn't like her, let alone love her. But like always, he didn't really care. I shoved the nightmarish idea of what life would be like with her as my wife, and now, my queen, from my mind long ago. Every once in a while, it resurfaced, following with trips to Avran's room and him trying to console me because he too agreed his twin sister was unbearable. It didn't help that she was, as Avran put it, "completely taken by me." She made sure I knew too. For all too often she would come at night, wearing lace and nothing else, and bat her lashes. It didn't help that once, perhaps a couple years ago, I had fooled myself into thinking I loved her. Back then I would have let her run her hands all over me, I would have let her kiss me and undress me. But now, just at the thought of that, I died a little inside.

It's not that I hated her. She never broke my heart, despite her having done what she did with me with numerous others. Maeghalin, I came to find out, did not want love really. She just told herself that. What she really wanted was power, and she already had it, from her father's status. But she was hungry for more, greedy for more. She no doubt had thought about being queen, perhaps even going as far as trying to seduce Verena. Or maybe that's where her limit was. Because for whatever reason she turned angelic around Verena, but set her sights on me. Even after I had told her, various times, that I did not love her. That I never had. That I had been young and beyond stupid, but not in love. Of course, that didn't stop her and sooner than I wish never, my father had betrothed me to her. Without asking me, he just one day, at a ball, announced it. Maeghalin was overjoyed, perhaps with the thought of all the power that came with marrying me. I was quite the opposite. Even then my father knew of my dislike of her. But it hadn't mattered.

And now Verena was dead. Our future queen was dead. And that left me as king and Maeghalin as queen. She would become the one thing I knew with all my cold heart she wanted. And I disliked her even more for that. If she wasn't a soul mage I could possibly hate her more than the damn blood mages, or the Rithlorens themselves. But she was one of us, and as greedy and bitchy and whiny and commanding and completely terrible as she was, she was a soul mage. And we, above all, stuck together. For better or for worse, and I swear it, it felt more like for worse.

Maeghalin and her entourage of excessively loud ladies would be in the White Hall, the one that housed the most important people and their families. And Maeghalin, daughter of our general army commander, much to my chagrin, lived with us. If only she didn't, then I could more easily escape her clutches.

And to get to the White Hall, also known as the worst one, I had to pass through the Grey Hall. Here, the floor was stone, cold, and it felt as if it was sucking all the heat out from the rooms. This hall used to be decorated in elaborate paintings that no doubt took hours upon hours to finish. But that was back when I was younger, and the day my mother died, Father ordered all the paintings, and the flowers and all the colorful things my mother had placed here, to be carried away and stored in the cellars below the dirt. My father made this hall nothing but grey as its name and cold like him. It was harsh, with jagged stone walls and iron torch holders lining the walls. The windows had no curtains; there was no carpet here either. It looked like a brightly lit prison, all the wooden doors leading to a cell instead of my father's office, my mother's abandoned one, and other rooms I'd forgotten about. And as I walked through it, I missed the color, I missed the life this hall once had. And I remembered there was a secret entrance somewhere here, I had forgotten where, after my father had the painting that hid it removed.

But I remembered it led to the kitchen. To where my sisters and I would sneak off in the middle of the night to eat freshly made cake and bread. My favorite had always been the blackberry cake. It was sweet and bitter, and I used to think it was like me.

As my feet carried me through the White Hall, I wished that I didn't have to be here. The only reason I didn't totally avoid this place was because Avran's room was here. Though now, since the formal announcement of the engagement between me and his sister, he and I chose to be in all the places that weren't in the White Hall. Where Maeghalin and her ladies-in-waiting were always gossiping and ordering around poor servants to bring them more cake, more sweets, more tea, more clothing, more this, more that. The list was endless.

I often wondered how a place could be so void of emotion, of something, anything really. The White Hall was the epitome of places that were empty of any personalization. Here, the floors were white stone, the walls were white, the curtains were white, the tapestries that hung on pale silver rods were also white. The threads were stitched into intricate patterns and designs were even different *shades* of white. Because apparently that existed. The flowers were always in white vases on white tables and were usually white roses.

Praise Darkness, I hated roses. Their smell made me sick. It was sweet, but too sweet. The kind of sweet that made you feel faint. The other halls, despite their names, had other colors. The Silver Hall had tapestries that sung with color, and the flowers in the other halls, though usually roses as well, were not only white. They were blood red, pink, pale yellow and there were those that were white, with red borders, as if they were bleeding. Simply said, there was color in all of the halls save for this damned White Hall.

As I walked on, I eyed a singular vase with white roses dipped in silver. Curious, for I had never seen them before. But, despite this unusual sight, my mind quickly turned to Maeghalin. As much as I hated it, it would be rude to appear to her empty handed. I scanned the hallway, at the other roses in their identical vases. None of their soft petals were touched by silver. I smiled, wanly, as I plucked the bouquet from the vase and set it back empty. One of the servants would soon see to it.

The all-too-high-pitched voices of Maeghalin's many friends rang through the halls. I calmed myself, telling myself that it would all be fine. I would walk into that room, hand her the flowers, kiss her on her deathly pale cheek, tell I was leaving and walk out unharmed. All would go extremely smoothly.

Ivar, if you believe that, you are stupid.

I almost laughed at my thought. False hope, to think, it would all go smoothly. It never did, never would. Not with Maeghalin. So, I let my ears guide me in the direction of screams and laughter. They led me to the parlor of the White Hall, the biggest room in this section of the palace where tea was served and there were sweets and pastries on the tables always, all day. There were three large fireplaces, one giant chandelier and chaise lounges, and large upholstery, which were, of no surprise, all white and ivory. The paintings in this room had some color, all white-washed and overly pastel; at least they were painted in something other than white. Or ivory. Or pearl. Or even eggshell, as Maeghalin liked to use to describe the color of the curtains in this room. I always wondered why she bothered with the nitpicky colors. Eggshells were white. And so were the curtains in the room.

My betrothed, dressed in a stark white gown that went incredibly low on her chest and seemed too tight for her to breathe, with pearls attached all over the skirt in a sort of fading effect, was lounging her with her friends drinking tea and eating, no doubt, cake. I forced a smile on my face. Usually they didn't hurt; this one did. No sooner did I step through the threshold of the damn door did her head snap in my direction, and she squealed and made her way towards me. She bunched up her skirts in her hands as she walked over towards me, and before I knew or thought or even uttered a word, I felt her thin arms envelop me. She pressed herself against me, but all I did was give her an empty hug back. She detached herself from me, after too long, and batted her lashes as her grey eyes looked into mine.

"My love!" She giggled, blowing me a kiss. I fought the urge to run, to curl into a ball and fall asleep forever.

My love. My. Love. She's called me that before, a lot. Each time I hated it.

Dearest Darkness, take me now. Please.

"Maeghalin darling, how are you." I said as I spat out those words; they felt so very forced to me. But a smile remained plastered on her face. She eyed the flowers in my hand.

"Are those for me, Ivar sweetest?"

Kill me now.

"Yes." The word sounding, without question, forced. I thrust the roses into her hands, and she all too eagerly took them. My eyes glanced over at her friends, girls I had seen once or twice, barely at all. They came here at the balls we rarely hosted and that was that. But I neither came to this room often, nor did I care enough to know who they were to want to converse with them at a dance. They all eyed me, cautiously since I was Maeghalin's fiancé, but still, I saw something swirling in their grey eyes. My eyes snapped back to Maeghalin who smiled at me, sweetly. Too sweetly.

"Ah, what a prince you are!"

Yes indeed. What a prince I am.

"Listen Maeghalin, I'm going to leave early tomorrow morning."

At this she turned her head, feigning sadness, her brows furrowing together as they did when someone was sorrowful. "Why?" She mumbled.

"To go to the Twin Cities." Her eyes sparkled once again, as if they were never filled with fake sadness.

"Take me!"

"I cannot, I'm sorry—" *No I'm not.* "I have to leave on a time sensitive trip, to recover some information that will be vital in the war."

She looked sad again, but she managed to look up at me and smile. "Very well then, I cannot force you to take me with you. I need to stay here and help in any way I can, right?" There was something in her eyes, some relief, or perhaps mischief.

"Right yes," I smiled at her again.

"You must stay a bit then, before you go."

No. Nope.

"Alright," My lips formed a thin line. Much to my chagrin, I knew I couldn't deny Maeghalin this.

"What were you talking about, I could hear you from all the way down the hallway." It was a cheap attempt at a conversation, but she had already looped her arm with mine, tightly, so I wasn't going anywhere.

Avran, you ingenious bastard...I need you.

I uselessly, yet mentally prayed for my friend to somehow magically show up and usher me away because of some absolutely atrocious thing that had just happened. We more often than not had to save each other from her.

Remembering he had said not to ruin his clothes because he needed to look nice later destroyed any hope I had that he might come. Whomever he was with was no doubt taking up his entire attention.

It looked as if I would have to brave this one on my own.

Maeghalin led me to the chaise lounge where she had been laying. To the left there was a small table, where a silver tray held a white tea pot and a small tea cup with a blackish steaming liquid inside of it.

"Kasla!" She shrilled; a maid popping her head out of a nearby door came only seconds later. She bowed once seeing me.

"Your Highness," she said. Her voice was soft spoken, almost afraid. I couldn't blame her. Half the staff feared me even though they respected me. Not only me, but also my father, well...mostly my father. After all, he *had* killed two servants only minutes after coming back from Meris—the first time.

I bowed my head in her direction and watched as Maeghalin thrust the flowers into her hands, just as I had done to her, but with more force. As the poor flowers lost petals, my eyes followed their drifting path instead of Maeghalin who screamed at Kasla to get them in some water immediately or else. Or else what, I wondered. What would Maeghalin do to her?

"Well, my love," my head snapped in my betrothed's direction, her words breaking my thoughts. She sat down, patting the space next to hers, motioning me to sit. I sat, every second wanting to walk out the door. Which wasn't even that far. "We were talking about what happened. Haelis was the only one that was with me, as were you obviously, but she and I have been telling the other of the atrocities that happened." The other girls nodded; all were displaying shock on their pale features.

"I just cannot believe the nerve of that bloody princess; how dare she disrespect you." One girl with dark brown hair shook her head in disbelief. I almost snorted. The princess of Meris hadn't dared anything. She had a perfectly good reason to scorn Maeghalin. As much as it pained me to take her side, we had been in her kingdom and her voice was higher than ours. We were in her territory, and as much as we hated her, we couldn't disrespect her without being in the wrong.

Haelis, perhaps Maeghalin's best friend, nodded, her eyes darkened with hate for the blood princess. "I agree. But you know what really set me off? That she's pretty. I hate her for it. She is too powerful and too pretty." Now that argument just confused me. I looked at her, trying to hide my thoughts from creeping onto my face and turning into a readable expression.

"I know, but I'm so much prettier." Maeghalin rebuffed, "and I have power too. If not more than her."

Now that was a lie. And I knew Maeghalin knew it was a lie too. She might have doubted the princess's abilities before having met her, as I would have, but after the display of today, all the rumors speaking of her magic, or her uncanny power over blood, reigned true.

But if she knew it was a lie or not, she didn't let it show. She only reveled in her friends agreeing with her, showering her with endless compliments. And then Maeghalin turned to face me.

"What do you think my love, don't you think I'm so much prettier than that horrible bitch princess?" She even sounded sweet when she said that, no doubt faked.

I feigned a smile, another one. One day just I had to keep count of how many fake smiles I gave people. "Yes, Maeghalin, you are." The words came out of my mouth in the emptiest way possible. I leaned in and kissed her cheek, lightly, just a touch. Nothing more. I barely wanted to do this. But unless some miracle allowed me to live my life not married to this woman, there was no escaping this marriage. I had made good things out of terrible things; it was hard, impossible. And now, I would have to do it all over again.

"See Maeghalin, you do not need to worry. You are beautiful." One of the girls interjected as I stood up. The other girls nodded and Maeghalin, her eyes still on me, just waved a hand dismissively in the air at them. I could tell she wanted me to do more. To kiss her. But I wouldn't. I would delay that for as long as possible.

"Yes, that princess is not as beautiful as you," Haelis agreed, smiling, sipping on her tea. But her compliment was almost void of emotion, as if her words were not her own.

I escaped the room, to the hall, thinking of why of all things they were so desperate to be the prettiest. I told Maeghalin she was beautiful. They all had.

And that was the truth. Maeghalin was indeed pretty. But the truth was also that the princess of Meris was a breathtaking thing, even more so than Maeghalin. Because the princess had a harsh beauty that came from pain and darkness and it *interested* me, she interested me. It was the truth, and a truth that I immediately ripped up and turned to ash.

I couldn't, wouldn't think of that, of her, or of anything for that matter. Not when I had a city to go to, a Neithisis to find, a truth to uncover and then, a kingdom to destroy.

VII : SIVREHYA RITHLOREN

The Twin Cities
Sunsier

First and foremost, if there was something I hated more than anything, or more than a lot of things I should say, it was the heat. Not all things that exuded a warmer temperature, but the uncomfortable heat. The one that stuck to your skin, that made you sweat and melt and beg to anyone or anything for a drop of water because even if you downed a glass of water two seconds before, the heat sucked it all out of your body, making you feel hot, sweaty, smelly and faint.

I *hated* it.

And of course, that was what the Twin Cities felt like.

Cue the internal screaming.

I had been there, perhaps two minutes, past the large golden gates that led to the outer portion of the city, past the tall trees whose large pale green leaves offered much needed shade, past the fountains spewing water out and past the grassy area, and I was already thirsty for water. Enough so to kill someone for it. Maybe.

All of the green and lovely shade stood behind me, and in front of me was well, a *desert*. This was the Merchants' Quarter, also known as the Outer City. It was where those who weren't Scholars, or students of the prestigious academies lived and worked. The ground was a mixture of gravel and reddish orange sand. The buildings were mud red, brown, light tan, tan, and if they had been colorful at one time, the paint that had been used was mostly gone. Leaving in its wake a pale, pastel color of what it once was. The smell made up for the heat. The aroma was of spices, baked goods, food, perfumes in large ornately designed glass bottles, and hanging fruit in the shapes of a million things. Stands filled to the brim with things were everywhere. Colorfully woven tapestries were hung strategically in order to keep the sun from ruining whatever merchants were selling, or stopping it from melting people right where they stood. And today, as others before it, people were running around holding rolls of fabric. Others yelling orders at others. Some were trimming the plants, planting plants, making them grow with their gold-yellow glowing magic. Solar magic. Solar mages. Mages of all kinds lived here, save perhaps for blood and soul. And obviously chaos. I knew why everyone was in a frenzy, they had a few days left to prepare for the biggest festival that ever took place in any of the cities or kingdoms or villages. The Festival of the Midnight Sun. Where solar and lunar mages alike turned an already magical city into a land of fantasy, a world beyond our own. Ever since I was a little girl, I've dreamt of seeing the festival. Not just hearing stories of it from the lips of our people, but to actually see it. Experience it. I would be lying if I wasn't a little excited that even though right now nothing in my life was going the way it should, I at least was able to experience this even a little bit.

Stands filled the streets. Every single piece of wall that wasn't taken up by doors, windows or plants was where the vendors placed their wares. And the people, oh, the people were another story. If the market added the aromas and the wonder, the people added the color. Their clothes were of every shade of every color, each one different than the other. Some were plain; others had bright hues atop other bright shades. Others had bells jingling metallically or small mirrors sewn into the fabric, and still others held ornate beading that was no doubt heavy.

My mind wandered back to my kingdom. Where there, my family and I wore red and black. The guards in their garbs of the same colors. The soldiers in their garb of the same colors. The people who wore muted, dark colors. Faded colors, colors with barely any life in them. I didn't hate it; fashion wasn't my forte anymore. When it came to dresses, it wasn't about the beauty, the fabric or how many beads made of obsidian could be sewn onto it. It was about a flowing skirt, about something with pockets, that wasn't too tight, that allowed me to look like a princess and also gave me the ability to move however I pleased. After all, fights happened. And I wasn't about to let an overly fancy dress get in my way of killing someone.

However, looking at all the people around me, each in their colorful outfits, with unique designs and shining fabric, I couldn't help but gaze in awe. My outfit, drab as ever, consisted of a thin black dress that fell just below my feet with sleeves that reached my elbows, and black boots, laced up and of course hiding within them were two throwing knives. My hair, no doubt flaming hot to the touch from the sun above, was tied up in a sturdy bun encased in braids. My maid, Lissa, had insisted on doing my hair this way. And I was glad I didn't stop her. If my hair had been down, I would have been dying even more than I already was. I was already wearing jet black, the dress was loose, sure, but that didn't really matter. In fact, nowhere around me did I see a single person wearing black, and judging from the quick looks in my direction from people who wore bright colors, I was unquestionably a foreigner.

Fabulous. Off to a great start.

Inside my bag, which of course was also black. Good hell, I must look like death and Darkness personified seeking out my next victim.

In Meris I could wear all black, walk the streets of any village and no one would bat an eye. Mostly because they would also be wearing all black. But here. Here I would need new clothes if I wanted to fit in. I was here on a mission; I wouldn't let people question me based on my outfits about where I was from. The people here, by rumor, were nice. Too nice. They smiled too much, laughed too much, talked and sang too much. And above all, they were curious; they soaked up information like sponges, begging and thirsty for an even a tiny sip of crisp and refreshing knowledge. Not that I wasn't like that, as I loved learning and above all, I wanted to know so many things. That's mostly why when I wasn't training, I was reading books. Any books, so long as they gave me more knowledge of anything really. I wasn't picky. However, the clear distinction between these people and me was that I didn't walk up to complete strangers, grab them by the arm smiling and ask them to literally just tell me their life story over a cup of goddamn lemon tea.

And that *just* happened. A woman in orange skirt, with gold details and a matching top, paired off with a magenta see-through scarf that was wrapped around one shoulder going diagonally down to her waist, walked up to a young couple on the street, looped arms with the woman and guided them to a small shop. She shrilled out "three lemon teas please." I rolled my eyes. If someone did that to me, a spear made of out their own blood would end them, I swear it.

Being nice was overrated. Being friendly got you robbed, or worse. Being kind got you killed. Maybe in this city not so much. Maybe this city was a door to another world, one that didn't live in the one I did. Because in my world to survive one must be ruthless, cunning and smart. One must be willing to murder, to torture, to lie as if telling the truth and to trust only a few. And if that trust was broken, make them pay and move on. There was no time for mourning, no time for sadness and all the icky things. Our world was cold, dark and dangerous and above all unforgiving. To survive you had to become the flesh version of our world. Match your wickedness with its own.

The smells and sounds carried on into the smaller streets, the capillaries of the city, allowing people to pass through from one end of the Quarter to the other, from behind a building to the front of another one. They, unlike the larger streets, were empty of vendors. Here, the streets still held their fair share of people, bustling around, but it was quieter, more peaceful, and cooler, thanks to the shade. I escaped into one of these smaller streets, knowing that as pretty as the city was so far, I came here for a reason, and I was going to see it through.

The hotels and inns were all over the city, each of them grand and fancy, colorful and bright, each seemingly trying to outmatch the others in secrecy. Each were decorated much like the rest of the Quarter, with golden suns and silver moons painted on walls, hanging in the form of tapestries. Swirls and majestic patterns painted in navy blue and silver on the walls of each building, flowing from one to another glowed and *moved* almost, pulsating underneath the paint. No doubt enchanted by magic.

A tap on my shoulder broke my trance. I whipped around, spinning on the heels of my boots. A girl, about my age, with dark brown hair tied up in a twisted bun decorated with golden flakes, stood in front of me. Her brown skin shone in the light, the gold beads of her ivory-colored top and skirt matched the gold amber color of her eyes. Solar mage then. If her eyes hadn't given it away, it would have been the shiny embroidered suns on the fabric of her clothing, or the simple fact that she was wearing gold and yellow. The girl looked regal, more royal than I looked right now. I was a sweaty mess of Darkness personified. She'd better not be one of those who kindly demands my entire life story over some exotic flavor of tea. She smiled, ear to ear, despite carrying a basket filled with what looked like stones. Shimmering blue, pearlescent things. I blinked.

"Yes?"

"Oh, sorry miss, I just said 'excuse me,' I need to get past." She nodded past me, and smiled still. How did her face not ache from it? I, having to pretend to avoid undesirable questions, feigned a smile.

"Right, of course, yes, I'm so sorry." I batted my lashes, showing my teeth, trying very hard to seem less monstrous.

The girl just laughed it off lightly, waving her free hand in the air, "Oh don't worry miss, it is alright," but something in her features changed. Her carefree face turned into curiosity and surprise. She reached out, her hand coming too close for my liking. I stepped back, eyeing her, perhaps even glaring at her.

She shrank back, noticing my glower. "Sorry, I do not see many blood mages around here." She looked around, turning her head and her gaze stopped for just a second on a bloody tea shop. Panic flurried through me.

Oh no. No. No. Absolutely not. I am not having damn tea with some stranger.

"Say, would you like to get some tea with me?" To the untrained eye this would seem like an innocent invitation to drink simple tea and have a simple conversation with a lovely stranger who was very nice. But I knew better. The moment we'd sit down she'd berate me with endless questions on my life, asking for more and more details because her knowledge-thirsty mind wasn't getting enough. And I would be damned if I said yes.

"No thank you, but I was wondering where the nearest inn is?"

The girl grinned again, as if my decline of her invitation sparked no sadness in her. "Lotus Flower is the pink one back there, Moonshine Inn is not far from that one. There is also Sunrise which is no doubt full. After all it is the nicest inn in the entire city. Most inns are marked by their rather big signs, I wish you luck, as this is high season. Unless you requested a room in advance there might not be any left." And with that she smiled again, and made her way through the narrow alley, disappearing into the sea of people on the other side. I huffed. She was right, I hadn't thought about it being high demand season right now. After all, the festival was the grandest event in all the lands. I was screwed. Great.

"I'm so sorry ma'am. I am fully booked." The lady behind the counter looked at me through her silver rimmed glasses; she was sad, she pitied me. Ugh. I forced a smile and waved a hand through the air dismissively.

"It's my own fault for not thinking in advance. Not to worry, but would you mind pointing me in the direction of the nearest inn."

The lady's expression changed instantly, into delight, "Yes! Of course, yes. But first," she bent down, disappearing from view for a couple seconds before popping back up and extending out her hands. In them was a small clear orb with something floating inside of it, gold swirling, magic perhaps. "Here, take it, I feel terrible. This is a pocket light of sorts. It will illuminate when you need it to, when there is no other light around. Please take it."

I forced another smile before finally taking the little orb and slipping it into a pocket in my dress. "Thank you," I managed. Did these people always give gifts to amend problems that weren't really theirs?

I was so close to the door before she yelled out "wait." I shut my eyes, praying to the Dark Mother she wasn't going to ask me what a million others did before her.

"I noticed your red eyes..." Praise the Darkness, hail all the evil on this woman. "Are you perhaps a blood mage? We don't get them there often! It's always exciting seeing one."

My features became a scowl, or perhaps, more like a death glare. Dark Mother how much I *hated* nosy people who didn't mind their own damn business. But nevertheless, I turned to her, faking my ten thousandth smile today and nodded, rushing out the door before she could utter one more fucking word. My face ached from all that smiling. How in the bloody Darkness's name did their faces, that held grins all day long, not hurt like hell?

The next inn, Moonshine, was also full. As was the Sunrise, the Sunset, Blue Night, and even the shabby one called Silver's. I huffed, defeated. Damn the festival. Damn me for not thinking about booking a room in advance. Not that I really could. I didn't even know how to. I had one last hope, one last inn that might, if Darkness was on my side, still have a few rooms available. The owner of the Silver's Inn pointed in the direction, and as he did, I began to think about how sad this inn must look. If the Silver's Inn was full, and this inn, called Stone's End, (a rather strange name, it didn't seem to fit with any of the other names) wasn't full, or so rumored to not be, what was its appearance? Ah. Whatever. It didn't matter. I wasn't planning on wasting away my days there anyway. I just needed a place for the night. The day would be saved for finding the ones who could tell me where the damned Neithisis was. I had one week, two at most. And I needed to get moving. So, holding tightly to the bag of necessary things and clothes I'd probably have to replace, I marched on to find the Stone's End.

~

I found myself silently praying to the Dark Mother as the burly man, dressed in loose-fitting ivory-colored clothing, flipped through the pages to see if he indeed had some spare rooms. The Stone's End Inn was unlike any of the other inns in the outer city. It was a grey stone building, with a wooden door. The front was marred black, perhaps from some flame. Inside, it was drab in comparison to the others. The fabric of the furniture was mundane and plain. There were two large fireplaces, and their burning amber flames were the only thing besides other candles that provided light. It looked like it belonged in Meris. Not in the Twin Cities.

The man finally took off his glasses and looked at me, his deep brown eyes unfazed by my glowing red ones. *Good, one less person to pry.* I had noticed others in the city whispering, looking, with awe and terror. As far as they knew I was just a blood mage, so I could be a weaker one. One that couldn't bend blood with my mind, my hands. But I wasn't, I was Rithloren. Not that they knew. Not that they ever would. Let them be afraid. Unless one crossed me, I'd leave them be to live their colorful happy lives.

"I have three. Two of them are conjoinin'. So just don't open the damn door and you'll be just fine. Otherwise I have a private room, more expensive though." His voice was rough and brutish, deep and scratchy. His words didn't flow into the accent that all those who I've heard in this city have. He didn't even look the part, much less his establishment.

"I'll take the private room." I replied, eyeing with wariness, the snake, curled up on the counter by the man.

"How long?"

"One week, perhaps two, maybe less than both?" I offered, not really sure how long I was going to actually stay. If, by chance, if Darkness was on my side, I would find the Neithisis within a couple weeks and be back in Meris with the truth.

The man just stared, and sighed. "Fine then, pay me by the week. That'll be easier. It'll be three hundred Kronas per week." He held out his hand for the payment. Right. That.

I bent down to open my bag and pulled out the red velvet pouch that held the Kronas. I pulled out three hundred and handed it to the man, who counted it and then grumbled as he put them away. In return, he handed me a silver key.

"Room number is on the key, don't lose it. Every lost key is ten Kronas. The stairs are on your left, enjoy your stay." And then he walked away, sat back down at his chair and went back to writing something. I stood there, blinking. This man, whoever he was, was not a native to here.

I picked up my bag from the floor and walked towards the stairs. They creaked and moaned as I put my weight on the steps. This building was either ancient or just poorly built. At the top, the floor was covered in orange and brown colored carpet. It looked like vomit. Whoever designed this place was, well, they didn't have the best sense of style. I looked at the silver key, turning it in my hand, looking for the number.

203.

Before me, was a wooden plaque. Rooms 201 through 210 were on my left, the numbers after that were on my right. I turned, making my way down the long, darkened hallway, narrowing my eyes to make out the numbers on the wooden doors. The hallway was illuminated, or, more like slightly, barely, not even really illuminated, by a few oil lamps that hung from the ceiling.

I found my room and put the key in the knob, unlocking it, turning the knob and with a bit of force, I opened the door. Darkness spilled all over me, and what little light was in the hallway crept inside the room. I narrowed my eyes but no such luck, the room was pitch black. Dark as the Darkness itself. I sighed, remembering suddenly the light orb the woman from the Lotus Flower Inn had given me out of sheer pity. I set down my bag and fished it out of my pocket.

How does this work?

I mentally slapped myself for not asking her before leaving. I gave the orb a good hard shake, nothing. I threw it on the ground, and nothing. I threw it up in the air, again nothing. I cursed. Useless piece of shit. But I tried again, this time speaking to it, willing it to light up, foolish really, I couldn't conjure ligh—

Yes, I could.

I put the orb back in my pocket, and dug my hand in the other one, this time taking out my beloved dagger. It was a lovely thing, given to me by Daemon and it was something that I always had with me. I brought it to dances, to the villages, here. My brother said every blade that draws blood needs a name, and I remember for the longest time I couldn't think of a name and until it had one, I refused to use it. But now, the blade I held, the blade I've used countless times to bring the demise of so many, to assist me in most anything I could will with blood, had a name.

Lancenor. The name of a famous artist from Otrina, the once proud kingdom that fell in a day from Darkness. One of my favorite history tales. Lancenor wasn't a mage, he had no magic, but he had the ability to make art into anything he wanted. He painted his wishes and dreams and they, according to legend, came true. I speculated he traded something valuable for an enchantment powerful enough to do that. But the truth was lost to history, lost when Otrina fell and nothing of the kingdom remained. Legends were all that were left.

But nevertheless, I brought Lancenor up to my hand, touched the tip to my skin and with it drew a straight line across my palm. Seconds later, red welled from the wound, slowly, streaming across my hand. I closed my eyes and imagined the symbol for illumination and I willed the blood to follow my thoughts, to turn and move and bend into what I wanted it to. And when I was done, I opened my eyes and in front of me was a small symbol with intricate lines and ornate symbols within. The blood was thinned into a delicately narrow line and then once in perfect place it glowed and glowed some more until there was light. Content with myself and the light, I put the dagger back in my pocket and quickly performed a healing spell on my hand.

I looked up at the room. It was a small thing, with one bed, a nightstand, a dresser that barely fit, a fireplace and then a door, for the bathroom I wagered. Picking up my bag, I placed it on the dresser before falling into the bed and yelping. The bed jolted me up, before sinking me in. I grimaced, trying to position myself in a better way, to perhaps be a little more comfortable. No such luck. This bed was hard as a rock while also being extremely springy.

Maybe I would just make this bed disappear and conjure up my own. I might only be sleeping in here, but if it was something I hated, it was sleeping uncomfortably. I was about to take out my dagger again, to perform another spell but then I heard a noise. Not from inside the room. From outside, to my left. It sounded like a moan? Or a groan? Or both. From pain maybe.

"Alright Siv, let's conjure up a new be—"

A scream. And then another, this time it sounded like a name. But it wasn't a scream one made from pain; it was a scream—

Oh, Mother of Darkness. You have got to be kidding me. The beds are crap! How could—never mind.

I shut my eyes, focusing on the blood inside me, on my power, my magic. I felt it thrum inside me, filling me with warmth as it flowed without falter. I raised Lancenor to my hand and was about to cut myself but another scream. Another moan. A plea. And I paled.

"Are these damn walls made of paper?" I groaned. I was *not* listening to that during the night. I swiped the key from the nightstand, grabbed my things and rushed down the hall and down the stairs, back to the man who was still writing something down. I gently rang the bell, startling him. He turned around, eyed me and set down his pen.

"Yes?"

"Sorry to bother you, it's just that, well, the room next to me. There are people there who are rather *busy*. And I'd rather not have to hear how incredibly busy they are, especially when I'm sleeping, or at least, trying to."

"Meanin'?"

"Meaning, I would like to, if it's possible, to switch rooms."

"They might very well not be as busy every night." The man spoke with a tired yet haughty voice.

And I just glared, not having the patience. But still, I forced a smile, "And they might very well be busy *every* night. And I'd really rather not find out."

"You'll be in a conjoining one. Just know that, if some 'busy' person decides to rent it, well, then you've lost."

I didn't think of that. "Then I'll deal. But I'll take the chance." I would just pray to the Darkness that that doesn't happen.

"Fine then, keys please." I handed him the keys, in exchange for others. This time they were pale gold. "Also, here's forty Kronas. The conjoinin' rooms are two hundred sixty a week."

I nodded, thanking him and taking the money back. Making my way to the new room, hoping, really hoping, if anyone took the room next to mine, it was someone who appreciated silence and peace.

VIII : IVAR THAEGAN

The Twin Cities
Moonsier

I arrived near midnight. But the city was more alive than ever. Very much unlike me. I was ready to fall onto the ground from exhaustion. Don't get me wrong, flying on a peryton is fun and all, really, but they were stubborn creatures who want to do what you don't and for whatever reason didn't need any damn sleep, so they squawked all night long. And I lost precious sleep. So, for the past few days, I hadn't slept more than a couple hours. My muscles ached from having to keep the peryton from straying from the course, my mind tired from having a hold on its soul and coaxing it to go where I wanted it to.

But I was here. *Finally.* In the Twin Cities, in what was once Sunsier, but now was Moonsier. A city that transformed for the night, a time where solar mages retreated and lunar mages rose from the shadows. From what those who lived in the day called Sunsier, into what those who lived in the night called Moonsier. It was a spectacular city, beyond what words could truly hope to describe. I was told, before I came here, that you had to see it with your own eyes. Stories from others, words written down, didn't do the Twin Cities justice. Past the golden silver gate at its entrance was a different world, just as magical, perhaps if not more, but definitely brighter. If there was Darkness here one had to know what Darkness looked like. What faces it took, what guises it wore, what it could be if it wished. Most who were born and raised in this magical city didn't. And so, they lived their lives unknowing of the dangers that lurked in the shadows of their endlessly bright city.

There were those that claimed Sunsier was prettier. The city came alive with gold, and yellow, flowers, spices from markets, colorful clothing, glowing magic the color of marigolds. Those who said that were usually solar mages. There were of course those who favored Moonsier, the city at night. The city that was alive despite the dark. The city that glowed with silver, with cool breeze and metallic outfits that shone in the moonlight. With flowers whose petals glowed in the dark, with shimmering magic casting the color of the moon's reflection on water in the night. Those who favored the night were usually lunar mages. I, neither a solar nor a lunar mage, favored the night far more than the day. Both were wonders to behold, both were beyond what the word "beautiful" could entail, but there was something about Moonsier that struck *something* in me.

I had been here twice. Once out at day, once in the cover of the night. Once with my mother and sisters, once alone. I had fled with vengeance and revenge on my mind. I had accomplished both. This time I was on a mission, one I would have to accomplish, or more likely, I would very much like to accomplish. Because in truth, I didn't know how much the fate of the kingdoms would change if I discovered the truth or not. I guess it depended on what it actually was. On what actually happened to my sister and the king of Meris.

"Excuse me," I whipped around at the noise that broke my endlessly tumbling thoughts. There stood a young woman, not much older than me. She was no doubt pretty, with black hair that was braided into thick braids atop her head, adorned with golden accents. Her gold eyes bore into mine with some fiery intensity. She smiled, almost smirking, as if suggesting something.

"Yes?" I tried my best not to sound too harsh. The people here were known to be very nice, and gossips. If someone heard twenty people talking about someone who looked very much like a soul mage and was nothing but cold to them, rumors would fly. Perhaps all the way to Meris, where my enemies could easily find me. It was better not to risk it.

The girl batted her lashes, and flashed a smile, enough to light up an entire room. I was willing to bet everyone in this damn city had a smile like those. I never saw anyone who didn't. "I was wondering if you were a soul mage. From the books I've read at the academies about the kingdoms they describe soul mages as having silver hair and silver eyes that glowed when they used their magic."

I looked at her, my eyelids heavy. "I am indeed a soul mage. Now go away before I do all the terrible things that you've read about." At that she yelped, and scampered off. I smiled lazily. I did not have the brain power, the will nor the patience to deal with people like her right now. I was tired, my body ached, and all I wanted was a fucking bed.

But this after all was a city of knowledge, that prided itself in having the most history, the most information on everything, and the people here were ever so thirsty for information. Perhaps it was because most, if not all, had never been outside the city walls, past the golden and silver gate that allowed people to enter. I pitied them for it. They learned so much of the outside world, everything they could, and yet, they saw it only from pictures and heard it from words of a stranger's tongue. They never saw the world they knew so much about. But maybe that was for the better. These people, who smiled through everything and were too nice to even those who weren't to them, wouldn't last seconds out there. At least not in the Kingdom lands. Maybe in the Lands of the Free Cities. But where Lysmir and Meris reigned, it was better for these people to not be there. For there were assassins, thieves, and people with rather terrible intentions everywhere. Not that everyone was like that, but most that lived there were either soul or blood mages. And that meant one horribly terrifying thing, a piece of Darkness was inside of each and every one of them. Inside was a cruel, evil little thing that made each and every one of us, darker than most. And of course, we were at war. That definitely didn't make things any better.

And then suddenly someone else was right in front of me, and I stopped, wondering how the hell she just appeared. I was walking, and—she just—popped out of nowhere...

"Are you a—"

"Yes I am." I finally answered her, exasperated. She was the fifth one in the mere hour that I had been here who looped arms with me, asked if I were a soul mage and tried to coax me into telling them my life story, but after the first girl, I just walked away. They didn't seem too terribly upset, of course, they flashed their smiles, waving their hands in the air dismissively saying it was so perfectly alright. 'Another day' they said. *Absolutely not*, I thought.

"You would like to get so—"

"Some tea," I finished for her. But not because she was lacking which words to say but because my patience was running very thin.

She perked up, her face lighting up. "Yes! Some tea, we have so many to choose from and we could get to know each other, I've never met a soul mage before, you should tell me all about yourself and your life and your magic, it's all so incredib—"

I held out a hand to stop her, my finger barely touching her lips. My mouth twisted into a smile, but there was something feline about it, something dark and perhaps dangerous. She shied away, only just a bit. I could tell from the excitement in her eyes she still would get tea with me even if I screamed at her. This is how desperate they were to get their hands on anything they could. I often wondered why this city, which was so spectacular, was such a bloodbath when it came to finding knowledge on something. It's as if they struck a deal with the Darkness itself, a deal that gave them something at the cost of information.

"No." I mused, "I'd rather not." And with that wicked smile plastered on my face I spun on my heel and walked away. I didn't turn around to see her face. I didn't care. If she was like the rest of them, then her face would be lit up with a smile. I wondered if they were fake, no one can be always happy, and yet they always appeared to be.

A large clock, on all four sides of a white tower adorned with golden and navy swirls, struck midnight. With it, the bells rung, heavy and loud. Metal striking metal, like a dance, only this sounded like a war. I tossed my head back, staring at the sky, the indigo sky that was littered with silver stars that twinkled. My body sagged, it ached, and my mind was heavy. I wanted nothing more than to just drop onto a bed and stay there until the sun came. But there was no bed around here, in the square where the center of the market was, where the tower that stopped chiming its heavy bells stood, towering over all the other buildings like their goddess.

And then there was an unexpected tap on the shoulder that took me off guard. Then the gibberish that came from the young man's mouth, beautiful and flowing words that I had no idea what they meant. He spoke in the native yet rarely spoken language of this city, Sunmoric. Erdaen, the language of Otrina, had caused most of the ancient languages that existed before it to disappear—

I felt a sharp pang in my stomach. I staggered, falling back as I groaned in pain. Another blow to the side, and in that instant all my fighting instincts kicked in. My mind, once frazzled, empty and focused, becoming eerily clear.

Then a second stranger rammed into me and pushed me to the ground. In the mess, my bag fell from my hand, as I coughed up the sand that found its way into my mouth. I wiped it off with a once white sleeve, now light tan. But that didn't matter, I felt deep down my power waking up, surging through my body, warming my veins and I looked up, my eyes no doubt glowing. But the men were gone. Around me were people who had been too busy with their marvels and their lives to notice me. Part of me was glad, as it would have been rather terrible for so many to see someone scream in anguish as I ripped a piece of their soul off.

My breath was ragged and heavy. I brought a hand to my side and winced. Blood stained my formerly white shirt, my palms. I grimaced, cursing those bastards. I shook my head, sitting up, scratching my eyes, hoping to rid them of the sand that conveniently landed there. I ran my hands through my hair, ridding it of the dirt that got caught within it.

And then I noticed my bag was *gone*. It wasn't anywhere near me. It wasn't anywhere at all. I looked down, relieved that at least the satchel with the remaining food I had was still on me.

My mind quickly twisted with thoughts, trying to focus on the face of the young man that had spoken to me. I turned around, over and over, walking forwards a bit, trying to find the man. He had on a bright yellow shirt, his eyes had been a dull brown, his hair was curly and long. The other one, from what I managed to see in the two seconds he was there, wore an ivory-colored head wrap and his skin was olive tan. But I was the middle of the square, and that was where the night market thrived the most. There were too many of them here, men with curly dark hair that was half hidden by their head wraps. I frowned. Something inside me wanted to chase them down through the dusty streets of the Merchants' Quarter and take back what they took from me. But my body was tired, and now because of them it hurt more than it already did. I knew I needed rest, and in order to do that I needed to find a damn inn that wasn't full. I had kept my coin pouch in my pockets, for what reason I wasn't sure, but now I was thankful. A cheap bed for a few days was fine, the sandy ground wasn't. Before I moved, anywhere, I brought my hand around the pendant hanging on a thin chain from my neck, and held it tightly. It was an instinct I had after any fight, anything that could cause me to lose it. This at least hadn't been snatched. If it had been, I would have tracked the thief down however long it took. I would have found them and made them give it back no matter the cost. It was a simple charm, a small transparent ball that held inside of it a string. The string of a soul that used to be iridescent until it was destroyed.

Because of me.

～

"I'm so sorry, sir. I am unfortunately fully booked." The lady behind the counter looked at me through her thick glasses with sad eyes. She probably pitied me.

"It's my fault for not thinking ahead of time," I insisted, hoping for her to stop feeling bad for something that wasn't her fault. Another flaw of the city's people. Too emotionally sensitive. Dark Father, they'd be so easy to crack, to break, to destroy. "Would you mind giving me directions to another inn?"

The lady's expression changed instantly into delight, "Of course, yes! But first," she bent down, disappearing from view for a couple seconds before popping back up and extending out her hands. In them was a small orb with something floating inside of it, illuminated gold, iridescent of sorts, perhaps enchanted. "Here, take it, I feel terrible. This is a pocket light of sorts, it will shine with light when you need it to, when there is no other light around. Just spin it around on a flat surface to light it up." Her arms stretched out further, "Please take it." She sounded as if she was pleading for me to accept it. As if some part of her would break if I didn't. Not wanting to cause another scene, I forced a smile and took it, shoving it into the nearly empty satchel that hung around my chest.

"The other inn?" I craned my head and looked away, feeling slightly uncomfortable from her eyes boring into mine. She had this inquisitive look on her face, I paled.

Good freaking Dark Father, I swear to Darkness...

If she so much as mentions "soul mage," information, or goddamn "tea" I would lose it.

"I do hope you don't mind my asking, it's just, it's only strange seeing a blood mage and soul mage on the same day an—"

I stopped listening to her. I turned around and walked out the door the moment she said "blood mage." I'd find the next inn myself then. No, I didn't know where the absolute heck the other mage was, but that wasn't what worried me. There was a blood mage out there, in the same city. I tensed, hatred bubbling inside me. What the hell were they here for? Our kingdoms were at war, so unless they lived somewhere besides Meris, or were too chicken to fight, then I didn't know why they had any reason to be here.

Though technically, I shouldn't be here either. I should be in Lysmir, at home, with my father, with Avran and the General and all our soldiers and our citizens, planning and plotting the demise of those blood demons. And now, one of them was *here*. How grand. Could the world get any more fucking complicated?

My feet, despite how tired they were, carried me through the streets where lanterns burned and the aroma of spices and laughter of people filled the air, and then through the smaller streets further away from the center of the Merchants' Quarter where they were lit by only candle light in the windows. There wasn't a single inn in the sight. My body was slowly shutting down from the long day, the long couple of days. If I hadn't been so tired, I would have been able to fight off those bastards who took my things. I swore that once I slept well, I would find them and take back what was mine. Part of me wished I had waited for that woman back at the first inn to just tell me where the nearest one was because I was lost in a sea of color and people. People shoving sweet bread in my face, yelling out prices. Others who spritzed scented water from ornate bottles, also yelling numbers my brain couldn't comprehend. I lost count of how many I bumped into, how many bumped into me. No one seemed to care nor notice. It was only when I saw a small sign, hidden by the arch of colorful flowers, that my spirits lifted just a little and my dying body, or not really dying but extremely tired body, perked up just a bit.

The Moon Flower Inn. The sign was written in a fancy script, illuminated by some enchantment. The door was open, letting the soft orange glow from inside spill onto the street, just as the light from the lanterns seeped in. The lights meshed together, forming a golden glow. I stepped inside, breathing in the scent of lavender and other flowers I couldn't fathom names for. The furniture was dark blue, the walls the color of ivory. Moonflowers in silver vases were everywhere in the room. They were rather large flowers and their petals the color of violet, with each petal that was closer to the center a shade darker. Their stems were a faded green, almost grey. Around the atrium of the inn there were other flowers, in other vases, but the moonflowers were the ones that shone with color, with drooping petals and thorns bigger than leaves. It seemed more like a flower shop than an inn. But it didn't matter, as I brushed a hand through my hair and prayed it had at least one room left.

IX : IVAR THAEGAN

The Twin Cities
Moonsier

P art of me wanted to scream and tear the world apart. The other part of me wanted to scream in the open air. The last part of me, the one that pounded at my head for being stupid, made me stop wanting to rip the world in half. Because after all, the festival of the Midnight Sun, the grandest festival of all, in which people from all over travelled to see was in a few days. And of course, all the inns would be full. And of course, this one, the one that looked more like a damn flower shop than an inn was also full. *Of course. Of course. Of course.* I knew that really there was nothing I could have done about it. There was no way to book a room in advance without being in the city, and even just a week ago, when the last rooms were free, I didn't know I had to come here.

But there was nothing else to do than to keep looking. The Merchants' Quarter was known for its famous never-ending market, its endless tea shops that sold countless varieties of colorful teas and the number of inns. All were small in size, and most were grand and fancy, filled with gold and sparkling lights. But I didn't care much for grandeur, not when I knew my objective was to find a mythical creature that may or may not actually still exist. I didn't care for fancy beds and breakfast with exotic fruits. After all, those rooms were no doubt the first to be taken, but also, I knew I would be spending most of my days, and perhaps even nights searching. I could settle with a cheap bed.

Of the last nine inns I visited, none had spare rooms, and all directed me in the direction of other inns that too were full. And all the people behind the counters had been like the lady in the first inn. Sad and all too eager to give me something in hopes it would make me feel better. I now had a light orb, a handmade leather bracelet, a gold chain, a small bottle of black ink for tattoos, a free tea at some tea shop, another free tea, and then another one and perhaps one more; I lost count. This last man handed me a sack of *biscuits* of all things and with sad eyes, directed me to somewhere called the Black Moon.

It was an onyx black colored building with greyish silver curtains and large black double doors. It was one of those that looked grand on the outside, and on the inside, it was a little less grand. But from the look the man at the counter gave me once we made eye contact when I stepped inside, I knew it meant two things. From his pity, the inn was full. From his awe, he realized I was one of them. One of the ones he had read about in books and perhaps, if the author did their job right, have nightmares about. After all, we soul mages are not known to be nice. We are ruthless and cruel if we have to be. This world, the one outside those walls and that gate, was never kind to any of us. It was cruel, mean and it made us each into monsters. But I didn't mind. Because in this world, the heartless survived, the strong were ruthless and the cruel did not waver. Those who were kind, those who had hearts, who loved and cared too easily, were usually found dead. Or worse.

I had stepped out of the inn, letting the doors slam shut behind me before the man could speak. Before anyone else could notice my damn silver eyes. Anywhere else, literally anywhere else, my eyes, my hair wouldn't have been an issue. In Azaneh, no one could care less; in Pyatov, no one would stare; in all the nine Shao Yun Islands, no one would loop their arms with mine and offer me tea. The only other place where I would be questioned would be none other than Meris. Obviously. A soul mage in the kingdom of blood mages, their sworn enemy, had a death wish. Even the strongest soul mages have no hope against a kingdom full of enemies.

But never mind them and their damned everything. My body was beginning to burn, from my muscles doing what they would much rather not do, move. So, I shrugged off the cold that was beginning to creep up and walked on, this time to find an all-too-friendly stranger that was all too willing to be nice and helpful.

Do I dare? I asked myself, over and over as I walked throughout the streets in the direction that a man selling naan bread showed me.

I wasn't known for trusting people I knew, much less strangers. I had grown in a world that didn't allow one to trust too easily. If one did, that usually meant death, torture and other horrible things. I remember trusting a person once, too quickly, too boldly. It ended badly for everyone, or for most of the people I cared about. It was then that I never again let myself trust anyone so easily. The memory flooded my head, threatening to control me like any bad memory did. They had power in themselves, to make you weak, make you cry, make you *feel*. I hated them for that reason, for the reason that they made you less of who you needed to be, and more of what you had been. An all-too-trusting-bastard, who learned his lesson too late. I had heard and read that sometimes bad things needed to happen in order for us to wake up, to realize that maybe we should change, or that we should do something else. As much as I wanted to deny that terrible truth, it was just that, a terrible truth. One I learned all too well. And in this world, I still knew it well.

It had been a foolish mistake, one made by a half-drunk man who had been drinking his feelings in order to avoid showing them on his face. That night, my mother had passed. And the kingdom hadn't known yet. But I, after too many amber colored drinks, had been swaying in the streets and a man had walked up. He didn't recognize me because he had the audacity to persuade me to follow him. And I did. Into an old building, where he gave me water. Only it hadn't been water, but something stronger and a lot more bitter. I remember little from that night, but I remember we talked and I spilled the death of the queen and the death of my youngest sister, the kingdom's angel. And then that man told me he'd keep the words I said to him a secret, and I trusted him. I should have killed him. Because the next day, the kingdom knew everything and my father had decided that whipping me wouldn't suffice. So, he made me do something so much worse. Whip Avran. Who I was sure would never forgive me. But he had, for better or for worse. Sometimes I wondered if Avran and my youngest sister were the only soul mages with hearts. They seemed so much more understanding, open, than the rest of us.

But for now, I pushed the memory away. Time had helped and the years faded the feelings. But only faded, they were still there, and always would be.

And despite that promise I had made to myself I was now contemplating doing that very thing. Granted, lives wouldn't be put at stake, lives wouldn't be ruined, people wouldn't die, people wouldn't change if I decided to trust the man who told me where the nearest inn was. If anything, I would find nothing, and I would keep on searching. Yet, despite that being the only outcome should the man have lied, I still racked my brain trying to figure out which way to turn. Back then, I hadn't thought of all the outcomes. Perhaps I hadn't because I didn't care. Or didn't think I needed to care.

The young man was the first of them that didn't look at me like I was some beyond valuable foreign treasure that had been lost for centuries and was the key to saving the goddamn world. He *had* been surprised, but not nosy. Maybe he sensed the impatience dripping off me as I talked to him. Or maybe it was because his eyes had been a dulled blue, almost lifeless. There was nothing magical floating in them, nothing enchanted swirling in their color. The man had been a nonmage, a human. Those who had been skipped by magic, which went by bloodline, usually. Perhaps that's why he had made no motion of questioning me, because he wasn't worried or couldn't care less about something he didn't possess or understand.

After all power was a weird thing; one would think if your parents both were mages then you would be as well. And usually you were, but magic liked to play wicked tricks sometimes and skip people or make them unbelievably weak or curiously strong.

My mother had been skipped, much to the disgrace of our father, whom she had been arranged to marry. But what she lacked in magic, she made up for in ruling a kingdom. While my father ruled the armies, the battles, my mother ruled the people with an iron fist. Rumors were rooted out within days. She was just as ruthless as anyone with the ability to control a soul, if not more. For that, my father had been able to respect her, maybe even admire her. Despite my mother's constant reassurances, I often doubted that my parents loved each other. My father was what many considered heartless, and he made all his children that way. My mother, though she never spoke about him, had a lover before her marriage to my father. Perhaps her heart had belonged to him, and always would. And then of course my father, just days before, said he never loved her when I had asked him.

I let my legs carry me to the nearest inn, the Stone's End. The man told me it was a cheap little place, shrouded in darkness for it was forever under the shade of all the trees surrounding it. It was in the outskirts of the Merchants' Quarter, past all the shops, the markets and even the people, who seemed to occupy every corner of the outer city. Here the night started to look like an actual night, not a magical city that transformed the night into its own day. Here the streets were dark, the windows were covered in curtains, forbidding the light to spill into the streets. Here, the people spoke in hushed whispers, wearing thick scarves to keep the cold out. Here there was no smell of a thousand different spices, or the light from a hundred different colored lanterns. This part of the city was like any other city at night. Almost lifeless. I wagered even in the daytime, when the city transformed into Sunsier, this part of the outer city would still be quiet, would still be lifeless and dull compared to the rest of it.

I passed by dark houses as I made my way towards a small building, unlike any of the other buildings. Those were colorful, decorated with paint that shimmered against the lights, with patterns that had magic pulsating beneath. Those were methodically made, perfect rectangles or squares, crafted from mud, stone and magic. They had flowers decorating them, colorful tapestries, light streaming from all the windows and all the open doors.

This building seemed, well, dead. It was made of large bulky stones, their grey color either faded with age or darkened by something that perhaps had been a fire. Judging from the windows stacked up atop each other, it had two floors. At that I began to doubt this place had any rooms left. But perhaps it did, considering it was a ways away from the center of all the movement. And it *did* look dead and rather questionable as a building.

The windows were covered in black curtains, letting no light, if there even was light, filter through. The door was wooden, tarnished and old. Battered by the years, however many they were. There were no flowers around it, no color. Just grey and black and mud brown. But its despicable appearance didn't bother me too much. I would only be sleeping here, not spending the next of my however many days. I sighed, my spirits long washed away from all the previous owners that had been painfully sorry for all their rooms being occupied. My hand was cramped from holding a muslin bag filled with things they gave me, out of pity.

I pulled on the door handle and opened the door, letting a gust of warm air flow right into me. There was nothing special about this place then, I thought, as my eyes glazed over the boring features. There were two fire pits, burning brightly. There was a counter, with no one standing behind it, and that was it. No colorful furniture, no unique aroma, no music from fancy instruments filling the air. It was so mundane, it seemed to be out of place in such a city like this.

I made my way to the counter, where a small and tarnished silver bell sat. The moment my palm pushed on the top, the bell rang out this awfully loud ring, filling the entire room with an ear-splitting sound. Seconds later a burly man, in colorless clothing, walked out from a door to the side. He looked at me, dark circles under his eyes, which were void of any sign of magic. They too were a dulled color like those of the young man who directed me here. However, his weren't blue, they were a mud brown.

He was a human, I wagered. But he held no kindness to him, unlike the young man who had been sickly sweet. This man was rough around all the edges.

"Lookin' for a room then?" His voice was deep, scuffed. I nodded, slowly; my head suddenly felt so much heavier.

"I am, yes." There was a half sigh in there, my shoulders sagging. Drowsy. I hated feeling drowsy; it made me feel weak. And above all I hated feeling weak.

"Yer lucky, I have one last room." My mind did a flip. I didn't quite believe I heard the man correctly. I blinked, then blinked again. Silence started creeping in as I looked at the man, my face no doubt expressing relief, or maybe something else. For his features showed nothing but confusion.

"Well," the man pulled out a small metal key with a thin loop of rope attached to it, "it's conjoinin', if you don't mind."

"No, no, that's just fine." I responded, hurriedly. Not even knowing why, as I should be relaxed, or at least more relaxed. Instead, my heart was racing and I felt stress creeping up from underneath me. Through it all I yawned, my body begging for rest.

"How many nights?"

"I'm not sure, one week at most, less preferably." At that the man just looked at me, a glint in his eyes. As if he was experiencing this for a second time, perhaps even a third.

"Right then," he pulled out a piece of paper, "pay me by the week. It'll be easier for the both of us, eh?"

"Indeed yes," I began fishing for the Kronas in my pocket,

knowing with absolute certainty I had brought more than enough, but still internally panicking at the impossible possibility that I hadn't.

"It'll be two hundred sixty Kronas then, a week of course." The man held his hands out, as I placed two hundred sixty of the paper money in my pocket into his hands.

"Sorry for the money being crumpled, I've had a long journey." A lie and a truth. For one, I most definitely wasn't sorry, I couldn't have been bothered to give a damn. Money was money, crumpled or not. The man would have to deal if he was vexed by it. The second part was true, I've had a ridiculously long and tiresome journey and all I wanted was some sleep.

"Thanks then," the man took the money, a plain look on his face. Perhaps he gave little for the sad state of the Kronas, maybe even less for my pathetic excuse for an apology. I was sure it sounded empty as I said it. "Here is the key. The room is on the second floor, enjoy your night." He handed me the key, and wrote some gibberish in purple ink with a quill.

"Thank you," I wrapped my hand around the cold little key, the key that would lead me to a bed and some much-needed rest. I turned to leave but then the man spoke.

"Just one question," I turned around, our eyes meeting, his boring into mine. "Are you someone who tends to be busy in the evenin'?"

Huh?

"I'm sorry? Busy?"

"Yes, busy, as in, entertainin' yerself loudly, with," he paused, looking around mindlessly, perhaps trying to think of what to say next in the least worst way possible, "another person." He finished. My cheeks heated up, my neck, my mind rattling for a reason as to why this man would ask me something like *that*.

"No sir," I faked my millionth smile that night, "I'm quiet at night. I prefer silence. Why?"

"No reason." He responded, and walked away, slamming the door shut as he disappeared through its doorway. I stood there for just a little while, pondering where the hell this man was from. He was cold. And people from here weren't cold, no, they were naively happy and warm. This man, whoever he was, hadn't lived his life here. He'd lived in the outside world. The real world. The one that was cold and harsh and oh so terribly cruel.

X : IVAR THAEGAN

The Twin Cities
Sunsier

Waking up to a sun whose rays seemingly burned through the curtains and streamed into the room like it would have if the world was destroyed and it could finally breathe again, was something I wasn't used to. In Lysmir, the grey curtains that hung over my windows blacked out any light that might have wanted to peek in my room in the mornings. I fell asleep in darkness and woke up in it.

But here, the light bombarded into the room, peeling my eyes open to see its spectacular light. I yawned, stretching on the lousy bed. It creaked and groaned, like a dying man. There had been no light in the room last night, save for the small light orb the woman from the first inn had given me. Spin it around on some flat surface, she had said.

So, last night when I had been blinded by the darkness I had spun it on the floor. The small glass ball illumined instantly with a bright yellow glow that lit up the entire room. With it I saw that there was a bed, or more of a cot, a bedside table, a small dresser, a dusty window and two doors, one leading to the other room, the other to the bathroom. No wonder this room was so cheap for an entire week.

I turned around, closing and locking the door behind me. I dropped my belongings on the floor and let myself fall onto the cot. I yawned, stretching myself like a cat on the cot. My muscles were still aching from the mess that was dealing with the peryton.

And then, suddenly a thought crossed my mind. Even though it was a traitorous thought, a thought that if spoken aloud would result in the immediate transport to the castle, followed by a whipping from my father himself; the selfish impossible thought of wanting, for just a moment, the ability to heal myself like the blood mages crept into my head.

I hated myself for it. But no one could deny, not even my father I suspected, that being able to simply heal yourself whenever was extremely useful. And while mages did indeed heal much quicker than those who weren't blessed with magic, we still needed time. Unless of course, you had the power to use blood to your will. Then the pain would only last from the moment it was started to the moment the spell was finished. Which from what I heard took less than a minute.

Healing spells, as the books said, were among the easiest spells for a blood mage to perform. And as forbidden as it was, the thought of wishing I had their damn magic still lingered in my mind. My father wasn't here, and even when we would have been together, he couldn't read my mind. No one could. So, unless I said it aloud, I was safe. Anyone was. The only person I had dared, while drunk, to spill the traitorous thought to was Avran. Who had agreed with me. Whom I made a silent pact with to never say a word about what we thought. What, in time, we wished for.

But here, I was alone. And with that thought in my mind I sighed. My muscles would stop aching by tomorrow and by this afternoon the pain would only linger a little.

I willed myself to get up, moving like thick sludge. Messily, slowly. I yawned again, and I shook my head. My silver hair was a tangled mess, falling at awkward angles. I ran my hands through it, trudging towards the bathroom, that the word "small" was not enough to describe. In the mirror, I blinked at myself. I had worn the clothes I had worn throughout the day yesterday to bed. And now they were more of a mess than they had been before. New creases showed more than ever.

I knew that once I stepped outside the doors of this inn, heads would turn in my direction, faces would scrunch up in judgement.

For as angelic as people were here, fashion, above many things, was held at the highest regard. Almost as much as knowledge. Almost.

But I had nothing else to wear. And I wouldn't until I tracked down those bastards that stole from someone they *really* shouldn't have. I had been dreadfully tired and sore last night. Too drowsy and dazed to strategize and orchestrate an entire attack. After all, I'd have to *find* them first, then somehow lead them or make them go into a less populated place.

The last thing I needed was a bunch of overly curious Sunsierans to witness a soul mage attacking some of their own. If that nightmare happened, I would be instantly bombarded and berated with endless questions and maybe, should these people have soldiers in charge of securing the city, I would have been detained for attacking citizens, guilty of a crime or not. Maybe I'd even be banished if I killed them, because to be honest, the thought of doing just that had already crossed my mind several times.

But, instead of attacking in front of an audience, what if I followed the traces of their souls, and trailed them to the dark alley that they, no doubt, were in? I could kill them quickly without anyone noticing. Not until it was far too late and they were already dead, and I was long gone from the crime scene. And with that swimming in my mind, I bent into the large ceramic bowl that was filled with chilled water and washed my face. Magically, the water bubbled and disappeared, refilling brand new and clean. I snorted. So, this sad inn did indeed have a touch of enchantment here and there. I reached for the nearest towel and patted my face dry, staring once again into the mirror. My skin was a touch pink, from the frigid water, but I looked and felt a little more alive than before, so I couldn't complain.

My outfit on the other hand, I would have to brave the faces holding looks of pity and judgement until I found my bag. That's if everything was still where I last left it. But, when it comes to criminals, professional or not, that usually meant that things weren't.

Luckily for me, there was nothing particularly valuable in the bag. I had my money with me, my amulet hanging from my neck and the clue, the tiny clue, of where to find the Neithisis floating in my head. But, now that I had arrived in the Twin Cities, the clue's helpfulness had ended. It brought me here; the rest was on me.

One week, I thought.

One week to find the people who knew of the location, to find the Neithisis, to get the truth from it. However hard or easy. I gulped, my heart racing inside me. Coming here was a foolish waste of time. My father knew that. Avran knew that. The general and Maeghalin all knew that. Even I knew the chance of finding out the truth was extremely and painfully slim. But the part of me that craved the truth was stronger than the part of me that thought this whole ordeal was foolish. And so here I was, with my heart racing and a few robbers to track down before I started searching for what happened.

A clock chimed in the distance. The bells were ringing through the entire city, the inner and outer. I put down the towel and made my way towards the window, pushing the muslin curtains aside. Below, what was a once still and eerily silent street was now filled with hundreds of people, each dressed in a different shade of color it seemed. They carried, pulled, and pushed various items, screaming and laughing at each other. New people opened the doors of the buildings and spilled into the sea of individuals, and others from the smaller streets. In Moonsier this street might have been an abandoned little thing, but it seemed I was wrong to think it would be just as dead. Because in fact it wasn't, now, in the light of the morning; it teemed with never-ending life.

I looked from the scene below to above, where the darkness of the navy sky was fading into amber, orange and a mixture of golden yellow. The moon, ever glowing silver, was slowly descending from the fading darkness. The millions of stars that dotted the sky were barely twinkling, their sparkle fading.

I opened the window, just a crack, feeling instantly as the magic, the one that symbolized the transformation, hit me straight in the face. It washed over me, filtering into the room. My eyes strained to see it, to see the tiny little bursts of light that lasted just mere seconds but had been there nonetheless. That was what the magic looked like, it made the air seem alive and glowing with some unnatural power. Something like this could only be seen here, and the first time I had, I almost cried because it was so beautiful. It was the same, or almost the same, every time. And for a second, a minute, a few of those even; I let my mind slip from the ever-pressing mission of finding the robbers, of finding the Neithisis. The transformation barely lasted ten minutes. I could wait that long.

I watched, leaning out the window, letting the cool air caress my face. The silver blue glow of Moonsier slowly faded, the enchanted cerulean designs that decorated the buildings turned gold and champagne colored. Each moon, each star turned into glittering suns. The swirls, lines and waves were an ombré of navy and saffron. Moonflowers, blue roses, flowers that relished the night slowly shrunk back and, in their wake, the red roses came, the yellow ones, the pink and orange ones. Daisies and marigolds and all the other hundreds of flowers that bloomed within seconds from the magic that was filling the air. The light in the lanterns, that hung between the buildings, faded away. The aroma of countless spices, plants and pastries, the never-to-be-forgotten teas, soon wafted through the air. I inhaled the familiar scent, closing my eyes. I missed this place, for as unreal as it was, and seemed to be, I loved it.

But just as quickly as I let myself relax, my body stilled and tensed. I couldn't relax. I had six days to find the Neithisis. Five if I had to spend all damn day finding the robbers who stole my clothing. Even if I had enough money to buy new ones, and even if there was nothing of extreme value in the bag, I refused to let them get away with it. Those bastards didn't deserve it, and if it meant sacrificing a day, so be it.

Although, to my disadvantage, the city was *huge*. Despite being a city, it was half as big as Meris, the largest kingdom. It consisted of three sections. The Outer City was also known as the Merchants' Quarter. The Inner City housed all the Scholars, the prestigious academies, the museums and the largest library this world had ever seen. The smallest part of the city was the Port, the section of the city that touched the sea. Where ships came and went filled with a million new things. Silks and fabrics from the Shao Yun Islands, weapons from Pyatov, and spices from Azaneh.

With that in mind, I focused on what the robbers had been wearing. From the loose thin clothing I remembered, they couldn't be Scholars. Scholars wore tight, white robes with thick metallic belts. They rarely left the Inner City, and they also wouldn't dare steal anything. The Scholars of this city were like the royals in any of the kingdoms, or the governmental bodies of any of the other free cities. They were noble and dignified, holding a code of conduct they lived and breathed by just like the Head Mistresses and Head Masters of each of the four academies that governed the city.

So, I could eliminate the Inner City from my search, which in it of itself eliminated an entire half of the city. That left the Port and the Merchants' Quarter. None of them had smelled like fish or water. Their hair, which was matted and sparkling, was more likely to have been because of sweat and not salt water. The scent of the unforgiving sea was nowhere on them, which meant if they were from the Port, they would have needed to magically take away their scent.

My mind shifted from going to search the Port or not. It was the smallest section of the city. If I eliminated it, it'd barely make a dent, unlike the Inner City.

"Merchants' Quarter first." I spoke softly, retreating from the window and closing it. If I didn't find them here, I'd look in the Port.

The clock chimed again, signaling the ninth hour of the day. I looked up at the clock tower that loomed over me and the entire city, casting a long shadow. I watched as the bells chimed, the noise filling the air as it always did.

My eyes moved from the clock tower to the scenery around me. People, even more than last night, dressed in even more colors, were all around me. Children ran, screaming and laughing. Women and men stood, danced all over to the music that thrummed in the air.

I made my way around the tower, waking up my magic, letting it spill through me, filling me with a feeling of warmth and cold at the same time. Each soul was different, the silver strings that made them up were tangled in a different way. A million different patterns were here, all glowing. I looked at each one of the people now as no more than glowing silver spirits. It was this ability that my father taught me. Whenever he needed to find someone, he twisted his magic to allow him to see only the souls of people, the silver things, that evanescence within each one of us. He taught me to not only see them, but to sense them, to be able to follow a soul's specific string.

And that was just what I planned to do. I let my power roll through me, focusing on the souls that belonged to the men that had robbed me. And soon enough, I saw a string, and then another and another, until they formed a tangled line where I was standing through the crowd of people. I raked a hand through my hair, hoping it could cover my eyes just a little. Whenever a mage used magic, their eyes glowed more than usual, glimmering with magic. And usually it didn't faze me, but here, in a city where eyes weren't silver, but instead violet blue and gold, I needed to be careful. Should anyone of them notice my eyes, they would ask questions, maybe become afraid, and I didn't have the time for that.

The line weaved through the people, and I did as well, always looking down at the ground and never at anyone else. My body bumped into countless people as my eyes focused on the glowing strings. I ignored the apologies given by people, strangers, when in reality they should have probably been given by me. But that would take time, and feelings and a heart. I had none of those things, least of all now.

And then I collided with someone, and I felt my body hit something hard. I stopped, and stumbled. My eyes, traitorous as they were, looked up. In front of me was a tall man, taller than me, taller than any man I had ever seen before. His eyes, like tarnished amber, narrowed at the sight of me. I let go of my powers, my magic waning quickly.

"You should watch where you are going, young man. This city might be lovely, but pretty things always hide the worst secrets." His voice was rough, almost *foreign*. Even for here. His words didn't glide as smoothly as they should. But I didn't have the time to do anything but blink in silence, as the man, whoever he was, pushed past me. I looked behind me, something awful twisting inside me, as if it was a warning. But I pushed it down. I knew not everyone in this city was a good person, if good people even existed at all. Sure, it was filled with those who did nothing but smile all day and laugh, but the man's words were true.

Ignoring it was the best option, so I turned my head around, and again, I stumbled into someone. A smaller, softer frame. I was about to spit out some nasty curse before a wave of black shrouded my vision and I heard a gentle yet ice cold voice whisper "sorry." A wave of something hit me, magic, but darker magic. Like my own but so different. I twisted around, trying to make out where either of the people had gone. But there was nothing, because just as quickly as the Darkness inside me sensed something like itself, it vanished, and was replaced by the magic all around me. I shook my head. Perhaps I was seeing things, imagining them; after all my mind was scattered in a million different directions. And perhaps I also shouldn't keep my head down. I'd have to settle with hiding my eyes as best as possible with my hair.

I willed the magic once again to roll through me, and in an instant the world faded and blurred. Silver and grey took over once again and the strings I had been following before reappeared, more tangled than before, but still there, so I let my feet carry me in their direction.

～

The sign that hung from the edge of the roof was beyond ancient. The wood was chipped, burned in some places, covered in green fuzz in others, and faded in different shades of what the natural color for wood was. The words that were so brutally carved into the decaying piece of wood spelled out what I assumed was the name of this *fine* establishment.

The Golden Crow.

If I had just heard the name, I might have envisioned a fancy place. One that reflected the name. But that wasn't the case at all, because I stood in front of the most rundown piece of shit I have ever seen. The building was on one of the roads that led from the Merchants' Quarter to the Port. It was a wide street. On one side there was the wall of the Outer City. The one keeping the outside world where it belonged, out. The other side held the wall that separated the rest of the city from the Inner City. Each side held houses, rundown shops and small buildings that were dark and were no doubt gambling dens filled with liquor. The state of several people outside their doors led me to that conclusion. They were either passed out on the ground, in the process of vomiting their guts out, or red faced from anger and hollering slurred curses at someone in the building. Drunk and unquestionably several hundred, if not several thousand, Kronas less rich.

The smell here was rancid. I tried my best to breathe as much as possible through my mouth so I wouldn't have to inhale the stench that filled the air. For as pretty as the city was, this alleyway was the worst part, the darkest part. The Port, from what I had seen, was just as nice and clean as the Merchants' Quarter. The way to go to it, however, wasn't. At least not on this street. There were two more that led from the Quarter to the Port on either side of the city. Of course, the robbers were in the street that was drenched in alcohol, illegal gambling dens and thieves. Maybe even murderers, monsters. After all, nowhere in this land was there somewhere without a drop of Darkness. It was everywhere, even in the fantastical Twin Cities.

I sighed, letting the power within me wither. The strings led me here, The Golden Crow. It was a building made of black wood with a golden door, and no windows. Outside I spied a group of young-looking men, not much older or younger than me, drunk and smoking. The scent of sick sweet smoke filled the air around the den. But the strings didn't belong to them. They belonged to people inside the damn place.

I scrunched up my face. Never once in my life would I have dreamed of ever stepping in a place like this one. It was hideous, dirty and a wildly different monster. But I wasn't afraid. I was a soul mage, and I was someone who was trained to kill and to fight with bare fists should it ever come to that. Perhaps that was the only thing that made me walk up to the door, twist the handle and let myself inside. The fact that I shouldn't be afraid. I was a monster, this terrible thing with a terrible power. I wasn't safe, but I wasn't someone the people who were in here could easily kill.

I had even gambled a little back in Lysmir. Though it was more for fun and games like everyone who did it, unless you were Avran. Then you would *actually* gamble. And lose. Then cheat and maybe win.

A smile crept onto my face as the memories of my friend flashed in my mind. But I forced my muscles against the motion. This wasn't the place where one smiled unless they were baring their teeth with evil intention. And though I did have a similar intention, no need for drunks to know.

So, I squared my shoulders, donned a glare of cold death, and walked past the black velvet curtains and down the spiraling stairs that led me into the center of The Golden Crow.

～

The moment the stairs ended, there was a small room, lit by two fireplaces on either side. In the middle there was a man standing in front of another set of black curtains, dressed entirely in black, wearing a mask made of golden feathers covering the upper half of his face. A jagged scar, bright and pink, ran from his left eye, which was colorless and white, down to his jawline. His remaining eye was a golden brown. He was a large man, no doubt a veteran of countless fights. But I didn't waver. I walked towards him, my stride solid.

I was entirely aware my wardrobe was inadequate for The Golden Crow, aware that I seemed less like a gambler and more like a lost dog in the wrong part of town. But I hoped that the way I walked, the confidence I wore, would make him look past my appearance.

My power buzzed, humming inside me. It was telling me he wasn't the only one in the room. There were more, two behind me. Dressed no doubt in black clothing and a gold feather mask, shrouded by the shadows. I wagered they were guards, security of some sort.

"You need something to gamble," the man in front of me spoke. There was no kindness in his voice. A feral smile edged itself onto my face.

Finally, someone like me.

I fished the remaining Kronas from my pocket, each piece of paper worth progressively larger numbers. I showed the man, who took them, his singular eye glowing with magic. His hands moved to make a symbol in the air, one to make sure the money was real.

"You'll need a mask." His rough voice shattered the silence that had settled between us. He handed the money back and with it a mask made of golden feathers, just like his.

I took both, stuffing the money back into the small bag and into the inner pocket of my trousers. The mask I lifted onto my face, tying the black ribbons behind my head tightly so it stayed in place.

"Never remove it while in there." It seemed like a warning, but the man said it just simply as a statement. Then he stepped back and opened the black curtains, leading me into the room that seemed too large to be real.

I stepped through it, and felt the curtain fall back into place behind me. My eyes scanned the entire room, from the golden pillars holding the ceiling up, to the girls who were dressed in very little clothing and laughing very falsely. There were large round tables filled with masked men and women whose hands held playing cards. My eyes narrowed; the cards teemed with magic.

So, they're charmed cards. I smiled. That only could mean one thing: enchanted illegal gambling.

All bets were off then. One could cheat, and if they weren't caught, then they were in the clear. But if they were, well, that's when I assumed things got a lot deadlier. I had my fair share of gambling practice with and without magically induced cards, but it was never real, never high stakes. But here I was, putting a lot of Kronas on the line, just to get close to a bunch of robbers.

My magic rolled through me once more, just enough for the strings to lead me to a table in the back corner. There the threads untangled and led straight into the bodies of three masked men, dressed in ivory clothing. I eyed the table, my spirits dropping just a bit when I saw there were no open chairs.

Well then...

I lingered by the table, hidden from view but close enough to hear their conversations. If there wasn't a chair open, I'd *make* one open.

A devious smile edged on my face as I whisked a champagne flute from the passing girl holding a tray of them and leaned against the pillar, surveying the table. Which one of these people should I send on their merry way? None of three robbers were an option, so that left nine more players. There was one woman, with stark white hair, whiter than mine, and blood red lips. Her eyes, in slits, were boring into another player. Perhaps that man had cheated; after all, she seemed to be plotting his murder in her head just now. The other players were all men, tall and bulky. They hunched over the table, hands filled with cards, gleaming with unpredictable magic. They seemed like the ones that the table would least miss. So, I eyed one, a random one dressed in dark blue, and I woke the terrible power within me.

The man buckled, groaning. The rest of the players eyed him curiously, half bored.

"Leave if you feel unwell. Don't make the rest of us sick you bastard," the woman spoke with a sharp voice. Her eyes had moved from the man to the cards in front of him. He turned them over. And she sighed, mostly at their hand value. A mere 8. From what I could see the bet was placed on the player, and the player just lost.

"We need new blood here; this game is as enticing as an empty wallet." One of the three robbers sneered as the man I was crushing fell over, dropping his cards on the floor. I smiled, crushing the man's soul even more until he gasped for air and then, he fell over, whimpering. Another man, dressed in the same black clothing as the man behind the curtains, picked this one up with ease and led him away. The woman at the table brushed her hair aside and sighed.

"He's gone. One of you find someone to complete this set." She flicked her wrist at one of the silent players and he stood. Now was my chance. I downed the champagne, set it down on the table next to me and spun on my heel.

The woman was the one in charge; the three robbers were the ones I needed to charm and kill. It wouldn't be easy; hell, I needed to make sure all the cards were played exactly right. Time to show these bastards who I was.

So, I stepped out from behind the pillar and my eyes found the woman's. And I smiled, a wicked thing, and when she mirrored me, looking me up and down with glowing eyes, I knew I had earned a seat at the table.

XI : IVAR THAEGAN

The Twin Cities
Sunsier

"Call me Mahin." The woman purred. *Purred*.

"Mahin," I mused, my mouth twisting into a smirk. "A lovely name."

The woman, Mahin, simply tossed her head back and laughed. "Thank you." She motioned to the seat that was now, thanks to me, empty. "Please, sit."

I walked past the man she had just sent to find someone to fill the seat, and sat in it. It was golden, covered in red velvet. While I had torn my gaze from her, I felt Mahin's eyes on me the entire time. I instead paid more attention to the robbers, who sat, looking at me with curious eyes. I hoped my disguise was enough, even though it was just a mask. And I hoped that in the hurry of things, they had paid little attention to my eyes or my clothing.

"So," Mahin beckoned the cards to come to her so she could shuffle them again. As she did, her golden eyes glowed, eerily dark. Without turning towards me, I knew she was about to address me. "What is it that they call you?"

I grinned, "I'm called a lot of things, Miss Mahin. Would you like to hear all of my names," I mused, making my eyes seem particularly interested in her. I felt her falter underneath my gaze, and internally my spirits triumphed. That's half the battle. The other half was winning this game, taking all their money and then when they leave defeated, following those three bastards and taking what's mine.

Her eyes, never leaving mine, sparkled with mischief. "Perhaps just your name, we can come back to all the others later?"

This woman had no shame; I almost laughed. But instead I just leaned back in the chair and nodded. "Very well then. You can call me Sovan."

"Sovan," she mused quietly as she shuffled the cards. "Well, we are, or we *were,* playing a game of enchanted baccarat. I am the dealer. Cheat with magic if you want, but *do not* get caught." She paused, looking straight at me, "Are you in?" There was a hint of a threat in her voice.

"I'm in."

Mahin continued smiling. "*Wonderful,*" she said, as she handed me my hand of cards and passed the rest to the other eleven players. I hadn't played a game of baccarat in years, much less the enchanted, illegal and high stakes version of it. But the rules were still ingrained in my memory, and even though I didn't have the magic to change the card's design at will like I suspected Mahin and some others had, I did have a lovely trick up my sleeve. My own magic. Which made it possible for me to turn the odds in my favor.

"How much are you betting?" Her voice broke my mischievous thoughts.

"Is one thousand Kronas enough?" Eyes widened at that. To them, that meant I was a new and inexperienced player who didn't know how much to bet, or I was a professional player and I knew that I wouldn't be losing any money. I'd be winning it all. I kept a stoic face; there was no need for them to think the former more than the latter. Sure, I didn't have half the experience these players did, but from their eyes, none of them were soul mages, so none of them could do or even feel what I was about to do.

Mahin's face shifted from wicked to pleasantly surprised, but there was a darkness behind it. One I knew well. She was thinking of all the ways she would cheat me out of it. I almost pitied her; if I had a heart, perhaps I would. She was just the dealer after all, but she had the cards at her will and she dealt them with magic, and by the looks on the faces of the other players, I wasn't the only one who knew this deck was going to be magically wild.

~

In the span of one hour, I had lost almost half of my money to other players. By now, each looked down on me as some easy pawn they steal from. But let them think that. By the end of this game, I would have all of it back and much more.

Mahin had taken all the cards, and shuffled them twice again before dealing them out to the players and the bankers. One of them was new, a girl, with light pink hair, no doubt from an enchantment. Her eyes were burnished gold, another solar mage. The girl, who said her name was Sabah, had replaced one of the players who was accused of cheating by Mahin. I saw the smirk of triumph as she caught him cheating and was able to prove it to everyone else, it was as if she had been waiting for the moment. She had motioned another man to find some new blood, and he had come back, minutes later, with Sabah. Her arms looped with his, a small plump bag underneath her arm and in her free hand, a half empty champagne flute with a purple lipstick ring. She had sat down, bet on the player with one thousand Kronas, and won the bet plus five hundred more Kronas at her first sitting. She made the game more interesting. Sabah was someone who knew how to play the game, especially if it was enchanted, who no doubt had managed to cheat a few times.

Mahin leaned towards me, her eyes glowing as her hands moved the cards as they floated in the air. They glittered with her magic, as it spun them, shifted them into a new order.

"As charming and mysterious as you are, Sovan, you are not faring well, if at all. You have bored me, and you better be careful. This is my game. If you bore me, I might have to make you leave." The threat in her voice was clear; she didn't want me here. But just like Sabah, I knew how to play. I knew how to cheat in the shadows.

She showed them, us, what she was capable of. I let them think I was small, and nothing.

So, I leaned back, taking the two cards she handed to me, my magic pouring through me. I didn't like to let them know that I'm strong, so I let them think I'm weak. And then, when the time was right, I would show them how powerful I can be.

At that, Mahin seemed content, "Hurry then, darling Sovan." She grinned again, and I mirrored her, while twisting my power into my own little weapon. "How do you bet?"

"The rest of my money on a tie." I spoke the words loud and clear, and everyone at the table stilled. None had dared bet on a tie; why would they? It was a risk none were willing to take, at least not in a game that was enchanted. If one was smart, they would know that Mahin would probably have made sure the cards would never be able to tie. If one was smart, they would also know that it was impossible to use magic discreetly enough to charm all the cards into their favor. But I wasn't interested in being the smart they expected.

So, when all the other players placed their bets, all higher than the ones before on the player and banker, I fought the urge to smile. Half the players bet all their money; the others bet most. If I did this right then I would be given nine times the number value and the money of everyone's bet. That was the wicked twist Mahin had spun onto the game. The player, be it player or banker, with the hand value closest to nine who placed a bet on the right rank got all the money. If not, then the bet money went evenly to everyone. It was a rather odd way of planning the game. For the first few hands, it tangled up my ability to fully grasp the game. But now, after enough times of playing the game with Mahin's own little spin on it, I figured out how to win.

"If he wins, he will empty the pot, and most of the players will be out. The game wou—"

"The game would finish," Mahin cut off one of the other players, "but not to worry, that will not happen. Ties *never* happen. This poor young man will learn the hard way," she turned to face me, a feline grin on her face. But I didn't let it faze me, instead focusing on my power as it welled inside me and did as I willed it to, as I commanded it to.

Everyone stilled. Everyone in the *room*. Silence settled quickly, and I stood up, waving my hands over my head and tightening my hands into fists.

Let's make them dormant for a little while.

That was the lovely thing about souls. They were the very essence of the body, of all magic save for blood magic that flowed in the veins of blood mages.

I undid my hands, slowly, lifting all the souls from their bodies, leaving all of them lifeless, rotting and decaying things. For now. If I was quick enough, nothing would happen to anyone. The only thing they would notice was a small jolt when their souls were put back into their bodies, a tiny little prick of pain, barely noticeable.

I stood up and turned over each card. Mahin was right, there was not a single tie on the table. But that didn't matter, I would show her that ties were possible, if one tried hard enough, if one knew how to make them happen. I reached for the deck of cards, replacing the cards in each of the player's hands until they all had the same hand value.

I looked over at Mahin, her perfectly glowing face seemed to dim with the seconds, minutes. Her body was dying, everyone in the room was. I returned the deck back to its original spot, and made sure every deck was a tie. And then I turned them all over, including mine, and I sat back down. Whilst raising my arms above me again, willing the souls back in their respective bodies, I felt a wave of wicked triumph. Should Mahin suspect anything, there would be nothing she could do. Absolutely nothing, because you couldn't just accuse someone of cheating, even if it was obvious they had. You had to prove it with concrete evidence. And she would have *none*.

I smiled at the thought. My body ached the moment I let my arms down and my hold on the souls disappeared. I was used to controlling a lot of souls at once, and for a while too. But there had been well over two hundred people here, and it had taken a toll. Nothing major, I was strong, and the small headache would fade away soon enough. A bleeding nose, a blurry vision, a killer headache were the signs when someone over exerted themselves.

The noise started instantly, as if no one knew or noticed what had happened to them. Even Mahin, whose face was stretched in its usual devious smirk didn't falter in the slightest.

"Turn them over lady," she nodded her head in Sabah's direction, "and gentlemen." She continued. And then everyone did, including me. And in seconds people gasped, shock filled everyone's eyes as they slowly found me. I turned to face Mahin, whose own eyes held the same emotion, but within hers there was a fury, a primal fury.

I smiled. Like a bastard. "Well, well, look at that," I motioned towards the cards, "looks like ties can happen after all."

"You cheated!" One man shot up from his chair with so much force the chair fell behind him, cracking. He pointed a thick finger at me, his eyes forming slits containing no doubt a glare.

I stood up, menacingly. "Prove it," I countered, and he knew, I knew, we all knew damn well he couldn't prove it. No one could. Not even Mahin herself.

It felt damn good undermining each and every one of them, especially Mahin and the three robbers, who ever so slowly stood up and walked off like everyone else at the table. The man cloaked in black handed the money to me and even I walked off. I didn't stay to really see all the emotions being felt by those at the table. They no doubt wanted to kill me, or worse. But I wouldn't let them, so I weaved my way out of the room, making sure to leave my mask with the man that had given it to me.

"Won big?" His rough voice filled the room. I flashed him a smile.

"Perhaps."

And then I made my way up the stairs, letting my power form once again the strings that belonged to the robbers.

~

They walked for what seemed like ages. The street going from the Merchants' Quarter to the Port was much longer than I realized. Or remembered. The last time I had gone to the Port it was from the other street. The one that was filled with the same magic and spirit as the rest of the Outer City. Perhaps then, as a child, I had been entranced with the magic, with the vendors who sold fish and foreign goods instead of the goods one always found at the vendor stalls in the markets of the Outer City. It was there, I remembered, that my mother bought me a doll, that was filled with smaller dolls inside. It was from a vendor who came from Volkova, the capital city of Pyatov. The doll was decorated in spiraling colors, in flowers carefully drawn beside silver blades. It still remained on the top of the bookshelf in my room, overlooking everything. I had put it there so my sisters, who were so keen on taking it to play with because they had been so foolish to pass up the chance to get one themselves, wouldn't steal it. I smiled at the fading memory, of them, of the doll and the vendor that may or may not be on the complete other side of the city, wishing I could be there.

Because I wasn't there, I was in this shitty street, stalking robbers. I had stuffed the money in the pockets of my trousers, and was now walking behind them at a distance. So far no one dared follow me out of The Golden Crow. Not even Mahin herself, though I wagered she had people to do that. And yet, there wasn't a soul behind me.

The men stumbled a few times; they were drunk then. Not that I was surprised, as throughout the entire game they had been the ones who consistently ordered drinks and downed them in seconds. I followed them, keeping to the shadows, turning corners when they did and going deeper into the darkened street. From the distance I could make out a tall gate, ornate and heavy, like the one I passed through to get to the Merchants' Quarter. Here, the air was tinged with the faint smell of salt water and fish.

We were close to the Port, and from being unable to smell the ocean on them, I wagered we weren't going into the Port. Then the men stopped suddenly, one disappearing into a building and the other two carrying on. I pushed aside my annoyance, and continued following the two that walked a little while longer, until they too entered a building. Or more precisely, a house. I waited a while before inching forwards, taking in the buildings. Even in plain daylight it looked morbid, daunting and eerily ominous.

It was made of a similar black wood as The Golden Crow was. But this one didn't have a golden door and did have windows. The glass was shattered and cracked, dusty and definitely old. The door was a faded green color; the paint was chipping off everywhere. I took the small rusted handle in my hand, and turned it whilst I felt for the magic that swam within me. I knew it was there, but even so, I checked it out of habit as I walked into the dark room. The men were nowhere in sight. But there was a door, another one that looked in the middle of full-on decay, right in front of me. I walked on the stone floor that was cracked in some places. Whatever happened here, whatever the history was, it wasn't a pretty one. I strained my ears, my instincts alert. Despite the men not being mages, from what I gathered from their rather dull colored eyes, they were dangerous. Perhaps not dangerous like me, but they were all the same.

I inched closer to the door, carefully and slowly opening it. The two men were standing in front of a table. The room was in shambles. On one wall there were countless paintings leaning against it, and on another wall there was another door. Ancient looking furniture was scattered randomly around the room, and a large chandelier was covered in a musty white cloth. Mirrors were stacked up on the wall near where the door I came through was.

I slipped through, into the shadows and behind a large mirror. And there I hid, not even knowing why. I could just demand them to hand over what they had taken. I wasn't afraid of them; I shouldn't be. So, I slipped back out from the mirror and walked towards them.

But the moment I opened my mouth; I felt a mind-numbing pain and then I felt myself falling onto the floor and into darkness.

~

My eyes fluttered open, my head throbbing with pain. I winced suddenly as my body became aware of the pain in my wrists, that were bound by another pair of hands. I smelled alcohol, a lot of it. Whoever was holding me reeked of it. The room I was in was the same one I had walked into. Except now the men were facing me, or two of them at least. They held smiles, drunken wicked smiles.

"We should thank you," one of them spoke roughly, pointing to an object heaped on the floor, "at least now we got all your money. Which was a lot, so in the end, thank you also for winning the game." This time he showed his teeth and praise Darkness, I wish he hadn't. They were blackened and dirty. I fought the urge to gag.

"Look at this! Nooran, the bastard found *us*. We didn't even need to go looking for him." He seemed overly amused, overly happy and definitely a little drunk.

The other man, they said he was called Sarun, stood up from his seat, violet silver eyes gleaming. Lunar mage. My eyes narrowed, as I tried to figure out how I missed them back at The Golden Crow. In the dimly lit room, they seemed so much brighter. But I didn't let it worry me too much. It was daytime, and lunar mages needed the presence of the moon to use their magic. One of their greatest weaknesses, likewise for the solar mages. Without the sun, they were powerless.

In the man's mouth was a cigar releasing a rather disgustingly sweet aroma. He also chuckled, taking the cigar from his mouth and making his way towards me.

"Ishan," Sarun nodded to the man holding me hostage, "good job. She'll be proud."

She?

My mind went straight to Mahin. After all she seemed, she *was*, the one to have others do her dirty work. Perhaps these were her men. Sent out to kill me, to find me, only I had made the job so much easier now. Or, of course, so they thought.

"Where should we put him?" one sounded from the darkness. I closed my eyes, focusing less on their voices and more on my power, letting it awaken once again. It warmed my body as it pulsed in my soul, body, veins.

"We need to make a spectacle of him, for her enjoyment. She likes it when it's especially bloody." Ishan tugged on my arms, harshly. I let out a feigned whimper.

"Weakling," he laughed. Still gripping my wrists, his thick fingers cut off my circulation. Ishan led me, or rather *pushed* me, past a door into another room. Darker than the last, but no less musty and dirty. He kicked at my feet, letting me tumble beneath him, to the floor. Their sick laughter filled the room. I heard the pop of a bottle of some type of liquor being opened.

"Don't you speak?" one chided, his face lost to the shadows.

"Yeah he speaks, he was so smooth at the table, but now look at him," this man spoke. Whichever of the three it was, kicked me. Hard. I resisted the urge to kill him right then and there. After all, I needed my money, and my bag. And dead men would serve me no good.

"Ah, I did not know when I woke up today that I would be torturing someone." The one who kicked me walked off, and I slowly sat up, willing myself to look weak for them, to let them think they'd broken me and shattered me. Let them think they'd won. It was a trick my father used, my mother used, it was a trick everyone outside of the Twin Cities probably used. It was a pity really; these men and I were so similar. Despite the fact that I would never drink while torturing someone, I have tortured plenty of people in the past. My eyes flickered open, adjusting to the darker environment. One of them pulled a sharp dagger from a black bag, a pearl shined in the ray of sun that bled through the dirty windows.

Wait.

That was *my* bag. *My* dagger. I recognized its white blade and pearl encrusted hilt anywhere. I eyed the bag on the table. Other than the man pulling the blade from it, it seemed untouched. But I had brought my sword in it and I saw that was no longer there. The fury bubbled inside me at the idea of them selling off my sword to the highest bidder. It wasn't my favorite one; no, I had left the best blades at home. This one was a nameless blade I had taken from the weaponry. It was a standard short sword that many of our guards held.

"Hey Sarun, doesn't he look a little familiar? I feel as if I have seen him before." One of them, hidden in the darkness spoke in slurred words.

"Doubt that," another one of them shot back.

No, I assured them silently. *You've seen me before. And you're about to wish you hadn't.*

The moment they turned around I stood; a wicked smile appeared on my face. And the moment I unleashed my power, their eyes must have widened in fear, in inexplicable pain. Because they no doubt saw my glowing silver eyes, they had no doubt heard of all the terrors of what we soul mages could do. And they knew they were powerless to stop me from doing whatever I was going to do.

I tightened my hands into fists, and one by one they fell to their knees. A scream tore through the silence, from Ishan. He was easy to kill, a weak little thing. He slumped over in just seconds. His body falling at awkward angles, his eyes frozen in fear and fully black.

The other two cowered, screaming, not daring to look at their fallen friend. My smile remained etched on my face through it all.

"Who—the *hell*—are you?" the one named Sarun, screamed, trembling beneath my hold.

And Nooran seethed, poison dripping from his every word, his eyes holding death itself, "*What* the hell are you?" As if he didn't already know.

I am Prince Ivar Thaegan of Lysmir. A soul mage, your nightmare, the bringer of your deaths.

But the words were left unsaid, because instead of speaking

them aloud, I simply smiled my malicious grin and tightened my fist, tightening my hold on them. Slowly crushing their souls, destroying them, until the light left their eyes and their lifeless, decaying bodies flopped to the ground. A few thuds and then silence.

The power inside me fizzled out, becoming dormant for now. I made my way to the table, picking up the dagger that they had left on the table and stuffing it back into the bag. Inside were still my clothes, my hairbrush and toothbrush. Even the soap, and the sword, buried deep under all the things.

"Well, well, guess you didn't have time to sell it." I smiled at the fact that it was still there despite it being just a regular sword. I brought the bag's flap overhead and covered it, tightening my fingers around the handle.

Time to get out of this hellhole.

I pushed open the door, ignoring the throbbing pain in my head and making my way out of the house. Down the dark and terrible street and back into the Merchants' Quarter where *someone* knew how to find the Neithisis.

XII : SIVREHYA RITHLOREN

The Twin Cities
Sunsier

Moonsier transforming into Sunsier was said to be something beyond magical, if that even existed. The night before I had been too busy trying to repair my awful room accommodations, and then I fell asleep. How, when the bed, that was more like a cot if anything, was beyond uncomfortable, I didn't know. All I knew was that I didn't want to miss the transformation, knowing well that this wasn't my last chance, but I didn't care. I pushed aside the curtain and walked, or tried to at least. After all this room was a hole. It was about the size of a prison cell, and just as appealing. It smelled of something, something like ash perhaps. I didn't know. Part of me didn't *want* to know.

But the moment I woke up, I had pushed off the sad excuse for a blanket and knew three things. This room smelled worse today than last night. I needed to conjure up an actual fucking bed. And, the transformation, by the looks of the faded streams of light through the sheer curtains, was about to happen. I thought, perhaps something beyond magical could brighten my dull spirits. I was going on an impossible search, with absolutely no place to start. Might as well try to cheer myself up.

A clock in the distance rang its bells. Loud, clear and crisp sounds filled the air, the city. I pushed aside the muslin curtains and looked out into the street below. Though yesterday, this street was almost deserted, this morning it was slowly filling with people. Each spilled from the doors, from smaller streets conjoining with this one. Soon enough, the boring scenery of beige and mud brown buildings was changed into a teeming crowd filled with colors and sounds and smells. There were no vendors in sight, no stands. But I saw the people carried large bags, bundled cloths, vases on their heads, under their arms, in carts they pushed or dragged behind them. Perhaps this is where the vendors lived, and now, at the eighth hour of the day, just as Moonsier was becoming Sunsier, they came out from their homes and off they went to their many stands.

My eyes shifted from the scene below and up to the sky. Where slowly, the sun rose and then, the sky glowed. Magic teemed in the air, filling it entirely. I felt it brush past me the moment I opened the window. I inhaled the scent of the magic. It was sweet and foreign, smelling almost like one of those spiced teas. The air was crisp, and within it, I could see the sparkle, the magic that touched the city as the sky glittered and the sun rose ever so slowly. Soon enough the buildings stopped glowing silver, the bluish tint of the city died and in its wake was gold. And yellow, and warmth. As if the city was turning into summer after winter. The lanterns that hung on thin strings between the buildings fizzled out, the moon-flowers that lined the buildings shrank back and in their place were marigolds, and roses and hundreds of other flowers I couldn't name.

Like magic, the buildings became covered in champagne-colored designs, ornate and spiraling in the shape of the sun. They glowed from within, pulsating with magic, the same one I had seen yesterday.

The people cheered, as if seeing this for the first time. Their eyes filled with awe and wonder. They were happy and for a small moment it reminded me of just a couple days before, when my siblings and I went to each and every city in our kingdom to tell them of the war, to tell our people to not worry. They had fear in their eyes, trembling in their bodies, just like the hatred for the ones we were going to war with. You could smell it in the air, in each city, every time stronger than the one before. But despite all that, some I knew had been secretly happy. Because, even if it meant mutual destruction, they had a chance to torture their worst enemies, to kill them, to unleash what dark desires bubbled beneath their skin. Years of being on the brink of war, years of the water of hatred boiling over the edge, years of the lid staying on the pot.

And yet, through it all, I couldn't help but think of how terrible their happiness was. Because it wouldn't last. And as I watched these people, I knew theirs wouldn't either. It never did, as the world drowned it out before it became too powerful. But maybe things were different here. After all it seemed like another place entirely. Though I knew there was Darkness everywhere. However big, however small, wherever it hid, it was in all the places. It was out there; it was in this city. And these people, who always seemed so happy, also seemed to not notice.

I stepped away from the window, walking towards my bag that lay on the dresser. I had packed a dress with a long skirt, that went down to my feet, the skirt of which had two pockets and five times as many folds and layers. The top was loose, with tulle sleeves and a neckline that went a little too low for my liking, but it was the only dress I had brought with me that didn't have long sleeves. I rolled my eyes at the dress, wishing I had brought a spell book on altering clothing with me. It was never something I had really bothered to learn, other than changing a dress into more of an armor, with enchanted metal plates and such. That was the only clothing-altering spell I knew, and it was useless now. I had kept to learning more practical things: how to conjure a fire, how to torture people in various different ways, a variety of curses, more than I could count. Portal spells, healing spells, protection charms, those sorts of things. The clothing-alteration spells were mostly used by our handmaidens, the ones who made our clothing, and partially by Rhi, who had always been fascinated with fashion, as was I. It was the subject we could talk about for hours: guessing the new trends for the year, what would be in style, what wouldn't. When we were younger we'd host our own fashion shows and beg the soldiers to take us to the high-end shops in Meris.

As we got older, my interest faded and hers grew. And while the kingdom still named us the most fashionable women of Meris, no one could argue that Rhiannyn was the Rithloren who wore the more extravagant outfits, the one with the most beads, the most intricate designs. I liked my dresses to be simpler. Not so much as plain pieces of cloth, as I liked a little adornment here and there. But it was nowhere close to Rhi's adoration for being covered in beads, gemstones and dyed pearls.

I slipped the dress on and knew the moment I stepped outside I would probably melt from the heat. The only reason I wasn't now was because I was bidding my blood from the wound I had just made, into the symbol for cold. It took a long while, but slowly, the air temperature began to drop. I remember my father using this symbol to cool down a soup our kitchen had made for dinner one time that was far too hot. He had burned half his tongue and the cook who had prepared the soup had practically begged the king for forgiveness. And he forgave her because he knew she had not meant it.

At the memory, my body started to ache, and before any tears could come out, I pushed them down and away forever. No crying, not here, not now, not ever.

I focused on putting on the boots and placing throwing knives into each one. I lost count of the years I've been putting throwing knives into my boots, and the reason why I started was lost to me. I think it was from my favorite novel series I had read once, of an assassin, who had knee-high black boots that each held two throwing knives. Granted, I didn't have knee-high boots, and only two throwing knives, but perhaps I had started putting them in my shoes because she had done it.

I made my way to the mirror, a large, cracked and ancient-looking thing. It was once in a frame, but it seemed to have been ripped out of it, if that were even possible. I looked at my reflection, and those bright red eyes that stared back at me. Those eyes that gave a clue to all the magic that sung in my veins. The eyes that raised too many questions and turned far too many heads for my liking.

"No more questions," I whispered as I lifted both of my hands, one empty and opened, the other holding my dagger. And then, I touched the tip of the blade to my palm and pressed. I didn't wince; the wincing stopped so many years ago, after I had gotten used to the constant pricking and cutting of my flesh. I remember when there was a time it hurt, when I ached, but that was when I was a child. And I wondered if maybe the pain went away because I was used to it and maybe, because blood mage bodies through the centuries had gotten used to being cut open so often.

I waved my fingers in the air, watching as the blood rose up from my wound and into the air. It formed, quickly, a spell, incredibly intricate. In the circle was the vague shape of an eye, lines and curves all over, smaller symbols attached inside and out, until finally the spell was finished and it locked into place, glowing red for just a second. My eyes found themselves in the mirror once again, only this time they weren't red, they were a dull light brown, with no trace of what they once were. The blood fell back onto my hand, splattering, and I used it to heal myself.

Though I knew I would take away the glamour of brown eyes soon enough, I hated them with a passion. I had always been a fan of my scarlet eyes. But for now, I would bear these. No longer would people here see me as a vault of hidden knowledge. I would be a simple, pale-faced, black-haired, brown-eyed, nameless girl. A nobody and that was what I needed to be.

Lastly my hair was a mess from when I woke up. I looked in the mirror again, and pulled the brush from my bag. Some other spells I didn't know, the ones to style hair. Those were second nature for people like Lissa, who used them on my hair. She taught me one, long ago, but its lines and curves were long gone from my memory. And even if I still remembered it, it didn't help, since I most certainly didn't want my hair up in a twisted complicated thing with red rubies everywhere. It had been a regal hairdo, one for a ballroom dance. Certainly not for tracking down a secret in a foreign city.

So, instead I grabbed a red ribbon and tied the end of my thick black braid. It was a messy thing, but it would have to do. And there, I was ready.

Ah. Wait, the money.

It never hurt to have it, and after all, I needed to buy new clothes to survive the blistering heat of the city. Because my dresses, all black and dark red and long in nature, would do me no favors. I didn't have time to faint from the heat while I was here. My time was already cut impossibly short and the pressure, the weight of a looming war, itched at me like a scab.

Oh fuck, the letter!

I mentally cursed myself as my eyes glazed past the little piece of parchment paper still on the dresser. The same one I had meant to send to Daemon and Rhi last night. I must have been extremely tired and too pissed off to remember. Quickly, I fished out the dagger again, cutting a shallow line into my skin. And this time I bid it to form another symbol, more intricate this time, filled with twists and loops. And when it stopped glowing, I took the parchment in my hand detailing my safe arrival and threw it through the portal, watching it disappear from sight.

The inn was quiet as it was last night, the halls just as dark. And the stairs, I noticed as I walked down, were just as loud, if not louder. In my hands I gripped the small metal key, the one I would have to give the man every time I left the room. Speaking of the man, he sat at his desk, shuffling some large stack of papers, humming to himself. He wore a light brown shirt this time, with dark brown pants. A belt, with what I assumed was a dagger hanging from it, clashed with the other colors with its black hue. If there were two colors that I found did not go well together, they were black and brown.

"Ahem," I coughed lightly, the moment I reached the counter. The man turned around, his eyes sparkling with recognition.

"Ah, come to bring the key back then. Thank you." He took the key that was in my outstretched hand and put it in some box, in some vault.

I was about to turn around and leave when he spoke once again, his voice scratchy.

"Yer lucky miss, the young man who is in the room next to yers is not one to be busy at night, or at all."

And I froze. Solid.

Hold the bloody hell up.

I looked at the man, my eyes wide, and just blinked. Because apparently, I had lost all my ability to do anything else. "You *asked!*" My voice hit a high note, enough to shatter windows.

"I sure did miss." He seemed overly pleased with himself. Then, his face shifted, his eyes narrowed as he looked me in the eyes. I gulped.

"Is something wrong, sir?"

"No, no. It's just, I swear it to the Sun Goddess herself, that yer eyes were a different color yesterday."

"Oh? Well, that would be dreadfully worrisome, but thankfully no." I waved a hand through the air dismissively and handed him the key to the room. "My eyes have always been brown." A smile carved itself onto my face, in hopes that he'd believe. I wished I had changed my eye color before stepping before into the city, but I had no idea that every one of them would be overly taken with a blood mage of all the mages.

The man said nothing, just nodded his head and returned, wordlessly, to the desk. And I turned on the heel of my black boots and made my way out the door and into the street that was filled with people.

∾

If the streets were busy, the Square at the center of the Merchants' Quarter was *saturated* with people. The scene seemed like lava from a volcano. The clothes were the wild reds, vibrant oranges, golds and whites and ivories they had yesterday. But for some reason my black dress seemed to bring out little attention, which I was glad for.

I found out yesterday that the Square was where most of the shops were, whether that be for tea, for souvenirs, food or clothing. I knew next to nothing about this city, but I wagered this would be the best place to start looking for some clothes that wouldn't make me melt.

And then I sensed it, and goosebumps freckled my skin in an instant. A wave of Darkness, of magic, of power like mine. And it was strong, but foreign. I twisted around, trying to follow it. And I weaved through the sea of people, focusing on the scent that was too similar to my own. Someone else was here, someone who had magic touched by the Darkness, but was different from blood magic. And then, I stumbled, having made full contact with a strong, solid form. I blinked, silver and ivory clouding my vision, before I finally muttered an annoyed 'sorry' and continued on my way to uncover who the scent belonged to. But in the mixture of spices and tea, in the sea of a thousand people, it vanished. I huffed.

Perfect, I rolled my eyes.

It was probably nothing but my imagination. So, I continued making my way through the mass of people and once I was free of its grasp I was in front of a small clothing store. I smiled. The golden sign sparkled against the sun's light.

Miss Fara's Boutique.

In the windows were dress forms, wearing all sorts of colorful clothing. There was a dress, yellow, with tulle sleeves and a long skirt made perhaps of silk and tulle. On another was a coat made of tulle, with a scarlet color. It had sleeves that reached above the elbows and the bottom of the coat reached to the floor. Underneath it was a skirt, the same length, made of billowing soft fabric, just a touch darker than the coat. It was adorned with simple yet beautiful gold patterns that hung off the sleeves. Gold designs lined the skirt, matching those of the coat. My eyes did one sweep of that dress-coat-skirt ensemble and I walked into the store.

A lady, of middle age perhaps, with faded yellow eyes and rich brown hair streaked with grey, wearing a pale-yellow skirt and top outfit and circular gold rimmed glasses, practically jumped out at me once I stepped through the threshold. I yelped as the woman looped her arm with mine and lead me further into the store. I had no time to protest or even have a chance of ripping my arm away because she had sat me down on a champagne-colored ottoman and herself in one across from me.

"Hello!" She said too cheerfully, "It's been so long since a foreigner has come into my shop. My name is Miss Fara, and how can I help you today?"

By not being that *nice.*

"I really liked the red coat and skirt outfit on the dress form outside in the window," I rushed out before I would say what I had thought.

"Ah yes!" The woman's eyes sparkled and she practically bounced off of the ottoman and to the windows where she took the clothing off. I barely had time to even ask the price of it before she shrieked out "one hundred and ten Kronas" before thrusting the clothing into my hands and pushing me into a dressing room. I hadn't even thought about trying on the clothing. It's a good thing this woman had thought it for me, because to have a dress that didn't fit after paying was a rather awful fail.

I took off my black dress and slipped on the new one, turning around to face myself in the mirror.

"You like red!" The woman shouted from the other side of the yellow velvet curtain.

"Yes! All shades of it," I replied, not really knowing why she asked. The dress fit, really well, right in the places it needed to be and loose in others. I was just about to slip out of it until the curtain was suddenly wide open and Fara stood there, beaming like the damn sun itself, holding a pile of reddish clothes and a nude colored underdress in her arms.

"Here then, try these on." She shoved them in my chest, since my arms were my sides and once again closed the curtain. For the moment, all I did was stand there, having caught the clothing before it all toppled onto the floor. My mouth was open, for just a bit, from shock. And then I shook my head and decided since I was already here, I might as well see what she brought me.

I did need more than one outfit, but this woman had given me ten. I just needed four, five at the most. At least all of them were shades of red, though none dark like I usually liked and wore, but they were just fine. I slipped out of the coat and dress and set them aside, going for a transparent red one with ornate bead patterns.

I stepped out of the dressing room, five dresses in one hand, six in the other, my face flushed from all that changing and my once messy braid now even more of a mess.

"Did you choose which one was best?" The woman replied, turning her attention from a young girl in a rich yellow top and skirt ensemble and a tulle shawl around her shoulder which went down to her waist. Her hair, rich brown like her skin, was pinned back with a few golden hair clips that matched her eyes.

I tore my gaze from her and looked at the arm with five dresses draped on it. I lifted it, "These five, I'll take." The woman looked bewildered, certainly not expecting me to buy so many.

"All five!"

"Yes, yes, yeah, mhm." A rumble of words, but the woman smiled anyways and took them.

"Dearest girl, would you mind helping me with the other dresses." Fara turned to the girl she had been talking to and the girl sprang into action. She walked towards me and took the remaining dresses from my arm, smiling as she did it.

"Thank you."

Her face lit up even more, "Oh no worries miss...what is your name?"

Ah, my name. Right.

I couldn't very well use Sivrehya. Most everyone knew who Sivrehya Rithloren was.

"My name is..." I wracked my head for anything, any name really, "Tess...eria." I finished, flashing a smile for effect. An I-was-definitely-not-at-all-lying kind of smile. But they seemed to take it because both the girl and the woman named Fara smiled.

"Tesseria, after the queen who took back her throne and her kingdom. My, you have a strong name." The woman's eyes crinkled as she spoke, leading me to the front. The other girl walked away, putting the dresses where the woman had gotten them from.

I nodded. Indeed yes, besides our Matron Queen Maehra, Empress Tesseria was my utmost favorite person, idol, inspiration, the list goes on. I had first read about her when I was eight, in a book, solely for children. It had pictures of her, of what they thought she looked like. She was depicted as being exceptionally beautiful despite her colorless skin that was quite literally *cracked*. It was from the Decay Disease she had contracted as a child. It cracked skin, weakening the host until there was nothing left but a pile of dust. I often wondered how in the name of Darkness she could have survived it, because no one did, not for long anyway. And yet, she was the best and longest reigning monarch the Empire of Otrina had ever known.

I loved her the most for despite being weak and fragile, she had the strength and courage and the capability to be just wicked enough to take back what her family had so cruelly taken from her. She had been the heir, the Crown Princess, until her younger brother, for reasons of greed and thinking her much too weak to rule Otrina, threw her to the Darkness to die. Only she didn't die. She managed to learn from the Shadowbenders, a race of mages who were now long lost to history but could control the Darkness itself, and in the end, she rose up and took back what rightfully was hers. And so, from her reign came an age of Shadowbenders, who effectively destroyed the Darkness...well, almost did. And for all that, I admired her. Sure, she was decaying, and always on the brink of death, but she never once let that stop her.

"So Tesseria," the girl's voice came from my left and effectively broke my train of thought. "My name is Junah. It is a pleasure to meet you. Where are you from?" The girl's eyes were hopeful, and so, I flashed a smile and took a deep breath in.

"From Meris." I said it bluntly, and because I didn't feel like telling an overly orchestrated lie where I was from some nonmage Free City like Ferreow. Because I had never been there, and should this girl pepper me with questions as I knew she would, it was best to stick to the places I knew best.

Her eyes widened at that. "Meris, like Meris the kingdom of blood mages, like the mages who are beyond evil and wicked and terrible."

I fought the urge to roll my eyes, but in reality, I couldn't blame her thoughts towards us. We were known to be just what she had said, and so much worse. And we were.

"I'm from a city," I paused, no. Rarely had any nonmages lived in the Merisan cities. "A small village I should say, actually. It's mainly just nonmages that live there. There's really no blood mages at all, if that can be believed." I continued, spinning a lie from a truth.

"Oh, is it Risno? I've heard of a village in Meris where only nonmages live." At that I nod my head. I had been to Risno a few times when I was younger. It was the custom for all of us Rithloren children to visit each village, each city in our kingdom every few years. Risno was the furthest from the royal city of Maeh, and the nearest the end of Meris and the beginning of the fallen kingdom of Vylara. I liked Risno, it was simple yet elegant and just as dark as any city in Meris. And despite consisting of only nonmages they seemed to like the fact that they lived in a kingdom filled with ruthless blood mages. And it was probably because they were just as ruthless themselves. There were thieves prowling the streets, murders happened perhaps once or twice a month, and there were more than several dark alchemists who drew on the books of blood mage spells and tried to recreate them without magic. It would always prove fruitless. Anyone could draw out a symbol meant to do anything out of blood, but unless one had magic in their own blood, the scarlet symbol would simply sit there and dry up, a useless thing.

"Do you like it there?" Junah probed me with another question. I nodded, taking the bag the woman put on the counter and handing her the Kronas. "Is it scary there, knowing you live near such terrifying beings?" She spoke as if she wasn't capable of becoming one herself, which of course, she probably didn't even think about, but solar and lunar magic was similar to blood magic. Only instead of blood to cast spells and charms and curses, they used the sun or the moon. I had always read it was weaker than its blood magic counterpart; after all, blood could be bent and shaped into anything, if you were strong enough. And solar and lunar magic could only go so far, but that didn't mean it didn't have the capability to create massive chaos and evil just like my magic.

"Sometimes, but the royal family never tries to hurt us, no blood mage does. We're peaceful." As much as I wished for her to stop talking, I knew she wouldn't. Miss Fara held her hand out; a paper slip laid in it. I took it and stuffed the slip into the brown paper bag with the boutique's logo on it.

"I am just curious, because I am a lover of all things dark and twisted, as weird as that may sound."

For here maybe, but for outside those city walls...not in the slightest.

I looked at her, and she smiled again, beaming. I wondered if her face ached from it, or if she was so used to it, it didn't hurt anymore.

"Oh really?" I began walking out, and she followed. Maybe I should have just said goodbye and spirited out the door.

"Oh yes, see I am a Scholar at the Sunsier Academy of Magical Studies and Art. And there I am majoring in the studies of mythical and magical creatures."

She's what?

I froze.

"It is awfully interesting learning about those things." Her fingers fiddled with her long skirt, "I know it is weird, and should be so unlike everyone here, but I do not know, I have always been fascinated by them and such things."

"No, it's fine. I think it's cool, actually." Her face lit up at that. And she looped my arm with hers.

"Goodbye Miss Fara," Junah called out to the woman and she led me out the door.

"Bye darlings!" The woman called out, waving her hands, smiling her radiant-as-the-sun smile.

"Come Tesseria, there is a place I want to show you." And with that, out the door we both went.

The Twin Cities
Sunsier

At first, I had just smiled, going along with the girl named Junah, who looked at me like less of a precious piece of information and more like a delicious pastry. Well, at *first*, I had suppressed the urge to turn her into a lovely statue made of stone just so she would stop talking. But then, she mentioned being a Scholar, studying mythical creatures of all things and so, I allowed her to loop her arm with mine. Carrying the bags filled with Sunsieran clothing, I let her guide me wherever.

Which happened to be a tea shop. Because of course.

"I like this place the best," Junah brought us to a table, round and small, though no doubt heavy as I saw it was made purely of marble. With cracks filled with glittering gold and specks of crushed silver. In its center was a glass vase, a peculiar one, since it was completely shattered, yet perfectly intact. In it was a stem of lavender, a nameless yellow flower and a singular branch of those small white flowers. I searched my brain for their names, but I wasn't a botanist. That field of study belonged to my mother, who besides ruling a kingdom with a sharp mind and an iron fist, grew the most splendid garden. My father always offered to help using magic, but my mother always refused. Our garden was impeccable, perhaps because in the end it was real, it hadn't been created with magic.

"Because the teas here are served with biscuits," she continued, "and I am someone who absolutely needs biscuits with her tea."

I snapped my head in Junah's direction, realizing that for a second, I had forgotten that she had even been there. My eyes found the golden metal chair she had pulled out for me, and I sat down, across from her. Her golden amber eyes bored into mine, and I wondered if she would look at me with far more curiosity if my eyes were still red, if I hadn't enchanted them to look a dull brown. There was no doubt in my mind she would. After all, she was a Sunsieran, and a Scholar no less, and I knew how much Scholars above all the people who lived here craved knowledge.

"Biscuits," I suddenly say, hastily picking up the menu in front of me, blocking Junah's view of me. I didn't like the way she looked at me, like she wanted to devour me whole. It set off this uneasy feeling in my bones.

"Y—yes," the girl stammered. She paused, "I'm sorry, have I made you uncomfortable?"

Slightly.

"Why would you ask?" I lowered the card down, my eyes still strained on it, on the lavender mint tea. Interesting.

"Well, it's just, I'm sorry. You're very pretty..." She trailed off and I simply blinked.

"Oh, thank you." Everyone who had called me pretty in the past made it sound empty, like a compliment one got for wearing a usually pretty gown and looking good in it. I think only Rhiannyn and Lissa actually meant it when they said it, but from the way Junah said it, from the way she suddenly became shy I wondered, maybe she had meant it as well.

"Of course," the girl smiled again, her eyes darting back to the menu card.

"So," I started. My own eyes searching blankly, my mind not caring to actually understand what was written there, despite the fact that I could read it perfectly. "Was that woman your mother?"

"No," the word came out trembling just a bit. I looked up at her, but Junah's eyes held to the menu in front of her. "Miss Fara is a family friend."

A young man came up to us, holding what I assumed was an enchanted quill, as I saw no ink pot nearby and an ivory-colored pad of papers. He wore a small golden band around his curly mass of black hair. His golden eyes matched the ring and his rather plain clothing. He must be the server assigned to the table. I looked once again at the menu, trying to decide in the span of ten seconds what I should get.

"Good afternoon, my name is Fardin, and I will be taking care of you both." He flashed a smile in Junah's direction, and she offered one back.

"I will take a lemon tea, please." Junah handed him the menu card and I fought the urge to roll my head. Clearly lemon tea was all the rage here in the city. Or maybe it always had been, who knows.

"And I'll take..." My eyes scanned the card, and landed on the Orange Tea with Hibiscus Saffron. What a combination. "I'll take the orange hibiscus saffron tea please."

"Wonderful!" The man, Fardin, quickly wrote down the order, took the menu cards and bowed, his eyes darting to Junah, who once again gave him a smile. He blushed brightly, and stumbled just a bit before walking away.

"He seems to be quite taken with you." I said, after a few seconds of silence.

"Perhaps yes, I come here often and he is always here," Junah nodded. "Unfortunately I am taken with someone else at the moment, or—well, for a long while now. And it is not him."

"Who then?" the words coming out more like a demand. "If you don't mind my asking," I rushed, trying to lessen the bluntness of my other words.

Junah waved a hand in the air dismissively, "No it is alright. She is over there actually," she motioned with her head behind me, and I turned.

As if it were magic, a girl, with bright golden orange hair and dark olive skin, seemed to glow. She was sitting at another table, with an older woman who shared her vibrant hair. This girl was not subtle. She wore an ivory-colored skirt with golden accents, and her top matched. She wore several golden armbands and bracelets, matching her thick necklace. In her hair, she wore a band with a singular sun in the middle and dark orange stone around it. I blinked. She seemed regal.

I turned back to face Junah, whose eyes were still on the girl. She seemed to be in a daydream. I coughed, making sure it didn't sound like I was having trouble breathing but more of a soft cough, to pull her from her trance.

And it worked. Junah blinked, shaking her head a little, smiling at Fardin as he placed down a golden tray with two steaming tea cups and a plate of freshly baked biscuits.

"Thank you," I told him. He nodded, bowing his head just a bit before he took his leave.

"It is hopeless." Junah sighed, bringing the glass cup to her lips and sipping the steaming tea. I reached for a biscuit and dunked it into the tea before taking a chunk out and letting the spices and rich flavors dissolve in my mouth.

"And why is that?"

"Because her name is *Feba*." She said that as if I have every damn idea who the hell Feba is.

But I softened my features, and spoke, "and you cannot be with anyone named Feba because let me guess," I waved a hand in the air, "you're cursed and all named Feba that you love will be ripped apart limb by limb before dying a terrible bloody death."

Junah froze, her eyes wide. Oh, maybe I went too far.

"I'm assuming I'm wrong then, judging by your paled face," I tried to lighten up my voice a little, making it sound less morbid. But no such luck. After nineteen years of sounding like cold death and threatening someone at least once a week, my voice couldn't be molded into something comforting.

"Yes," Junah laughed. She laughed, and with her laugh, I relaxed just a bit. "You are quite the imaginative person. I say, are you some sort of gory fiction novelist back where you are from? You add such detail, really!"

"One could say I am the storyteller of some pretty bloody deaths," A stretched truth. Sort of. But it seemed to satisfy Junah, who set down her tea cup and looked back at the girl, Feba, behind me.

"She won't get cursed, it is just that, she is basically royalty." Junah started, fumbling with her napkin, "She is the daughter of that lady who is with her. And that lady is the headmistress Soha, of the Sunsier Academy of Historical Studies. It does not help that Feba herself is her mother's own Hand. A mother and a daughter, in charge of the city together..." She took a bite of her biscuit and chewed it, her face scrunching up in thought.

"I've heard that the Headmistresses and Headmasters basically govern the city, and therefore are seen as important figures."

Junah nodded, "They are. They run their own academies and the city. I wonder how in the name of the Sun Goddess they are able to do all that, but I guess not needing sleep helps."

I furrowed my brows. Not sleeping?

"They don't sleep?"

"Oh no, the Headmistresses and Headmasters do not require sleep. They have a different magic, more powerful. There is a fifth academy that teaches one how to be a Head of the Cities. It is rigorous, and few survive it. " I raised a brow, and at that Junah flustered, "Oh no! I do not mean they die; they just do not pass. The magic it takes to not ever sleep and never need sleep is hard and very powerful. The lessons are exhausting and treacherous, but it is to be expected. After all you are training to be the next Head of the city and an academy."

"And if they pass?"

"If they pass, they become apprentices. Each Head has two. In the end, only one is chosen when the time is right to become the Head. The other is the Head's Hand. They help the Heads rule the city and they make up the Small Council. Though in the end it is the Heads that choose the verdict, the Hands hold a lot of power and are able to voice opinions."

I let the knowledge filter into my mind. It was an interesting way of doing things, and the very first thought that came to my mind, after thinking it was a strange method, was jealousy. Two apprentices, who have gone through hell perhaps to become a Headmistress or Headmaster. And then, after all those years, one gets picked to make all the important decisions and one is cast to the side, as a Hand. A helper.

"Do the Hands ever get jealous?" I probed, making my voice as nonchalant possible.

"Jealous? Oh no, never, being a Hand is just as much work and prestige as being a Head." Junah sipped her tea again, but I just let mine sit. It was no doubt already cold, I watched as the herbs floating around it spun around my spoon as I absentmindedly whisked it around. I needed to get some information on the Neithisis, and even though she might not know the exact location of it, I could still get some information out of her. She seemed willing enough to answer my questions. All I had to do was guide them in that direction. I dropped the spoon suddenly.

"Junah," I asked, her eyes found mine.

"Hm?"

"You mentioned being a Scholar, at one of the academies, where you study mythical and magical creatures, correct?"

She set her cup down, now drained of the piss yellow liquid. "Yes, when I was younger, I admit I wanted nothing more than to be a Head, or a Hand. I even went as far as taking a short course, a preparation of sorts, for the Fifth Academy. But," she paused, her eyes looking at in the sky, something distant, something that wasn't there at all. "My sister, Sabah, also dreamed of becoming a Head or Hand. Mostly a Head. So, she took all these courses to help her become ready for the classes at the Fifth Academy. In addition to being viciously hard, the classes are extremely expensive. But she knew, she knew it would pay off. So, she applied and got accepted. That year, twenty-nine others got accepted. There are never more than one hundred Scholars training at once." She paused again, ripping another piece of the biscuit off and eating it, slowly.

"I don't know all the details of how the Fifth Academy works. My sister never really went into detail. But, anyway, she was accepted and at first, she did well. After all the classes started off hard, and she was one of the best Scholars to ever come out of any of the academies. But then the classes got harder, more strenuous and she could not take it anymore. She was so close to being chosen as an apprentice that she continued, but in the end, she was not chosen. And that broke her. She was no longer the sister I knew. And my mother, who was sick, resented her for spending all the money on the academy and then failing. Sabah tried to make it right, she got a job, a good one and started paying for everything. But our mother died soon after and my sister thought it was all her fault. She fell into a phase of sadness, so strong she could no longer keep her job. And ever since I have seen less and less of her, and when I do, she is usually drunk and with a new hair color." Junah stopped her story, looking at me, with sad eyes. And if I had a heart, if mine wasn't ripped open and torn apart so many years ago, I would have pitied her.

"I'm so sorry," was all I could manage. Junah forced a smile, the first forced one I saw on anybody in this city.

"It is alright. I assume she has found another job. After all we are not homeless, we still have very nice things, and she seems to be better. She seems to be a little happier which makes me happier. But after all of that, I did not dare try to enroll into the Fifth Academy. So, I began to study about the thing that interested me the next best, and that would be mythical and magical creatures."

"That's—that's wonderful Junah."

Her eyes sparkled, "Thank you."

And then an idea popped into my head.

"I was only asking," I started, choosing my words carefully, "because I'm writing a novel."

Her spirit piqued with interest, "Oh!" She clapped her hands together, as if we hadn't just talked about how her family fell apart moments ago. I admired her for that, and in that moment, I saw a sliver of myself in her. Of all the times I too flashed a smile seconds after going through hell. "A novel!"

"Yes, yeah. A novel, on—well it's going to be a story about a girl whose family disappeared while hunting dangerous creatures in their homeland. And so, she must find them, but she has no idea where to start, and so she goes looking for the only thing she can think of, the Neithisis." I stopped, to survey Junah's expressions. At the name of the creature, her eyes sparkled with recognition.

Wonderful.

"And," I continued. "I know nothing, or barely anything really on mythical creatures, especially the Neithisis. And I am one of those people that likes to be as close to fact as possible in my novels, so I was wondering if you could shed some light on it. Or maybe point me in the direction of where I can get more information on it."

"Oh Tesseria! That sounds positively wonderful, you must let me read it once you have finished it!" She clapped her hands again, her eyes, her whole body practically bursting with joy. "And yes, of course I will help in any way I can. It would be my pleasure!"

My body relaxed, for the first time in a while, completely. Finally, I was getting somewhere.

"I must admit, I do not know much about the Neithisis. That lesson has not been taught quite yet, but never fear, I can help you gain access to the largest library in the world!" She smiled wide, almost as wide as her arms stretched out in happiness. "Or at least in Rodessa," She laughed lightly. And I mirrored her.

"Thank you Junah, really, I don't know what to do or say."

"'Thank you' is enough for me. Here in the city we pride ourselves on being selfless and above all helping and kind. Plus, I get to teach someone all I have learned." Her smile faltered just a bit, "Many Scholars think I am weird for choosing to study such dark things. After all, none of the mythical and magical creatures are creatures of light. I swear they all stem from the Darkness themselves," she lowered her voice at that part, darting her eyes to see if anyone was watching us.

"Not everything can be good." The words came out of my mouth before I would stop them. The thought had swirled in my head for a few minutes before deciding to come rushing out.

"No, they cannot." Junah shook her head in dismay. And I

couldn't help but think what she would think of the world outside the city walls. The one where creatures like those lurked everywhere. And far worse, like mages and blood mages, like *me*.

She raised her head, our eyes once again meeting, her mouth once again forcing a smile. "Tomorrow morning, I will be in my classes, but after that I should be free."

"That's fine," I said. In the meantime, I could go around the city to see if I could find some other person, some other clue to finding the beast.

"Splendid, shall we meet at the gates to the Inner City? You can get in if I am with you."

"That sounds good," I offered her another smile.

She clapped her hands once more, her smile brighter than ever, "Ah, wonderful! Shall we say at the twelfth hour of the day, midday, how does that sound?"

"Perfect," I was the mirror opposite of her. She was all bouncy and I remained calm. Perhaps too calm, as she was helping me after all. But I didn't have half the energy she did, and what I did have, I wouldn't spend on being overly joyous.

"I must go, Sabah will be home soon and the light is getting low. It is time for the transformation soon," she winked. This girl winked at the most random of times.

"Oh right, yes, I saw the transformation this morning, it's lovely. I really have no words for it."

She laughed, "No one does. But this transformation is also quite something, I suggest you watch it." She stood up, opening her clutch purse and fishing out seven Kronas.

Ah the tea, I had completely forgotten about it. Mine still sat in its cup, cold and brown. The vibrant orange color had faded away. I pulled out my own purse but a warm hand on my own stopped me. I turned to face Junah.

"No need, it is my gift." When I didn't say anything, because I couldn't think of what to say, she continued, "See you tomorrow then!" And she waltzed away, passing by the table where Feba sat, and I swore, as I watched her go, she had tensed just a bit as she walked by the girl's table.

"How nice it must be, where the worst thing you have to worry about is talking to your crush." My voice didn't sound like my own, my thoughts didn't feel like my thoughts. I was raised by monsters, I was made into one, living my whole life around them, around others who were much worse or just the same. And all my life I knew who and what I was. I accepted it, because there was no other way. But in that moment, I wondered, if I had been born here, raised here, would I have been different? After all, monsters aren't born, they're made.

No, I thought. Different or not, it was better to be a monster. Better to be cruel and wicked. Darkness was everywhere, and evil followed it. If you were nice, you'd be ripped to shreds, reduced to nothing, all the while feeling terrible pain. At least as a monster I could survive it, I have survived it. Over and over again.

And yet, I was just a little jealous that this city never had to, that Junah never had to. And never would. Because maybe after too many years of pain and torture, I want some years to be filled with fantasy, filled with things other than Darkness. But as quickly as the thought came, I pushed it down, I squashed and burned it.

No Sivrehya, you're thinking useless things. You are a monster. That is who you are, and you like it.

And that was the truth. I did. For as terrible as it might be.

~

Moonsier

The daylight faded, and the sky, once bright cerulean, turned slowly darker, into an inky navy weaving together with vibrant red orange, golden yellow and a fierce shade of violet.

I walked, bag in one hand, the other in the pocket of my skirt, fingers playing with the hilt of my dagger. Today had gone by in a way that I could have never in a million years imagined, but at least

I was one step closer to finding the Neithisis and finding out the truth. And yes, I had to put up with a Sunsieran, but she was far from terrible, and I wondered why she was so different from all the others around me. Maybe because the others I had encountered weren't Scholars, and maybe because since she was one, she didn't need to get information from strangers. She had access to a library filled with priceless knowledge, she had professors who knew more of the world than anyone. But Darkness knows if that's the reason she was different. Whatever it was I was thankful. For as nice as everyone was, they were far too nosy.

I made my way past all the strangers, who just like this morning paid no attention to me, or my eyes, and if anything only noticed my outfit. That rich black skirt with countless folds in it and beads and all the things typical in a Merisan outfit. I was surprised no one questioned me for it. Perhaps it was because I didn't have red eyes, no hint of scarlet anywhere in their enchanted brown depths. Perhaps they saw me as just a regular human who happened to be wearing a Merisan-looking outfit, and nothing else.

Slowly, my skin prickled, feeling the magic that started to seep into the air, that started to fill it entirely. I looked at the clock tower first, and within seconds the bells rang out, signaling the twentieth hour of the day. As it did, the city began to glow and the sky began to shift into shades of dark and brilliant blue. The sun met the moon halfway and suddenly the stars appeared, still weak but growing stronger each second. The city began to shift and twist. Golden designs now silver and purple. Flowers of warm colors turning blue and white and lilac. Fewer and fewer solar mages were seen, as now the streets began to fill with lunar mages. With mages dressed in cool colors, with eyes of glowing indigo with hints of sky blue and their hair adorned with silver moon and star shapes.

And when the transformation ended, and the lanterns all glowed gold with light, and the city was a nighttime fantasy of brilliant sparkle, I came face to face with the dull inn that was the Stone's End. I had thought about staying in the Square, with the clock tower. After all, I had never seen nor experienced Moonsier.

And it was only the twentieth hour of the day; I didn't need to sleep just yet.

So, I went into the inn, asked the man for the keys to my room and in minutes was back out again. I hadn't bothered changing into one of the dresses I had bought; those were too bright and sunny for Moonsier. I felt as if the black dress I had on would fit better in the newly transformed city.

This time the Square was saturated with people, unlike before when just a few had trickled in. Moonsier was just as lively as Sunsier, if not more so. I felt the cool air flow around me, thankful that the blaring heat of the sun was finally gone. I could breathe, wear this dress and not melt.

I weaved through the sea of people and indeed it looked like a sea. Everyone wore glittering outfits, beads that shone in the light, pearls that shone simply because they were pearls. There were teal and blue, cerulean and white, black and violet, forest green and light green, and all the colors in between in all the forms of clothing.

I made it to the outer section of the Square, where the shops all were. None were closed; instead they had transformed with the city itself. Even the signs, once glittering gold, were written now in silver, in names that beheld the night and all its wonders. I walked into one, the one that held all the trinkets, the things special to the Twin Cities. While I was here, I might as well bring something back for Rhi and Daemon and Mother, who all were taken by the city's glamour. Though only Mother had stepped foot in the city, Rhi and Daemon had always loved it. My eyes glanced over all the shelves, filled to the brim with all sorts of things. From cloth bags filled with special tea blends, to necklaces made of stardust and enchanted moonflowers in silver vases that never died. There were small glowing balls, similar to the one the lady from the first inn had given me. These shone with a silvery white light. Other shelves held books, bound in silver and white covers with illuminated scripts on the Cities' history and magic.

I walked further in, inhaling the sweet scent that came from the teas and candles that lined the wall to my right. There was a small sign that said once lit they would always burn. And I couldn't help but think that was a fire hazard waiting to happen. But if they were enchanted to burn forever, perhaps the fire it created was not the kind to burn everything, should anything happen.

I checked my pockets for the pouch filled with paper and coin Kronas, but they were empty. I stilled.

Darkness save me.

I had left the coin purse at the inn. I mentally cursed myself. How in the name of the Dark Mother could I have been so stupid, not to mention careless? I wagered, I could always portal back there and back here. But I thought against it. I was here for a few more days, I could get something for my family then. After all, searching for the Neithisis was my priority, but if I had some free time, then I'd come back here.

I rounded the corner, seeing an ornate staircase with glowing stars, and I walked up them to the upper level. Here there was more of what had been downstairs, and more in general. An entire wall was made of windows, side by side, from the ceiling to the floor. In the middle were tables filled with baskets, filled with other little things. I weaved through them, picking up small vials of stardust and something that looked like purple water. I narrowed my eyes to read the small label.

Sleeping Potion.

I almost laughed. This was no doubt made with the intention of taking it when one had a restless night and couldn't for the love of Darkness fall asleep. It certainly wasn't made with the intention of using it to make someone fall asleep against their will. But of course, that is what I thought of using it for, what I would use it for, should I not have my magic to do it for me. I put the bottle back.

Behind me there were tall aisles, filled with—

I stilled. I had sensed something, something familiar and dark. I had sensed it before, in the Square, just this morning. It was a faint thing, but it was there, and my skin prickled at the sense of it. I turned around, my eyes looking at all the people, at everyone and everything. The sense, growing stronger. I tried to decipher it, trying to see what it could be. I twisted on my heel once again, this time making my way towards the aisles. It was stronger, and it smelled so terribly like magic. A darker magic, like mine and yet different. My feet carried me down into a hallway, empty but just as ornate as the rest of the shop. I walked down, my skin prickling, my magic humming, my instinct curling into itself. There was a walkway, made of stone, encased in glass, and on the other side was a door.

That slammed open.

And then I saw *him.*

And he saw me.

Dark Mother... fucking bleeding skies. How and why the absolute living hell. What the fuck. Praise Darkness. Let it save me. Darkness save me please. Mother of all living and dead creatures. Holy fuck. Seven hells and goddamned graces of Darkness. What. The. Actual. Fu—

I swear, if there was a spell to rip the world apart or perhaps make it disappear into oblivion, if it even existed, I would have slashed my hands open and died to make it happen. Because *he cannot* be here right now. He. Cannot. Under. Any. Bloody. Circumstances...be here right now.

Prince Ivar fucking Thaegan of Lysmir stood in front of me, dressed in plain ivory clothing, a sheath with sword at his side, a dangerous and lethal glimmer in his silver eyes that caught the light of the lanterns. His own silver white hair mimicking his eyes. I did nothing but stand there, shocked and utterly wordless.

His deep voice cut through my circulating thoughts of sheer panic, confusion and utter, well, animosity, "Your Highness." He didn't bow his body nor his head. He simply glared daggers in my direction, countering my gaze of death.

"*Your* Highness," I responded curtly, feigning a small smile. He mirrored me and stepped forward, tense but also graceful. The movements of someone who was wary, who was ready, perhaps, to kill.

"I didn't at all expect to see you here." Despite his smile, his words dripped poison. "I imagine you didn't expect to see me either?"

I clenched a hand into a fist, my nails digging into my skin, but I ignored the pain. "You imagined correctly." I seethed through my smile.

Still tense, "What are you doing here?"

"I could ask you the same." I jabbed, lacing every word with poison. Our eyes narrowed, smiles showing teeth, but less of smiles and more of wicked grins that spelled someone's demise.

"Would you believe me if I said it was to relax?"

I scoffed, "No. We're going to war in a mere few days. There is no such thing as relaxation, not now anyway."

"Fair enough." He continued looking at me, into my eyes, noticing the difference. "Your eyes," his voice was matter-of-a-fact. As if more of a statement than a question.

"My eyes." I responded, bluntly.

I could see the gears in his mind turning until he realized why in the name of Darkness my eyes weren't their usual gleaming red. "You're hiding from them."

"Of course, I am, do I look like I want attention from strangers when I need to—" I stopped, freezing, tensing, just a bit. But the prince just stared at me, expecting to finish.

"To what?" He probed, one hand behind his back, the other on his sword's hilt. As if he needed the sword to fight someone anyway, but perhaps the prince liked to fight a battle with both magic and blade. One to destroy and other to make them bleed.

"To nothing," I replied, holding my head higher, my body still tense. My magic continued to hum inside me, a tiny voice in my mind telling me to unleash it. On him. To destroy and burn and kill him. But I willed it down, for now. The prince only looked wickedly amused. He knew I was hiding something, but not that he could judge me for it. He had refused to tell me what he was here for, not that I expected he would.

"My father already said it," The prince took one step forward, his eyes never leaving mine. I remained rooted in place, my own hands behind my back, my fists clenched, my magic pulsing inside me widely. "But I'll say it again. Meris will fall. You will pay for what you have done to my kingdom, to my sister."

I urged myself not roll my eyes, or scoff or do anything of the sort.

"We didn't *touch* your sister, just as you claim you didn't touch my father. But what of it, we're going to war, and as our kingdoms are pretty evenly matched, there is no way only one of us is going to fall. Lysmir and Meris will fight to the death, and both of us will fall. I know it, you know it. And I'm sure we're not the only ones who do. So, Your Highness, if you're going to threaten me, do it properly."

Our eyes never left each other. Burning into them, perhaps hoping that one of us would falter and look down, to the side, away. But neither of us did. Our bodies remained tense, alert, poised with the unyielding grace of a royal, and yet, ready to attack, like a cat stalking a poor little mouse. Except neither he nor I were mice. We were both cats, beasts more like it, bodies crafted with lethal grace.

"Oh, don't worry your pretty little head about anything, I will threaten you properly, and then, I will kill you properly." The crown prince of Lysmir raised his hand, unsheathing a long blade, gleaming in the light the window gave way to. He grinned, a malicious sparkle in his silver eyes.

I shook my hand, my eyes reverting back to his, "Wherever are your manners Your Highness, threatening an unarmed opponent? So rude."

He laughed. Lightly. Falsely. "I'd apologize for it, but it's you, so I don't have to."

"How charming," I batted my lashes, flashing a fake smile. One he mirrored to me, and as he did I clenched my jaw, masking the pain I was about to inflict on myself. The dagger I usually used to slice my skin was burrowed in the folds of this skirt. The piece of absolute shit had too many goddamn layers. So now, I was forced to clasp my hands behind me and turn small amounts of my blood into a needle shape, with pointed ends, and poke it through my skin from the inside and will it out. A slender, small spear of sorts, double-sided with no hilt and tips shaped to puncture soft flesh. I willed the blood to form into a solid line in my palm, finding the right vein. The sharp point poked through my flesh; my eyes never straying from the prince's despite fluttering from the pain. I watched him take out a handkerchief from his breast pocket and wipe down his already impeccably clean blade. His eyes never left mine. He must have done this a thousand times, staring his enemies down while wiping a blade filed to cut through skin and bones without slicing off his own fingers.

Two small strings of crimson ebbed and flowed from my hands, and without ever taking my eyes off him, I directed my blood to form into two doubled-sided spears, sharp and wicked, and then I willed the blood to solidify. It obeyed my silent command and they floated in the air by my hands. The small pinprick holes still trickled blood and required a spell to stop. A spell that with a single drop of blood from either spear I performed quietly. Once the wounds were shut, I grabbed the blades and held them tightly, my grip turning my already pale skin paler.

"That's a nice sword." I said plainly, nodding towards the blade he held.

The prince tucked the ivory-colored square of fabric back into his breast pocket and shrugged, "I'll use it to cut you open, Your Highness," A devilish smile crept on his face, eyes glowing, sword positioned, his body ready for a fight to the death, "I want to see you bleed."

I smiled, a wickedly evil thing. And then he realized his mistake, as I said, "No, you *don't*."

XIV : IVAR THAEGAN

The Twin Cities
Moonsier

I mentally slapped myself for being stupid. Of course, I wanted to see her bleed. I wanted to see all my enemies bleed. The blood running down their bodies, taking their lives with it. I liked the way they begged, and squirmed from the pain. It was a natural death, one my family, or any soul mage with people to kill, rarely used anymore. But there was something wickedly fascinating about slicing someone's flesh, watching the crimson fall, their strength along with it. I was known to make those who vexed me bleed. I broke their souls first. Tearing off little pieces, just enough so they would still feel the pain of my blade digging into their skin and ripping it apart. I wanted them to hurt, to suffer, to bleed. All those I hated.

But even though I hated this princess more than the world itself, I knew that deep down she was right, I didn't want to see her bleed. Because she wasn't a normal enemy. She was one who could take the crimson flowing out from her and turn into something fearsome and terrifying. But I knew, if she bled or not, it wouldn't truly matter. She could simply force someone to bleed with a simple swipe of her own blade, fashioned by metal or blood. Or perhaps she could even do it without it. She, after all, could solidify blood in someone's body. She, if she wanted to, could force the blood out of someone. And that scared me. I cursed the world, the Darkness, for manifesting this terrifying power. Blood mages had an infinite supply from which to make whatever, do whatever they pleased. With some limits, my father always said. But now, staring at the spears in her hands, I wondered if there were limits, or if that was simply a lie everyone who wasn't one of them told themselves to feel safer. Because being on the bad side of any blood mage was worse than death.

I ignored the fear rising inside me and positioned my body to move. I was just as good as her, if not better.

"For the sake of the people and this lovely shop, perhaps we shouldn't try to kill each other here and now."

I scoffed. Rithlorens. Always thinking of the destruction, the aftermath of a battle. Always thinking of the people that could get hurt instead of just running into a fight and *fighting*, with the sole thought of winning, defeating, surviving.

"You do know I don't care," I responded, gripping my sword tightly, eyeing her small spears made of blood.

"You know," she stepped forward, slowly, "I used to think we were both the worst monsters of all." She took another step towards me, and I took one towards her. "But now, I think that you, Ivar Thaegan, are just a little worse."

At that I smiled a feral grin, primed, seeping with hatred and anger. "Good."

And then I lunged, but I fell into nothing, my sword, hitting air. I spun around, and the princess, looking ever so regal, spears in hand, just stood there smiling like a demon.

"But then I think of all those times when we did things that even made you *pale*," she walked towards me again, "that made you almost *faint*, do you remember that?"

I did. I did remember that moment, so many years ago, when I had been ten. It was the first time I had stepped foot into the royal city of Maeh, in the kingdom of Meris in general. We had been there because my father had killed a blood mage envoy, a person close to the entire Rithloren family. And it was then that the blood queen, in front of all of us, killed our royal envoy, in the most torturous way. In the end, there was a body, in seven different pieces scattered across the floor, splayed out like a sacrifice made of flesh and blood. And when she was done doing her demonic magic, the queen gave each of us who had come to the castle a piece of the man she had just killed. But, of course, she wasn't finished. Because after all, my father had not only killed an envoy, he had also killed a royal court member, Visiria Faraday, the general's wife. And for that, the Crown Prince Daemon, Princess Rhiannyn, the king and the queen and of course the general took their turn ripping apart and slowly killing Alanna Salvaen. The wife of our general, and Avran and Maeghalin's mother. We watched, unable to move, unable to use any of our magic, as the Rithlorens did what they did. And Sivrehya I remembered, a child smaller than me, had stood watching it all with us, her magic the one humming beneath us on the floor, drawn out in a grisly symbol that made us powerless.

It was that day when I had turned a sickly white, where Avran fainted, and I would have followed had my father not beat the urge to faint out of me. Another one of his whipping sessions.

"I remember." I seethed, the memory fresh in my mind, feeding the fury inside me. Deep down, I knew they had just been repaying the favor my father had given them. An envoy for an envoy, a wife for a wife. But the wife, Alanna, had been a mother. Avran and Maeghalin's mother. And for that, I would never forgive them, or her.

"Good, because it's thinking of that that makes me remember that we are just as wicked."

I raised my sword, as I focused on her, on her blades of blood. "Alanna Salvaen was a mother, and you killed her. She was innocent. I thought you didn't kill innocents."

The princess laughed, "Innocent? Please, if you believe that you're a *fool*. Alanna Salvaen was far from innocent. After all she was the one who wanted to kill our envoy in the first place, wasn't she?"

I cursed. I should have known, remembered, that stupid spell Sivrehya's mother had conjured up to learn the truth of what happened. The queen of Meris, before beginning her revenge, had made a spell to make sure my father spoke the truth.

"And besides," her voice broke my train of thought, pulling me back to reality. "You think Visiria Faraday wasn't a mother. She was. A mother of two, and one died from grief. And the other one almost did, but he knew he couldn't. Because in this world mourning isn't allowed, at least not for the ones who want to survive."

I couldn't argue with that, and now that I knew that the woman my father killed had also been a mother, the anger and hatred inside me threatened to simmer.

"Are we going to fight? Or just keep talking?" I looked at her blankly, and she shrugged. But I didn't leave time for her to answer, because I lunged, bringing the sword above my head and slamming it down. A soft clink. But not of metal on metal. It was metal on solid blood. Underneath me, Sivrehya smiled, wickedly. Her hand up to block my blade.

And then I felt a pain, a terrible pain in my side. And I felt warm blood, my blood spill out of me. I staggered back, grunting, but not bothering to look down. I had forgotten about her other spear. Damn her. Damn *me*.

The princess wasted no time as she ran up to me, throwing her spear at my chest. I caught it. My hands trembled. I spun around; she was behind me, panting. I narrowed my eyes, her spear still in my hand. And then, searing hot pain, like fire, blossomed in my hand. I yelped. Jumping back, letting the steaming spear fall onto the floor.

"Playing dirty, princess?" I ignored the burn on my hand, contorting my face to hide the pain from her.

"When have any of us played fair, prince? After all," she lunged, and I lifted the sword, both blades coming in brutal contact, "playing fair gets you killed."

And then, I couldn't move, and I felt the blood inside me thicken, slowly, and freeze into place. But I searched for my power, as I dropped the sword, and unleashed it on her. But it found nothing, because the princess stood in front of me, grinning; an intricate circular symbol, glowing red, was floating right beside her.

"What is it? Magic making this too boring for you?" I didn't respond; I only delved into my mind to find something to help me defeat her. She must have taken my silence as a yes, because slowly I could move again. And I could bend down and pick up my blade. I looked up at her.

"Fine, no magic."

"No blood blades made out of your blood then, princess." I sneered, looking at the one spear in her hand. I smiled, wickedly.

I wanted, expected to see her falter, but she didn't. Instead a mischievous glimmer shone in her eyes.

"You should learn to be less specific with your requests sometimes." She let the spear and the symbol, both made of her blood, loosen in the air, and go back into her body, sealing off in a dim red light before her wound was gone.

And then I felt it, my blood, slowly leaving me, but not in the way it had before. I looked down, watching it float towards her in a line. I grabbed at it, but nothing, it dodged my hands. Even as I covered the wound with one, it continued making its way towards the princess. And then it stopped. And our eyes met.

"Give it back. I said no blood blades," I seethed, knowing perfectly well she fashioned two more from my blood.

"I will, maybe, when you're done being an ass who always wants to fight. But you said no blades made of *my* blood, you never said anything about yours." She smiled, sweetly, innocently. Praise the Darkness, the Dark Father, all of hell. One of these days I needed to lock myself in a library and teach myself all the tricks a blood mage could pull from their sleeves, all the loopholes their magic allowed and all the damned ways I could avoid them.

"You can't do that."

"Oh?" She raised an onyx brow, "But I can." And then, in a flash she was on me, spear in hand, both tearing into my skin. I pushed her off, swiping the sword from the floor and driving it into her leg.

No grunts or groans of pain. I blinked; the sword had cut into her layered skirt, not her.

But she again wasted no time.

"You want a fight, Thaegan, I'll give you a war." And then my leg exploded with pain. A mother freaking spear lodged in it. I gripped it, yanking it out, throwing it to the side.

"Fuck you." I spat, raising my sword again with one hand, with the other reaching for the dagger behind me.

"Fuck you too."

And I threw the dagger at her shoulder. The princess shuddered in pain, before wiping her mouth of blood and launching herself into the air again. I moved to the side, watching her land nimbly on her feet, like a cat. And I was on her again, pulling the dagger from her shoulder. And smiling at her scream of pain.

"Fuck," I spit out, doubling over, falling beside her. She kicked me right where it hurts, with her knee. If only I had on my armor, the pain wouldn't have been so severe.

My hand flew to my other dagger, launching it in her direction. She dodged it, letting it fly straight into the window. A loud crack silenced us. And suddenly the crack, like lightning, drew itself all over the glass, decorating it in a beautiful spider's web. And then, when she wasn't looking, I jumped up and ran into her, into the window. It gave away with our weight, and I heard a grunt of pain and screaming.

And then a thud, and more pain. I looked up, standing before her, covered in dirt and surrounded by people filled with awe and shock.

The princess stood, panting, bleeding, and dripping with anger. I mirrored her.

"I'm going to kill you," I told her, sword in hand, magic flowing inside me, begging to be released.

"*I'm* going to kill *you*," she countered, holding her own stance, ignoring the questioning looks of everyone around us. Her hair stuck out at awkward angles from her braid, her pale cheeks were flushed with color, her black dress torn.

Around us, people started moving. They started ignoring us, started becoming less worried, or rather, less interested. And soon, the street we crashed onto became what it used to be, busy and al—

There was a scream, feminine and young. And then people gasped and started running away, frenzy erupting around the princess and me. My eyes darted around for only a few seconds before landing on her again.

But then someone yelled "robber." Over and over, and the princess's eyes left me. She turned, and she launched her remaining spear into the air. I saw a thing red and blurred flying through the air before someone, a man, dressed in brown stopped, stumbled and fell. Blood seeping, pouring from his back, where the spear went through.

No one seemed to know where to look. After all, only I had been watching the princess to notice she was the one who threw the spear. She huffed, turning back to face me, anger, old anger, for someone else etched into her features. My grip on the sword relaxed, just a bit.

"Was that not meant for me?" I motioned towards the man, who was slowly being surrounded by more people. The spear was gone; no doubt she had let go of it the moment he fell to the ground. Letting it blend with the rest of the blood that poured from the sizable hole in his back.

"Trust me charming, there is plenty more where that came from." The princess smiled again, pushing the loose strands of her hair behind her ear before walking away.

"That's *mine*." She stopped, turning only enough to see my face.

"What's yours?"

"The blood you used and threw at him." I put the sword back in its sheath, realizing she wouldn't give a good fight, not until we were on the battlefields. She would give an easy fight, and I hated those. If we were going to fight, it would be unchained, with magic roaring around us, metal crashing and both of us fighting to the death.

"Right." She eyed a small stain on the ground, her eyes lazily found their way back to mine, "and I should care because?"

I tensed. My thoughts teeter-tottering between crushing her soul and ripping it apart, imagining both scenarios playing out, her screams of anguish ringing in the back of my mind. But I willed the thoughts away, as nice as they were and said, "I'd like to have it back."

She laughed, but just as quickly as she broke into laughter her face changed, her features becoming stoic and plain, "you'll unfortunately still survive without it." And with that she spun on her heel and walked off.

All I could do was stare. There was no point in killing her amid people who didn't know who she was, people who didn't care for her. It would be so much more gratifying doing it when her family, her people, watched. So, for now, I would have to settle with letting her live. But the thought, the promise of the future when the kingdoms were at war, soothed my anger. Because then I would do what I pleased. I would use my magic, my blades, my mind and my all of my strength.

And then, I would watch her die.

The street, the one I took back to the inn, was silent as the night before, as it was perhaps every night.

My hand was on top of the wound on my side from our short yet bloody ordeal. Ever since I watched her walk off, my thoughts were filled with four things; how and when to kill her, why in the name of Darkness had she thrown the dagger at the robber and not into my eye socket, and the final thought was more like a string of curses. At her, and my pain. I managed to make her bleed, a stab wound on her shoulder. But that was not likely to pain her like her cut pained me. She had probably healed it already, unlike mine which had seeped through the fabric of my clothing, and filled the air around me with the stench of iron.

I opened the door to the inn, ignoring the man's eyes as they traveled from my dirt-stained face to my hand that was pressed up against the wound.

"The hell happened to you?" He bellowed, handing me the small metal key. I walked off, making my way to the stairs.

"A blood demon," I called back, not caring to turn around to see his expression. Instead I made my way up the stairs and down the hall to my room. Near it, was a figure of a woman in a black dress.

I saw that it was the door to the room next to mine, the one conjoining to mine. I grimaced, as the dress came into view. I knew that dress. I fought the person who wore it.

Ever so slowly, as if sensing I was behind her, the princess turned around.

I stilled, again. Her unnatural brown eyes boring into mine.

"You have *got* to be kidding me," I seethed, as my eyes saw her hand on the door handle that led into the room that was...right. Next. To. *Mine.*

"Trust me charming, I would very gladly trade almost anything to change the situation." But instead of trying to kill me, she simply opened her door and slammed it shut. The floor shook, just a bit. I wasn't going to survive this, was I? And so, I stepped into my own room, and sat at the edge of the bed, staring, practically burning a hole into the door.

I raised my hand just a bit and let my power roll through me, and then I clenched my hand into a fist. But nothing. There was no screaming, no agonizing sound, and even with my power, I felt I was grasping onto nothing. I shook my head, falling back on the bed.

Clever little blood demon.

XV : SIVREHYA RITHLOREN

The Twin Cities
Sunsier

Bloody mother, Darkness praised, bleeding skies.
I was going to fucking scream at something, at someone, at *anything* at this point. It was not even that early in
the morning, the city had already transformed into Sunsier once
again, and despite the air being cold, the sun was still peeking only
a little through the darkness. People were already squealing with
joy and laughter. It was an irritating sound, especially when it rang
in my ears as I was trying to sleep.

But forget sleep. I couldn't with these buffoons yelling as if all
good things were being showered upon them. Weaklings. Each one
of them were weak. I had the strong urge to throw them all out into
the real world, the cruel and dark one. The one where you had to
be strong to survive, where you had to become something worse,
something twisted, before you were ripped apart. These people
wouldn't last a week. I envied them for that, for the happiness,
however false it was, that they had.

I slipped out of the bed, groggily, my body moving like thick
honey. And though my eyes absolutely refused to open, from the
light, from me being tired, I didn't know; I could still make out the
door that didn't lead to the hallway outside, but instead to the
conjoining room. The room that held my enemy. How bad would it
be if I just...squished the room? If I were to just maybe, blow it up
and then set it on fire, or maybe first set it on fire and then blow it
apart. Either way he would be dead. I had thrown the spear at the
robber, not his face. I hated myself for that, for the memory that

came tumbling back, flooding my head the moment the woman screamed "robber." I hurled that blade of solidified blood right into his back, and the man, whoever he was, was no doubt dead. And despite him having stolen something, he hadn't been the one I wanted dead. The crown prince of Lysmir was. And he was probably just past that brown wooden door with the navy stain on it. It would be so easy. So bloody easy to just...

Stop it Siv. You're not here to kill him, you're here to track people down.

Although he will complicate things.

I should just kill him now, I thought, raking a hand through the bird's nest that was my hair.

No, no killing him. Not yet. The moment he knows, the moment he feels something, he'll use his damn power and it'll be a bloodbath.

I sighed at the voice inside my head. I knew it was right, that killing him would have to wait. Or maybe it didn't have to...

Ah, curse the war inside my own head. Kill him, or not kill him. Let him live. Let him live so I could take him down on the battlefields. Which would no doubt be a better way for us to play this out. On the field, in front of everyone. Or most everyone. At that I smiled, a small grin.

The thoughts continued raging in my head as I dressed into a plain bright red dress with gold beads. It normally would have been something I wouldn't even think of wearing, but maybe, if the people here saw me as one of them, they'll pay less attention to me, and therefore not ask me to drink damn tea with them in hopes of telling them all of my life's grand adventures.

I hated the fact that it was practically sheer. If I didn't have anything underneath, it would show—things. The beading did more hiding than the red fabric, but nonetheless I had slipped on a nude underdress I had also gotten, silently thanking the saleswoman who had practically demanded I get it because it was on sale and she oh so wanted to get rid of them. Now, I looked down, there was nothing to show, or that should be seen. The dress itself was loose, hiding what little shape I had. But it allowed me to move, to stretch my arms, to run and, if I needed to, it allowed me to fight. If there was something I couldn't stand it was tight clothing that constricted my movement. There was no point to something that looked pretty if it blocked your ability to move, or sometimes even *breathe*.

The boots, the ones I came here with, though black, were the ones I would wear for the rest of the days. Judgement or not, I could run miles, and scale walls because of their rubber soles. And trading them for some sandals, however lovely they might have been, was something I refused to do. So, I slipped them on, grabbed Lancenor off of the pillow and strapped him to my right thigh. I would have preferred to have the dagger closer, in a more easily accessible area, like a pocket, or my arms, should they have been covered in something more opaque. But alas, the thigh would have to do. I just hoped I wouldn't need it, but with a soul mage, who was more specifically my mortal enemy, I knew at some damn point I would.

The tea shop, called The Rising Sun of All, which in and of itself was a rather interesting name, was practically full. But in the far corner, by the golden fence that enclosed the patio section in front of the shops, there was an empty table. It was circular like the one I sat at with Junah just yesterday. This one, though, had cracks filled with navy and silver. As if someone had scooped up a piece of the night and crushed it up. In its center was a vase, shattered yet intact, like all of the vases on the tables. Lavender stems poked out of the vase, their vibrant violet color matching the blue of the table. The chairs were even silver, and as I sat down and scanned all the other tables, I noticed most were all matching, with a theme. This table looked like the night, the table I sat at yesterday looked like a sunrise, and the table next to mine was mixed with light pink and turquoise, with the chairs a rose gold color. It looked like the sea, a magical one, in the peak of morning.

I looked down at the menu, my eyes glancing over all the countless teas they had, the food, the everything really. My eyes rested on the orange with hibiscus saffron tea. Yesterday, I had completely forgotten about its existence until it was cold and the color had turned into a mud brown, as if it was mad at me for not drinking it. I grimaced. Maybe another tea, or perhaps none at all. I turned instead to the food portion of the menu.

There were hot potatoes served with an ornately named spice. There was Idli, which by the description underneath were small rice cakes made of black lentils and rice. Underneath that was a variety of hummuses, with different spices and oils, each served with pita. Kaak bread was also an option, said to be served warm. There were falafel and stews flavored with spices and herbs, and countless other things. I scanned the menu, my stomach grumbling as I read each item carefully. They all sounded amazing, and I wished I could just order each one and eat them all. But I decided against that.

"Hello," a cheerful voice broke my train of thought. I snapped my head in the voice's direction. It was a girl, with a pad and a quill, in a plain uniform. I smiled at her, and she mirrored me. In her other hand was a newspaper. My eyes darted to the other tables. So many of them had newspapers, people either ignoring them or sticking their faces in them while sipping tea.

"Hi," I forced out.

"My name is Cyra, what can I get for you today?"

I looked back down at the menu, my mind spinning and spinning and spinning. "I'll get the Kaak bread."

The girl nodded, writing it down. "And tea? We have so many," she looked back at me.

Right....tea...

"Can I suggest something?" She asked gently, as she smiled and tapped her rainbow quill on the pad of ivory-colored paper. Its edges were marked with brilliant gold that glowed with magic. It seemed far too pretty to be a simple pad for writing down people's orders.

No. No, you cannot. But you will anyway.

She took my silence as a yes. "Lemon tea, everyone loves it."

Ah yes, I'm sure they do.

"It's a popular flavor now."

Is it? Huh.

I was about to scream; inside of course, I already was. Lemon tea. Fucking lemon tea. I hated the idea of it, all of it. Curse the stupidly annoying thing that was lemon tea. It looked like piss.

"No," I smiled sweetly. "I'll take the orange hibiscus saffron one."

The girl smiled and before she left to attend to the others, she placed the newspaper on the table, by the small vase of lavender. I picked it up, feeling the weight of its thick stark white pages with dark marigold-colored script. The pages were covered in little drawings and filled with articles on everything: the festival, the news of some Scholar from this one academy in the inner city who did this one thing that wowed everyone. But nothing really truly interesting, no mind-bending murders, no impossible robberies been made possible, no one going mad, no one dying. Just success, and happiness. And yet, I should have expected that. This was not Meris, a kingdom in the middle of a very real, very dark world. This was Sunsier, a city in the middle of a fantasy world.

"Good morning." A voice, unmistakably *his*, came from behind me. My blood froze. I froze, my hands gripping the pages of the newspaper with the grip of death itself.

Oh, for the love of bloody Darkness.

I had expected to see him again, to once again cross paths with the bastard, but *now*? During breakfast, in a restaurant when there were so many? Just fabulous. Just truly, ah...an urge to break something started bubbling inside me; the urge to turn some measly drop of blood into a tiny sharpened spear and just stick it through his eyes, his throat, and down where it hurts. I smiled behind the newspaper, thankful for its existence, so at least I wouldn't have to meet his disgusting silver eyes and his damned face that was too handsome to belong to *him* of all people.

"Oh, it's you, what a pleasure," I forced myself to say in a sickly-sweet voice. Might as well entertain him. He'd leave sooner or later. "Whatever have I done to be graced by your presence?" I sneered, flapping the newspaper down a bit, just enough for our eyes to meet. My curiosity had gotten the best of me. His silver eyes weren't glowing, unlike when he used his power. Then they indeed glowed, metallic magic flowing with them, in between threads of black darkness. Just as the eyes of anyone who had the power, the malicious magic sprouted from the Darkness itself.

He forced a laugh, and said, "Funny." His features changed instantly into a deathly serious look. I just looked at him, batting my lashes as if his sarcasm had gone over my head. Silence settled as he sat down, across from me.

Why? Leave. Leave, go away, don't make me want to tear you apart more than I already do.

If we weren't in the middle of a café, surrounded by innocently made people who would probably faint and never wake if they witnessed a fight between a soul mage and blood mage, I would have already stood up and wrung him dry of all his crimson liquid. After boiling it, of course, and cooking him from the inside out. Melting his pretty little face off, turning his crisp silver-white hair blacker than my own.

"Why are you here?" I asked finally, pushing the thoughts aside. For now. Though I still kept the newspaper up, this time blocking my view of him.

"To eat breakfast," he deadpanned. I rolled my eyes behind the paper, pretending to be very interested in this article about muffins. Not that he could see me.

"I mean why are you with *me*. There's plenty of seats, even more," I flipped to another page. Ah, an article on *rose water mint muffins*. Well isn't that just something. "There're a million tea shops and cafés and out of all of them you choose this one."

I could hear him leaning back on his chair, sighing, "I'm here because we need to talk."

Hm?

I stilled, to the point where I could *feel* the blood in my veins rushing through me as if it realized my greatest enemy of all the damn time wanted to talk...to me. And then I dropped my arms, bringing the newspaper with them. Our eyes locked. Silver against brown. Silence, just for a few seconds, as we simply stared at each other. Finally, I said, "We need to nothing." And I lifted the newspaper again.

"Well, we need to not kill each other," he said, and sounded bored almost.

At that my curiosity soared. Now, why in the name of holy Darkness, would someone who hates me and my kind overall, want to *not* kill me? I smirked, "Not yet." I whispered. Just high enough for him to hear, but no one else to.

"Ah, Sivrehya Rithloren, do I sense murderous thoughts for me?" He mused, and for whatever reason, a reason I hated, I loved the way my name rolled off his tongue so easily. Maybe it was the way the Lysmirans spoke, softly and harshly at the same time.

At that moment, the girl, Cyra, chose to show up. In her hands she held a plate with bread, a glass plate and a teacup with a steaming golden liquid. She set them down on the table, her eyes finding Ivar's. She stilled for just a moment, no doubt at his silver eyes. I almost laughed at the thought that he would get berated with questions, and I was free of that.

Bless blood magic for being able to let me enchant my eyes a different color.

"And...for you? Sir." She seemed unsure of herself all of a sudden, her smile no less big, but much less genuine. I looked at her, at the emotions swirling in her gold eyes. I swore I saw a tendril of fear in there somewhere.

"I'll get the butterfly pea tea," he said as he flashed his handsomely devilish smile at Cyra and handed her the menu card. The fear in her eyes, if it was ever there, disappeared and she blushed bright red, against her dark skin. She walked off and I looked down at my tea.

I set down the newspaper, avoiding his silver eyes and folded the pages. Sighing, I picked up the teacup and sipped a little of the tea. It was sweet and spicy, exploding with flavor. The taste was strangely wonderful, and I looked down at the liquid, a brow raised; wondering what kind of magic made this tea taste *good*. I set down the cup on the glass saucer and we once again locked eyes. A smirk twisted itself onto my face, as I responded to his ever-pressing question. "You've read my mind, you ingenious bastard. I do want to string the life out of your *worthless* body. Tell me you haven't thought of the same for me."

He leaned over the table, smirking wickedly, "I dream of killing you every night," he whispered. "In fact, I would be lying if I said I didn't try last night."

I felt, heard, the resentment that hid in his voice. Resentment from failure. I smirked again, this time, for real. Proudness washing over me.

"You know, it's a wonder really, we're much more similar than I thought. Because, see, I dream of killing you. In fact, I dreamed of killing you just last night. Your screams were the best part if I do say so myself. As for trying to kill me, good luck, because as a soul mage, you stand no chance against my protection spell." I confessed, bringing the cup to my lips. Calculated mischief swam in my eyes, and he could see it. Good. I drank some more of the tea, all the while my eyes were on his, as his were on me. He leaned back in his chair, eyes sparkling.

"A protection spell," he sounded slightly amused, his own eyes glittering with something dark and playfully evil. "Are you *that* afraid of me, that you must hide behind a simple blood spell?"

At that, I want to laugh. "*Simple*, Thaegan? You know nothing about protection spells, do you? Or blood magic in general, I assume. Not that it's a subject you would be interested in. But let me correct you, nonetheless, that the protection spell is not a simple one. It's rather difficult, creating the spell, line by line, curve and design, to be exact."

He raised his brows, as if bored.

"But despite its difficultness, I am not afraid of you, Ivar Thaegan. I am merely protecting myself from an enemy. Making a move, to make sure, you'll have to try a whole lot damn harder to squeeze the life out of me. I suggest you do the same, because for all your power, Thaegan, if I have managed to stop you from using yours against me, you stand no chance against me when I decide to kill you. And I am assuming, you don't want to take that chance, but we both know that I have the advantage here. And you, so terribly, do not."

He looked defeated, but no less feral in his gaze. He was still eyeing me when Cyra came by again. This time she remained wordless as she set down his cup of blue steaming tea. My eyes found hers, and hers remained on him as if she were entranced by his appearance. In love and curious at the same time; at least that was what was written all over her ogling expression. I scrunched up my face as she walked away, my eyes finding their way back into his. The prince raised a brow while picking up his teacup and sipping the purplish-blue liquid.

"What are you doing here, Sivrehya?" My name, like a toxin on his lips. He had probably grimaced at the thought of it.

"As if I'd tell you."

At that, the prince's demonically glowing eyes turned to me, "I'm assuming your protection spell is only for your room at the moment, and if you know anything about me, it's that I don't care who is around me if an enemy is so damn close. So, for the sake of your life, which I'm assuming you don't want to lose so soon, tell me..." He paused; his eyes boring into mine. I would be lying if fear wasn't slowly growing inside me. But I snuffed it out and challenged his glare with one of my own. "Tell me, what the hell are you doing here?"

I leaned forward, baring teeth in a feral smile. "As if. I'd. Tell. You." And then I leaned back, my eyes still on his, as I reached for the teacup and sipped some more of the tea.

"Fine then, don't." He shrugged, setting his own cup down. "But don't think that I won't make sure you'll be torn apart and screaming for the sweet release of death."

My feral smile remained, unfaltering, plastered on my pale face. "Then I'll make sure to be ready, Ivar Thaegan. For you, and all your henchmen you plan to send a letter to for some added force. But wait," I pushed a piece of hair that had fluttered loose from the braid behind my ear and broke eye contact with the prince. "It would take at least two days for the letter to reach them, and if your father is willing to spare the mages, at most three I'm guessing, then it would take about two more days to get them here. Which means it would take four days total for you to get the entourage you needed to help you defeat me. And in that time, should you still be alive, I would have found what I came here for and I would have left." I paused again, this time looking him in the eyes again. "Am I wrong?"

"No." But he didn't sound defeated, "I guess I'll have to deal with you myself for the time being then."

"It appears so," I grunted, rolling my eyes, making sure to lower my head so he wouldn't see. I knew the Thaegans, the soul mages, and I knew most had short tempers. They were quickly vexed and were just as quick to use their magic. From the incident in our throne room, this prince, who had been silent and composed the entire time, perhaps was an outlier in his family, his kind. Much like Rhiannyn was in ours, for as much as I loved her, she didn't seem to possess much patience. Nevertheless, I didn't know this prince; perhaps he was an outlier, perhaps not. I didn't want to risk it. The Thaegans might be known for killing innocents when necessary, but we Rithlorens weren't. We may be monsters, but we didn't kill for the fun of it, we didn't kill innocent bystanders who were caught in the wrong moment at the wrong time. We killed monsters, lesser monsters, ones worse than us, but monsters nonetheless.

"I wonder," his deep voice cut my thoughts, "why haven't you killed me?"

His eyes, features, didn't crease with wonder, but perhaps more of knowing. As if he knew why I hadn't killed him yet. And maybe he did. After all, I was a Rithloren through and through. So, I looked down at the tea cup, the amber liquid diluted with the tiny amount of tea left. I picked up the spoon and swirled it inside the cup. "Here is the difference between us, Your Royal Highness. You, above all, want to kill me right here, right now. But I would find no real pleasure in torturing you and killing you in a place where no one knows you." I paused, narrowing my eyes just a bit.

"But on the field, in just a little under two weeks, we'll be at war, and I will kill you slowly then, in front of your father, your people, and that, that will feel very good," I mused, smirking slowly. "See, you like to kill quickly, right then and there, but I, I like to wait for the right moment, the moment that will last the longest, with the biggest impact."

Silence. In which he just stared at me, his silver eyes glowing with something other than his power. "You sure know how to properly kill people, Your Highness." He spoke slowly, a malevolent smile etching itself on his face. "I'm going to enjoy breaking you. You're a proper rival."

I acted surprised, placing a hand on my chest and ever so dramatically fluttering my lashes. "Am I? I'm honored."

He stifled a laugh, his eyes going from mine to somewhere in the sky. "No kindness intended." His voice, ever so deep, ever so deadly.

I lowered my hand and smiled sweetly. "Oh, no kindness taken. I'll kill you one day too, slowly of course. After all, there's no fun in quick deaths."

His eyes snapped back in my direction, still glowing with dangerous magic and something else just as dark. "No, there isn't." The prince flashed a wickedly handsome smile. I watched it linger, cursing the world for making my enemy so freaking beautiful. He was my mortal enemy and yet he looked like a god. This world liked to be cruel in all sorts of ways.

Silence fell around us, and with both our cups empty, we started for the bread. Well, I started eating the bread. Should he touch it, I'd break more than one finger, in public or not.

All around, people talked, laughed. About a million different things. Marriage was a popular topic. I assumed it was because it was the season of the Midnight Sun festival which no doubt inspired the unnecessary feeling of love and all that stuff. Blah. I shook my head, letting the thoughts tumble away into oblivion.

I was about to blast a string of angry curses at the prince for not leaving and just idly sitting there. I mean, was he trying to make me *want* to kill him? Just so he could have me put up a good fight and kill me as soon as absolutely possible?

But then, I heard a word, 'Neithisis,' and I stilled. And ever so slightly I turned my head, raising my ear to catch onto the other strings of words being spoken.

"...the journal of Kason, the only one who has ever seen the beast, at least in our lifespan."

"Really, that's...how much do you think...sell for?"

"I don't know...thing...the Neithisis is...creature of great..."

I leaned back in the chair, careful not to fall, but just far enough to perhaps hear a little more. Should these strangers be telling the truth, then, maybe, I've gotten my second clue in finding the beast. I almost smiled at my sheer luck since being here, and just as quickly I frowned. No, better not think that way. This city might be strangely different from the real world, but that meant nothing in the end.

"...the auction is today...have to go...at the Palace Iishraq..."

"...can't go..."

I relaxed my neck a little bit, sensing the prince's eyes on me. I coughed lightly, leaning forward, the rest of the conversation which now was spoken in Sunmoric, faded away into the sea of endless conversations.

"I need to go," I spoke suddenly, standing up. I set down a small handful of Kronas coins and pushed the chair back under the table.

"I need to go too." The prince mirrored me, standing too, his clothing shimmered in the sunlight, a cold silver color.

He was about to leave but before I thought entirely of the words that left my mouth, they did, and he stopped.

"You never told me why you're here."

"You never asked," he retorted bluntly.

"And if I had?"

"*As if* I would have told you." He flashed another grin. I sneered but all the same smiled at what he had said.

And then someone approached us. Gold eyes. Shimmering. A solar mage.

"Hello there, I noticed you're with him," she pointed to Ivar, her eyes never leaving his. Another poor soul captivated by his silver eyes and pale angelic complexion. Surely, she must know the myths, the rumors of just how terrible soul mages were. She shouldn't be probing for questions; she shouldn't be looking at him with eyes that held admiration. She should be afraid, very afraid. She should scream and run away, as far away as she could. But yet, here she remained, as they all did. "...and he's a soul mage, and you two were talking and I was wo—" But I didn't let her finish.

"No damn questions!" I hollered, my voice laced with anger and from the patience that was no longer there.

I didn't wait to see the girl's expression, or Ivar's or anyone else's for that matter. I just spun on the heel of my boot and marched away. Maybe the people here let their thirst for knowledge cloud their judgements, their instincts. Because clearly, they did not see a glare holding death and throwing daggers when they were given one. But I knew them, very well, and that was the look on the prince's face when she came up to us, when perhaps any of them came up to him. He may not have killed her, but I knew, deep down, a war was waging within him, whether he should or shouldn't. After all, the same war had, for just that small moment, raged inside me.

XVI : SOMEONE TOUCHED BY DARKNESS

The Twin Cities
Sunsier

Darkness is a funny thing. A terrible thing. A wonderful, beautiful and very deadly thing.

There used to be a time when the Darkness was feared, when the stories, legends, myths of how it was a force of pure Darkness, of pure evil that twisted everything it touched. That turned everything it came in contact with into a spawn of Darkness, each wicked and cruel in different ways.

We have never feared the Darkness; the time for fear is long over. We are spawns of it, we have it within us, swirling beneath our sickly pale skin, our bronze eyes, our feral smiles. It is a part of us, we are a part of it, we are one.

∽

The city, the one so many rave about, is nothing like what they will make of the world once they have taken it. As we walk, alone, dressed in foreign clothing, smelling foreign scents and hearing foreign whispers, we remember what she told us, and we smile. One day, this would all be ours, hers, his. This city will be part of the new world, of the one that they will make.

We make our way through the people, who are laughing over trivial things, to our first prey. To the first, in this city, all the cities, that will mark the end of an era and the beginning of a new one. We had his name, the name of all eight, who in the next few days would all fall and leave the city in beautiful chaos.

It would be easy, she said, while sitting on her throne. Ending them would be easy. And we believed her. We had the advantage of being a secret in the shadows no one was aware of. We had the power to make everyone see things that weren't there, or the power to make them blind to those that were.

It would be easy to make them fall...asleep...forever.

As we make our way down the street, nearing the tall gate leading us to our prey, the light of the sun set everything aglow, and we cannot help but think how it would look so much prettier shrouded in darkness, in shadows, in chaotic power.

And at that thought we smile once more, baring our teeth. To anyone here, it would probably appear as an innocent smile, for the people here are so naïve, so innocent.

Oh, if only they knew of the greatness that will soon come.

The spiced air will smell of death and ruin, and then power. The flowers will wilt but grow once again, reborn with ragged spikes dripping black. The animals remade into breathtaking creatures with lethal claws and an insatiable thirst for blood.

We often wonder if the people here are ready for such a world. If anyone is. Because we are ready, so, so ready. We continue walking past people, smelling the air filled with foreign scents. And then, we smell one, no, *two*. Two dark scents, dark magic, just like ours and yet so terribly different.

And then we see her onyx hair, her red eyes just slightly brown, and pale skin. Some of us are afraid, for we have heard...we know what she's probably capable of. What her kind is capable of. Things being wicked, beyond cruel. But the other part of us smiles, knowing that we are so much worse and that one day, very soon, this girl, her kind and her kingdom will fall.

And we will be the ones to demolish it.

XVII : SIVREHYA RITHLOREN

The Twin Cities
Sunsier

ivrashmo Street was past Central Square, past the
section of endless inns and in a quieter part of the city,
should such a thing exist. But that was exactly where this
so-called Palace Iishraq was. Here, the colors were dulled, dark
earthy tones. The aroma of spices were well faded, and here there
were no clothes draped from building to building as to shield
people from the sun's transparent intent to burn everyone alive.

I walked past the houses, the mud-brick buildings with terracotta rooftops, past the people who were strangely silent. I could
never imagine anyone in the Twin Cities being utterly silent. But as
I made my way down further down the street, the darker it became.
There were less people dressed in brightly ornate clothing and
more dressed in rags, stained brown, dark red. I noticed heads turning, slowly in my direction. I had enchanted my eyes brown, so it
couldn't be for that. It was for something else then. My outfit? I had
dressed in traditional clothing. Or perhaps because I was a stranger
in traditional clothing?

No, that's not it.

I shivered suddenly. Not from the cold, from something close to
fear but not quite. Instinct. I turned my head slowly, my eyes scanning the scenery. Decrepit buildings, people doing a mixture of
walking and dragging themselves across the sandy ground.

I inhaled, and I smelled the pungent odor of strong alcohol and
fish. So, *this* is the secret darkness that the city keeps hidden. I
smiled.

"So, this auction is an illegal one, then?" I smirked, not caring to hide it from the prying eyes of half-drunk strangers.

Suddenly a clammy hand placed itself on my shoulder and someone spoke, deeply. "My, my, what a pretty little thin—" I stopped listening and, quicker than lightning, my heart burst and my body convulsed. I turned around, bringing my hand in his, encasing it and twisting it just enough to hear a soured yelp of pain and a groan. I smiled, my hair obstructing my view. I kicked at something, only satisfied when hearing another groan. I pushed whatever or whoever it was with my foot and brushed the hair from my face, my mouth.

The man, young-looking, not much older than me, looked at me with terror in his dull-colored eyes. I narrowed mine, raising a brow.

"What is it that you want?" I demanded, my hands at my hips, my magic churning beneath me, ready to strike like a viper.

"I—" he stammered, clearly afraid. "You're just very—um pretty and uh...well..." he trailed off, trying to seem apologetic. Bastard. I rolled my eyes.

"If you thought I was pretty, you could have just said so *without* touching me, thank you, or perhaps you could have kept your thoughts to *yourself*. Because that too is something you can do. Make sure not to forget that." I had the strong urge to make him hurt more, but he seemed genuinely afraid. And after all, I had a suspiciously illegal auction to attend; there was no time for master-minded torture.

~

Palace Iishraq

The sign was as colorless as the building itself. And the sap, or whatever the sickly amber-colored liquid was slowly dripping from it, was not doing anything to help the situation. I grimaced, trying my very best to not inhale through my nose for the danger of losing consciousness due to the horrid smell.

The building was the tallest on the long mysterious street. But it was just as sad. The door was no longer there. In its place was a thick curtain, velvet perhaps. The once purple color long had faded into a colorless lilac. Outside there were flower pots filled with soil and long dead plants. Broken alcohol bottles lay scattered around them. And the windows were either stained or shattered or both.

Bleeding skies, Darkness be praised, this place was death personified into a building. I turned around, my back to the face of the Palace. I closed my eyes, tuning out the coughs and slurs from around me.

Go on then. Go in that hellhole and get that stupid journal and be out of this place as quickly as possible.

And then I smelled it, something other than fish and liquor. something stronger and darker. My eyes flew open, my chest suddenly tight and my magic became alive inside me.

In front of me stood none other than Ivar Thaegan, the prince of fucking Lysmir. Well wasn't this day just grand.

"You," he seethed, his eyes throwing daggers in my direction. I huffed, hiding my annoyance. But what to be expected, we're in the same city, confined to only the outer portion of it. Still, it was rather irksome seeing his face.

"Me," I deadpanned. I couldn't bring myself to put emotion into the word.

"What in the name of Darkness are you doing here, Rithloren?"

"I could ask you the same, *Thaegan*," I replied, crossing my arms and smiling wickedly.

Suddenly, behind me, there was a loud crash. A waterfall of glasses all fell onto the floor, shattering into little shards. My eyes darted to the side, and from my side vision, I could see the blurred building from which the sound came. Seconds later someone screamed; it was a male voice. Another screamed, in fear, begging. And then, as fast as one could blink, there was another scream, from the same man who was begging; it was ear-splitting this time, and it died midway. There was a soft thump and then silence.

My eyes snapped back in the prince's direction, a wicked grin on his face.

"Well, someone met their end today," he retorted, walking past me. Pushing me aside as if I were simply no one. I rolled my eyes.

"You never answered my question." He stopped, and ever so slowly turned around. This time there was no evil on his features, only amusement.

"You never answered mine, Rithloren."

Okay, so he had a point.

"Now, if you'll excuse m—" He was about to turn around when a human-shaped blur knocked him into the mud and ran away into the dark street, hidden by a black cloak. Two others followed, huffing. One held a sharp dagger; the other screamed something. I strained my ear to hear, completely ignoring the Lysmiran prince who was about to set fire to the world from his anger.

"...journal...Neith—" I stopped trying to listen. I broke into a sprint, focusing on the disappearing figures. Deep down I delved into my power, slowly waking it. Behind me, there was a matching pair of footsteps and, though I was too preoccupied to see who it was, I sensed it was the prince.

The three cloaked thieves, crooks, whatever the hell they were, rounded a corner unexpectedly, their feet almost skidding in the muddy water in the potholes of the stone street. It was as if they took a new route, an improvisation. Because they knew they were being followed. They probably thought I, or I should say *we*, were people from the Inner City, tracking them down.

Another turn. And suddenly there were only two cloaked figures.

Inside me the natural panic of realizing one was gone hit me, slowly creeping up from my chest into the rest of my body. But I ignored it. Should they try anything with me, I'd show them exactly who they're dealing with. From the looks of it, they weren't any mage who could create a portal to another place. Otherwise, they would have already done it. So, blood and solar mages were crossed off. Lunars were powerless in daylight, so if they were in fact mages, that left fire, water, and soul. But let's be real, any fire mage that committed a crime would have set the place on fire to avoid any capture. A water mage would have used the vast amount in the damp air or even in the puddles on the street to create some diversion or attack if they knew they were being followed. And a soul mage wouldn't have bothered running away. They would have just killed us.

Another sudden turn. Another gone, only one left. And suddenly I slowed down, knowing exactly where the other two had gone. I furrowed my brow and then made sure the single cloaked person left stopped mid-track and grunted in pain. I turned around, and saw Ivar, smiling wickedly, more devilishly than ever. I crossed my arms.

"Have you destroyed their souls or taken them out so their bodies slowly rot?"

Then he too stopped, only feet away from me. The prince ran a hand through his hair, the glowing light in his eyes slowly fading away.

"You're rather educated on soul magic," he huffed, catching his breath.

I shrugged, "I know the basics."

He nodded to the stranger behind me that was moaning deeply in pain.

"And them?"

"What of them?"

"You're clearly holding them down, why?" He stepped forward, and continued, "in fact, why bother chasing after them at all?" Another step. "They didn't knock you into ice cold mud that ruined your clothing, now did they?"

"Why should it matter to you why I'm chasing after them?"

At that, he barked out a hoarse laugh, "Oh please." He sneered, his eyes narrowing. "You and I have our obvious differences, but in the end, we're both monsters. And monster to monster, I know that

I only pursue those who have done something or who have something I want."

I stood there, my eyes remaining on his, but I was silent. He took it as permission to continue.

"Now, given that they didn't even realize you existed until they saw you chasing them, I doubt you were pursuing them because they did something. Which leaves one thing, they have something you want." His glare could kill. "Am I right?"

I let the stranger go for one simple split of a second and the moment my mind was free from my power I clenched my fist, letting it once again surge through me. The cloaked thief grunted again, mumbling an incoherent string of curses, words, whatever.

"So maybe they do, what of it?"

"What is it they have that you want?" He crossed his arms, eyes narrowing. I scoffed.

"What is this?" I took a step towards him. "An interrogation? I don't owe you any explanations."

"I'm simply curious, Your Highness, that's all." The prince forced a smile, slim and serpentine.

I mirrored him, and said, "Well then, be curious for all I care." I turned around, pushing my hair back. "Just don't expect anything to come out of it," I added, as I made my way to the limp body on the floor.

The person, whoever they were, was drenched in their blood and quite dead. I blinked, staring blankly at the figure cloaked in a faded black cape. I hadn't meant to *kill* them.

I heard footsteps behind me. The prince. I ignored him, even though I knew he could very easily just break me from the inside in seconds if he so wished. But in that moment, there was something just a bit more important than fighting for my life. The journal.

I prayed to nothing really that this person had it. After all, they were the first to run out. But that didn't always mean they were the ones with the prize. I pushed aside the flimsy fabric of the cape and scanned the inner pockets until one stood out. It had the shape of a small rectangle. I gingerly stuck out my hand and reached into the pocket, pulling out a grey leather-bound journal with a red splotch that looked suspiciously like blood.

And it was still wet. The strong smell of iron hit my nostrils. If there was one thing I genuinely disliked about my power it was the metallic scent that burned in my nose, in my mouth.

I stood up; my nose still wrinkled in disgust. I opened the little book and flipped through the coffee-stained pages. There, on the first page, written in indigo ink that still shone, was:

Kason Rajmani.

The only man who supposedly had seen the Neithisis in our age, according to stories of the streets.

I almost smiled, almost let myself settle for just a little bit in the warmth that spread inside me. In just a matter of a day, really, I had already found a major clue. But I pushed the good feeling down. There was no time to dwell, no point, until I found the beast and learned the truth. Maybe then, and only maybe, would I allow myself to feel proud and accomplished.

And then the moment of silence I had to focus on the journal was shattered into millions of pieces when a hand swiped the journal from me. My head snapped in the direction of the thief and my eyes landed on the prince. I blinked, having completely forgotten that he was there.

"Give. It. Back." I threatened, my eyes slightly aglow, in warning.

"You were chasing them for the journal." At that, I stilled. My mind suddenly stopped spinning, or maybe it was the world.

The prince's face remained emotionless as he asked me. No, because he hadn't said it like a question, but more like a statement. And he said journal. Which means...

"What?" I breathed out, utterly confused.

"Did you chase them for this?" He held up the hand with the journal and waved it.

I could lie. I was an excellent liar. But I was also exhausted.

"Yes, why do you care?"

"I *care* because *I* was chasing them for this."

Excuse me. What?

"You—" I stopped, not being able to think of what to say next. "You...you were chasing after them for the journal?" I was in complete disbelief, my body refusing to move properly.

His eyes flashed silver. "Why the hell did you think I was chasing them?"

"Because they knocked you into the mud!" I flung my arms up into the air, exasperated.

He blinked, looking me over before looking down at the terrible state of his attire. "That too, I also chased them for that." He paused, his eyes now on the little journal. At that, my heart leaped and I tensed. No way in hell was I going to let him have it.

"What do you want with this? How do you even know about it?" He demanded. I glared daggers in his direction.

"I don't need to answer any of your damn questions, Thaegan. Now hand it over." I held my arm out. His face glowed with amusement.

"You really think I'm going to let you have this? No. It's *mine*."

"Like hell it is." I lunged towards him, landing on the ground.

The pain blossomed inside me, spreading like a wildfire. I stood up quickly, seeing the prince making a run for it. Fool. I smirked and started after him, picking up a couple drops of the person's blood, forming them into an arrow.

"What do you want with it?" I made sure to keep my voice trained and calm, menacing also, almost threatening. The prince stopped, and before he turned around, I bent my arms, my eyes narrowed on the hand holding the journal. "And how the hell did you even come to know its existence?"

"And why does it matter to you! How did you find it and what do—ah!" He yelped, jerking his hand away, letting the journal fall from his grasp. I grabbed for it, swiping it before it hit the ground.

"Give me the journal, Rithloren." Poison dripping from his glare, his words. He lunged for it, but I was faster, moving my arm out of his reach.

"What do *you* want with it?" I asked, raising a brow.

He didn't answer, reaching out again at lightning speed.

"Ivar Thaegan, answer my goddamn questions." I almost demanded, having little patience left for the abomination in front of me.

"You never answered mine!" He yelled back.

I paused, hating how right he was.

"Okay, true, I didn't," I offered. He simply rolled his eyes, reaching out once more for the journal.

"Wait, wait." I stepped back as he huffed in annoyance. I could tell his patience was wearing dangerously thin.

"What?" He demanded venomously.

"Don't you think it's a bit too much of a coincidence that we both come here at the same time to the same city and then meet again to find the same journal?"

He looked me over, confused, as if it were pure coincidence for him.

"Sure," he shrugged, "whatever though. Give me th—"

"*What* are you doing here?"

"Fine, do you really want to know?" He seethed, "I'm here because we didn't kill your father, because I want to know what really happened to my sister since none of your bastardous kind has the courage to say it to our faces. I'm here because I want to know the truth, and only one thing, a beast, a mythical creature can tell me. So, give me that damn jou—"

In that moment, the world froze. The silence prevailed. I couldn't even blink, my heart hammered inside my chest and I looked at the prince. In shock. Because he was...he was...oh Darkness...

"You're—you're here for that *too*?"

At that he stilled. His eyes went from me to the journal and back to me and to the journal and back at me, before staying there.

"That is what I said..." The bastard. He trailed off, taking a deep breath in, as if to carefully choose what words to say next.

"I'm here because we didn't touch your sister and I want to know who killed her and my father. I—I want the truth of what happened. And the only thing I could think of that could tell me was the Neithisis."

And then seconds passed, and minutes and maybe even hours before either one of us spoke or even *moved*.

"You," the prince started, relaxing just a bit. "You don't think we killed your father?"

"I don't *know,* Ivar," I sighed into the words, letting them fade away slowly into the air. "I—I don't know anything right now. It's all a mess." I paused, looking at the journal still in my hand, "But I do know that I need to know the truth."

He stayed silent. Part of me wanted him to talk, to say something, anything.

"I need to know too." He finally whispered, just loud enough so I could hear.

I forced a smile, "We're going to get in each other's way."

His head snapped in my direction, our eyes meeting, no longer aglow.

"What do you mean?"

"We both want the truth and to kill each other more than anything."

"You're not wrong." His silver eyes twinkled with Darkness. "But what of it?"

Now that, that was the question.

I slowly closed my eyes, for just a second to quickly curse at the world for being particularly cruel this past week. First, my father being gravely ill and then being killed, my mother weakened with grief, our kingdom threatened and this fucking war, and now this. How—how *grand.* And great and just overall amazing. Good Darkness, if I could, I would fight the world. I would fight it; I would tear it apart and make it hurt. I'd make it hurt the way it hurt us. Slowly and then all at once.

And then, in the midst of the red-hot insults and impossible wishes a terrible, terrible idea slowly creeped into my mind. The other thoughts faded away and I was left with just this one. I was left to contemplate it; and realized, as much as I hated admitting it, it was a good one. In a cruel way.

"I have an idea..." I trailed off.

The prince raised a brow. "Go on."

"But you're not going to like it. *I* don't like it."

He simply nodded, silent, expecting me to go on. But there was a hidden threat in his metallic eyes. One that spoke of murder if I didn't continue, as if his patience with me, should it even exist, was wearing dangerously thin.

"I propose," *Holy shit, I cannot believe these words are about to come out of my mouth, Darkness save me.* "I propose we form an alliance...of sorts."

His brow remained raised. "An alliance? Between you and me?"

"Yes..." I elongated the word, my doubt, hatred, all the negative feelings I had about this terrible idea were heard as I carried out the 's'.

He was silent.

"I think—I believe it would be better if we..." I took a deep breath in and with my breath out I jumbled all the words together and managed to spit them out as one.

"...ifweworktogethertofindtheNeithisis."

"I *cannot* believe those words just came out of your mouth."

That makes two of us.

"I can't either. But listen, if we want to find out the truth as soon as possible, it's probably best we work together. If we can set aside our instinct and desire to kill each other until we find the truth, it'll make this a whole lot easier. I have one week, two at the most to find this Neithisis creature. Two minds are better than one."

"Always the rational one."

I laughed. "That's actually my brother."

"Well you're not the impulsive one."

"No, that's my sister."

"What are you then?"

"I'm the reasonable one." I smile at that, and for whatever

reason the prince does too. "So," I hold out my hand for him to grab, "do we have an agreement?"

"You're asking a lot from me, Your Royal Highness, " he said as he took a step towards me.

"I know. Trust me, it will take some serious composure for me to not break this, but it's *only* until we find out the truth. We both want it, after all, and we're more likely to get it if we work together, as painful as it is to say so."

"I hate myself for agreeing," the prince muttered, shaking his head in disbelief. His eyes left mine and went down to my hand.

"So?"

"Deal," he responded, taking my hand in his and shaking it.

"Good."

"Great."

"Fabulous."

"Now give me the journal." The prince demanded, his hand out, ready to snatch it from my hand.

"You could ask nicely," I spat, rolling my eyes and crossing my arms, keeping the journal from his reach.

"Or you could just give it to me."

"You're maddening," I seethed as I chucked the journal at his face, hitting it squarely in the middle. I stifled a laugh, but a smile broke free. The prince stumbled back, his hands flying to his nose.

"You damned woman!" He cursed, swiping the journal from the ground with one hand, the other on his nose.

"What?"

"You could have just handed it to me," he scolded, shaking his head.

"Yeah I could have, but I also could have thrown it, so I did."

He looked at me, so much amused hatred practically oozing out of him. "I hate you." He spoke quietly, almost threatening. But I smiled.

"And I you. Now that we've cleared *that* up, because it wasn't obvious before, read what this Kason has to say about the Neithisis. We don't have a millennium."

"You know, Sivrehya Rithloren," my name rolling off his tongue, "you're the authoritative one, not the reasonable one."

"Because *you* didn't just demand I give you the journal about a million times?" I raised a brow, eyeing him questioningly. He rolled his eyes, choosing to be silent, and flipped through the book instead.

Silence prevailed once more. A soft wind flew around us, filtering through the fabric of our clothes and our strands of hair. I looked at the prince keenly, hoping to see some sort of emotion from him. I had only ever seen him silent and brooding, back at the palace, but I'd always heard that the Lysmirans were very emotional people when it came to one thing. Anger. They seemed unable to keep it hidden, to keep any source of it hidden. Lashing out instead, with their silvery magic.

But now, as I looked at the silver-haired prince with mud-stained clothing, all I saw were brows that were scrunched together in complete focus and fingers quickly flipping through the delicate pages.

I looked beyond him, my eyes researching our surroundings, once again taking them in. I had chased him back to about where we first encountered each other, the Palace Iishraq. But just a little beyond, closer to the colorful, innocent side of the city. Or perhaps not innocent, just more naïve. After all, I'm sure more than one person knew of this part of the city, the part forever shrouded in shadows, where broken bottles of alcohol littered the streets and the smell of it tainted the air. And the decrepit buildings threatened whoever lived inside every day with the sheer chance of falling down in a cloud of dust. This was the dirty part of the city, the dark part, where illegal gambling, thieves, and perhaps even murder thrived.

As much as I loved my kingdom, I couldn't help but think that the darkness this part of the Twin Cities held was similar to the darkness in most of the cities in Meris. Perhaps in my kingdom the cities and villages were prettier, much prettier. But as lovely as they could be, there were just as evil, if not more. And that was expected.

I was certain that it was the same in Lysmir. Even the same in Vylara perhaps, though many, many years ago.

My eyes found their way to the silent prince who still stood, focused as ever, his fingers gingerly turning every page after briefly scanning it.

"Anything?" I asked.

His eyes remained glued on the book, his head down, his silver hair covering half his face. I forced myself to look away, into the desolate streets that looked so lonely and empty but were full of prying eyes hidden behind dusty windows and molded crates.

"No..." He dragged the word on, as he continued flipping the journal. He was about halfway through it already and still nothing. To be fair, I didn't know anything at all really about the author of the book. The alleged man who had seen the Neithisis. Perhaps his journal was filled with other magical creatures and his findings on them.

And then suddenly he scoffed. My head snapped in his direction. I stepped towards him, craning my neck to catch a glimpse of the page he was on.

"What?" I probed, mentally wishing he'd move his goddamn hair out of the way. "What is it? What did you find?"

He said nothing. Instead he shook his head, his eyes wide. And then the prince laughed, but it was forced, and hoarse as if in mocking of something. In sheer agony and disbelief of something. I yanked the journal from his hands and flipped to the page he was at.

I cleared my throat, the words not making sense. Or perhaps it was me not wanting them to make sense because if they did, then the world might as well end.

I have travelled far and wide in search of new magical and mythical creatures in this wonderful world. But the Neithisis, the most elusive of them all, remains a mystery to even me. I have seen many caves, all empty of such ancient and magical life. The Neithisis, as best as I can

say, may or may not still exist. From what I have found, or from the lack
of finding anything, perhaps it no longer does.

"Well fuck."

"Indeed." The prince muttered.

"This..." I searched the air for words, my eyes looking every-where, the sky, the building, the mud, for an explanation. "This can't be real."

"And yet it is." The prince mumbled, raking a hand through his hair.

"But it—it just *can't*. It, no, no." I shook my head, refusing above all else to believe what the ink spelled out was true. "No. I didn't come here for nothing. I couldn't have. No. No. No. No. There's— the beast is out there; it *has* to be. It has to be because I need it to be out there. I need to know what happened."

If I was at home, in my room or at least alone I would have crumbled to the ground in grief and laid there, staring at some-thing and wondering, thinking, hoping for another ending. Another clue, a hint, that somewhere in this world there was a goddamn bloody Neithisis that could tell me the truth.

But I wasn't at home, in my room. I wasn't alone. I was in the slums of the Twin Cities with the prince of Lysmir only feet away. So, I stood firm and tall and clutched my hands to stop them from shaking with anger and pure denial of the horrid truth.

"No. No," I started, "This isn't the only thing in the entire city that has some information on the Neithisis. There's something else we can do, there has to be."

The prince turned to me, his face calmer, more stoic, like usual. He frowned. "Your Highness, there is no 'we' anymore. This was a dead end; the deal is off."

Haha. What? Oh, I could murder him right now, I could just boil his blood right now.

He was about to walk past me but I was quicker, moving in front of him to block his path.

"No. The deal is *not* off. We're still here, in the Twin Cities after all."

"Not like it matters much now; the journal is fucking useless. It's a dead end."

And yes, this was a dead end, but there was something else out there with information. I breathed in, centering myself the best I could under the circumstances, "We both want to find the Neithisis, yes? And know what actually happened, right?"

He nodded, slowly, painstakingly slow.

At that I smiled and turned around, just slightly, to allow him a view of the city that lay beyond. Of the terracotta roofs that glittered in the sun, of the trees that shined in the light. Of all the secrets kept hidden in millions of different enchanted places. "This is the city of *knowledge*; I doubt there are any dead ends."

"Oh, is that so? And do you have some miraculous idea that will help us to find this elusive beast that might or might not still, but most likely doesn't at all, exist?"

I rolled my eyes and huffed, letting go of the journal in my hand and letting it fall into a puddle. The soft splash sent my mind elsewhere, into the sky that was slowly starting to become darker, greyer with clouds.

And then, somewhere in the distance where the sun reached the buildings and everything was filled with awe and wonder, the clock chimed the twelfth hour of the day.

And I turned to the prince.

"Yes."

XVIII : IVAR THAEGAN

The Twin Cities
Sunsier

We. We.

It's strange to think about, and even stranger to realize that it's real. An actual thing that actually happened. Darkness save us all, because Sivrehya Rithloren and I are now a 'we'.

Though thankfully not in the way so many would think. We had a deal that was thin as a thread, fragile as ice. And as *we* left the sector of the city that was darker than the rest, I simply looked ahead at the princess who weaved through the crowds of people in blocky moves as opposed to everyone else who had fluid, soft movements. She was stiff, tense, perhaps alert that I was walking right behind her and, though we shook hands on a deal, she thought I would strike at any moment. Which, in her defense, was true. My own alerts were high into the sky, knowing perfectly well she was having difficulty not luring me into a darkened alley and torturing me until I begged for death. Or maybe not. She had refused to fight me the day before because she insisted on killing me on the battlefield. Which was understandable. There is nothing more satisfying than watching an enemy fall in front of all the people they love.

I didn't know if she was loved in her family, if she cared for them deeply, if they were close as a family. I only hoped she was;

that way it would break them to watch her die by my hands in the grasses of the battlefield. If she were to kill me, my father wouldn't waver. He wouldn't cry or shed a single tear. He would only see me as a failure. But that was nothing new. Avran would be the only one to miss me. The only one who would perhaps mourn, if not in public, then in the privacy of a dark secret passage that no one else knew existed.

Because my father did not mourn. Not ever. Perhaps the only time he ever came close was when my mother died. He had lost a wife, but he had not cried and been angry for that reason. He was angry because he had lost a strong-willed ruler who governed with an iron fist. He knew of no one who ruled the kingdom the way my mother did. Perhaps he had never truly loved her, but he had respected her. And earning the respect of my father was basically impossible. But she had done it, and when she died, well, a part of him died too. And perhaps, there was nothing of him left when she died. So he became colder than ice, should that be possible.

My sisters mourned. They cried, oh, how they cried when Mother died. I remember years ago when Verena had cried for three days straight after her cat died. On the fourth day, our father whipped her dry, and she never cried again. Ever. At least not where my father would see it, hear it, sense it. And Avran cried too. He mourned his mother's death, and the murder of his only other friend, Pieter, on the streets one night three years ago.

So, if I died, when I died, in whatever way, should it be by Sivrehya's hands (which I sincerely hope not because I'll kill her first), or by old age, by disease, whatever. Then I knew one thing was certain. Avran, should he still be alive, would be the only one to mourn. Oh, and perhaps Maeghalin, but only for show. I know that deep down she couldn't care less about me. Her one true love was the silver diamond encrusted crown of the Lysmiran queen.

～

And suddenly a pale blur of a hand appeared in my vision. I blinked, stopping mid-step and almost falling on my face. As my eyesight cleared and focused, the princess came into my view.

"What?" I scolded, shaking the previous thoughts I had away.

"Who put salt in your tea this morning?" The bloody damned demon of a girl raised a brow, insultingly.

I, unfazed by her apparent judgement, rolled my eyes and forced out a smile. "Right, sorry, what is it that Your Royal Majesty requires?" I batted my lashes for an added effect and it got me only an eye roll from her.

"We're here," she responded flatly, and I looked up. And there, in front of us, was a wall; tall as the sky it seemed. A gate, silver and gold, as high as the wall if not higher, loomed beyond us. It was built with sturdy intricate designs of suns, stars, moons, swirls and other patterns. There were ten squares, each containing a different design, a different story. The top right one was nearly void of anything, and slowly each square had more. A building, a tree, then two and three and then people and then there was a city made of silver and gold. And I realized that the sections on the gate doors told the story of the Twin Cities. Of its history, its magic.

"It took ten years to make," a feminine voice to my left spoke out. The princess.

I turned to face her. "And this gate is going to help us how?"

At that her eyes met mine and she made a face, a face that perhaps meant to ask me if I was serious. She took my silence as a yes, which it was.

"We're not here for the gate. We're here to meet someone."

Now *that* interested me.

"Meet someone? Who?"

"A—" she stopped as if the word she was about to say didn't sit well with her for whatever reason. "Someone who can help," she finished saying. Like her answer told me much.

"Who?" I asked again, hoping she'd give me a name, a profile on this mystery person.

The princess sighed, her patience wearing thin. "Her name is Junah, she's a Scholar at one of the academies in the Inner City. She studies mythical and magical creatures and she has access to the biggest library in all of Rodessa and probably in the entire world, surpassing even the one in Soteros."

I had to admit that it was a relief to hear someone had access to the one place where information on almost anything could be found.

"And the museum," the princess continued, "she has access to the Scholar Museum of Rodessian History, the one that connects to the library. And technically so do we, but it's a maze, and she's been there a million times. She'll know exactly where we need to go."

"Wow, impressive, Your Royal Highness." I boasted, widening my eyes and acting in total shock.

"You know you don't have to call me 'Your Royal Highness' all the time."

"What should I call you then?"

The princess looked away from me, her eyes searching the sky for some answers.

"Blood demon, okay?" I asked, a cheeky grin plastered on my face. Her head snapped in my direction, her eyes meeting mine, this time dangerously aglow.

"*No.*" She seethed. But I simply shrugged.

"Too bad."

She would have killed me if not for a dark-skinned girl with amber eyes, a red-orange dress and dark brown hair that was pinned back with a golden clip, who walked up to us from the other side of the gate. She yelled something in Sunmoric at the men at the gate who had the ability to open and close it. And slowly, the gate opened, creaking just slightly before widely welcoming us inside. The princess and I stepped back, just enough to not be swept under the gate like the little mounds of sand squashed by the bottom frame of the doors.

"Ah!" The girl squealed when her eyes met those of Sivrehya.

She opened her arms and stretched them out engulfing her into a hug. I bit back a laugh when I caught a glimpse of the princess's face. Her eyes wide and her mouth just slightly open.

The girl, Junah, as Sivrehya had said before she stepped back, was taking us in. "Hello, hello, it is so good to see you again Tesseria!"

Who now?

"You as well, Junah," I watched the princess flash a smile, wrinkles forming at the sides of her eyes.

At first, I had thought this mystery girl was a friend of the princess, but clearly, Sivrehya had given this girl Junah a fake name and a fake smile just now. So, these two, whatever they were, weren't friends. Which probably means that they met either h—

"Junah, this is Iv—"

"Sovan," I finished for the princess, quickly, careful to not let my real name slip through her lips. She had probably chosen a fake name for the same reason I had, discretion. And I might as well keep it.

"My name is Sovan Grey, a pleasure to meet you."

Junah's eyes lit up, in something other than magic. She turned to Sivrehya. "Tesseria, you never told me you had a lover."

And death has come for us all.

Silence fell, and panic and shock and a mixture of other emotions. Sivrehya coughed, her eyes bulging like mine.

"That's...that's be—because I don't have a lover." The princess stammered, getting herself back together.

Junah looked at her, then me, then back to her and nodded, a glint of mischief in her eyes. "Right, of course, I am so sorry."

Sivrehya waved her hand in the air dismissively. "No, no, it's alright, don't worry about it."

Junah nodded, accepting the princess's forgiveness. She rocked on her heels back and forth. "Who is he then?" This time she turned to face me. I gulped.

"I am a..." I trailed off. The word " friend," though a lie, didn't sit well with me. But I obviously couldn't say mortal enemy, her future killer—

"He's a friend."

Of course, she said that.

But I can't blame her; I would have had to say it too.

"You have a soul mage for a friend!" Junah exclaimed. Her excitement could be sensed miles away. "That is so very cool!"

I closed my eyes, breathing in and out and readying myself for the imminent probing questions that this girl was about to drown me with. But none came. Instead, she simply held out her right hand for me to shake. I took it, slowly, shaking it while offering her a small smile.

"Pleased to meet you." Her smile, unlike mine, was very real.

"Pleased to meet you," I repeated, not really knowing what to say back.

"I do not know if Tesseria here has told you anything about me, but my name is Junah, and I am a Scholar here at the Academy for Magical Studies and Art where I am currently learning about this world's mythical creatures, but mainly the ones who are Darkness cursed. Because I have always been interested, I do not know why. I mean, they are just so interesting, so evil and you know...just malicious and *evil*." She smiled all the way through, and I began to wonder if her face ever ached from all the smiling. She beckoned us inside the gate, thanking the men for opening it. She lead us down the arched hallway filled with golden and silver shining patterns mixed in with vibrant turquoise and vivid orange colors.

I followed them, leaning forward just a little. "What do you mean by 'Darkness cursed?'"

Junah turned around and cocked her head. "Oh, for example, the Taenebris Wyvern or the Obscurae. Two creatures created from the Darkness many centuries ago. We say here that they are Darkness cursed for that reason."

I nodded, taking the information in. I knew about those beasts. The winged wyvern that was almost entirely black save for the yellow eyes that could see anything in the darkness. They were the monsters that preyed on anything living and could hide in every shadow, in the darkness of night. Their claws and teeth were said to be as long as daggers and sharp as swords and always covered in fresh blood. But the Obscurae were worse, if that could be that believed. They were the ones that had an insatiable thirst for magic, the ones that consumed it, sensed it from far away and could run with immense speed to devour it all. They were the beasts that had no thoughts other than to kill, to destroy, to consume.

From the drawings in the books, they were hideous things. They had the body of a large, gangly wolf with coarse fur, and along their spine and down to the end of their tails there were spikes, sharp and deadly. Their claws were short but just as lethal as their teeth that were the size of a grown man's middle finger. Their eyes were white, a creamy color filled with no emotion. Perhaps because they had none. It was rumored that their saliva burned through flesh like the fire they were afraid of, that their tongues were so coarse they could lick the flesh right off you, and that anything that made light would send them running away.

Or so, that's how the story and history books went.

I shivered, trying to shake the image of the beasts away. I could only thank Darkness that they no longer existed. Neither of them, not anymore. They had once roamed the land before the Darkness changed it. They had once been wolves or some other forestland creature changed by the horrid thing that was the Darkness. But no matter how fearsome, how terrifying they were, in the Kingdom Lands one doesn't say they are Darkness cursed, one says they are Darkness *blessed*.

~

If the Outer City awed you, the Inner City might make you faint with its endless unique beauty. But the word beauty, I soon realized, was not enough to describe it. In fact, I didn't think there was a single word in the Erdaen language that could encompass all of what was the Inner City.

"This, it's...I can't even think of a word..." Sivrehya trailed off, seemingly having the same issue I was.

"In Sunmoric, there was a word made just to describe this kind of beauty," Junah called out, walking in front of us as we made our way through the smaller gates at the end of the arched hallway and into the Inner City. "*Lahyievash*. It means a heavenly allure."

Heavenly allure was right. The Inner City was a world of its own. The buildings were all mostly ivory-colored, with blue and brown shaded accents. Arches and pointed domes with metallic spikes could be found everywhere. Here it didn't smell like spices and the air wasn't filled with the constant bustle of everyone yelling and laughing and pushing past each other only to stop and say "sorry." Here it was quiet, peaceful and the air smelled like freshly cut grass.

There were sectioned off areas, bordered with marble as if to protect it from the gravel walkways.

The buildings were majestic, each with stained glass windows and pointed archways, gold and silver accents, and metallic navy and lilac patterns painted on the walls. Just as in the Outer City, the paint seemed to pulsate with magic, seemingly as alive as any of us.

We continued walking down the walkway, passing many Scholars dressed in their plain ivory robes with only a belt to determine which academy they belonged to. Rose gold was for the academy of historical studies, gold for the academy of magical studies and art, silver for the academy of foreign affairs and trade, and navy for the academy of literature and languages.

"I thought all Scholars wore robes," I spoke, as I saw a few others wearing colorful beaded ensembles. "Why aren't you?"

The girl beamed, "Oh! They do, or I should say we do. But only when we have classes. We are free to wear our normal clothing outside of our class hours."

I nodded at her words. They made sense. Back in Lysmir, I would wear outfits for training that I wouldn't wear normally.

"The Scholar dormitories are right over there," Junah pointed to a light blue building, outlined in a darker shade of blue with a golden-domed roof. "That part of the Inner City is what we call the blue sector. It is where the dormitories are, and the residence of all the other people here, other than the Heads and Hands of the city. As well as the professors. They live right over there." This time Junah pointed to a stark white building with a metallic finish and a domed roof that donned the city's iconic symbol. The half-sun, half-moon symbol, representing both Sunsier and Moonsier.

"They all live in one building?" I asked, looking beyond her finger to where it pointed.

"Oh no, that is just one of the buildings they reside in. But their houses are around this building over there."

"Ah," I nodded, looking back around me, glancing over my heavenly alluring surroundings. I was still in complete awe at it all. The tea shops here seemed to be just as common as in the Merchants' Quarter. But here there was a bookstore on every street. There were no street vendors, there were no carts, no food stands. There was simply peace and quiet, tea, books and of course Scholars.

We reached the shaded part of the Inner City, where the trees grew tall and proud. Here, in the coolness that the shadows offered, I could actually breathe and not die from the blazing heat of the sun.

Junah turned a corner and we followed her, through the maze of brightly painted buildings, past the sections of grass filled with Scholars studying, past the tea shops that were always full of people. I kept my head down as much as I could, without missing too much of my surroundings. If out there, in the Merchants' Quarter, where people that didn't study for their lives were overly curious about my eyes and hair and general self, I could only imagine how one in the Inner City would react if they saw me.

Or maybe they wouldn't really react. After all, Junah is a Scholar and she hadn't asked me a single question. Maybe she still would. I couldn't believe she didn't want to tear me apart to find all the answers to her countless questions.

Junah reached behind to pull the princess to her side by

looping her arm with hers. I stepped closer, to overhear their conversation, which wasn't hard. The girl didn't talk, she almost screamed.

"You will be very proud of me, Tesseria." She said, excitedly, jumping a little.

Sivrehya turned to look at her, and said, "Oh, really?"

"Yes! I have talked to Feba." She squealed, and I swore as Junah turned to look at Sivrehya I saw a blush on her dark cheeks.

At this, the princess's face lit up just slightly. "That's great! What did you talk about? Political history, magical history, perhaps about the weather if it was a shorter conversation?"

"No, no," replied Junah, "We did not talk about any of those things. But this morning, she was going to her classes and we crossed paths as I was going in the opposite direction of her, and I said hi. And she replied with 'hello'."

Sivrehya stopped in her tracks, taking Junah with her, who stumbled just a bit. "You—you just said hi?" The princess asked, unlooping her arm from Junah's.

The girl nodded happily, a smile brighter than the sun on her face, "Yes! Is it not extremely exciting? I have made such progress!"

Sivrehya offered the poor girl a smile and nodded. "Yes, yeah, you've done good Junah, keep it up."

"Thank you Tesseria!" The girl clapped her hands together and her eyes lit up once more, "Come now, we are almost there!" She took the princess's hand in hers and led us through the small alley, and around a corner, and another, and into a courtyard of grass that was a shade of green that couldn't be real and a building that was too tall.

"Tada! Beautiful, is it not?" Junah beamed, her smile growing on her face, spreading from ear to ear.

"It—it is." Sivrehya nodded, her eyes traveling up and down the building in complete awe.

"Yes, it's quite the sight to behold," I cleared my throat, lowering my head again as a pair of Scholars walked past us. "What is it exactly?"

I looked at it again, closer this time, as the two Scholars had walked away, and I was safe to show my eyes. By its sheer size it could be mistaken for a castle, or a palace of some sort, even a glorified fortress. It was a soft white color, with large black double doors in the shape of a pointed arch in the middle. On each side were two large stained-glass windows, one with an image of a sunrise, the other side an image of a sunset. Well above the doors were nine windows, the same shape and the door, all made of stained glass. The two end windows were of the same design, a starry night sky, filled with purples and blues and greens. The windows in the center depicted all the phases of the moon, with the full moon, a large stark white circle in the upper middle of the picture, at the center directly above the double doors.

Around the front of the building, the castle, the fortress, was grass so green and cut to perfection that it definitely was done by some kind of magic. Tall trees shrouded the place with a lovely shade. To the side, in the middle of the grass, bordered by a frame of marble, was a pond or pool perhaps. Lotus flowers floated on the tranquil water. Their vibrant array of colors contrasted to that of the turmeric-colored marigolds that lined the walls of both white buildings and continued onto the second, which was just as grand but made almost entirely of glass. The windows made up most of the buildings, every other being made of stained glass. Those windows held passages, probably relating to ancient famous texts in the Sunmoric about the history of the Twin Cities, the famous fables and legends of the people.

My eyes went back to the building looming above us in a graceful yet almost mocking nature. It was as if it was alive, boasting its beauty and grandeur to us tiny, insignificant beings. I gulped, unable to peel my eyes from whatever this place was. An enchantment seemed to have washed over me.

"This is the Museum." Junah's voice broke my trance. I shook my head slightly, turning to face her.

"The—this is..." I trailed off. This massive building was the Scholar Museum of Rodessian History and just beside it, in all its magical and mystical glory, the place holding our key to the Neithi-sis. Connected by a colorful overhead pointed archway passage that was ornately decorated was the greatest place of knowledge in all of Rodessa and perhaps in all of the world.

The Library Grand Splendid of Rodessa.

XIX : SIVREHYA RITHLOREN

The Twin Cities
Sunsier, Inner City

Junah led us inside the Scholar Museum of Rodessian History, showing her metallic Scholar badge to the woman at the front desk before leading us down the great marble staircase, down under into the illuminated underground.

"The Neithisis, from what we know of..." Junah started, as we reached the last stair and into an endless room filled with glass cases floating in the middle of the room. On the walls were tapestries, paintings, glowing trinkets and illuminated manuscripts protected behind enchanted glass. She continued, "...is the most ancient creature that might still be alive today."

At that my spirits flickered.

"Junah, what do you mean 'might'?" I was almost afraid to ask, mainly because I was too afraid of what the answer might hold. If this was a dead end, I might actually cry of desperation.

"I mean, we know a lot about it, but not if any of them are still alive."

"Any one of them?" asked the prince, suddenly stopping. "You mean to say there's more than one?"

Junah grinned, "Well of course, there is not ever just one of a creature. Though there probably were never that many Neithisises to begin with. We do know that they live a very long time, and it is even said that they live forever. But of that, we cannot be sure. And from various renderings, we know they have at least eleven heads, each with one eye, containing mysterious magic. And if they are opened, well, no one knows exactly what happens then." She continued walking across the seemingly never-ending room, passing by all the encaged enchanted items and artifacts as if she knew each one by memory. Which she probably did, considering she studied them.

"Is this the floor for magical artifacts?" I asked, my eyes catching the glimmer of an illuminated manuscript with a picture of what the illustrator thought an Obscurae looks like. I winced. On one side of the page the artist drew just the face. The drawing of the creature growled and opened its mouth. Its sickly white eyes were slits and blood dripped to the bottom of the page from its mouth. On the other page the Obscurae was running in a field, its hind legs propelling it further and further in place, to absolutely nowhere. I moved along, trying to forget its hellish face, its demonic appearance. It was truly a creature of the Darkness.

"No, the floors are chronological. This floor starts with the chronicles of Tesseria's Conquest to when Empress Fiona of Otrina gave birth to the Dark Crowns or the three siblings," Junah replied. Ah, the famous conquest of Empress Tesseria Aslaria Solavon of Otrina. I loved that part of our history more than anything.

It had all unfolded when Crown Princess Tesseria fell so gravely ill when she was young that she almost died. She didn't but the illness left her eternally weak and in a slowly decaying state. When she was close to turning twenty-one, the year she would be crowned empress, her younger brother, jealous that his weakened sister would rule the kingdom instead of him, plotted against her with their mother and had her thrown into the Darkness, the force at the edge of the kingdom that corrupted and destroyed everything it touched. Her lover, a poor stable boy who she had written about in her diary that became a famous book (that I had read a hundred times over), was killed slowly. Tesseria, though, survived and met the Shadowbenders who learned to control the Darkness and keep it at bay. With time, in a span of five years, Tesseria too had learned to manipulate the Darkness. With the help of her newfound allies, she took back her crown, her throne, and slayed her own brother by cutting off his head. And she was the longest reigning monarch Otrina ever had. The best too, as she brought the famous Age of Shadowbenders, who after a century successfully destroyed most of the Darkness.

It was her tale of a weakened girl who rose to become the greatest empress that I loved. I saw a lot of her in my mother, in my sister, and maybe a little bit in myself. Tesseria had always been my idol; from when I could read as a little girl, I dreamed of being strong like her. She had been weak, but she still fought, and she took back what was taken from her.

"Oof," I huffed, my body ramming into something soft.

"Ow," a feminine voice squeaked out. I sprang back, blinking, focusing my vision.

"Junah! Oh, I'm so sorry, I—I was so focused on all the amazing things here I didn't notice you were there. I'm sorry," I said hurriedly, but Junah just smiled.

"Oh! It is alright, do not worry!"

"Alright," I said as I still smiled, not knowing what else to do.

Junah turned around and pointed behind us to the staircases on either wall that led to another room under this one. "The history from the Dark Ages through the Age of Kingdoms is down there. I recommend seeing it one day, it is very interesting. But if you would like to know about the Neithisis, that floor will not be of much help. It is half the size of this one, and this one is not the largest of the rooms in this museum." With that, she turned around again and continued walking to the end of the room where there was a stair-case that at the top branched into two, both leading to the room upstairs.

Junah turned around, still smiling. "Come," she beckoned us, "Let me show you where you might find something."

~

The next room was much larger. At the other end of it was the same set of stairs branching off in two directions, leading to the next floor. Here were the large windows that seemed small from outside of the museum, depicting the eight phases of the moon, with the new moon design at each end. The purple-blue light that filtered through the windows gave a perfect effect to the room, making it appear as if it were in an eternal night, much like when the siblings shrouded the whole world in an age of nighttime during their conquests.

The three siblings, Maehra, Luthyn and Vaehlys, who were born as Darkness then made flesh, killed their mother, Queen Fiona. Each had been born with one of the dark powers: Maehra with blood magic, Luthyn with soul magic and Vaehlys with chaos magic. They were thought to be the first of our kind, the first to wield the three dark magics of this world.

Though no one knew for sure how they truly came to be. Many believed Queen Fiona came in contact with a little bit of the Darkness that had either never been defeated or slipped through the cracks of its fall when she was pregnant with the siblings. Others thought the Darkness attacked her when she gave birth. Others thought other more bizarre ways on how the siblings came to be, but no one was truly certain. The only thing we were certain of was that these siblings were spawns of the Darkness, like me, like the prince. With them, Otrina and the world they knew fell at their hands, our kingdoms were formed, the three races of deadly mages were formed, and a little piece of the Darkness was left within each of us.

"Here?" I asked as Junah made her way across the room. My eyes kept catching interesting objects, pieces of illuminated texts that yearned to be read by my eyes. I made a mental note to come back here and spent a full day, or more, as soon as possible. I had never thought this place could be so magical; it was like one of my beloved history books come to life. I couldn't wait to just admire all the words that were the enchanted objects, all the pages that were the walls, and all the chapters that were the floors. I could feel a blossoming feeling of excitement rise inside me.

"No," she responded, leading us up another set of stairs and then to the left. "It is on the top floor, which also connects to the library."

The prince came up beside me. "And what does the top floor have?"

"The history of the War of the Dark Kingdoms up until the deaths of Sierah and Florek." At that, the prince and I looked at each other and stumbled in our steps just a bit. Their deaths happened a little more than a century ago and they had been what started the tension, the intense hatred that had just gotten worse over time, between our kingdoms in the first place.

Princess Sierah of Meris and Prince Florek of Lysmir were madly in love and conveniently betrothed. Two weeks before the wedding, they both disappeared without a trace and both kingdoms had been confused. They were in love, they were getting married, they were the darlings of the kingdoms and yet, they had vanished. Soon conspiracies sprouted, rumors of foul play, but the royals dismissed it as a common joke. After all, the two were known to play harmless tricks from time to time. But then, three days before the wedding, Sierah was found on the palace steps at night, her body decayed and rotten, her soul destroyed. How she got there in the first place with no one knowing was a great mystery that, to this day, had never been solved. The prince, Florek, was found having been bled dry, in his room that same evening.

The soul mages blamed the blood mages for the murder of their beloved prince, and the blood mages blamed the soul mages for killing their darling princess. And thus, the kingdoms ended their friendship, they weren't allies anymore, but instead mortal enemies. But their deaths only led to tension, not war. The death of my father, of Verena...those...those deaths, they had led to war.

"Tesseria!" I jerked my head up, my trance shattering. In front of me was the prince. I blinked, staring at him like an idiot.

"Yes? Hm, what, yeah?" I mumbled, stumbling on the words. Hearing him call me anything either than "Your Royal Highness" or his new clever nickname, "blood demon," weirded me out.

"Are you alright? We need to move to the top floor and you just,

I don't know...stopped?" His facial features were blank, his back to Junah, who looked concerned. And then I understood why he even asked. To Junah he was my friend, and to some degree he'd care for me. To not completely ruin this entire delicate ordeal we'd have to be civil with each other, at least in Junah's presence. Great. Here I thought the only things I'd have to do were not kill him and tolerate his presence.

"I'm perfectly fine, thank you," I offered the prince a reassuring smile and started walking towards Junah who had already started again.

This last floor was just as big as the one below it. Here, the large tapestries hanging between the red stained-glass windows, that depicted a red-eyed woman with short brown hair and pale skin and on the other, a pale, silver-eyed and white-haired young man, indicated that this was the floor for the War of the Dark Kingdoms, and ended with the story of the fallen lovers.

Near us were different swords used in the week-long battles that caused a once mighty kingdom to fall to our own two. It was the bloodiest war in the history of any Rodessian war. It was the war that ended the Kingdom of Vylara, where the chaos mages had reigned and thrived.

The three kingdoms had always been friendly. After all, since our matrons and patron had been siblings, it only made sense that the kingdoms were also in close friendship with each other. And for about four centuries that remained true. Until the rule of King Harren and Queen Nessamira Wysterian of Vylara, who for whatever reason, wanted more than what they already had. They wanted Lysmir, they wanted Meris, they wanted all the Kingdom-lands for themselves. And so, ever so quietly, the rulers and their children turned all their people to their side. Killing those who didn't turn, imprisoning and torturing all of the blood and soul mages living there for the fear that they were spies working against the Vylarans.

And then they attacked at night, without a warning that they were coming, that they were going to destroy us both. But Lysmir and Meris allied and destroyed Vylara, the Wysterians, and the chaos mages until all that remained were burning villages and corpses lining the streets of a once powerful kingdom.

The war killed so many of our people, but it made our two king-doms closer. Until of course, the murders of Sierah and Florek, which to this day had always bothered me. And now that it had happened again, the unsolved mystery was itching at the back of my mind and it felt like it would never go away.

"Here!" Junah pulled me and the prince along with her to the left wall, near the red-stained windows that gave off the glow of blood, dark and menacing unlike so much of the city. And it suited the floor, as it was about war and death and a lot of spilled scarlet.

In front of us was a display of a famous Lysmiran author who was killed in the war. All his chronicles, his discoveries were here. And one, from the looks of it, was about encountering the Neithisis.

I almost squealed with joy.

"Most everything we will learn on the Neithisis is here. Torin Elfaed was a great explorer who discovered many creatures, and we discovered that he was the only one who had seen a Neithisi—"

"How long ago?" Ivar suddenly cut Junah off, a trace of venom in his voice. I could feel the anger slowly start to radiate off him. Junah blinked, still smiling. I looked at her, but there was no sign of hurt, or surprise. Or perhaps if there was, she didn't show it.

"Oh, just recently, only two years." She replied triumphantly.

"Two years." The prince repeated.

"Yes, two years." Junah nodded.

"Why didn't I know about this?" He snapped, and the moment our eyes met I scowled at him and gave him the slightest, smallest shake of a head, careful to not let Junah notice.

"Oh, well..." This was the first time I had seen her at a loss for words.

"I'm sure it's because the Free Cities have no contact with the Kingdomlands. It's only logical really," I butted in before the world turned into chaos. I turned to the prince, "*Isn't* it, Sovan?"

He looked at me and his eyes spoke of murder, but I dismissed it entirely. I was not about to let him and his emotions ruin all this. Not when we could be so damned close.

"Hm?" I raised a brow, hoping Junah wasn't sensing the tension between us.

"Hm," he repeated, in agreement with complete dissatisfaction.

"Well, then," I clasped my hands together and forced on a smile, "let's start reading, shall we?"

I stepped forward to one of the cards on the wall, and on it was a rather long biography of Torin Elfaed. It was weird that his own kingdom never knew or was never told that their decorated war hero and famous explorer managed to find a Neithisis.

A Neithisis. It still sounded weird to say. In all the books I've read, it's always been written as "the Neithisis", alluding to the idea that there was only ever one. But no, there were always more than one, which meant our chances of finding one increased.

Somewhere in the distance, a clock chimed and Junah jumped.

"Ah, I must go, I have a class soon," she twitched, hurriedly trying to fish something out of her pocket. In her hand was a card, golden and shining. She handed it to me, basically thrusting into my hands. "Take this, this will help you gain access to the library. Let us meet tomorrow, at the ninth hour, at the Rising Sun of All! You can return it to me there!" And she was off before I could reply in any sort of way.

I turned the card over in my hand and it seemed to shimmer, changing color ever so slightly in the light.

"How the hell did we not know he found the Neithisis?" Ivar spat the moment Junah was out of sight.

I raised a brow, eyeing him. He seemed betrayed, as if under all circumstances, Lysmir should have been informed. In a way, they should have. Torin Elfaed was one of them, after all. His findings were just as important to Lysmiran history as the history of Rodessa or the world.

"What?" The prince demanded, as his eyes fell on my judgmental ones.

"Hm," I looked away, "oh nothing just—just trying to figure out if we should go to the library now or look at the exhibit more closely."

He didn't seem at all convinced with my answer but said nothing to oppose it.

I motioned with my head where I wanted him to go. "You read over there, and see if you find anything and let me know. I'll do the same."

"Fine," he scowled.

"Oh," I stopped him, "and please try *not* to reveal our identities?"

"Why the hell do you care so much about keeping our real identities secret, hm?"

"Because maybe no one thought Torin Elfaed finding a Neithisis was worth telling anyone about in Lysmir, but the moment someone finds out about a Lysmiran prince and a Merisan princess in the Twin Cities, *together*, word will spread like wildfire and that word will *definitely* reach our kingdoms."

"And?"

And? And!

He said it like to him it didn't matter that his father or his kingdom might find out he was with a mortal enemy, start to question him and maybe send assassins, maybe start the war sooner.

"Because, let's just say, when it comes to our kingdoms who are currently being ruled by two hot-heads, prone to serious damage if only slightly irked, it's best to not let them know about this."

"You would compare your mother to *my* father, my what the little demon you are." He smirked ever so slightly.

"Not my mother, you grand imbecile, my sister. I love her but she can be a volcano sometimes."

"Such a lovely thing to be compared to."

That's it. I curled my hands into fist and punched him, straight in the nose despite the floor being occupied by others.

The prince stumbled back, covering his bleeding nose with his hands, his eyes blaring.

"Stop it, Thaegan, get moving. We don't have a million years to find this creature."

"You just punched me." He spat, wiping the blood on his sleeve.

I flicked my wrist and just as quickly as his nose started bleeding it stopped, in a dim flash of red. "I'll do it again if you don't start moving." I shot back, and turned around, walking away from the prince.

I turned my focus on the wall in front of me, where an enchanted painting of Sir Elfaed hung before me, a description on the side. I stepped closer to read it quickly, trying to take in everything.

There was nothing, nothing of actual use anyway. I continued down the wall that was covered in the color of blood from the light shining through the stained window. It fell almost perfectly on the portrait of the chaos mage, who had belonged to one of the most powerful noble houses in Vylara that had slain Torin. His copper eyes were set aglow with the red light, and it made it seem as if the portrait were bleeding the blood of all those he had killed.

I knew him from past history books that I'd read when having nothing else to do. This chaos mage was Abriel Vasstrid, one of the more powerful ones and perhaps the one that had killed the most of my kind and Ivar's kind during the War of the Dark Kingdoms. No one knew what became of him after the destruction of Vylara, but many liked to believe he had died with all his people when their kingdom fell at the hands of its enemies.

Only a few believed he had survived and lived the rest of his days alone, in the midst of crumbled buildings and burning villages. I wasn't one of them. Abriel had died, just as all his people had, some time in those four weeks of battle.

"A handsome one, is he not?" A meek voice from my left pulled me back from my endless thoughts. I looked, and there was no one, and then my eyes floated down to meet those of a little girl.

"Um, hello." I offered her a smile, not entirely sure if she had been the one who had spoken to me, or if anyone had even spoken to *me* at all.

"Hi! My name is Biva!" She replied in a bubbly voice, balancing back and forth on the tips and heels of her shoes. "I just saw you admiring the portrait of Abriel Vasstrid, and, well, I think he is rather very pretty. Do you?"

Admiring? She must not have seen the hatred swimming in my eyes the moment I had seen the portrait of that damned chaos mage. And for pretty, yes, he wasn't hideous, he was dangerously beautiful. As so many cruel and evil things were.

My parents always told me and my siblings that the beautiful things are the ones that held the most Darkness inside. I've always believed it to be true. And Abriel Vasstrid was no exception.

I looked at the picture of the mage again and back to the girl who looked at me with hopeful eyes and a smile too big for her face. She cocked her head just a bit, blinking, staring at me innocently, so patiently waiting for my answer.

"Yeah, yes, he's...good looking." I offered her another small smile before leaning back up and making eye contact with the mage's eyes once again. I hated how alive he looked, as if he could blink at any moment to show me he never died all those years ago. As if he could at any second reach out his arm and wrap his sickly pale hands around my neck and make me see whatever he wanted me to see.

"I wish I could meet him."

What?

My head jerked to face the girl, who no longer was looking at me but instead at the chaos mage with eyes of a lovestruck girl.

"You..." I couldn't bear to form the words in my mouth, much less my head. She couldn't possibly have been serious. Please, Darkness, tell me she wasn't serious. Did she not know what this man did, what he was capable of? He would laugh as he tortured her, he would take pleasure in hearing her screams of terror, in her begging for him to stop. And she wanted to *meet* him. This little girl was mad. Or perhaps too entranced by his wicked beauty to recognize the evil that hid underneath.

"He's a terrible person." I finished finally, not knowing what else to say to her.

"But he's so interesting, and so very pretty." This girl was a lost cause. I bent down to meet her eye to eye.

"There is so much more to a person than their beauty. Has no one told you beautiful things, beautiful people, are the most dangerous ones?"

She pursed her lips and furrowed her brows as if in deep thought. But in a matter of seconds, another smile, brighter than the sun appeared on her little face. "No, never!" She bounced cheerfully.

Darkness save me, save *her*.

"Well, they are." I pushed, not bothering to smile this time.

"But you are so pretty, and you are so nice to me. You are not evil!"

Oh, darling, if only you knew.

My heart clenched as she said that. And I stood back up, wondering how she would react if she knew who I truly was. I knew almost all the people here were into the idea of meeting us monsters, of having tea with us and learning everything about us. But I knew something they didn't; we wouldn't have tea with them. We'd corrupt them, torture them and make them see the world and us as it is, as we are. We would shatter their perception of reality, and we could leave them crying on the floor after we'd broken them.

"Thank you," was all I could say, and I plastered another grateful smile on my face, knowing she'd never see through the guise. "But that doesn't mean that he isn't a monster."

The little girl laughed, "I know, but I still want to meet him, or someone like him. Or maybe even the princesses of Meris, my goodness, I want to meet them so much!"

She was attracted to Darkness and corrupted things like a moth to a flame.

"No, you don't."

She looked at me with those big bright eyes full of dreams and just smiled, walking away, completely oblivious she had just met one of the monsters she had romanticized. The people here had the courage to want to come face to face with us mages that are Darkness blessed, but it was that very courage in false dreams that would get them killed.

I watched her walk away, disappearing down the stairs. My mind wandered from her, back to the wall dedicated to Abriel Vasstrid. I shook my head, focusing back on what mattered most. Moving from the portrait of the murderer, I came upon pages of the famous exploration journals containing pictures and descriptions of what he saw.

On one page there was a tree, drawn in purple ink. It had a face of a man forever trapped in fear. According to Elfaed, this tree was a Timorae, a tree that fed on fear. It consumed the body hosting the fear, its face becoming forever engraved into the tree. I grimaced. These trees were found in the Sourielian Forest, the forest that surrounded Vylara and all its cities. I had heard tales of these trees; they were the warnings in my bedtime stories that my mother had read to me as a child.

Underneath the page, on a metal plaque, were words my mother always said to us Rithloren children:

Do not let your fear be used against you, never. For these trees do just that. They harness it, make it into your enemy. You must turn your fear into your greatest ally, your greatest strength.

I smiled, for real this time, at the thought of my childhood. At the memory of hearing my mother gently drill this lesson in my head, my sister's head and my brother's head. Even my father's sometimes.

And at that thought, I dared to laugh. Just a bit.

"Found something?" The prince's deep voice coming from behind me snapped me back to reality. I leaned back upright, whipping around to meet his curious gaze.

"Nothing of any use to us." I spat out, tensing immediately.

He didn't try to pry any further and he didn't look suspicious, but bored if anything.

"Well, I did." The prince turned around and I followed him to a display right beside the red stained-glass window. Behind a panel of enchanted glass, there was a notebook, with most of the pages singed black but it was open to one with a drawing of a Neithisis.

And I stilled.

It was *hideous*. I had known the monster had eleven heads, each with one large eye that remained closed, rendering it blind until it opened them and a surge of magic came to life. But this drawing was a messy rendering of the creature. It had the body of a dragon, with strong clawed hind and forelegs. The neck was thick, separating at the base into eleven smaller necks, covered in scales. Along its spines and down its tail were dagger-sized spikes, jagged and uneven. I gulped. How this man came to cross it without dying was a mystery to me. Torin Elfaed was a powerful soul mage who no doubt could render a Neithisis immobile under his command. Or, perhaps despite their monstrous appearance, they were actually quite friendly. Though, I doubted that was the case.

I turned to face the prince. "Did he write anything on it that might help us?" I sounded too hopeful for my liking.

"Yes, over here." Ivar pointed to a large piece of once folded paper, stained with coffee rings and what appeared to be blood. "He wrote that he encountered two, in the Raven Mountains, inside the biggest caves on the tallest mountains. He wrote that they prefer the cold and the darkness."

So, should this man be trusted, we could find a Neithisis, in a cave, on an incredibly tall mountain, in an enormous mountain range.

Easy, I told myself.

"He even drew a map, but most of it is destroyed." The prince pointed to a once crumpled piece of paper, ripped in various places and stitched back together with some magical spell.

"This could help us. We need to go as soon as possible."

The prince laughed, "Slow down, Your Royal Highness, we

need to do more research. I'd like to say I trust him but I never knew about this. It could be that the people here put it up for show and awe."

And there went my spirits. I hated to admit he could be right. "Dammit! We were so close to actually getting somewhere."

"Maybe we did, we just have to be sure." He sounded like he wanted to be reassuring but I didn't buy it. Him, reassuring? Please. "On another note, I guess you're right about word traveling fast."

I snapped my head in his direction. "What do you mean?" I narrowed my eyes into slits, preparing myself for a terrible answer consisting of our identities being discovered, the kingdoms going to war tomorrow and sending assassins to kill us both.

"I passed by the symbol that was above Verena's bed displayed in a glass case just over there. Looks like the museum is adding the murders of my sister and your father there."

That's...odd. So fast?

"But how did they get the piece of paper your father drew the symbol on if it's somewhere in my palace? And there's no doubt that the blood has already been washed off of your sister's wall, right?"

At that the prince stilled, looking past me to where the display was. I turned my head to follow his gaze.

"I—I'm not sure..." He trailed off, something changing in his eyes.

I made my way over to the case, where in the center was a piece of parchment. And the moment I saw it, the entire world stilled.

It was drawn out in blood, not in ink like the symbol drawn by the king. But that wasn't what caught me off guard; it was the symbol itself. Because it was the *exact* same one above the murdered Lysmiran princess's bed. And how anyone outside our kingdoms got their hands on it truly confused me.

I looked down, to the metallic plaque where the description was. And it was as if the world folded in on itself and stopped. It was as if I was pulled into oblivion.

I blinked once, then again, and again. But the description never changed. My eyes went from the symbol to the plaque and back again. And my hands flew up to cover my mouth, to silence my gasp. My body trembled, and my mind started swirling with endless questions.

Here is an exact copy of the symbol found on a handkerchief on the body of Prince Florek Thaegan of Lysmir when found on the floor, in his bedchamber.

But...but that is, should be, utterly and completely impossible.

XX : SIVREHYA RITHLOREN

The Twin Cities
Sunsier, Inner City

"How...how is this possible?" I breathed, shaking my head, stumbling back. "This, no, it can't be."

"What are you talking about?" Ivar came up beside me, looking down at the symbol drawn on the paper.

"This..." I trailed off, catching my breath after suddenly feeling faint. "This...this isn't the symbol from your sister's room."

"Of course, it is, look at it, it's exactly the same."

"I know," I whispered, "that's the problem."

"How it got here after only a few days is a mystery to me, but someone must have spilled about her murder an—"

"Look at the description," I demanded, extending out a shaking arm to point at the plaque.

The prince looked at me, a brow raised, clearly annoyed.

"Just look at it." I pleaded, ignoring the fact that pleading with him of all people should be below me.

He leaned down. The moment he read the sentence he tensed, slowly, his head raised, his widened eyes meeting mine.

"I..." He shut his mouth, stood back up, his eyes never leaving mine until he was upright and they flew back to the symbol. As did mine, and my breaths started getting heavier, labored. My body felt heavy, my head felt impossibly light. I closed my eyes, shook my head, wished for it to all go away.

Silence fell between us and the only noise around was that of the other people there who seemed to be so happy, so carefree, so unaware that our world just split in half.

"No one, *no one* messes up exactly the same." I whispered, low enough for only the prince to hear.

"What do you mean?"

"I mean no one messes up the same way. It's impossible. If you make a mistake, you can correct it, but you don't do it again." I shook my head in disbelief. "It's why this doesn't make any sense. How, with something as complicated as this symbol, could it be drawn wrong the exact same way? The line, the same line, is different in the same way in both. The two symbols are the same, they're both wrong. I just—I don't understand how that can be possible..." I trailed off, still in shock.

"Maybe..." The prince ran a hand through his hair, "maybe whoever did this didn't think they messed up. Maybe, if indeed it wasn't a blood mage who killed Prince Florek or my sister, it's possible they thought this is what the symbol looked like."

Oh. Oh fuck. If someone doesn't know they're messing up, it's likely that they'd mess up the same way again.

"I just, I don't know. This doesn't feel right for some reason."

The prince stayed silent. His opinion, whatever it was, remained in his head.

"What bothers me is," I said as I started walking around the glass case, never taking my eyes off the piece of parchment, "... that Florek was bled dry and so was your sister. This means in both cases someone would have to manually cut them up and bleed them dry which might take about fifteen to twenty minutes depending on the person. I just—" I paused, taking a deep breath in and out, "Why would someone do that twice? I just don't get it."

Ivar offered, again, nothing. Not that I could blame him; he was just as confused as me.

"Does it say anywhere the state of Sierah's body?"

The prince didn't have time to answer before I took off to look at all the other displays in the area of the exhibit dedicated to them, weaving through each, my eyes darting from one to another, until I found a drawing and journal entry in a glass box that held my answer. I leaned in, closely, to read the cursive Erdaen, hoping to decipher what it said.

Having no such luck I bent down, to look at the metallic plaque.

Princess Sierah, found on the front steps of the royal palace, was in a state of decay. Her body, pale and ashen, slowly turning to dust. There were numerous cracks all over her body. Her eyes, colorless white, were still open, as was her mouth. Her face was contorted in fear, her last and final emotion before her soul was destroyed.

"Come over here!" I raised my arm, beckoning the prince to read the description. He walked over, slowly, as if still in a daze of confusion.

"Read this," I demanded the moment he bent down beside me.

"Shit," he whispered.

"What? What is it?" I turned to face him, my eyes meeting his.

"It says here that her soul was destroyed but her eyes were colorless white."

"And that's..." I trailed off.

"That's not how the eyes are after a soul is destroyed." He finished, freshly pale again.

"What do they look like?"

"The eyes are gone, they become black voids." He breathed out. "Your father's eyes...they were white too."

Holy fucking Mother of Darkness. Daemon had said...

"So, my father and your sister were killed in the exact same way Sierah and Florek were, with the exact same mistakes?" My voice trembled; my brows furrowed.

This makes no sense, no bloody sense.

"It appears so."

"A little over a century apart, same mistakes, I don't—I don't understand. Does this mean there's only one killer, that there's only ever been one?"

"Perhaps, but, but why now? Why ever? Nothing good came out of those murders. Sierah and Florek were loved, your father and my sister in their respective kingdoms." He shook his head, throwing it back to look at the domed ceiling that was covered in little intricate designs. "And if it is just one person, *who*," he asked as he rubbed his eyes, "kills someone again when they're over one hundred years old? I mean, let's just say they were at least fifteen at the time of the murders. That would make them around hundred fifteen years old. If anyone made it that far in this age, I'm impressed."

It wasn't strange for a mage to live past one hundred years; most all of us could. Our bodies aged slower than those of nonmages. If the Darkness and curses and killers didn't get to us, we'd die of old age around two hundred years of age. But no one got that far. No one decidedly powerful that is, or no one I knew of. All died and they had either been murdered or they had sacrificed themselves. It seemed as if this world didn't approve of dying a peaceful death at an old age, but was more content with bloody, heroic or tragic deaths that involved swords and daggers, vengeance and violence, broken hearts and fallen crowns.

I huffed, pushing a stray hair from my braid back into it, and stated, "This decidedly bothers me."

"Understandably, but we're *not* here to investigate conspiracies." The prince turned his head from the display and walked back to the display of Elfaed's drawing of a Neithisis.

I followed him, slowly, my shoulders slumped. My mind was a spinning mess, words flying around, thoughts circulating. But I let them fall away into the back of my mind. The prince was right. I didn't come here to investigate something that was probably just my elaborate imagination.

"We know where to find one, or where we'll likely find one, should they still exist." Ivar stared intently at the drawing of the Neithisis, the lines of ink that drew out its hideous terror.

"But we need—*must* be sure. We can't waste precious time searching every single cave in the Raven Mountains and then turn up with nothing."

The prince nodded, "Right."

"Should tomorrow be left for checking our sources?" I didn't even know why I was bothering to ask for his opinion. It wasn't as if I cared what he thought.

"Sure," was all he said before turning around and heading for the stairs.

"Where are you going?" I asked, but I stood in place, rooted by Elfaed's display.

He didn't answer. And with the hearing of a mage, there was no way in hell he hadn't heard me.

Fair enough prince charming, I thought, rolling my eyes. I probably would do the same thing.

~

The Twin Cities might have seemed like a different world, but the library was a different *universe*.

I stepped through the doors, having shown the golden card to the man at the desk, and the moment I pushed aside the thick, heavy curtains, I almost stumbled, my jaw dropping to the floor.

I was on a balcony, made of marble, with an ornate golden railing. A design that was clearly inspired by Lysmiran architects I had read about. There was a staircase on both sides, also made of marble, leading to the floor of the library.

My hand flew over my still open mouth, a gasp stuck in my throat. I almost squealed like a little girl from the sheer excitement of being *here*.

Oh Darkness be praised!

From here, I could see all the aisles, the maze of bookshelves that held near-infinite information. The library was circular, with large stained-glass windows and a domed ceiling also of stained-glass. The design, a sun with golden rays surrounded by a starry night.

The blue color of the glass set the entire library aglow as if it were underwater. Floating just below the domed ceiling were tiny silver orbs, reflecting the light filtering through the glass. And hanging from the very center of the ceiling, there was the famous astrolabe, golden and shimmering. It moved, ever so slowly. In the center, a larger yellow orb was glowing, lighting up the symbols on the metallic circular bars surrounding it.

I could feel a smile edge itself on my face the moment my eyes found it. I had read about it in books, seen simple renderings of it from various artists, never knowing I'd see it one day in person. It was *beautiful,* but in the moment "beautiful" didn't do it justice. Once, it was used on a regular basis, before the technology of the city advanced and with it, its magic. The astrolabe, though unused, now hung in the middle of the largest library in Rodessa, an ancient yet not obsolete machine.

I gathered myself, mentally, trying not to squeal like a little girl. The library in my palace was huge, and it was my safe haven, but this...this library was *massive,* and perhaps the dream come true I never thought of.

I made my way down the stairs to the left. All the while, my eyes were looking over every inch I could see. There were so many levels to the library, stairs that led to ledges that stuck out from the walls. There were balconies with chaise lounges and small tables. There was a section, to my left, against the only part of the wall without books, save for the windows, filled with tables. I could see the Scholars huddled there, scrolls all around them, rolled up or open. Stacks of books, feathered quills and ink jars scattered amongst them.

"Wow," I whispered. There must have been *thousands* of books, tomes, stories here. A thousand tales of history, of magic, politics...The smile on my face stretching from ear to ear now, my face almost aching from it. But it didn't matter. I was in my own personal heaven. Or hell...it was hard to decide which one it was, knowing I had a time-sensitive mission out there, which would tear me from this place far too soon.

The moment I reached the floor, I looked around me, up and over me. To where I would possibly find anything on the Neithisis. From the balcony, I had seen a large book, on a pedestal, in the middle of the floor. It stood in the middle of a circular painted map of the world, painted in various shades of blue. But more specially, the marble pedestal was in the middle of Rodessa, in a large, seemingly endless field, that would soon be soggy with blood when the war comes. I saw Meris on the map, and Maeh, and even the tiny rendering of a castle they painted. And I had smiled, remembering home.

I made my way to the center, having wagered that the book served as a catalog for finding anything in the library. But it was *huge*, and just by walking up to it and seeing the thin layer of dust, I knew I was the first to use it in a good while. Not that I was surprised. After all, this was the Scholar Library, and the ones who came here already knew what they needed and where they needed to go to find it.

But when I stopped just in front of the book, panic seized me. I could feel the nonexistent stares burning into my back as I gingerly lifted the book's large and heavy pages.

"Fuck it," I muttered after momentarily deciding whether I should accept the curious stares that were given to me as I looked at the book, or run out of the place from sheer embarrassment. I knew I shouldn't be self-conscious. I might not belong here like all the others do, but I'm sure they've lived through their fair share of non-Scholars.

I looked at the top of the page, where a single word was written, "magic". I blinked, wondering to which page I should turn. Perhaps I should have done some research beforehand.

"Miss?" A small voice from behind me spoke. I stilled, dropping the book's pages and hearing a low thump. I turned around, and there, an elderly man, dressed in clothing similar to a Scholar's but dark blue and lined in silver thread, stood behind me.

"Yes?" I responded, hoping I wasn't about to be thrown out. Come to think of it, I hadn't seen anyone from the balcony not wearing Scholar ropes. I froze.

No, please let me stay. Don't make me leave, I silently prayed to the Dark Mother.

"Do you need some assistance?"

I blinked. Of course. *Of course*, he wasn't going to throw me out, and of course, he was asking if I needed help. I almost laughed at myself. How could I have forgotten this city was filled with overly generous and nice people?

"Um," I considered it, knowing fully I hated above anything asking for help. But then again, I didn't have a million years, and the quicker I found the information, the better. So, I nodded. "Yes, I need help to find books or scrolls on the Neithisis."

The man nodded, "You are a rather odd one then." He gave me a proud toothy grin, and from that I knew the statement had been a compliment, despite it sounding slightly like an insult.

"Yes, yeah, that's...that's me." I forced out a small laugh, on the side serving a smile.

"Follow me," the man said, beckoning to me. We walked past countless bookshelves, each filled to the brim with colorful books of all sizes. There was a winding staircase. This one was made entirely of copper, the railing made of ornate designs of the sky at both night and day. It led one of the tallest ledges in the library, as well as some in between.

The man stepped aside, letting me pass, and walked onto the staircase first. "There, at the very top. That is where you will find books on all the mythical creatures."

I turned to thank him for his help, before taking a deep breath and preparing myself for the large number of stairs ahead.

And then suddenly something jerked, and the stairs came to life. The railing started glowing and slowly, the stairs moved, in a circular motion around the metallic pole holding them together, taking me higher and higher. And then, I reached the top, and I stepped off, onto one of the tallest ledges. I looked down from the railing, surprised at the sheer height I was at. It seemed so far down where I had been just seconds before.

Behind me were shelves, reaching all the way up to the edge of the domed ceiling, filled with books and only a few empty spaces here and there. Rolling ladders stood, waiting, ready to be used to reach the higher shelves. I made my way towards them, slipping the golden card I had been clutching into my pocket and taking a deep breath.

"Let the search begin," I whispered, taking in every one of the books, any one of them that might be able to help me.

∽

Moonsier

The library suddenly became a spectacle of golden lights as each little orb, seemingly floating near the domed ceiling, lit up one by one. I tore my eyes from the current book I was reading to tilt my head upwards and watch as the orbs came on, shining their light down on all the books.

The hours had flown by as I buried myself in any book that seemed remotely helpful to my cause. So far, I had found tiny little footnotes on the Neithisis. Because finding a lovely thick book filled with extremely helpful facts on this creature was far too much to ask. It was like the world was mocking me, laughing at this very moment as it watched me get lost in the maze of bookshelves trying to scour anything.

But most importantly, what I found out was that the Neithisis, at any point, at this point, did not, above all things, want to be found. The term "elusive" was simply not enough to fully capture how little was known of the creature or to describe how much it wanted to be left alone.

Obviously, the one thing that could help me find out what really happened and maybe stop a war that would end us all, would be nearly, if not completely, impossible to find. *Obviously.*

"Miss?" A deep voice behind me startled me, pulling me from the world of the book I was reading. I blinked, looking up and behind me. A Scholar, or perhaps someone of higher status from the dark shade of his robes, looked down at me, holding a gas lamp.

"Yes?"

"It is nearly the twenty-first hour of the day," He started. And I immediately looked out the nearest window. I swore that just an hour ago it was bright and full daylight. But when I saw the view, it was navy and purple. The silver moon, almost full, hung in the sky, setting the world aglow.

"The library is closing soon." The man continued, "I am going to have to ask you to leave now, Miss."

I rustled, closing the book in my lap that turned out to be useless to finding the Neithisis, but nonetheless was an interesting read about the longest reigning kingdom during the Age of Kingdoms.

"Yes!" I stood up too fast, my head quickly light, "Right, of course. I'm so sorry." I flashed a smile before sticking the book back in its rightful place on the shelf with a bit too much force.

"Nothing to worry about, Miss." The man smiled, "Do you need help finding your way back?"

Yes.

"No, I can manage. Thank you." And I walked off, leaving him in the golden light of the floating orbs. I was going to get lost. But to get help from him, from anyone for that matter, would simply not do.

Perhaps I should have swallowed my pride, set aside my fear of asking people for help as a sign of weakness, and let the man help me. My research had carried me to another ledge, where there were a lot more aisles than I had anticipated. And I cursed at myself for having paid too much attention to the books and not enough on where I had come from before finding them. Because now, I was most definitely lost and not getting out of this library before it closed.

"Darkness help me please," I whispered as I turned left again, and ended up at a dead-end for the hundredth time at least.

Oh, wait. Darkness. Magic, blood magic...my magic.

I rolled my eyes at myself as I stuck my hand in the folds of the skirt, fishing out my dagger, and pulling it out.

"You have the power to teleport, Sivrehya Rithloren, good grief." I sighed, cutting a shallow wound on the palm on my hand. And as the red spilled from it, I put the dagger back into my skirt. I willed the blood with a flick of my wrist and a dance of my fingers to form into the symbol for portals. I closed my eyes, thinking of my room in the inn and then opened them again, watching as the symbol set itself in place and glowed with magic.

And then, I stepped through it, letting the bitter cold of the void wash over me before stepping into my room.

It was dark inside, the light only slightly filtering through the muslin curtains. I quickly cast a light charm and healed my hand. The orb of pulsating gold floated to the ceiling, bumping only slightly and floating back down.

I looked at the bed and sighed.

Right.

There was still the problem of the bed. The one that wasn't even really a bed. I pulled the dagger once again from my skirt and once again pushed the tip into my palm. I would turn the bed back to its original state the day I left, but everyone needed proper sleep and it was impossible with a bed like this.

In an explosion of red light, enveloping the room like blood spilling from a gushing wound, the bed shifted. It creaked and groaned as it extended itself, growing, twisting and turning to make an ornate bed frame. The bed sheets became puffy, losing their mud brown color and adopting a dark red one instead, with carefully threaded designs decorating the pillow and the covers. And suddenly, just as quickly as the room was swallowed in a wave of bright scarlet, it became gold again, as the red dispersed into thin air once the charm was finished.

The moment it was done and in front of me was a large bed, I squealed at the sight of it. With my trusty dagger in hand, I fell on top of the bed. It was warm and fluffy, inviting, mimicking the one I had in my room at home.

At the thought of the word "home", I closed my eyes, at first smiling. And then, I stilled, my mind suddenly drowned in the perilous thoughts of all the terrible things that could happen.

Because what if I never found the Neithisis? What if I did and it killed me? Or kept me prisoner? What if the truth was that a blood mage had killed the Lysmiran princess and that a soul mage killed my father? What if the war wasn't based on a lie? What if...what if... The thoughts, the questions, no matter how hard I tried to push them down, away into oblivion, always came back.

I looked around the room, my eyes stopping at the pile of parchments and the quill laying on them. I sighed. It was time to send an update to my family even though there wasn't much they could be updated on. Walking over to the papers, I picked one out and I stared at it, quill in hand. I pressed the inked feather to the paper and nothing. I couldn't tell them just yet of what I had found out about Sierah and Florek. Because it might just be nothing, and I didn't want to worry them over nothing.

Better to keep it as general as possible, I thought, as slowly, words started flowing from my mind to my hand.

I found something...confusing. But I'm not sure about it. So far, the Neithisis is proving difficult to find, and for today I'm done looking. Good night, I love you both. Send my best wishes to Mother, Jace, Lissa and the rest.

I set the quill down, poking my skin with the dagger and letting the red scarlet flow into my palm and up into the air. I threw the letter through the elaborately designed circle, half hoping this time I might get a response from them. I've never been separated from them before. I've lived nineteen years of my life with them, my entire life, and now, I was alone, in this room. And there was this small ache in my heart, an emptiness.

You miss them Siv, I told myself. And as soon as I did, I shoved the thought away and walked to my bed.

I set the dagger underneath my pillow where it was whenever I slept. And then I dug my hands in my other pocket and pulled out the library card that Junah had given to me. Tomorrow at nine, at the Rising Sun of All I was to meet her to give it back. I was grateful for her help, wondering if she was this way with every stranger who needed it. The prince and I had managed to learn where to possibly find these creatures, and that was already more than I hoped for.

But my tireless search for more information had proved fruitless. Perhaps we would need to just search every mountain, every cave in the Raven Mountains, and hope that just once the world would not be cruel and instead would be a little kind. The sheer thought of the countless number of holes atop the mountains within which one might hold the beast was terrifying in it of itself. But at least that one I could push away, at least for now.

I laid back, my head on the pillow, my eyes glancing over the stained old ceiling, that no doubt held many stories and secrets, as all walls do. My father had told me that. Every time I hid behind a shelf of books in the corner of the library, my father would always find me, only to pretend he couldn't and then hours later, claim I was impossible to find. But I knew, he let me be, for the simple reason of having a little peace and quiet.

I had once asked him if I had become a secret the walls had come to keep. And he told me I had, and I remembered smiling like the happiest child he'd ever seen. And he smiled.

Oh, *Darkness*, how I missed his smile. And his laugh. How he'd bark orders around and then say "please" and all his men and women could just laugh and nod, and do as their king said. I miss the way he always lit up the room, and how even after a kill, a hunt, torture that lasted too long, he would find a reason to smile. For us.

A tear, traitorous and small, fell out of my eye. Then another. I wiped them away, sniffing my nose and closing my eyes shut.

"No crying Sivrehya. No..." Another tear. "No crying. No crying," I mumbled to myself, as I slowly curled up. "Stay strong, no crying," I repeated, hoping I'd fall to the lure of sleep. "No crying," I said once more, "No crying," I said again.

Please, no, no, no. I can't cry. No. I can't...cannot...

But a tear fell, and then another, and then five and then countless.

And there was a moment when nothing came out of my eyes and my chest hurt and I was aching all over and I just prayed that the world in this moment wasn't watching. Or hearing.

XXI : IVAR THAEGAN

The Twin Cities
Sunsier, Outer City

Blood lined my clothing, my hands and dyed my hair a sickly color.

All around me, people screamed in terror, yelled in anger, poison in all their words. All around me, there were piles, growing higher, high as the sky, of people. My people, their silver and ivory uniforms coated in red. Their swords either embedded in themselves like cruel irony or lost somewhere in the chaos that was all around us.

I stood up, only hearing my breathing, my heart still pounding heavily in my chest. I could smell the iron; I could taste it in the air. My eyes only saw death, as was spanned for miles, surrounding me.

In my hands, there was no blade, no shield. I looked down and felt as if my soul was ripped from my body. Below me, Avran laid, blood dripping from his mouth, his silver eyes, once aglow, were now a colorless white. His skin, cold, like ice.

And I screamed, I screamed. But I heard nothing, no one heard anything. I was trapped in my mind perhaps, or the world around me was too busy drinking the blood of the fallen to even care.

And suddenly there was salt in my mouth. I had been crying for him. For who else, I wondered, as I turned around watching the swords clash, the daggers being buried in flesh. I watched as scarlet symbols covered in the sky and glowed, unleashing their wielder's will. I watched as soul mages raised their hands and arms and bodies crumbled at their command.

My head lowered, my eyes gazing over my bloodied hands once again. And slowly I stilled, controlling my panicked breaths. The sounds of the war around me were getting louder, less faded, more real. I closed my eyes, and the senses came rushing back.

In an instant, the bloody world that was once quiet became a raging storm of spoken fury. A faint crying, almost as if from another world, seeped in and weaved together with the angry cries and the blood-curdling screams. I covered my ears, walking backward and stumbling over something.

And I fell into oblivion and then from the sky. But I couldn't scream as my body plummeted to the ground, the force of air pressing my armor flat against me.

Below I saw the war of red and silver, from all sides, as they meshed together becoming one and yet still separated. I watched figures fall, figures stand, figures break.

My tears escaped me, flying into the sky, and I closed my eyes as I readied myself for death. But the pain of being broken physically didn't come.

I opened my eyes and in front of me stood my soldiers, my people, looking at me, swords in hands, screaming. They rushed towards me, past me, and when I turned around, I saw the princess they all wanted to kill.

But she looked different in this dream. Her glowing red eyes were almost black, her hair red, soaked with blood, her clothing, ripped and dirty. But her look was none less than feral and lethal. She looked more than just Darkness blessed; she looked evil.

I could hear her laugh, as my men ran towards her and exploded in red. Their remains flying, their heads rolling, their blood staining the world around them. I tasted their blood on my tongue.

Then she walked towards me and I reached for my blade, but it wasn't there, where it should have been. I searched for my power but there was none.

She laughed again, and it was as if the air was filled with her taunting smile, her haughty glare, as she raised her arms and made her way towards me.

I stumbled back, my eyes always on hers. I could see, glistening drops on her pale cheeks, coming from her eyes, as if she had been crying. Or was.

"Watch as your kingdom falls, Ivar Thaegan." She boomed, and her voice could be heard for miles as if amplified by some magical spell. "Watch as we destroy it all."

Around me I saw all the silver specks that littered the grass; in the distance I saw a castle burning, I saw the smoke of a thousand fires.

My heart dropped because I knew I was looking at Lysmir burning.

My kingdom was burning, and I was powerless to stop it.

"Isn't it a lovely sight?"

I screamed, realizing the princess was now on me, her pale fingers closing around my neck tightly. She smiled, blood staining her white teeth, dripping from her mouth. She looked like the princess of death that she was, the blood demon that she was.

I gasped for air, unable to form words, unable to use my power. It had left me. I was nothing but a limp thing in her hands that remained coiled around my neck like a snake. My life in her clenched, white-knuckled fist.

"I think it is." Her feral smile bared her bloody teeth, and then she tightened her grip and I screamed. No noise came out but pain exploded in my body as her fingernails dug into the flesh of my throat.

And then I fell limp to the floor. Gasping for air as I stood up. I couldn't give up. I couldn't let her win. The princess laughed, throwing her head back for just a second before setting her lethal glare on me once again, her smile quickly dying.

And as if she had taken those pale fingers to dig into my mind, she spoke softly, "I already have."

"NO!" I screamed, "NO!" But there was no noise.

Why, why couldn't I speak?

She walked towards me again, stepping on the dead bodies as if they weren't even there, her eyes set on me. And in her hand, a long spear made of solidified blood formed, ever so slightly glowing.

She smiled once again, a serpentine smile, full of wicked promises. And then, I was trapped in my own body, my mind screaming for me to move, my legs refusing to listen.

And then, her spear found its way through my heart, and I felt my body tense and crumble.

I looked at her, tears forming, my eyes set on her wicked grin, on her *glowing eyes that were almost black. And then I looked beyond her, and clear as ever, I saw my father, standing, sword in hand, his armor shining silver and glowing, not a spot of scarlet on it. He stood regally, unbothered by the war, the blood, the death around him. His eyes bored into mine and ever so slightly, he shook his head, and then he turned around. And he walked away.*

The princess dug her spear deeper and deeper until it impaled me and I coughed up blood. And my mind became mush, my vision clouded and fading.

But there was no pain. Not as there should have been. Instead, there was the sensation of failure.

Suddenly, a feminine voice, strong yet gentle, as I remembered, loud yet faded by the surrounding screams, spoke out, "Get up, Ivar, get up."

Then darkness fell, and I did too. The voice, the last I heard.

It was the chiming of the bells at the eighth hour, signaling the change of Moonsier to Sunsier, that pulled me from my sleep.

I woke up, sweating, trying to catch my breath. The taste of blood was on my mouth and the weight of failure on my mind.

Head turning, my eyes focused on the wall beside me. The wall separating me from the blood demon in my dreams. I tried to shake her image from my mind, but to no avail. My mind had an imprinted drawing of the blood-soaked princess with her red smile and black eyes.

But that hadn't been the worst part of the dream. I had failed my people, my kingdom, myself and my father. I failed them all. She had won; she got her one true wish. To kill me, to watch me die by her hands in the midst of my falling world.

And then something twisted inside me. I had made a deal with a demon to not kill her, and I would keep it. But the moment we found the damned beast and got the truth, whatever it was, I would *tear* her apart. *I* would win, *I* would watch her kingdom fall and *I* would be the one to drive a blade through her heart.

My dream had been a horrid nightmare, but nothing more. Lysmir would not be burned, my people would not get slaughtered and Avran wouldn't die. I wouldn't. I...I couldn't.

~

The massive clock tower came into view, towering above all the other buildings in the Outer City. I narrowed my eyes, trying to make out what time it was.

I cursed silently; it was almost nine o'clock. Nine was when the princess would meet that girl and give her back the card to the library.

The girl had mentioned the Rising Sun of All as the meeting place, and even though I was there just yesterday, I had chosen that place because I had seen Sivrehya sitting here, not because I had intently searched it out. Which now meant that I had no idea where I was going.

I remembered it was near the Central Square, not too far from the clock tower and in the middle of numerous street vendors. But not like that helped much. I kept seeing tea shops, all not far from either the clock tower or the Central Square and all surrounded by vendors.

Great.

The bells chimed again, loudly, their clash cracking through the air, filling it entirely with their music. The ninth hour of the day. If they talked for hours, or perhaps longer than ten minutes I might still have a chance of catching them.

I quickly weaved my way through the sea of people that was slowly becoming larger and larger, as more people began to awaken and spill out their doors. It felt like a race against time as I started almost running into the Central Square, spinning around slowly, standing on my toes to look over all the people and see if I could find the tea shop. And I knew I couldn't be far. It had to be near here somewhere.

"Ah," I breathed out, colliding with a hard surface. I stumbled back, shaking my head back to focus. A man, close to my age perhaps, stood there, worried more for me than for himself. "I—I'm so sorry," I spat out, forcing a smile to make my apology appear more genuine. In part, I couldn't care less, I needed to find two people and a card.

"Oh, it is quite alright sir, are you okay?"

"Oh, yes, fine, I'm perfectly fine thank you!" I jumbled the words together. "Good day," I yelled out, before making a run for it. But an arm, looped with mine, stopped me in my tracks.

I turned around, to see a young woman with skin that quite literally *glowed*.

She batted her lashes seductively, "Hello pretty, how are you?" She mused, taking a strand of my hair and moving it from out of my eyes. She saw them, their silver color and for once second, she stilled before seemingly pushing the idea of me being a monster aside and pulling me into some dark and heavily scented building.

I blinked, taken aback by the strong sickly-sweet odor that filled the air. All around me were vases of flowers, of all kinds. Some red, some white, some blue, and some the color of the sky. Some glowed, some hung from the ceiling in bouquets.

Where the hell am I? I thought, just as another thought quickly took over, *Why the hell am I here?*

I turned to the girl, ripping my arm from hers. She looked a little startled, but brushed it off and pushed me back. I hit the wall, and a vase crashed to the floor, shattering into a million pieces, the blue roses once inside it now scattered.

Blue roses, roses that grew nowhere anyone knew about, but legend said they killed with a single touch. That their petals held enough poison to send hundreds to their doom. That their thorns bled a dark blue sap that turned your skin the same color in minutes before rendering you paralyzed, blind and with a slowly diminishing supply of oxygen. Rumors said they grew in the snowy Raven Mountains where the Darkness was said to have originated, because many believed they had been roses changed by the Darkness. But no one knew for sure, and if the stories of their blueish terrors were even only somewhat true, no one would want to know.

I gasped, looking the girl in the face. "How did you find those roses? They don't even exis—"

"Oh, for someone so pretty, you're a person who worries far too much." The girl mused. I scoffed. Was that meant to be a compliment or an insult?

"I'm not—"

"Shhh pretty boy, they're just white roses painted blue. No risk of dying darling."

The fact that they were just painted made me relax just a little, but not enough to let her do whatever she was planning to do to me. I pushed her away, gently enough.

"What do you want with me? And where the hell *am* I?" I demanded, glaring at her and only now realizing she was almost naked. I stilled.

Oh, sweet Darkness you cannot be serious. I'm in a—

"You should tell me what you want me to do with you." Her voice lowered, seductively and heat exploded inside my body.

I stilled, looking more closely at her eyes that were hidden by dark brown hair with streaks of orange. They were the color of orange and red with hints of yellow. A damned fire mage. Who happened to be a harlot. Darkness save me.

And then she winked, slowly extending her arms to grab me. My eyes had gone from her to around the room, where men and women alike laid unclothed in piles of silk cloth and on expensive looking chairs with exotic prints.

I bolted out of her reach, twisting my body away from her and from any other harlot who could claim me.

"Oh *no*, no, no, no, no, no. I'm sorry, so sorry, really, but no. There's something I have to do, somewhere I have to be."

"Oh, so you're calling me ugly?"

What? Why would you—

I wanted to just stare at her and ask her how in the name of the

Dark Father she thought I was calling her ugly when the very thing I was doing was saying I needed to go.

"No, no, of course not." I assured her, even plastering a smile on my face while I told her, "You're very pretty." *Too pretty for me to ever be able to trust you.* But those thoughts I left unspoken.

"I can make all your dreams come true," she whined, grabbing my hand before I could tear it from her reach. I stilled. A wicked idea forming in my mind. There was one way I was going to successfully make her disinterested in me without having to kill her.

So, I moved towards her, slowly, my eyes traveling up and down her body before landing on hers and I smirked. I held her hand in mine, bringing it to my cheek.

"Can you..." I paused, looking at her intently, at the eagerness in her fire-colored eyes, "can you torture and kill all the Rithlorens for me? And then perhaps drain them of their blood and spill it on every street in every city in Meris for all their people to see and smell? Could you seduce Prince Daemon and then slit his throat and give me his head?" She stilled, looking absolutely horrified. Her dark skin paled; her eyes widened in fear. She tried to yank her hand away but I held it firm. To make sure she didn't scream out for help, I rooted her soul in place, unable to move.

My smirk fell away, and I gave her a glare of death. I let her hand fall from my cheek after looking into her frightened eyes for just a few seconds longer. "Do yourself a favor. *Never* seduce a monster. We do not fall for it." I turned around but stopped, having another thing to say to the poor girl. "You do."

And then I walked out, letting go of her soul and hearing her scream of terror the moment I disappeared from view.

"Well, thank Darkness that worked." I huffed, running a hand through my hair and fixing my shirt that she had managed to ruffle up.

∿

The Square was saturated with people. But it was the moment I looked at the clock that I knew I had no chance of catching up to the princess and the other girl. It was already fifteen minutes past the ninth hour, and at this rate, I would get to the tea shop in about seventy hours. Should I arrive sooner, the two wouldn't be there anyway. Sivrehya was on a mission, one that was time-sensitive. She wouldn't waste it talking to a stranger unless it was absolutely dire. And I sensed that that girl Junah had given all the help she could give.

Out of the corner of my eye, I caught the image of a shimmering golden sun. I turned to look at it. It was the sign of a gift shop, the one where I had first seen the princess. And I had walked past it the morning I saw her at the tea shop.

I made my way towards it, pushing my way through the crowd, careful to not trip on any of the carts filled with goods that several people pushed in front of them.

Catching my breath and shaking the sand off the hem of my trousers, I escaped the sea of people and found myself under the sun sign.

Forward, I thought. I couldn't remember the exact path I had taken but the tea shop was close to the gift shop.

I spun around, my eyes narrowed and I saw, behind a cluster of vendors in the middle of a small plaza, a tea shop, with a sign, a half sun rising. The tables were made of marble, each with a broken glass vase in the middle and a single flower in each. My heart quickened its pace.

Please, please let them still be there, I thought to myself as I quickly looked back at the clock tower. Half-past the ninth hour. My chances were more than slim.

I passed the vendors and looked at all the tables of the tea shop, filled with people all laughing carelessly, sipping colorful tea. But none of them were Junah or the princess.

"Fuck," I muttered under my breath. I knew that I would probably not be able to catch up to them, but for some reason, a false hope had fluttered inside my chest and grew against my will.

"Okay," I breathed. I needed to think, to slow down and think. I had no idea where the princess would go after she returned the card. If she even returned it; perhaps she had asked if she could still use it.

Bah, that's not helping. No, okay, think Ivar, think. Whether the princess returned the card or not, Junah would probably, either way, be heading to class. Which is in the Inner City, which is where the library is...

Which means heading to the Inner City gate was the best bet to find Junah. Unless of course they made a portal there and were already past the gate.

Curse blood and solar and lunar mages for being able to just make a symbol in the middle of the fucking air and step through it and land somewhere, anywhere else.

But, without knowing what else to do, I took a deep breath in and out and turned around, making my way to the gates.

And of course, they weren't there. Curse the entire world.

I was about to ask the guards at the gate if there was any chance at all that they would let me through, and should they have said no, I would have made them open the gates, but I caught a whiff of dark magic. A scent of it, not far away. I whipped around, my eyes quickly scanning all the people below, and sure enough, in the midst of it all was a girl with onyx black hair and pale skin wearing a red dress.

"Got you," I smiled, but then, out of the corner of my eyes I saw Junah. Walking in the opposite direction. I stilled, my gaze going from one to the other. I could only follow one. So, I strained my neck, my eyes to see if perhaps Junah held the card.

A blossom of relief rushed through me when in her hands I caught sight of something shimmering and gold. The card to the library.

I bolted down the stairs, careful not to run into those who were making their way up to them. I couldn't have any more mishaps.

"Junah!" I called out, slowing my pace to weave through the people around me without knocking them all down like dominos. From the top of the stairs, I could see her perfectly, but from the ground, my view of her was obstructed by people taller than me, by people carrying folded fabric on their heads and various other things.

I huffed, slightly regretting my decision to follow Junah and not Sivrehya who could have easily constructed a portal from her blood for us.

In a gap between a group of people, I saw her. And I hurried to catch up to her. Junah turned the corner, disappearing into the shadows. I followed her into a smaller alleyway, the sun blocked by pieces of yellow fabric that hung between the buildings.

Slowly the number of people around me started to dwindle, and just ahead I saw her, between a small crowd of people.

"Junah! Wait, Junah!" But it was no use. She turned another corner and disappeared.

I stopped, catching my breath, this time delving into my power, this time using it to find her soul string. But before I could, a serpentine voice stopped me in my tracks.

"Hello handsome, remember me?"

I whipped around, my hand curling against the hilt of my dagger, cursing whoever had taken my power away from me, as I felt it fade away slowly. But as soon as my eyes met hers, I stumbled.

Because there, in front of me, dressed in golden robes that pooled at her feet, with her hair styled in a heavily adorned bun and a single golden feather pinned to it, was Mahin.

XXII : IVAR THAEGAN

The Twin Cities
Sunsier, Outer City

Mahin's face contorted into an evil smile, with eyes that spoke of murder. Around her, there were men, dressed in black, masks covered in black feathers painted gold like the one I wore at The Golden Crow.

"Mahin," I mused, steadying myself, readying myself for a fight. "How are you?"

"Fine," She made her way towards me, and suddenly the air was filled with a silent threat of death. I tensed, clenching my hands into fists. "Though I would be doing better if my men had not been killed though." She cocked her head to one side, batting her lashes, turning her smile into a sweet one.

"I'm sorry your men were murdered," I responded bluntly. She clearly wanted something from me, but what her murdered men had to do with it, I had no idea.

"Hm, I am quite sure you are. After all, it was quite a terrible way they died." She feigned the tremble in her voice, the tears that formed in her eyes.

"Oh?" I raised a brow. I drummed my fingers against my leg. I didn't have time for this. Why did the world keep sending people my way who wanted to talk to me when I very clearly needed to get somewhere?

"Hm yes," she mused, her eyes leaving mine as she paused, looking off into elsewhere. But then just as quickly they returned to mine, boring into them with lethal intensity. I stood firm, looking down at her small yet menacing form with the same level of intensity, if not more.

"Their souls were destroyed."

Oh shit.

"Have you ever seen a destroyed soul, Sovan?" Mahin mused, as I gulped, careful to not let her see the instant realization that rushed through me. "I have," she started again when I remained silent. She placed a cold hand on my shoulder, gingerly, as she walked around me, dragging her hand over my shirt. I remained tense but dug inside for my power.

But there was nothing.

I tried again, focusing, ignoring the chills that ran down my spine as Mahin continued walking around me. Again, nothing.

My eyes darted around me, to each of the men, and they met the eyes of the one in the middle. He was baring his yellowed teeth; in his hand, a small glowing symbol floated. I didn't know exactly what it was, but I could guess.

This damned woman and her henchmen just made me powerless. I cursed myself for rushing out of the inn and only bringing my dagger with me.

"The first and only time before this, was ten years ago, when the royal family of Lysmir paid a visit. Someone, if I recall, robbed the princess of one of her jewels and she made him *kneel* and *beg* and *beg* until she became bored of his pleads and killed him. Destroying his poor soul."

"Mahin. Let me go," I seethed, completely ignoring her story. My grip tightening around my dagger's hilt, my knuckles whitening.

At that, she laughed, wickedly, haughtily as if she were the queen of the world. I took it as an opening. I yanked the dagger from its sheath, and in a flash, I stuck it into Mahin's stomach. Only it didn't pierce soft flesh. I froze, my eyes focusing on my blade, that was lodged in the middle of a swirling symbol glowing gold and yellow.

"Oh handsome, I think not. You have just done another very,

very bad thing. And now," she stepped back, smiling like an evil monarch, "you must be punished."

Her smile faded away, and her arm raised. And then there was hot exploding pain at the back of my head, and then darkness.

~

Ice cold washed over me, pinning my clothing to my skin, pulling me from the darkness. I coughed, spitting water. And blinked, the pain from earlier still throbbing at the back of my head. I groaned, shivering from the cold water just thrown at me.

In front of me, Mahin stood, smiling, holding a rusted bucket. I looked around, sitting up just slightly, to take in my new surroundings.

It was dark and smelled of rotten things with a hint of spices. Which meant we couldn't be far from Central Square, or at least a place filled with people.

"Tell me why you killed them, Sovan." The woman demanded. I huffed, still catching my breath, as my eyes darted from her to the men behind her. All spoke of silent torture, of imminent death should I try anything with their leader.

Not that could. I was bound by rope at my ankles and wrists, enchanted no doubt. And my power was made useless from the glowing symbol still floating above one of the men's hands.

"I didn't know they were your men," I spat out, shutting my eyes tightly, hoping my mage body would subdue the pain exploding at the back of my head quickly. I had guessed they might have been, but she didn't need to know that.

"Would that have made a difference?" Mahin asked in a sickly-sweet voice, a feral smile plastered on her face.

Not a damn difference, I thought, knowing myself too well and hating that she did too. Because in the tone of her voice, I knew, she knew it wouldn't have made a single difference. She wasn't like all the other mages in this city; she saw me for what I really was. And a monster like myself wouldn't have given a single shit if those men had been hers or not.

So, I sighed and said, "No."

"What I thought," she said as she nodded, leaning back in her chair, crossing her arms. "Now, tell me why you killed them."

There was no point in trying to sugar coat my actions. Not to her, at least.

"They took something from me."

"And?" She probed, sensing there was more to the story.

"And they refused to give it back."

"So..." She trailed off.

"So, I took it back, forcefully, and they got in the way. So..." I replied bluntly and shrugged my shoulders.

"You are truly a cruel one." Mahin smiled, her face lighting up.

I mirrored her, baring my own teeth, "You should know from the stories of my kind. I'm sure you're well versed in what we're like."

"Hm," the woman looked off into the distance, considering her next words before standing up and flattening her skirt a bit. "It is a shame you killed them; I could have used you." She bent down, taking my face in her hands, cupping my cheeks.

She licked her lips.

"As if I would ever take orders from you," I spat. She was going to make me hurt; I knew that already. But I had been in pain before, terrible pain, and I somehow survived. I would survive this.

A blur of dark skin and gold and then a blaze of pain blossomed on my cheek. My head turned at the sheer force of her slap. I would feel the tingle of the sharp pain and tingles slowly turning my pale skin into a raw pink color. It was a downside of looking like a half-ghost. Every scratch, slap, wound, whip seemed to glow in red against pale skin.

"You think you are so above me?" She seethed, gripping my face in her hands, digging her nails into my skin as the princess had done to me in my dream.

I know I'm above you, you insolent bitch.

But I also knew I couldn't blame her. Every time someone killed or hurt someone close to me, someone important, I would do what she would do to me. I would make them hurt, suffer. Make them beg for their lives and then wait until they begged for death and then deny them both by breaking them just enough but not completely.

"You think that even with me being powerless and tied up, you have any power over me?" She released my face, pushing it away as she stood and towered over me. "You *do not*."

She walked away, to a table, and from it, she grabbed a whip.

And I paled, against my will, as a memory flashed into my head.

"Father! Father please, I—I'm sorry," I wept, sobbed through the words, making them barely comprehendible. "I didn't mean to do it, I swear, I—" A crack of a whip, a hot burning pain and I screamed. And my cries filled the air of the room, the air of the hallways, and the other room and the entire castle.

"Silence! You have failed me; you are a failure. I have no use for a fail-ure." My father bellowed, raising his arm again and bringing it down, bringing the singing hot whip with it. Another sharp explosion of pain ran through me.

"Stop," I sobbed loudly.

"Please," I whispered that time.

"Please..." I trailed off.

Please, I thought.

Please...

The memory shattered the moment the whip met my skin. But unlike when I was a child, unlike the first time, I only winced from the pain. Not even bothering to close my eyes, or to scream or even to cry. I remained inhumanly still.

"So," Mahin mused, "You are accustomed to this then?" She cocked her head, looking into my eyes, my soul. I simply stared back at her, not giving her the satisfaction of an answer.

She took my silence for what it was, the truth. She tossed the whip aside. "That is useless then. I rather hate when torture is dull. Don't you?"

Again, I remained silent.

"Oh, come now, all of a sudden you have become so...so, so boring." She huffed.

I looked up at her, shrugging my shoulders as if to say I was sorry.

She rolled her eyes, saying, "I want to make you suffer and I will. And at first, I was not going to use magic, but if I must..." She trailed off, raising a hand, and I watched as it started glowing gold. "Then I will."

My scream brought her pleasure. I saw it in her eyes, in her smile.

I had gotten used to being whipped, used to my soul being ripped apart, twisted inside me, I had gotten used to doing things against my will. But her type of magic opened the door for a million new ways of inflicting pain that I had never been through.

My body was trapped in itself and I was burning inside, screaming for an escape. She would break a bone, and then another until I screamed again. And then she'd tear open my skin, and burn it with bright hot light.

The world around me became a faded, colorless thing. I felt nothing but the pain constantly exploding inside me, and slowly that too faded. My screams became ragged and broken, my throat burning, raw and sore.

All the while Mahin laughed. Oh, how she laughed. And in the moments when I fell into darkness, I imagined all the times I had inflicted pain on someone, something and never once had I laughed. Perhaps I had smiled; no, I had *definitely* smiled.

Not because they were broken, but because I had gotten what I wanted.

And then, suddenly ice-cold water was thrown over me and the pain seemed to freeze in place, being numbed for just a second before exploding inside me again.

"Well, I quite enjoyed that. Did you?" Mahin clapped her hands like a little girl, she squealed, all the while smiling like the proudest mage.

I didn't respond. Against my will I had screamed out in pain, giving her far too much satisfaction for my liking. I wasn't about to give her more.

"I like you better when you're screaming." She frowned. "But I am going to give you some time to breathe before I continue."

Oh, how kind.

She walked to the same table she got the whip from, this time grabbing a wine glass and filling it with dark red liquid.

"Would you like some?" She held out the glass, offering it to me. But I was unable to even form my incoherent thoughts in a coherent way. She shrugged at my silent decline. "Fine then, more for me." And then she sipped the wine, just a bit, before downing it completely.

"This time, of course, we will try something a little different." She winked. Darkness save her.

I remained silent as ever.

Mahin sat back down, looking at me, her face contorted in focus. "I will give you a choice. Should I bleed you dry like all the blood mages like to do, surely you know what about that, right?" She smiled sweetly, cocking her head to one side, her eyes meeting mine. But never once did I make a noise. Instead I just looked at her, glared at her with blaring intensity, sending daggers in her direction.

"Or," she continued, having grown bored of my lack of responding, "I could skin you alive. With this dagger," She unsheathed her blade from its sheath at her side.

I was fully convinced this woman was beyond mad, just next to my father. They would like each other.

"Which do you prefer?"

Silence.

"You should answer people when they have questions, Sovan, it is only nice." Mahin scolded like a mother would do her child.

Silence. My eyes still boring into hers, my face still blank. It began to ache from not moving it.

Mahin sighed, impatiently. "I am being *nice*, Sovan. Answer me. Which do you prefer?"

In all honesty, neither. But that obviously isn't a choice.

"Actually," she said as she turned around, "no, wait." She put her dagger back in its sheath. And then made her way back to me, taking my face in her hands, gently this time. Uncomfortably gentle.

She leaned in; I could smell the wine in her breath. "Your face is much too pretty to waste in such a way. I think I am going to keep you." She bared her teeth, a faint tint of burgundy from the wine stained her otherwise white teeth.

Her hands traveled down from my face to my neck, and my collarbone, where she in a split second ripped open my shirt. Cold air caressed my chest. I winced.

Praise Darkness, curse the world.

I tried to remain still, to be unbothered by her cold hands all over me. But my traitorous body twitched at her unwelcome touch. Her thin long fingers crawled beneath my shirt, to my back, and over the healed bumps of my many scars. They travelled over the lines cruelly engraved into skin softly, but nonetheless I tensed involuntarily.

"Oh," She mumbled, looking suddenly sad, "Someone's ruined you."

Someone's ruined you. Someone's *ruined* you. My father with his whip, with his temper, his constant disapproval of my actions, and with his adoration of branding me a failure. He was the one who had ruined me.

Her snake hands moved to my upper back, and she slipped my shirt off. I twitched, jerking away from her, but she didn't stop or notice, she simply continued. I moved again, trying to inch out of her reach. Mahin simply laughed at my pathetic attempt to escape her, all the while moving lower, to my pants, where she slowly started to untie them.

All the restraint I put on myself cracked, shattering, and with all the force my weakened body could muster, I kicked her, wherever my legs could reach.

Mahin groaned, falling back to the ground. In an instant her men were on me, and the number of hits to the stomach, face and body were lost so quickly.

"Stop!" Mahin shrilled, "Stop."

All at once, as if under a spell, her men retreated back to their position. I coughed up blood, weakly groaning, turning over onto my back. If I were a non-mage I would have been dead already. The only thing keeping me alive was the fact that we mages are *very* hard to kill.

"Look at him," Mahin whined, "You have ruined his pretty face! He is a weak little limp thing because of you! I have to heal him now, wait until he gets better, before I can have my fun."

I could barely hear her. My ears could only focus on the weakened beating of my heart, of the pain that continuously exploded in my body, rendering it immobile.

Then she turned to me, and slowly, I lifted my throbbing head to meet her blaring gaze.

"And you, what do you have to say for yourself?"

I spat out blood, "Do not touch me."

At that Mahin laughed. "Oh, now you talk."

"Yes, now I talk." I seethed, "Torture me all you want, but do not think I will let you touch me like *that*."

"You ungrateful bastard! I offer you your life, but you deny me! Perhaps then I will kill you!" She screamed just as the door slammed open with such power that it vibrated through the walls around us.

"Don't you *dare* kill him," A feminine voice, laced with poison, stopped Mahin in her tracks. Like clockwork, she and all her men twisted themselves to face the person whom the voice belonged to.

I kept my head low, but my eyes followed theirs. In the doorway, dressed in a dark red skirt with a matching top, her obsidian hair tied back in a loose braid, her brown eyes glaring with a look worse than Death, stood the princess of Meris.

Mahin's face twisted into a lethal feline smile, her bright white teeth showing. But there was no kindness in it; it was a threat of a smile. But it did nothing to faze Sivrehya. After all, she was so much worse than Mahin was. Not that Mahin knew, and part of me pitied her for it. She was about to face the wrath of a blood mage. No, worse, the wrath of a *Rithloren*.

"And why not, lovely?" Mahin purred, moving towards her with a feral grace.

"He's *mine*," Sivrehya's voice was like cold death.

"Yours?" Mahin continued walking in Sivrehya's direction.

"To kill." The princess finished, her face brutally blunt, her eyes still brown. Yet, from where I was sitting, I saw the Darkness that began to swim within their depths.

But Mahin laughed, haughtily, as if not quite believing it.

"Get in line," a man scoffed, spitting in the princess's direction. He stood up, towering over her, but again, the graceful monster that was Sivrehya Rithloren remained perfectly calm.

Her own face shifted; a serpentine smirk appeared on her wicked face. Her hand was raised, and in it was a small sharp spear, bright red. "I'd rather not," she spoke, and then, with all the practiced skill of a killer, she threw her spear straight towards the man. And in the split seconds that it flew through the air, the spear was suddenly two, each finding one of the man's eyes.

There was a crack of a skull as two spears pierced through flesh and bone, a gasp of pain and then a thud. Loud and short. As the man fell, limp and dead.

Mahin's face of stoic calm faltered, *she* faltered, her eyes suddenly wide with fear. She turned to face the princess. "What —*who* are you?"

"That doesn't matter."

The woman pushed her hair back, unsheathing her own blade, the double-edged dagger she was about to skin me alive with, and in her other hand a small ball of light started to grow impossibly bright. "I should know who I am going to fight," she spoke calmly, as if the fear that washed over her just seconds ago was now nowhere to be seen. "It is only customary."

"We're not going to fight, darling," she replied in a bored voice, her eyes lazily meeting Mahin's. "After all, you're already dead."

"I am no—" and then Mahin's eyes went unnaturally wide, and blood came pouring, sputtering from her mouth as her hand, trembling, tried to reach for the spear that went straight through her neck. But it was too late to do anything, because Mahin dropped dead, just like the man before. I grimaced, my eyes switching towards the woman's limp body and the princess, who stood like regal Death.

Darkness save us all.

The spear, the one she lodged into Mahin's throat, had come from nowhere. Or so it seemed. I looked over the man whose eyes were long gone. One spear remained; one wasn't there. Sivrehya hadn't even so much as *breathed.*

I wagered she had willed the blood with her mind. Praise the Dark Father, because her power, her magic, would always scare me.

Sivrehya raised her hands, willing the spears made of blood to return to her; this time they twisted themselves into five. Five spears, then suddenly they doubled. Five remaining men, ten eyes. She looked up, still perfectly dressed, not a hair out of place, not a bead of sweat trickling down her face.

Another feline smile twisted itself on her face as she spoke. "So," she mused in her taunting voice, "which one of you should be next?"

XXIII : SIVREHYA RITHLOREN

The Twin Cities
Sunsier, Outer City

"What in the name of bloody Darkness happened between you two?" I asked, after retrieving the spears from the woman's throat and the man's left eye and all the other eyes of the nameless men piled on the floor. The blood floated in the air around me as I slowly willed it to return to me, but not before separating my own blood from theirs. I could feel his stare on me as I moved my fingers so slowly, as I let the blood return to my body, as I healed the cut on my arm.

Ivar, looking more princely than ever, looked at me lazily, coughing up blood in the process. "I killed," he started, coughing again. "I killed three of her men, after stealing all their money in a game of Baccarat that was both enchanted and illegal, both of which you shouldn't care, nor wouldn't care about. She mostly did this to me because she lost money when those men lost to me. To top it all off, I crushed their souls entirely. Leaving her with three less henchmen to do her dirty work. Pity." He scooted back, resting his back on the wall behind him, wincing from the pain but otherwise showing no other signs that all the bruises and cuts pained him.

So, he hid his pain. I could relate to that. Most of my family could, and perhaps any mage with dark powers living in a world where pain was everywhere would.

"You saved my life," he looked at me, amused. But my face remained blank, my lethal smile gone. "How does it feel to save an enemy's life?"

"I only saved you so I could kill you myself when the time comes." I edged a feral grin on my face, for him this time. I flung their blood away from me and brought my own back inside me, quickly healing the wound with a healing spell, before turning towards the prince.

"After all, I couldn't let her take away my prized kill, now could I?"

For the first time, the prince smiled, and said, "You seem so confident that you're going to kill me. You don't think that I could kill you first? "

"You'll be the first person I kill on the battlefield."

"I'm honored, Your Highness, truly. I guess you should know then that you are the first person *I* plan to kill."

"Then when the time comes, may the best mage win then. But for that to happen, you need to not die; all the fun of killing you should belong to me."

"I couldn't agree more," Ivar responded, still smiling despite his obvious pain.

"Good then," I moved away, pushing the braid behind me. I nudged Mahin's corpse with my foot. "She's quite the feisty one?" I eyed him, curious.

The prince rolled his eyes, "She was rather lovely when we were playing Baccarat. I even seemed to charm her."

"Ah of course, since you're ever *so* charming. But seriously, illegal gambling Ivar? *Seriously*? Don't you think you had more pressing things to do?"

"As if I would have done out of pure interest," he scoffed. "I had to win the game in order to get back what three men stole from me. She," Ivar motioned towards Mahin, "was unfortunately at the same table they were, so when I won, she lost a lot. And clearly, she wasn't too happy about that."

I looked once more at the woman, sprawled on the floor unnaturally, her dark skin stained a brilliant red, her magically glowing eyes, faded. Faded. Faded.

Colorless.

White.

Decaying.

I jerked my head away, the moment my vision became too clear. Looking away from her, I blinked, once, twice.

"How the hell did you find me?"

I jerked my head in the prince's direction, clearing my throat. "I —well, I after I returned the card to Jun—"

"Right," Ivar cut me off, I glared at him. "Why did you give that back? We need it to go to the library, which no doubt will be helpful."

"It wasn't."

"What do you mean it *wasn't*?"

"I mean, it wasn't helpful. What else does that mean?"

The prince huffed, trying to unbind himself. "*Wasn't*, being in the past tense implies you've already *been* to the library."

I simply stared at him. "Correct."

At that he laughed, coughing in between. As if he couldn't quite believe my answer. "Correct, she says. Correct," he shook his head, ripping himself out of the rope bindings. "Curse them," he mumbled. He turned again to face me, our eyes meeting. "You went without me? You were the one who proposed the deal, Rithloren, don't forget it." He stared at me venomously.

"And you *left* me, don't forget that."

He looked down, becoming quiet. Suddenly, he seemed extremely interested in the rope that was still wrapped impossibly tight around his ankles. I thought, surely, they had bound him with their magic, allowing him to be free once they died. But clearly, I had thought wrong.

"Where did you even go?"

He remained silent.

"Iv—forget it," I mumbled, clearing my throat. "Anyway, after I gave back the card to Junah, she promised to keep me informed should she find or learn anything useful. But I didn't have the slightest clue where to continue looking. If the library proved to be no good, then what would? So, I was simply walking around and then I saw her," I looked down at the woman again, this time, I centered myself, allowing my eyes to just sit on her body, "and a few men, carrying you into here. And I have to admit, at first, I didn't question it, I me—"

"Well thank you anyway," he blurted out. I stopped mid-sentence, my mouth still open. I looked at him suspiciously, wondering if his apology was genuine.

"You—you're welcome." I responded, "I have to...go." I turned around, and made my way to the door.

"Help me untie these ropes?" His voice rang behind me.

I turned around, "And why should I do that? I have things to do."

The prince scoffed, "As in what? You said you didn't know where to start?"

I rolled my eyes, "People talk here, charming, about anything. There's a chance they'll talk about the Neithisis."

"You're calling me charming," he said, as an evil twitch of a smirk grew on his face. "That's rather nice in contrast to me calling you blood demon. I wasn't aware you could be nice."

"Oh, forgive me, I thought we were naming each other things that we aren't. After all, I'm calling you charming precisely because you *aren't*."

"A misunderstanding then, because I call you blood demon precisely because you are. And besides, I can be charming. I am charming, just not around you."

"Oh, lucky me," I raised my arms in the air dramatically, "I get the cruel side."

"What side did you expect?" He raised a brow. I raised mine.

"I didn't expect you to even have *sides*."

He looked past me, then above and around me, looking for an answer. "Well...I do."

"That's great, good for you." I plastered a smile on my face, and twisted around, just stepping one foot out the door when the prince spoke again.

"You aren't going to help me?"

"No," I said bluntly.

"We're partners, aren't we? Partners would untie each other." He scoffed, bending his knees, holding back his groan.

I turned my head to look back at him, his eyes focused on the thick rope that bound his ankles. Inside me were a whirl of emotions, red and blue, but none of them was pity. So, I spoke. "I've saved your life, now untie yourself."

And then I walked out the door, and let it close behind me.

Once again, like every other day, the streets were saturated with people. I weaved in and out of the sea of mages and nonmages, threading through the tiny streets and larger ones, always keeping both my ears and eyes open.

But hours had gone by, and I was nowhere closer to uncovering anything about the Neithisis to tell me if Elfaed's words were true. And in all honesty, I was seconds away from properly saying "screw it all" and making a portal to the mountains and just beginning the search right now.

My days here were numbered, slowly dwindling to zero, and while we had managed to find out where the beasts live, should the word be believed, we had uncovered nothing more.

Currently, I was walking through a darkened alleyway in the Merchants' Quarter. The sun's light was obstructed by thick dark pieces of fabric, hanging open from one building to the next. Here, there were less people, less noise, less floating aromas.

In the time that I had been walking, my mind had gone off in a million different directions, yet it found its way back to the two mysteries clouding my head. Two impossibly tangled messes, and despite me trying my best to forget about at least one of them, it always came back.

Perhaps it would still when we finally found a bloody Neithisis, and after we asked it the more pressing question. I could ask how the deaths, that are centuries apart, are so similar.

"Come one! Come all!" And heads turned as the voice boomed from further down the alleyway. But bodies didn't, as if their voice captured their attention just a bit but not fully enough. I continued walking forwards until I reached the man who was hollering the infamous phrase. I looked past him and froze.

The man was standing in front of a store, shabby and darkened. But it was the window displays, as horrible as they were, that captured my attention. There, in the middle of a bunch of brown and black fabric, positioned and scrunched up to mirror the insides of a cave, was a sculpture. Of a beast. With ten too many heads and mouths, filled with dangerously sharp teeth and nine too many eyes.

A Neithisis.

I walked up to the man and tapped his shoulder. He turned around and gave me a toothy grin. I smiled to hide my disgust of his yellowing, partially black and chipped teeth.

"Good day miss, how are you?" He beamed, one eye burned closed. The scars were still pink, as if recent. His head was almost bald, if not for the dark short hairs that grew from it.

"Perfectly wonderful," I responded. Before he could mutter a single word, I pointed to the store and asked, "What is this place?"

"Ah," the man smiled, "this is the place to be if you want to know things, about anything dark and mysterious." He winked.

I raised a brow. "Dark and mysterious?"

"Oh yes, we have people who work for us, who travel to unknown places, who know things, and who are willing to tell, at a cost of course."

Of course.

"Are the people in here?" I nodded towards the store.

"My, my, for someone so pretty you sure seem desperate for some forbidden knowledge."

I huffed, my patience running dangerously thin.

"I don't have all day. Are they here or not?"

"Well," he smiled again, only this time it was different. Less friendly, more sinister. "That is no way for a lady to talk."

"A lady can talk however she pleases," I rebuffed, slowly clenching my fists. The Darkness inside me started bubbling, slowly coming to life, as if it sensed the same threat I did.

The man's face hardened, "Listen here, I can tell you where to find these men. But I don't give information for free."

"I expected no different," I managed to grit out.

"What will you offer me?"

"What do you want?" I asked, a plan unraveling in my mind.

"How about you let me have my way with you for just a bit, and then I will tell you what you desire to know." His sinister smile spread across his face again. He stepped towards me, I stepped back. His golden eyes were glowing.

Aw, poor thing. *You have no idea who you're talking to,* I thought, flashing my teeth with a feral smile.

"Hmmm, I must say. I don't like that deal all too much." I batted my lashes. He stepped towards me again, raising his hands, glowing bindings wrapped around my arm.

Fool. Fool, if you think these things can hold me.

"No?" He asked, feigning the hurt in his trembling voice.

"No. How about this?" I raised my bound arms in front of me and clenched my hands into fists. I focused on the power coming alive inside me and slowly, I bid his blood to pop out. The man winced a little, not caring enough to see where the small prick came from. But I didn't care, I told it to come to me, so it did. His blood floated out of his wrist, in a thin red line. And slowly, it twisted and turned and formed the symbol that would break my binds.

And it glowed red, and with the light, the magical binds shattered falling to the ground, reduced to dust. The man cursed beneath his breath, having seen the entire thing and finally realized who, or at least *what,* he was dealing with.

In a flash, the man turned, ready to make a run for it. But his blood, frozen in place, didn't allow him to move. He grunted, his eyes, once wicked, now filled with fear.

"Now, now, where do you think you're going? I was just about to propose a deal." I cocked my head to the side, baring my teeth again, like a wolf, grinning at its chosen prey.

"P—p—please let me go."

"Hmm," I looked off, pretending as if I was actually taking his plea into consideration. I looked back at him, my eyes boring into his. "No, I'd rather not. See, because I think you're going to quite like this deal of mine."

He gulped.

"I let you live, with all your eyes and fingers, and you tell me where to find these people."

The man shook his head, "I will never. Kill me, torture me, I will stay silent."

I glared at him as the symbol floating behind him, the one that stopped glowing with every lie, told me otherwise. So, I raised a brow, and still smiling, I asked, "Oh really?"

He gulped.

"Well then, what should I take first," I asked, raising one hand, in it a newly fashioned small spear of his solidified blood, looking down at it with dark happiness.

"Stop using my blood, you witch," he spat out, my eyes flashing in his direction once again. And though they were still the dull brown as I had charmed them to be, I knew he could see them darken.

"The eyes?" I asked softly, thankful that this far down the alley it was empty of people.

Suddenly, as if a switch was flipped, the man screamed, and shook his head and convulsed, trying to move under my hold. "No, no, not the eyes."

"No? Then the fingers."

He shook his head again, vigorously. "I'll tell you, I'll tell you where to find them, please, just, oh sweet Sun God, please just stop."

"I will. Once you tell me."

"I will tell you once you stop," he sputtered out, through gritted teeth. The symbol behind him stopped glowing.

"You are in no position to choose. Now, tell me where to find them."

"Why," his voice trembled, and tears started falling down his cheeks. "Why can't you ask nicely?"

I almost clenched my fist entirely and killed him then and there. "I did, you idiot. And you fucking refused." I snarled, "So now, we're doing it the hard way. Now," I demanded, seething, eyes blaring. "Tell me where I can find them."

"Fine!" A crack in his voice. "I don't know where they are, but I know where you can find the people that do. You can find them in the Port, at the Sea Sun, it—it's a bar. Down there you'll find them, just tell the bartender this: 'The sun never sets on our wisdom.'" My eyes flashed to the symbol above him. It wasn't glowing. I looked back at the man, clenching my fist more.

"Lying," I warned, "is not in your best interest."

"I—I'm telling the truth!" He cried out. I rolled my eyes.

And I'm an angel sent to save the world.

"We both know you are, let's not waste any more time. Tell me where to find them, and tell me the truth this time. My patience is wearing rather thin."

The man looked down at the ground, his head hanging, perhaps because he knew he was defeated.

"I wasn't lying about the Port," I looked up, the symbol glowed. "You'll find them there, not at the Sea Sun, but at the King's Port. It's right by the little cluster of trees. It's also a bar, and the bartender will know you want to meet them if you order water."

My eyes had been on the symbol the entire time, and all the time it glowed, bright and red. I released my grip on him and dropped the symbol. His blood crashed, falling to the floor with a soft splat.

"Now, that wasn't so hard. Thank you," I offered the man, who had fallen to the ground, coughing up blood, a smile. And then, I twisted on my heel and headed for the Port.

XXIV : SIVREHYA RITHLOREN

The Twin Cities
Sunsier, Outer City

E veryone in the streets was in a frenzy.
Two days left until the first day of the weeklong
Midnight Sun festival and apparently the thousand
floating lanterns, freshly enchanted and painted designs on every
building, newly blooming flowers and the literal ground glowing at
night for some reason wasn't enough.

The Twin Cities was already a glamorous city, however now, it
looked like a fantasy story world, with new colors rising from every
building as slowly they changed colors as the hours went by. Before
they might have been ivory or terracotta brown but now they bore
the color of blush pink, changing ever so slowly into an ombre of
yellow and sunset orange. Some transformed into lilac, slowly
turning into sea green. Others had painted scenery on them, which
started moving once a certain spell was cast.

The lanterns, which had fancy cutouts before and were hung
on thin threads, were now tripled and colorful, glowing brighter
and changing color. From gold to yellow to orange and blue and
green and pink. They now floated freely and slowly, weaving
between the people or flying high above them.

The flowers, either glowing in the dark or not, bloomed brightly
in a million different hues. And I swore as I walked through the
streets, that the city had turned into an explosion of color, and each
shade was part of the lava that was tumbling into every street, into
every single crack, every space. Until the city was a rainbow of its

own and seeing it now made the city before almost a colorless dull world.

The festival was only held in the Outer City; the Inner City remained the same pristine and clean place as it probably always had been. I had seen when I had been there that the Inner City was impossibly neat. No blade of grass was out of place, not a grain of dirt was on the marble borders cutting off the grass from the walkways. It was quite literally, picture perfect, too perfect. It seemed fake.

I made my way through the crowds, weaving in and out, drowning out the noise of a million conversations, keeping my eyes always ahead. The Port was close enough and slowly, I could see the colors fade into more neutral shades. The paint started to chip, the ornate little patterns drawn on all walls were faded with age, with neglect. The buildings weren't vibrant turquoise or pale lilac; they were mud brown, light brown, faded orange and the shade of pink at the crack of dawn. But underneath the numerous cracks, where spots were left behind from peeled off paint, there was stark white. These had been painted, years ago, by hand. Not by magic.

Up ahead was another wall, another gate, this one rose gold and decorated with fancy fish with scales that shimmered in the light. Each had little stars and suns and moons burned into them. I walked through it and ahead, there was a trail of sand and a wall to my left. And to my right, water, bright and clean, spanning for miles where somewhere past the horizon the nine Shao Yun Islands lay.

∾

Sunsier, Port

Officially, the Port was the second worst place in the Twin Cities. For as pretty as it was, in seaport city terms, it stank of fish. Dead fish. Burned fish. Fish that were barely alive. All mixed with the pleasant odor of seawater, rotted wood, and mud.

I had turned from my trance of losing myself in the sea and

walked all the way to the center of the Port, where somewhere according to the man, there would be a park where a bar would be. Where the people I needed to find would hopefully be.

All around me there were market stands, each with crates and barrels filled with ice and various marine species. Small fish, big fish, rainbow-colored fish, fish with no heads. Octopus tentacles, sea urchins, oysters, mussels, shrimp and tiny little creatures I had never seen before in my life. Hanging from pieces of rope from the bars above the stands were of course more fish, their lifeless beady eyes staring into my soul, shaming me as if I had been the one that pulled them from their peaceful existence and killed them.

On the ground were seaweed-clogged nets and piles of metal cages, some filled with crabs. If no one knew that the Port was actually part of the Twin Cities, they would think it was an entirely different place. It seemed too dirty, too filled with the scent of death and cooked meat to ever be able to be a part of something as ethereal as the Inner or Outer City.

I scrunched my nose and looked away, painfully aware of the stares I was getting. Clearly, people in bright dresses that were half sheer didn't frequent the Port much. But I pushed the thoughts aside and continued down the street.

Up ahead was the harbor, filled to the brim with ships, each bearing a different flag, each unloading or loading heavy crates on the backs of several men and women. From each boat was a different scream, a different arrangement of letters to signify a command. I made my way down the wooden walkway, eyeing the ships, breathing in the salted air.

"All aboard!" A whistle sang through the air, splitting eardrums. Not far from where I stood, a ship, bearing the white with a golden and red dragon flag of the Shao Yun Islands, detached all its ropes, sending the ends into the water. All around me, people walked, little kids ran and jumped over wooden crates, and horns blared, filling the atmosphere with an unpleasant sound. I closed my eyes, ignoring the consent blaring of horns and yells and whistling to signal a million different things. I walked, until the noises faded, and were traded for the sea side banter of all sorts of nations.

I looked up, past the bars filled with half-drunken sailors, and saw a cluster of trees. The park. It consisted of a half-dried sheet of uneven grass, maybe about six trees, a fountain that looked far too clean to be there and precisely one bench.

A small building, made from stone with a terracotta roof and golden designs painted all over it, stood beneath the largest of the trees. The windows were large, clean and tinted black. On the front face of the building, there was a sign, hanging from metal links, painted gold with an image of a large ship.

King's Port.

I smiled to myself and took a deep breath.

"Alright Siv, time to get some answers."

Outside a man leaned against the wall, smoking something, stark white smoke coming from his mouth in perfect "o" shapes. His eyes lazily met mine, and he smiled, lopsided and half drunkenly.

"Hell..." he blinked in the slowest motion, "o". Then the man burped. I stood there, my head cocked to one side, looking at him, trying to hide my disgust.

"Hi," I managed, before walking up to the bar door and pushing it open. The moment I stepped inside, the smell of strong alcohol and smoke hit me.

"Oh, sweet Darkness," I breathed, blinking, standing in the doorway.

This bar was *hideous*. Across the large room, where the floor was wood and scratched and stained with something dark brown that looked suspiciously like blood, there was the bar. Which was a slab of wood, on top of a short wall made of wood, with a wall of wood behind it filled with wooden shelves saturated with ornate looking bottles filled with colorful liquids. A dirty cracked mirror hung in the center doing a terrible job at reflecting anything. Stools at the bar were covered in ripped fabric. The tables in the center of the room were just as scratched as the floor, damp with old liquor that was never wiped up.

This bar looked like it belonged of the tiny villages of Meris, not the Twin Cities. Not Sunsier, not Moonsier, not a city where the walls glowed with magic and flowers never died.

There was not a single woman in sight. Only men, dressed in pale, earthy tones, baggy wrinkled shirts, a glass filled with the brim with brown liquid in their hands. All of them, as if under a spell, turned their heads to glare me down. Some of their eyes widened in shock, as if no woman had ever stepped foot into this place.

Not that I would blame them for never doing so. This place looked and smelled like shit.

"Well, well," one finally spoke, in a thick Sunsieran accent. He stood up, alcohol in hand. "Look at what we—"

"A woman." I cut him off, my patience for the males, females, people in general, already thin. "Surprising? Yes. But I'm sure you will all be able to continue your lives peacefully anyway."

I let the door slam shut behind me and made my way to the bar, where the man, the only one dressed in black, stood.

"This is not a place for ladies, miss." He spoke brutally, his dark brown eyes boring into mine.

"Sir, this isn't a place for *anybody*."

Someone behind me snorted. Alcohol probably spewed from his nose onto someone else, because just seconds later a man yelled.

The man at the bar rolled his eyes. "Only a woman would say that." He huffed, looking me up and down, "What do you want? A drink?"

"If you have water, and I mean drinkable water, that would be great. I'm parched, this heat sucks all the moisture out of you. I find it extremely annoying."

"Agreed!" Another stranger yelled, and then a shattering of glass. Holy Darkness this place was a shitshow.

"We do not have *drinkable* water here, miss, sorry."

I hid my displeasure. "That's alright, but perhaps you'll have the information I'm looking for."

The man shrugged, sipping his drink. "Perhaps we do, but no information is ever free."

"Never expected it to be. How much would you want?"

He stared at me so intently I was certain he started looking through me, not even at me. As if he was seeing the scenery behind me while gazing into my eyes. He blinked, cocking his head, in deep thought.

"Five hundred Kronas," he finally replied. This time I would have snorted out a drink if I had one.

Five hundred Kronas? Is he mad?

I sighed, "Alright, but first the information."

He shook his head, "No, the money first."

"Information *first*, money *after*," I repeated, staring him down, sending daggers in his direction. The man shifted uncomfortably, his eyes quickly darting from mine to look anywhere else but at me.

Silence. Not even the men behind seemed to be breathing.

Finally, he spoke, "Fine. What is it you want to know?"

I willed the blood inside my hand to harden and poke through my skin in a thin string. And slowly it twisted, turned and formed the symbol I needed it to and once the symbol started glowing, I looked back at the man, straight into his eyes.

"Where can I find the Neithisis?"

Silence. And then his head moved closer to me, in the way it would when someone didn't think they heard something right.

"What?"

"The Neithisis," I repeated, "Where can I find one?"

Now he laughed. "You, you cannot be serious."

"I assure you, I am *entirely* serious," I replied bluntly.

He stopped, blinking, looking at me intently. "What in the hell would you want with one of them?"

"Research purposes." I said, "Time...sensitive research purposes." I added, hoping he'd catch onto the fact that I didn't have all day for him to process the information.

The man narrowed his eyes, taking a fat gulp of his drink, downing it completely before slamming the glass down, shattering it. "You are going to be disappointed; I do not know where to find such a beast."

I looked down at the symbol floating above my hand. I could feel my hope dampen as I watched the symbol softly glow bright red.

"But I know who does."

My head jerked up, my heart leaping, pounding at my ribcage. I drew in a breath. "What?"

"I know who does." The man repeated, and my eyes darted down to my hand for a split second, enough to see the symbol glowing, enough to know he was telling the truth and that there was still hope.

"Are they here?"

He shook his head, "No. He lives in the Merchants' Quarter, near the..." he eyed me, "darker part of the city. If you know what I mean."

I forced myself to not roll my eyes. "Yeah, yes, I know what you mean."

"Then you know that you should not go there, ever. Unless you are accustomed to the place, to its people. It is a very different world."

"My world isn't like the Twin Cities, sir," I assured him. My world is very much like the darker part of the city, only cleaner. And with less alcohol.

He raised a brow. "Well then, walk in that direction until you get to the Stone's End. It is an inn, the building beside it, should be a dark building with a lot of trees around it and moonflowers. But do not let them fool you, a monster lives inside the house they surround. His name is Khadir. Blonde hair, wears only black, a large red scar down his face and his left hand is covered in burn scars."

This time I raised a brow.

The man chuckled. "Do not play with fire."

"Oh never!" I waved a hand in the air in total agreement. *I prefer blood anyway*, but those words, I left unsaid.

"He knows what you want to know, but be careful, he is a snake. He will twist words to make you take a deal that ends in his favor and not yours. He is a professional liar, a man who can spin your dreams into nightmares and still make them seem like dreams. He will seem loyal, he will make you trust him and you will see him as a friend, but he is not. Everyone who goes to him regrets it. They only go because they are desperate enough." He paused, eyeing me intently. "Are you sure, very sure, that you are desperate enough?"

"Yes." I nodded, keeping a straight face. I am desperate enough but I would never let this Khadir twist any of my words. I had dealt with professional con men who could say a few sweet things and weave a nightmare worse than any you've ever felt.

"Then I am truly sorry for you."

I ignored him. "Do I just walk in and ask for him?"

The man chuckled, "No, no. You do that, you are dead before you even see his face. No," he shook his head and snatched a bottle of thick liquid to his left. He popped off the cork and filled another glass to the brim with the drink. I fought the urge to pinch my nose from its potent odor. I didn't even want to fathom what it could possibly be.

"You," he continued, sticking the cork back in the bottle, "need to make an offer, one he cannot refuse. Go in, and you will see a woman. Make your offer. If she sits there, he is not interested. If she gets up to go to another room, Khadir is interested. And then," he raised his arm, sticking out his finger and pointing at me. "That is when you start to pray to whatever god or goddess you believe in because that will be the point of no return."

I nodded, mentally preparing myself to be ready for this man. He could be a mage perhaps, so I would need more than just my usual dagger. I could need extra blades in case this Khadir tried anything funny.

"If he comes out, he will ask you what you want, and until you make a deal that you both seemingly agree on, you cannot leave."

"Does he have magic?" I asked, innocently.

At that, the man glared at me and jabbed his finger in the air in my direction. "*Do not*, and I mean, *do not* use magic if you have any. Do not try. Do not even think about it. He is the most powerful mage I have seen."

"So, walk in, make my offer, and when he comes out, ask him to tell me where the Neithisis is. Where I can find one, correct?"

The man ran a hand through his thick curly hair. "Yes," he sighed, thinking I was no doubt mad.

"Well thank you very much." I looked down, this time bidding the blood to form another symbol. One that was a little more complicated than the last. "Five hundred Kronas, yes?" I asked again.

The man shook his head, "No," he held a hand out, shaking it. "You will need it to bargain with the worst mage alive."

At that, I smiled and looked into the man's eyes.

"You don't seriously believe he is the worst mage? Have you not heard the atrocities of the mages in the Kingdom Lands?"

"Oh yes, of course, we all have. But trust me, I know that he is worse than they could ever be."

I almost felt sorry for him, for Khadir too. For he, they, did not know just how terrible we could be. Or perhaps this man was right, perhaps Khadir was worse than us. But somewhere, deep down, a part of me knew that wasn't entirely possible.

"Well thank you, really, you've been a great help."

"You sure you do not want a drink? You might want to consider having some liquid courage before facing the devil, no?"

I stared down at the glass in the middle of us, the one filled with thick liquid, like starch. I gulped.

"No thank you," I declined. "I'm perfectly fine."

"Careful around him, miss," he blurted out when I stepped back to go. I nodded.

I assured him, "I will be."

"He's dangerous, miss," The man pushed. "He's not someone you want to cross. Ever."

"Oh," I shrugged, "I'm not worried." I made my way to the door and opened it, smiling sweetly at all the men who had no doubt been listening to our conversation.

As soon as I reached for the door handle, I turned around and the man huffed, shaking his head, perhaps asking himself how I could say such a thing and praying to his gods for nothing terrible to happen.

"You should be." He picked up the tiny drink in front of him and downed it, this time only setting the glass down and not shattering it.

"I know." I smiled, wickedly and walked out the door, letting it fall shut behind me, letting the men inside decipher the meaning behind my malicious smile.

XXV : SIVREHYA RITHLOREN

Twin Cities
Sunsier, Outer City

Slowly the sun began to set, turning a once brilliant blue sky into several shades of red and yellow. There were still a couple of hours left before the city changed into Moonsier, and as I walked from the Port and back into the Outer City, I could see the day life change slowly into the night. Market stands and vendors started packing their things up and hoisting their sacks onto their animals, piling them into carts or carrying them on their backs. As the solar mages filtered out, in came the lunar mages, carrying sacks filled with different trinkets and items.

And one vendor stand at a time, the night market began to come to life. All that was left now was the magic that made it seem truly alive.

As I walked through the streets, towards the Stone's End Inn where the man said that pretty house with all the deceiving flowers was, I regretted not taking the shorter route. According to the map I had seen painted on one of the walls of a building near the gate to the Port, walking through the dirty part of the city seemed to take less time. The city was built like a circle, with a fourth of it chopped off by the ocean. Had I taken the route through the darker part of the city, I would have reached the house without having to cross the entire Outer City.

Unless I found a place to hide. For just a second. For just enough time to portal myself out of here without anyone seeing. If only this place wasn't constantly crawling with people everywhere. Even in the thinnest alleyways where barely one person could fit there were people. Under vendor stands doing Darkness knows what, or even on the rooftops of all the buildings making a fire, cooking, hanging clothing...making out.

I immediately looked away from the couple that was eating each other alive. They were simply standing on one of the lower rooftops, completely unaware of the number of people giving them a raised brow look. I, among them.

Shaking my head, I continued down the road. If I didn't manage to find a good hiding spot, I'd have to walk an hour to get to the Stone's End Inn.

Curse me for not taking the shorter route through the slums, I slapped myself mentally. Because there, it would be shorter and easier to find a place where no one would be.

My feet might as well have been out to kill me.

I stood in front of the Stone's End Inn, looking up at the window of my room, sighing. Looking down at my shoes, I frowned at the worn leather, the burned orange-colored sand that imprinted itself on the material and would never get off.

And, I hadn't been able to find a single place to portal myself out, as every single damn dark corner, every shadowy area, every small alley had been leaching with people.

The scenery around the Stone's Inn was different, darker and quieter; everything was more still. There was still life, there were always people laughing, but there were no vendors, no children running around chasing each other. And the laughing was distant.

I stretched my arms out, squeezing my eyes shut to let the tension out and then I let them fall limp beside me.

"And so, the search begins," I whispered, walking past the Stone's End, and making my way further down the road, my eyes peeled for a pretty house with deceiving flowers.

My eyes settled on one building, black as night with silver curtains from which golden light seeped through. On the outside, there was a patch of impeccably well-kept grass and *flowers*. I narrowed my eyes, seeing their silver-blue and lilac petals that shimmered ever so softly. Moonflowers. My eyes floated back to the building, to the entrance. I took a deep breath in and out, closing them for just a second and feeling for my power.

I trusted it, I trusted in it, in myself. But every now and then I delved deep and checked, perhaps out of fear, or something else.

I opened my eyes, narrowing them at the door. This man was bad, terrible, horrific. He had magic. And no doubt would have some extremely complicated spell to make sure no one with magic would even step into his house without being cursed immediately. Which meant before even stepping into that building I needed a protection spell against him.

So, I raised an arm, opened my palm and I bid my blood to follow my command. Protection spells always varied in how complicated they were. The more specific, the harder they were, the more concentration and memorization it took to perfect every twist, line, and dot. Slowly the blood stopped glowing, and it hardened. Then, I felt a wave of warmth surround me, seeping into me.

I looked back at the house, performing a quick healing spell before my feet carried me to the door and my hand knocked on the wooden door.

Alright Siv, I told myself, taking a deep breath in and out. I could do this, I've seen worse, dealt with worse.

Slowly, so slowly, with creaks that made it seem like it was groaning in pain, the door opened. Behind it was a large room with white walls, lit by thousands of floating golden orbs bumping into each other. To my left there was nothing; to the right there was nothing. In front of me, across the room, there was a pair of black double doors and beside them, a lilac chaise lounge chair, on which a woman was laying. She had fading dark brown hair with silver streaks running through it. She wore a see-through silver dress and seemingly nothing underneath. But it was her eyes that caught me most off guard. They were golden, or used to be...they were milky, with some hint of silver in their depths. As if her eyes were covered in the same fabric she was dressed in.

"Hello?" I said, uneasily. I grimaced, tensing, the moment her eyes locked onto mine and she stood up, slowly, and started walking in my direction. There was something off about her. She didn't seem like herself, as if her movements were the commands of others and she was following them. She seemed like a marionette doll, with a fake smile plastered on her face.

"Miss?" I asked. The lady remained quiet, still smiling. I looked around quickly, trying to sense if there was something that could explain her incredibly odd behavior. She seemed to be possessed, and I seemed to have walked in the middle of a horror world. With ghosts and spirits.

"Miss?" I repeated, and then she stopped.

"What," she started, her voice eerily hollow, "do you want?"

"I," I looked around again, my eyes narrowing, as they glanced past an intricate symbol glowing on the ceiling. "I..." I trailed off, unable to take my eyes away.

"I would like to talk to Khadir. I need information."

I could have sworn that symbol looked impossibly similar to the blood magic symbol used to cloak magic. To hide its presence.

"What information?" The woman's hollow voice pulled me from my trance. She cocked her head to the side. I looked into her eyes with so much life yet none at all.

"Information on the Neithisis."

The woman continued to smile, like a doll. "That will cost you."

"Cost me what?" I stepped back, my back hitting the door. The woman seemed unfazed, but I was. The blood was rushing inside me, my power, coming alive, running around through my veins in a frenzy as if it sensed something I didn't.

She brought her head back to the middle in a stiff movement and took her eyes from mine as if she was pondering an answer to give to me.

"What are you willing to give for the information?" She asked, looking back at me.

"It depends if you have it," I responded after taking a little too long to think about it.

"Payment first, then information. What are you willing to give for the information?"

I huffed, rolling my eyes, and using the wall behind me to propel myself towards her. I stopped mere feet from her, eyeing her entirely before I caught a sniff of something disgusting. Like rotting flesh. Something dead was in the room. I shook my head, looking back at the woman, seeing for the first time the discoloration in her skin.

"No," I started, ignoring the smell and her ghostly appearance, "*information* first, then payment."

At that the woman said nothing. Instead, she simply turned around and made her way back to the chaise lounge. She laid on it, and then the moment her eyes closed the double doors slammed open, sending vibrations through the walls and the door.

From the darkness came out a man, with pale skin, sickly blonde hair, dressed in entirely black with a black cloth covering his eyes. The scar on his face, the one the man from the bar told me about, was practically glowing red from the light. His left hand was so brutally disfigured with bright red patches, pink bumps and black spots, that it barely even looked like a hand anymore.

"I must say," the man, Khadir, started speaking, his voice dangerous, but pleasant to listen to. Perhaps this was how he could trick so many people into giving him what he wanted with nothing in return. His voice was charming enough. "You are the first woman, man, first anyone to ever demand anything with such confidence."

I raised a brow. So, he had heard what I said to the woman. But how? I looked him up and down, trying my best to decipher the type of mage he was. Lunar or solar. His eyes, the biggest clue, were hidden.

"Am I?" I asked, plastering a smile on my face.

"Yes." He stepped forward.

"Then you know I want something."

"And you know, I want something as well."

"What do you want?" My body was still tense, and deep inside a pit of acidic agony grew.

"How desperate are you for the information, how far are you willing to go, what are you willing to do?" He bared his teeth, as the golden light of the room shrouded him in such a way that made him glow in wickedness, like a villain from the horror tales of my childhood. He spoke the way Jorus Darholm of Meris did. The *bloody* traitor whose name I had taken years to forget, the traitor whose memory still plagued mine, whose existence found its way into my dreams and twisted them into nightmares.

"Desperate enough," I replied, as bluntly as I could.

The man smiled. "Good, then perhaps you're willing to give me your name."

Excuse me what?

I was expecting money, a ridiculous amount of money. Sex. Him wanting me to steal this impossible object from an impossible place in an hour. But my *name*?

"I—I'm sorry?"

"A name is too much? Fine then," He sighed, "No information."

"No, no, no. I *need* to know what you know about the Neithisis."

"Then, give me your name."

I stood back, looking at him, staring at him right where his eyes would be. If they were visible. And I wondered if, through the cloth, he could see me with a brow raised, narrowed eyes, asking myself how mad he was.

Names didn't hold any magical power by themselves, but in the wrong hands, in the wrong mind with the wrong magic, they could. A name could be worth millions. A name could send chills down someone's spine or light up their world; it all depended on who knew it and what they wanted with it, what they could gain from it.

"Could I give you something else?"

He crossed his arms, and his head lifted, turning as if he was looking off in different directions for the answer.

"No."

"How do I know you're telling the truth?"

He pointed to the woman resting on the couch, whose eyes suddenly burst open and she immediately sat up, raising her hands in the hair, twisting them in some weird fashion until a golden symbol appeared in the air. And she looked at me and she threw it. The moment it hit me, I fell back from the sheer force and slowly it began to tear into me, trying to stab through the protection spell I cast. And once it was unable to it fell limp to the floor beside me, burning into the floor with a defeated squeal of smoke and flame.

"Well, well, a mage. How quaint."

I stood up, huffing. My patience was gone.

"Listen, I need to know where I can find the Neithisis, a Neithisis. So, tell me."

"And if I don't." He mocked, still smiling, cocking his head to one side. "What then?"

"I'll—" I started, but I clamped my mouth shut, knowing it was best to not say what I was about to say.

"Well? You'll what?" He repeated, pressing me for the answer. But when my mouth remained closed, he laughed. "What could you possibly do to me, anyway?"

I stood silent, all the million of answers to his question filling my head. But I didn't say a single word. Might as well let him think he's won, think that he is the king of the world and that I am just a dreamer who believed too fiercely in an impossible dream.

"She doesn't seem to want to talk." Khadir chuckled at his lady friend, who mirrored his action while twisting a chunk of hair around her finger. "Suddenly too shy?" He turned back to me, baring his stark white teeth in a feral smile.

No, I just don't really know where to start, I thought, remaining utterly silent.

The man laughed again, and it sent chills through my spine. I stepped back. There was something off about him, something darker than I expected.

He bent down his eyes, smiling the entire time, as his hands fumbled with the knot of the cloth behind his head. And suddenly it dropped to the floor, and he looked back up.

And then the world seemed to slow down and stop.

And everything seemed to make perfect sense. The woman's strange movements, her eyes, the man's strange request.

I gulped, doing my best to hide the fear that slowly started to eat me from inside. The shock that was bubbling through me as I tried to process what I was seeing. And what it meant. I blinked, my heart suddenly pounding, I could almost hear the blood rushing through my veins as my eyes met his.

His very glowing, shining, *silver* eyes.

XXVI : IVAR THAEGAN

The Twin Cities
Sunsier, Outer City

I looked at the house, staring it down like it was my newest enemy. If the words of the stranger from the slums were to reign true, then in here was another soul mage. One that apparently hurt and killed without reason. I sighed, clenching my fists.

I am worse. I am worse. I am always worse, I thought to myself, letting the words run through my head. They were all I was taught to believe in. To be the worst, the cruelest, strongest, the most terrible, the most wicked. That was how one survived. It was how I had survived my father this long, how I had survived living in a kingdom that was divided between people that idolized you and those who plotted to kill you.

I made my way up to the door and I tensed, sensing something dark. It seeped through the door, into the air, all around me. I closed my eyes. This scent wasn't mine; it was the scent of the soul mage beyond the door. So far, the words of the man reigned true. I took a deep breath.

I have fought plenty of soul mages in my life, and I have killed all of them except my father. But he was my father; no one who had fought him had ever won and barely any had lived. I was the exception and I was still surprised that I was.

My eyes floated down to the silver door handle.

Now or never, Ivar.

I could feel inside me there was a storm brewing; my power was coming to life again as if it knew it would be useful to me. As if it knew there was a fight coming.

Slowly I twisted the handle, the door opening, revealing...I froze. My blood froze. The world stopped.

The princess and a silver-eyed man were facing each other, looks of murder on both their faces. And on a chaise lounge behind them was a rotting woman.

"Ivar?" Sivrehya whispered, her eyes met mine for just a second before she let out a bloodcurdling scream and fell to the floor. Her eyes, once red, once brown, slowly turned a faded beige lined with silver.

My eyes moved from the princess who laid sprawled at awkward angles on the floor and a man who I assumed was none other than Khadir. He had the large red scar the man had told me about, his left hand was brutally burned, and his clothing was blacker than ink.

"Another soul mage? I must say, I haven't seen one of my own kind since I left Lysmir for good."

This time *our* eyes locked. His were a darker shade of silver, almost grey. His smile, baring his white teeth, held a lethal threat. Like an animal, looking at its prey, smiling as it imagined its fangs stripping through soft flesh.

"Do you not talk either?" He cocked his head to one side. I blinked, unable to figure out what to say. I looked over at Sivrehya, her milky brown eyes staring blankly at the ceiling.

Khadir had taken her soul hostage. She still had it, she was aware of everything, but it was his to control like a puppet.

I looked back at the man, my fists still clenched, my power still swimming inside me, making a storm, begging me to unleash it. To kill this man. But I ignored its pleas and stepped forward.

"You know her?"

Unfortunately.

"Yes," I said, my voice blunt.

"How?"

"That doesn't matter. You know why she is here?" I asked, teeth gritted.

"I do, *Ivar*," He paused, noticing my body tensed at my name. "I can call you that, right? After all, *she* called you that." He eyed the princess, forever sprawled on the floor, her red dress surrounding her like bloody flower petals. "And, as you are a soul mage, would I be wrong in thinking you're perhaps the prince of Lysmir?"

I relaxed my hand just a bit, but my senses were still on high alert. For some reason, I didn't think my name, what terrible history it held, would scare the man away. He hadn't even faltered when Sivrehya said it, and now, he seemed to be as calm as ever.

"No, you wouldn't be," I responded bluntly.

The man smiled again, stepping forward. "My, my, whatever have I done to be honored with your presence? Truly, I am shocked a mage of such high status would come visit a low-life such as myself." His devil-like smile contradicted any geniality the tone of his voice held.

"So," I took another step forward, "You're not afraid of me?"

I didn't have the time to talk with him, to listen to his casual threats and pretend not to notice he believed he was the most powerful mage ever. This game of his would turn in my favor.

He widened his eyes, putting a hand to his chest. I fought the urge to roll my eyes. Any more dramatic acting and I might lose it.

"Oh no, I'm not. I have heard the tales of your horrors, of what you have done. They are what make so many, if not all, fear you, but not me."

I hid my surprise behind my smile. If he wanted to act like this was a play being shown to an audience, so be it. "Oh, great. See, I came here for the same reason she did. And I really don't have the time for someone who is going to tremble and scream just from my presence. So, I mean, thank the Dark Father you are someone who isn't afraid, who I can be straight forward with and all."

The man stilled, blinking. His mouth opened, only for him to close it just as quickly. The shock on his face quickly masked with a lethal gaze and a serpentine smile.

"You're lying, clearly you're surprised someone isn't afraid of you. And here is the thing. I do have information on the Neithisis, but I need payment."

I remembered all the moments of breathing, of clenching my hands so hard that my nails dug into my skin, just so I wouldn't burst. But I didn't have time to waste. And this man might not know of the impending war that threatened to destroy half the world, but that didn't mean I had to deal with his bullshit act of him being the master of the universe.

Fuck it, I thought as I stepped forward, this time smiling for real, letting the wicked side come out.

"Your payment will be your life. Tell me what I need to know and I'll let you live."

Khadir was about to laugh, about to throw his hands in the air and laugh like a madman. But I didn't give him the chance. I took a hold of part of his soul and ripped it out of him violently, holding it above him, leaving the rest inside him shaking.

He fell to his knees, screaming. "No, no, please." He shrilled, thrashing on the floor. I knew the pain he was in; I had felt it once. It was like a fire eating you alive at the same time that ice was crawling all over you. It seemed like you were underwater because you couldn't breathe, and it was as if someone was stabbing you all over, your blood was leaving you and your mind was aware of it all.

"Tell me where to find the Neithisis, Khadir. I am not playing games. You want the rest of your soul, then tell me where the beast is."

He cried out, clawing at his eyes until they started bleeding. Until his fingers were caked in scarlet and his face was red. I clenched my other hand, stilling him. The rest of his pitiful soul under my control.

Suddenly the room was quiet, save for his panting, his soft crying.

"*Tell* me."

"You are a monster!" He shrieked. I rolled my eyes.

"Yeah, I know that. But tell me something I don't know, like the location of the *fucking* Neithisis."

"Please d—don't hurt me."

"Do not try to beg, it does nothing. Now, do not make me ask you again. I am perfectly capable of putting you through more pain than this." I managed to spit out through gritted teeth. I had his life in my fists, and he was so willing to beg, thinking I would listen. Or care.

I could see him reach for his power as he realized it was no longer his, but mine. He had left Lysmir, he left the real world and traded it for a fantasy. I was willing to bet he hadn't fought another soul mage in all those years.

"Please..." he mouthed, tears streaming down his face, catching the color of his blood.

"You got used to being the king of mages here in the city, where a soul mage would always be feared no matter what." I crouched down to meet his gaze, or what was left of it. "You were used to being undefeated, used to being the strongest, the worst, the darkest. Because after all, we are not like our solar or lunar counterparts. We are not nice. We do not fall easily into traps. We twist the game someone else is the master of, and we do not have hearts. You know that, but even if you do, you've forgotten what it's like to fight one of your own."

He hung his head, trying, trying to call to his magic, to escape from the reality of my words.

Suddenly someone screamed. My head snapped in the direction of the shrill only to see the woman who had been sleeping on the chaise lounge chair was lopsidedly walking towards us. Her eye color was a dulled gold, her skin almost green and pale with discoloration. Her teeth browned and chipped, her hair half gone from her head.

"Help, oh *gods*, what is..." And she fell, landing on her head, and a thick brown liquid oozed from her wounds. Flies appeared from nowhere, multiplying, as a pungent odor of rotten flesh and death filled the air. I gagged, looking away, letting go for just one second.

And pain. It exploded within me, and when I screamed, nothing came out. But someone laughed, a man. Khadir. He stood once again, over me, watching me fall slowly to the ground on my knees. My soul, slowly being pulled out of me. I winced, keeping a firm hold on my life source, half of his still clenched in my right hand, the dull silver light of it slipping through.

"Fool!" He bellowed, laughing. I rolled my eyes, standing through the pain.

"I think we *all* know who the real fool is, Khadir."

I turned around to face the direction of the voice, the pain rising inside me from my soul being pulled out flickered out.

There was a thud and Khadir mumbled, "How?"

Because standing, with eyes once again brown and a lethally calm face, was the princess. She cocked her head, smiling just a little, her eyes landing on me, then on Khadir.

"How the hell—"

She raised a hand, and the man doubled over, groaning, once again on the ground.

"I suggest you get better at multitasking." She spat, crouching down to meet his pained gaze. "Or not get so easily distracted that you so foolishly yet thankfully give me back my soul." She smiled wickedly and her eyes met mine.

"You b—"

"Bitch, yes, understood." The princess frowned, rolling her eyes.

I turned back to Khadir, "You need to accept that you have lost. Your empire has lost its emperor. Accept it."

The man spat in my direction. "Damn you all. I will stay silent. I may have fallen, but the truth you so desperately need will die with me. So, go ahead, do your worst, soul mages."

"Hold on," Sivrehya interjected, stepping towards him. "Did you say soul *mages*, as in both of us," she pointed to herself, then moved to me and back and forth, "are soul mages?"

The man nodded, his head hanging.

"How *dare* you, I am a blood mage. Not a filthy soul mage, please." She scoffed.

"Ahem," I coughed, glaring at her.

"What? Like you haven't called me worse." She shrugged her shoulders and moved the hair out of her face and behind her ears. "And on *that* note, let me just use some of your blood to work some magic, make a symbol to force the truth out of you by maybe burning you, no, breaking bones..." She continued in a sing-song voice, and with her head turning ever so slightly to meet the man's gaze, she winked. "That method never fails to work."

Khadir jerked back. "Stay away from me you demon, don't you dare cast one of your curses on me."

I almost laughed. As if saying that would do anything to stop the princess from casting her little magic trick.

"First of all, it's a *spell*, not a curse." She scowled, "Second, it will hurt, so..." Her eyes trailed up and down the man, considering him. "Prepare yourself."

I watched as she bid the blood from his eyes to form a circle, then another and another until they were more shapes in one and then lines and twists and little loops all glowing until it was finished. And the moment the light went out he screamed a blood-curdling, ear-shattering scream.

"It won't stop until you tell us." Sivrehya stood back up, eyeing me.

It. But what was *it*, I asked myself, watching in silence as the man writhed on the floor. Perhaps it was pain, pain that crawled inside him, plunging him into an infernal nightmare.

"Should I destroy half of his soul," I raised my still clenched hand, "to worsen the pain?"

Before she could answer the man screamed out a name. Both of us snapped our heads in his direction.

"What did you say?" I barked, pressing him to repeat.

"The Raven Mountains, in a cave. Any cave, it's impossible to tell. That is where you will find a Neithisis."

"Go on," I pressed, needing there to be more.

"Height," and then he screamed again. "They like height and the cold, freezing cold."

"So, they're more likely to be in a cave higher on the tallest mountains?" Sivrehya asked, her one hand still raised; her spell unwavering.

Khadir panted, catching his breath. "Y—yes, yes." He stumbled, groaning in pain.

Suddenly, the princess smiled, dropping her arm and the symbol fell with it, splattering on the ground. Khadir fell to the floor, whimpering, crying.

I sighed, letting go of his soul, having heard far too much ear-aching screaming to bear anymore. The moment the two pieces stitched themselves back together, Khadir seemed to relax, just a bit.

"So," I finally said once silence began to take over. "It takes one of your bloody spells to get this man to fucking talk?" I frowned, annoyed at the simple fact that Sivrehya was able to force the infor-mation out of him.

"No, pain does. He clearly didn't feel enough. If you destroyed half the soul to begin with, then maybe he would have spilled."

This time I let the silence filter in and settle.

"At least," Sivrehya started, brushing her hands through her hair. "At least now we know where to find this monster."

I looked at her, "Why didn't you tell me you found out about this place? Why the hell didn't you just *leave*?"

There was a foreign feeling in me, hurt, betrayal. I didn't know, but it was there, in the smallest amount, just floating inside me. I ignored it, just as I ignored the fact she wouldn't have had the slightest idea where to find me after she had found out about this place. Ignoring the fact that even when I found out about it, the thought of telling her hadn't crossed my mind.

She turned to face me; her tired eyes didn't search mine. Instead she just leaned against a wall and sighed, "I don't know."

I felt a wave of red heat wash over me slowly. "What do you mean you don't know?"

"I mean I don't know. I—I'm not used to this detective work, to having to walk around this damn city a million times a day just to find out something."

"And?" I cut her off, feeling my power once again start to sing with anger inside me.

"And *what*? I was—" She sighed, defeated and tired. And part of me understood her. I was tired, beyond tired of everything. Of trying to find this stupid monster, of the walking endlessly asking a million people for help. I hated all of it.

"You just left."

"Fine!" She pushed herself from the wall, "I—I'm sorry that I left. Does that make it better?"

I scoffed, "No it doesn't. You're the one who proposed this whole bullshit partnership and then you leave and not bother to say or do anything."

"I know, dammit," She threw her hands up in the air. "Look," She sighed , "Forget it—"

"Forget it? What the hel—"

"Yes, forget it! Tomorrow morning let's just go find the freaking beast, get the fucking truth so we can fight and kill each other, because I'm pretty sure not being able to do that is the whole problem!" She screamed in frustration as she yanked on the door handle, marching out.

I followed her, into the wooded area behind the house. "You know, I agree, not being able to kill my mortal enemy despite them being right in front of me is *really* fucking difficult."

"Right back at you!" She hollered, stopping in the middle of a grassy area surrounded by trees.

"This would be a lot easier if you didn't want to kill us all."

She turned to face me, marching towards me with a finger pointed at me as if it were a dagger. "How *dare* you say that?" She gritted out, her pale face red and tense.

"Whatever do you mean, *Rithloren*?"

"Do you think I *want* to eradicate an entire race of mages?" She countered, stepping back.

"You and your family are pretty hellbent on destroying us!" I shot back, stumbling back when she launched forward and pushed me.

"As if *you* and your family aren't hellbent on destroying us!" She pushed her hair out of her face, as she pointed to herself. "Look, I get it, you have no reason to believe me, but I don't want to eradicate all of the soul mages that exist. Despite the fact that I absolutely bloody hate you with all I'm worth, I really don't wish to destroy all of you. I might be cold-blooded and heartless but even *that* is beyond me. Beyond any of us."

"Then why are you fighting to destroy us? *Hm.*" I could swear steam was coming from my ears.

She stepped back, her body tensing up, almost trembling. "We're fighting to defend ourselves! And our people! Because my brother refuses to wage war on lies, and if he thinks for one second that you're telling the truth about not killing our father, then he won't fight to avenge a lost one, he'll fight to survive! Because *you* are the ones that want to kill us all, *you* are the ones that want to destroy us and all we're worth. Because *your* father, your king was the one who proclaimed war on *us.*" She paused, sighing, covering her face with her hands as she shook her head. "And while we all fucking hate you, we're really just defending ourselves. But if that means destroying your kingdom and you in the process, so be it then." She stopped, glaring at me. Her eyes might be a dull brown, but they were just as piercing as they were when red.

There was a silence, and in it, we simply looked into each other's eyes. Not to scavenge a lie, or see if we were being genuine with our words, but instead to just realize, for once, perhaps, we weren't so different from each other. But then Sivrehya looked past me, her face paled, her eyes glowing with pure fury, and was it fear? There was something foreign in her eyes, floating there like an imposter.

"Sivrehya?" I whispered, still looking at her, but she refused to turn her eyes back to mine. She remained perfectly still, like a statue. "Sivre—"

"Shh, be quiet, I heard something."

"Yeah, it's probably the steam coming from my ears. Because do you really expect me to think you just want to def—"

She took her eyes off from whatever and they landed on me, in the form of death. "No," she scolded.

"My n—"

"Shut up, will you?"

"Oh," I pretended to be hurt, "Excuse me? Manners?"

This time she smiled, deviously. "Oh right, of course. I am so sorry. Let me try again; Prince Ivar Thaegan of Lysmir, Your Royal Highness, would you please, pretty please, shut your fucking mouth?"

I glared at her, sending daggers in her direction but she simply looked at me, blinking, and shrugged.

"What? You said *manners*, not language."

"I swear to Darkness I wil—"

"Yes, I know. But be quiet."

"Why?"

"Because there's...I'm not sure, but something feels different."

Both of us stopped talking. Slowly, I looked around and back at Sivrehya, confused, but then she nodded to something behind me. I turned around and as I felt something drop inside, something else rose up. A bad feeling, itching me, eating me alive slowly. My magic spurred to life, the threads of silver and white tangled themselves in a frenzy. Magic was a strange thing; it could sense things you couldn't. The magic inside all of us, especially the ones touched by Darkness, protected us, or itself. It came to life inside of us when it felt something, anything, that could possibly harm us. It hummed stronger, pulsing in our veins, our bodies, begging to be released and do all the terrible things we could do. And right now, my magic sung, filling my body with heat. I turned around slowly, following her gaze into the darkness that shrouded the trees in front of her. Squinting my eyes, I could see nothing, but I did feel something. Something dark and dangerous. I could almost smell it, and when I did, it felt foreign.

Out of the shadows stepped three figures. In the dim light of the lanterns, I could make out dark hair, pale skin that seemed like the color of the White Hall in my palace. The sickly stark white that was devoid of all feeling and life. Their clothes were green, darker than the trees from which they stepped out. Gold designs decorating their garb sparkled in the fading light.

But my stomach dropped and my power roared when my eyes met the eyes of one of the figures. They were bronze, glowing and gleaming. All three had wicked grins on their faces, and their hands were clenched. Not in a way one would clench when angry, but instead in a way one would when they used *magic*.

The one in the middle, a girl, her hair in two thick dark braids framing her small face, stepped forward and spoke with an accent I had never heard before.

"Hello darlings." Her voice was hollow, sending a chill down my back. It was as if spiders were crawling up and down it, as if the air suddenly froze around us, as if the Darkness itself came and sucked the life, the light, and the noise out of the world.

XXVII : SIVREHYA RITHLOREN

The Twin Cities
Moonsier, Outer City

"I'm sorry, do we know you?" Ivar demanded, his body suddenly in a defensive stance, one hand clenched in a fist.

"Oh no, no, no." The woman's laugh was as chilling as her smile. She waved a dismissive hand in the air, her copper eyes glowing. "Not yet anyway."

"Excuse me?" The prince stepped forward, jaw tightening, body tensing. I watched him close his other hand into a fist.

"My name perhaps will mean something to you. I am Sylaria Aolaine..."

"Yes," I responded, nearly cutting her off.

"Yes?" Ivar turned to look at me, one brow raised. "What does Sylaria Aolaine mean to you?"

"Aolaine is a Vylaran noble hou—" I stopped, my blood chilling at an impossible thought. "Aolaine is a Vylaran noble house," I breathed out, so quietly I almost couldn't hear it myself.

"Really?" Ivar questioned, still looking at me, with the most confused look on his face.

"What do you mean *really*?" I almost laughed, "How do you not kn—ow." In that moment, I swore my heart had stopped.

Stepping back, I looked at the prince, one brow raised and two eyes narrowed. There was no way, no absolute fucking way he didn't know who the Aolaines were. Every royal did, every noble did. They, we, were taught about them, about the Wysterians, about the war that ended the kingdom they reigned.

And yet...

Something in me cracked, shattering and suddenly the world stopped, turning cold. My head turned slowly to face the three strangers. The woman, still smiling like a doll, cocked her head, blinking innocently. But behind those damned copper eyes I knew, I knew what she was doing.

Which shouldn't be possible. It couldn't be...I didn't want it to be.

"You're all supposed to be *dead*." I managed through gritted teeth; my hand clenched so tightly my nails began to dig into my skin.

She smiled, baring her snow-white teeth. "So, you've figured it out. Smart girl." She walked forward, raising her hands and then the world went dark.

I blinked, stepping back, stumbling over a...I looked down. A skull, and another and then I realized I was standing on a mountain of them, overlooking piles and piles across the horizon made of skulls, and hands, and feet, bodies. The sky was grey, a sickly shade of yellow fading in and out. All around me was the smell of death and in the distance, hollow laughter that sent chills down my spine.

I bent down, my chest heaving, my mind spinning until I felt sick.

No, no, no, this can't be happening. This isn't happening. No, they're dead. They're gone. Holy fucking Darkness no, no, no. Shit, holy Dark Mother, no, this can't be real...

I opened my eyes, my body shaking, and I could see the sky turn dark red and suddenly it was raining, red, blood. And the laughter grew louder and louder. I screamed, turning around and gasping for air before I felt myself being pulled under. A hand, and another, and another, grabbed at my dress, pulling me deeper into the mountain of bones. I shrieked, grabbing onto anything to pull myself out, but I couldn't.

"Killer. Killer. Monster. Monster. This is what you deserve for destroying us." Voices laughed, sing-song whispers clouded my mind. I covered my ears, thrashing my legs around, desperately trying to free myself from the bones around my legs, digging into my skin. I gasped for air, my eyes closing as the last sight of the reddened sky raining blood disappeared.

"Blood demon. You thought you could kill us all. You couldn't; we survived." Another wicked laugh, as cold seeped in, surrounding me, suffocating me. Once again there was nothing but darkness, and then pain. Something exploded inside me, burning me like a white-hot fire. My hands were bound in chains, and I could see them slowly start to glow yellow, then orange and red slowly started seeping in.

My voice was hoarse, my throat screaming. The blood I was covered in started steaming, my flesh burning. And all around me, there was laughter, there were angry screams, there were voices that I drowned out who were screaming of revenge. Of their return. Of their revival.

The chaos mages. Chaos mages. They're...Dark Mother...

They were chaos mages. They made chaos. They could make you see things, hear things, so lifelike you think they were real...but they were just illusions. I started breathing again, trying to calm down my heart that was pounding hard against my chest. I held a hand to it, breathing slowly.

"Illusion," I whispered as the voices around me got louder.

"Illusion," I sang, as they chanted revenge.

Illusion, I thought, as they shattered the cold around me and grasped onto me with bony hands.

With my eyes still closed, I focused on my power, filling it inside me, raging like a storm at sea.

How the fuck am I supposed to fight them, I asked, as I slowly opened my eyes, and I was suddenly falling through the sky. I held back a scream as my hair whipped around wildly and my clothes stuck themselves to me. I forced myself to turn around, and below me, there was nothing but water. Except...it was red. A sea of blood.

"Our blood. The blood you spilled, now drown in it you monster!" The voices laughed and screamed, threatening to shatter my eardrums, as I was plunged into the sea of scarlet. I flailed my arms, pushing myself up for air, but there was no hope. I was being dragged down, again. By a hand, a current of hate, I didn't know. I didn't care. Around me cold seeped in, my ears threatened to explode and the air was leaving me. My lungs screamed for it, for me to take a breath. But I couldn't, and slowly, my chest burst, burning.

It's not real, I thought. *It's not real, not real, not real, not real...*

Darkness clouded my vision, my chest heaved, and my body felt weak, slowly feeling like it was floating. I no longer felt the cold around me. Instead, there was a steady warmth. It was almost welcoming. I squeezed my eyes shut, ignoring my burning lungs, my brain begging for air and instead I delved deep into my magic and did the only thing my dark mind could think of.

I focused on the blood, rushing up and down through the body, to and from the blood. I focused on four bodies like this, and one was quieter than the rest, the blood flowing slower.

Ivar, I smiled to myself and then I picked out another one of the three remaining bodies and clenched my fist.

And then there was a scream, broken and scratchy. But it was not one of revenge, not one of anger, but of pain. I opened my eyes once again, and slowly, the sea of red disappeared and I gasped for air, as it came rushing back. I felt myself fall, my body still weak, still aching and shivering. My eyes fluttered open, and around me, I could see the night sky, alive with millions of stars. I could make out the trees, towering above me. The scent of fresh grass hit my nostrils, drowning out the smell of death that plagued me just moments before.

In the distance, I saw a man, dressed in green, on the ground, still screaming. A woman, *the* woman, crouching by him, caressing his face. The third was walking towards me, slowly, his hands in fists. I sighed, closing my eyes.

Rithlorens get up, Rithlorens keep fighting, I said to myself. The golden words my family always said.

Suddenly the man stopped, standing over someone who was gasping for air, his hands gripping to the grass for dear life. Ivar. I blinked, shaking my head, quickly trying to pull myself back to reality.

"What the hell did you do, soul mage?" The man in green kicked at the fallen prince. The words "soul mage" were filled with disgust as they rolled off his tongue.

I froze. They thought Ivar had done it. They thought he had hurt the man that writhed on the ground. And with that thought coursing through my mind I smiled and slowly I stood up, my eyes darting back and forth between the woman whose back was towards me and the man whose eyes were on the prince.

The fallen man controlled the illusions that trapped me. The woman seemed to be doing nothing and the man standing over Ivar, who was making him scream for mercy, controlled his nightmares.

My eyes remained on that man, and I clenched my fist, grabbing onto some blood that someone had spilled. Suddenly, the air was filled with another scream. But this time it didn't come from the prince. It came from the man who was drawing up hideous things in the prince's vision. The man, the one with a blood spear lodged into his left leg, impaling him, looked down, shaking, trying to grab at the spear that fell onto his dark clothes, staining them. And then he fell onto the grass next to the prince.

The woman jerked her head around, her copper eyes blazing and glowing. She trembled, shaking, anger seeping from her reddening face. She walked towards me, in the way a predator would stalk their prey, pointing a pale blaming finger at me.

"*You*—"

"Save your last words for something meaningful, Sylaria Aolaine." I cut her off, holding her still and slowly heating her blood, watching her claw at her throat with sharp nails until it bled. Her eyes were suddenly wide and muddled red as her blood vessels burst. Her pale skin cracked, turning pink as her flesh sizzled and burned. Melted. She opened her mouth to scream, to perhaps curse me and all I was worth, but she fell limp to the ground before she could.

I opened my clenched hand, releasing the dead woman from my magic. I gagged from the odor of it all as I waved the smoke away. Boiling blood never ceased to make a spectacle of itself. It left the person a pile of half-cooked flesh and burned skin. And it smelled *awful*, like death but worse.

I pinched my nose, making my way to the prince who was coughing, clutching his side.

"Get up, these people are fucking chaos mages," I whispered. Slowly he stood up, gasping.

"No shit, I just went through hell, fucking Darkness." He ran a hand through his mud-stained hair.

The two remaining men, eyes holding murder, stood like statues, their arms raised.

"We have to fight them."

Ivar tensed beside me. "How?"

"I don't know, just kill them," I whispered back, eyes still on the men who slowly walked towards up, baring their teeth. "And fast," I added.

The world became a blur as all of us suddenly broke into a run, arms raised. Out of the corner of my eye, was the one I had stabbed earlier, grinning, baring his teeth. I reached for the woman's blood, which was spilling out of her. And slowly in the air, flying, it formed a little spear, and then two and three. And they went flying, quickly, through the man's arms and his waist. His eyes widened as he coughed up blood. I dropped the spears, letting the sharpened form collapse onto the grass. The man choked, falling to his knees. I stopped in front of him.

"What the hell..." he gasped out, clutching at the solid red with quivering hands.

"Spears made of solidified blood, my specialty." I shrugged, smiling, holding my hand up and letting another one form in the air. "It hurts, doesn't it?"

"Fuck you," he said as he spat out blood, his brows furrowed, face red with anger.

Behind me, there was a grunt and a light laugh. I looked over my shoulder only to see the prince punching the second man in his face. I cocked my head, looking at the scene.

What...why...

"What the *hell* are you doing?" I seethed.

"Trying not to die, and fight." He shot back, throwing the man back, letting him fall to the ground. "What the hell are you doing?"

I stared at him, blinking. "Why, *why* are you punching him? And not doing your soul control thing or something more useful?" I flung my arms in the air in disbelief.

"Why can't I hurt him before killing him?"

What...you...Darkness save me.

"I suggest killing him as fast as possible, we don't have time for orchestrated torture."

Ivar rolled his eyes. "I'm going to fight and kill this man however I please, Rithloren," he spat out and I was about to scream in frustration but it was lost inside me.

Suddenly my vision turned completely black, sending me into darkness, and seconds later I was crouched, alone in a desert of red sand, pale-skinned, copper-eyed people walking towards me. But slowly, their necks bent at awkward angles, their faces hollow, limps gone, green armor caked in dried blood. They were dead, but their swords were still in hands and daggers raised high, and their lifeless eyes were on me.

Fuck, I cursed myself for not being more careful with the chaos mage lying on the ground. I turned around, as all walked around me slowly, some smiling. Again, voices filled the air, laughter and screams of revenge joined in. I looked up to the sky, covered in grey clouds, turning black, sucking the little light around me away.

Somewhere past my eyes, my heart, was a forest. And two men trying to kill me and the prince. The prince! A hope sprung inside me. None of this was real; if I screamed, he would hear me.

"Ivar! Ivar, I know you can hear me, get up!" I screamed, closing my eyes and covering my ears, ignoring the walking dead that loomed all around, ready to plunge their blades in my body.

"Sivrehya?" A confused voice came from somewhere to my left.

I jerked around, walking slowly. A laugh erupted from somewhere else. This one felt less hollow, real. I smiled, ignoring the feeling of pushing through a mass of dead people. Slowly they began to stab me, laughing, screaming. I ignored the pain.

"Ivar, where are you?" I called out beyond the illusion.

"She thinks this will work, she's silly..." A faint deep voice. One of the men.

"Make him appear...cast...off him..." they faded away and I stopped in my tracks. I should have known they'd try to add him in this sick illusion of theirs.

"Ivar!" I screamed in one last attempt, "Fight!" My throat burned as I screamed as loud as I could just as a blade made its way through me. I coughed up blood, my body suddenly panicking, my heart racing. I stumbled, unable to scream. My hand covered my side. I could feel blood, real warm blood seep out of me, and there was still the blade of a dagger inside me. I grasped the hilt, pulling it out, coughing, gasping for air. My mind was spinning, my vision breaking, the dead all around me faded in and out. I focused on my power, slowly stitching myself back together.

My hands trembled as the wound slowly healed and the pain slowly began to disappear. I wiped my mouth with my sleeve, swallowing down the blood still in my mouth, forcing back a gag. I blinked, shaking my head.

Someone screamed, deep and cracked. Another scream.

Rithlorens get up, Rithlorens keep fighting, I reminded myself, as I got up, ignoring my body's screams. My vision suddenly cleared, and I could make out the prince holding someone's soul in his hands. A silver thing, bright and burning, slowing being ripped apart. And then the man who had stood above me, shaking with the blood spears still impaling his body, fell, cold and limp on the floor.

I stared down at him, my heart beating so fast I thought it would burst any second. I blinked, my eyes going from him to the prince.

He had...Ivar had just...

But the thought was cut when my eyes caught a shadow behind the prince and before I could scream, Ivar's eyes widened and his ivory-colored shirt became red. His eyes dulled, he screamed a bloodcurdling scream, and he thrashed around on the ground. Another illusion. I looked at the chaos mage, the last one, his body trembling. I raised my hand, ready to burst all his blood vessels and veins, but his head snapped up, his copper eyes blazed and he gave me a bloody smile before he ran into the forest.

"Hey!" I shrieked, my feet taking off to run after him, into the forest, into the night, but when I passed the barely conscious prince, I stopped mid-step. In the distance, I could see the man in green still running and I could still run after him, I could kill him. Rip him to pieces. Or...I turned to look at Ivar, who was barely alive.

The man or the prince. I looked back between them, my magic itching to follow the man into the darkness beyond. My mind pushing me to stay.

Darkness save me, I thought, as my feet refused to move.

My eyes once again met the darkness as I searched the forest, but the man was gone. Part of me knew I should have gone after him, but the other part of me knew he wasn't the last one of his kind. If three had still lived, likely many more did before them and with them.

I walked over to the prince, his blood still gushing out of the wound, the dagger still lodged in his stomach. I winced; his pale skin was paler than any shade of white. An evil thought crossed my mind, one that two days ago, even yesterday, I could have let happen, but now, I couldn't. I bent down, reaching a hand out to touch his skin. It was cold.

"What the hell—" He coughed, blood. "are you doing here?"

"Talk some more and you're dead." I scolded him and stood up.

"You should have," another cough, "killed him, ran after him—"

"Shut up and save your words for when you're a bit more alive. I know I should have gone after him. Don't make me regret it by dying right now."

He closed his eyes, his chest ever so slowly going up and down.

I reached out, his blood following my command and slowly forming a circle, and another and another.

The prince coughed, slowly moving, "Oh, hell no, not my blood. You're not using *my* blood to perform your damned tricks."

Ugh. He was fucking *impossible.* Here he was, a dagger in his stomach, on the brink of *death,* and he was picky about which blood I used to get us the hell out of here.

I shook my head in disbelief, fighting the urge to just stare at him in utter confusion for eternity.

"Fine," I spat, splattering his blood that was hanging in the air on him. His face contorted with disgust as he spat out the scarlet liquid that made it inside his mouth. Served him right.

His silver eyes burned with a dangerous fire. "Why the hell—"

"Oh, my apologies, I seem to have accidentally flung your blood onto your annoying face," I batted my lashes at him as I stood up and reached out for the blood of the fallen chaos mages, and slowly, a symbol began to form.

"I hate you." He groaned from the pain behind me. *Walk it off,* I thought as I rolled my eyes.

"And I you," I shot back before grabbing his arms and pulling him through the symbol, out of the forest clearing and into the Stone's End.

XXVIII : SIVREHYA RITHLOREN

The Twin Cities
Moonsier, Outer City

His room was brighter than the forest. The light of the city just beyond the window filtered through the curtains.

The moment we were both through the portal, the blood symbol softened, being held in the air by my thoughts. I had kicked open the door to his room, quickly putting the prince down. He groaned, shifting over to the side in pain.

"Don't move!" I hissed, bidding the blood to soak into a random white shirt that laid on the bed. "You don't want that dagger to dig any deeper into your stomach, do you?"

This time the prince remained silent. As I turned around, his eyes were closed, his chest barely moving. I shoved the bloodied shirt on the bed aside, letting the rest of the blood still in the air fall to the floor.

"Screw you for being so careless," I whispered, as I gently turned him over onto his back, grabbing the dagger by its hilt. His pulse was weakening, barely even there. I yanked the blade out, the prince giving only a shiver and a slight groan as a response. Tossing it aside, I rose a small stream of his blood above him and formed as quickly as I could an intricate healing spell. Slowly the glowing symbol hardened and a small flash of red light lit up the room.

And then darkness and silence. Save for his breaths. Slowly his eyes fluttered open. I lifted his shirt, covering the entry wound, and though he was still caked in dried blood, the wound was gone. I huffed, sitting back, running a hand through my hair. My mind was still unable to completely grasp what I had just seen or done.

"What..." Ivar groaned, sitting up slowly, like an elderly man, one hand on his bloody chest. "...happened?" He asked weakly, looking at me, his hair half covering his eyes from me.

"You got stabbed, I healed you."

"No," He gasped for air, "B—before. Then, I saw them in the darkness, in the room...and the blood, there was so much blood and I smelled all of the death..." His head hung.

"Iv—they were chaos mages..." I looked around the room, "I think."

The prince shifted, brushing a hand through his silver hair, his eyes now meeting mine.

"That's impossible. They're all dead."

"I know," I leaned my head against the wall, squeezing my eyes shut, "But I can't—what happened, it was them. It had to be. No one else can do what they did to us."

"It was so real, and they knew, oh Darkness they *knew*." He shook, trembling, shaking his head in denial.

"Knew what?" I asked, trying to lock eyes with him but they remained glued to the floor.

"Nothing." He murmured. I closed my eyes again, sighing. "We killed two, what happened to the third?"

I shifted, pulling out my dagger and throwing it up in the air, watching it flip several times before landing in my hand. "One got away."

"Why?" He stood up, grabbing onto the bed for support.

"Because I..." I stopped, throwing the blade in the air again. *Because I decided saving your life was a better idea.* "Because you were about to die," I said instead, pushing my hair out of my face. I reeked of death and the strong odor of iron.

"So, let me get this straight, one of them got away because I was about to die?" He looked bewildered as if what I did was beyond his comprehension. Which I couldn't blame him for. I moved my hand in front of me to let the hilt of the dagger fall into my hand, before sending it once again in the air.

"Oh, you're welcome by the way, for saving your life." I rolled my eyes.

"You could have *killed* him," Ivar shot back.

"Yeah maybe, or he could have gotten away. I was *tired,* Ivar," I replied, exhausted, "He might have conjured another illusion, one I couldn't see past. And besides, if I had chased after him, fought him and killed him, you would have been long dead, and you are *no* good to me dead."

"Oh no?" He almost smirked, a dangerously curious sparkle in his eyes.

"No, no absolutely not." I caught the dagger again, this time aiming it towards him. I moved my arm back, bent my wrist and let the blade fly through the air. "I need you alive so I can kill you myself—"

His hand moved in a blur, the hilt on the dagger in his curled fingers, the blade a breath away from his face. This time he smiled, "On the battlefield in front of all my people, yes, I know."

"You remembered."

"No, it's just that that's how I plan to kill you. You know, maybe I'll even draw that little blood symbol on a piece of cloth and put it by your crumbled body to frame a blood mage for killing you."

I almost laughed, as something between a gasp for breath and chuckle erupted from me. "Oh really?"

"Of course, if I didn't want anyone to know it was me who killed you, it would be genius! Make it seem like someone else killed you so they take the blame and I'm safe in the shadows." He wiped the blood from his face with the part of the shirt left untainted by blood.

I laughed, covering my mouth with my hand, shaking my head. Until a thought crept into my mind and the world froze once again. My head snapped up, our eyes meeting. My face fell, my heart dropped, blood freezing. The world became quiet and I swore I could hear my panic slowly start to shift inside me.

"Holy fuck." I stood up too fast, the blood rushing, my head suddenly faint, but ignored it.

"What?" Ivar asked, "Did something happen?"

"Holy *fuck...*" I shook my head violently, gripping my hair. My feet carried me to the end of the room and I turned, pacing back and forth.

"Sivrehya?" The prince stood up, his fingers wrapping around my arms to stop me. "What's going on?" He demanded. I looked up, my eyes impossibly wide, my body trembling with the terrible realization.

"It was *them*." I said in a hoarse whisper. "It has always *been* them. All along. Oh shit, shit. Oh, fucking Darkness, holy Dark Mother." I covered my eyes, trying to breathe through the panic. But the air was stuck inside me, outside of me. It felt heavy and sudden, like a boulder hitting me straight in the chest. I huffed, wincing from the pain that came from breathing.

Ivar shook me, "Sivrehya, what is wrong?"

"I—" Nothing made sense; it felt as if the world was being ripped apart around me and I was falling, falling into the pile of skulls and bones from the illusion. Falling from the sky that rained blood drops into the red scarlet sea of taunting voices.

"Why aren't you breathing? Breathe." The prince shook me, looking at me, without a shred of worry in his eyes, or fear or emotion. I blinked, shaking my head, gripping my chest.

"I—I can't..." I stammered, walking back, falling onto the bed. I sank in, and my heart tightened, panic rising through me. The world seemed foggy, and I could hear the laughter of all those chaos mages who died so many years ago in the war, the laughter of those who survived knowing they would come back to destroy what destroyed them.

I started huffing, gasping, until I became light-headed from the air.

"I'm going to be sick," I breathed out, doubling over.

Ivar crouched in front of me, "What is wrong?"

"It was them!" I screamed, clamping my mouth shut, covering it with my hands as soon as the words flew out of my mouth. I shook my head again, taking a deep breath, trying to calm down, trying to drown out the voices dancing around my head.

"What do you mean it was them?"

Stop, stop interrogating me, I begged silently. I wanted to sleep, to be in Meris, in my mother's arms, or my brother's or sister's, or even my father's. But he's dead because a chaos mage killed him, because it was all of them. It was all of them. It was all of them. We never killed them all. We never destroyed them. The history I knew, the history everyone knew, was wrong.

The prince remained silent, still crouching. My eyes were on the floor but his presence filled the room. I squeezed my eyes shut, so hard that it hurt. I needed to tell him, to make him understand, but I couldn't even manage to understand myself.

I looked up, taking a deep breath in and out, and another, and another until my heart slowed and I stopped shaking. Our eyes met.

"What..." I searched his eyes for something to say, for what to say, as if I'd find the answer within their silvery depths. "What would you do if someone destroyed you?"

The prince furrowed his brows, "What?"

"If someone took everything from you, destroyed you, left you to die. What would you do?"

His eyes darted around the room, landing back on mine. He brushed a hand through his hair. "I'd wait, some time, until I was ready, strong enough to rise up and destroy them."

I closed my eyes, nodding. "Exactly."

"Exactly?" He repeated, "You're making no sense. What are you talking about?"

I huffed, our eyes locking. I looked deep into his, breathing slowly, the words forming slowly in my head. "There were once three kingdoms, right?"

He nodded, unsure of what I was going on about, "Right?"

"Two destroyed one, right?"

"Yeah, our kingdoms joined forces to destroy Vylara when their king wanted to take over our kingdoms."

"And they were destroyed, right?"

"The Vylarans?" He asked. I nodded. "Yeah."

This time I shook my head, holding it with my hands. My eyes floated down to my feet. "What if they weren't destroyed, at least, not completely. What if a few survived, in the shadows of their fallen kingdom? And what if they carried on the hatred and anger to their children, through the generations? And what if in that time they grew, they became stronger, until they knew they were ready enough to destroy what destroyed them?" I looked at the prince, who remained perfectly still. I could see his brain spinning behind his eyes.

"Sivrehya, you cannot possibly be saying....no." He shook his head.

"Ivar, they were chaos mages. They made these," I tossed my arms in the air searching for the word, "these, these illusions. That were so painfully real, no one, *no one* else can do that. No one."

The prince looked at me, "No, no that's not..." Whatever word he was about to say was lost inside him.

"It makes perfect sense, everything now makes terrifyingly perfect sense."

Ivar fell back, sitting, leaning against the wall, his face in his hands. "They're back." His voice trembled.

A chill traveled down my back and through me, into my blood and bones. "They're not back, Ivar," The prince lifted his head up, raising one brow. "They never left. They've always been there, just hidden. In the shadows."

"So, you're saying..." The prince started, eyes locking with mine.

"I'm saying, I guess, I don't know. I mean, it makes sense, too much sense. That it would be them, but we both know it can't be. Because they're dead, they're dead. They're all gone, we destroyed them..." My chest felt like it was enveloping a rock, hanging in my ribcage, slowly becoming harder, heavier. "But it makes sense, doesn't it, I cannot be crazy." I look at the prince, desperate for something, anything. A confirmation that he too thought the same, or him judging me for being, in fact, crazy and having an overactive imagination.

But silence settled between us, filling the room with a thick mixture of panic and realization.

Ivar stood up abruptly, sighing. "We need to leave tomorrow for the Neithisis. What you said, it makes sense, and it shouldn't. But... you know, we have to..."

I nodded my head. "It's late, we need to sleep and tomorrow when Moonsier becomes Sunsier we go find the beast." I stood up, making my way to the door.

"Sivrehya," He called out after me, I turned around. He clenched his jaw, a war in his eyes. "Th—thank you for saving me."

I gave him a tired smirk, "Like I said, how else am I supposed to kill you myself?"

He laughed. "Still so sure you'll manage to kill me first? Trust me, blood demon, when the time comes, I'll be the one to destroy you first."

"We'll see, charming, we'll see." I turned around, walking out of his room. But before I closed the door behind me I turned around, our eyes meeting.

"But thank you." I whispered. "For what you did with the soul mage, back there."

Ivar gave me a half-hearted smile, and our eyes never left one another's, as I closed the door.

I stood in front of my own door, sticking the key I had grabbed from downstairs into the knob and twisting it. I trudged in, yawning, stretching my arms in the air like a cat.

"Siv?"

I froze, my instincts flaring, I jerked around, my eyes meeting a pair of red ones.

"Daemon...how—what..." I looked at him, up and down, and

noticed a small orb of light glowing in the center of a red symbol floating above him.

He held one of my books from my bookshelf at home. One of his wrists was bleeding, a dagger slightly unsheathed hanging at his belt. So, he had used a locator spell. Something must have happened for a simple letter not to suffice. "Look, sis, I don't have much time but I ju—"

I cut him off, waving my hand in the air. "Wait, no. Tell me something, something only you would know about me." I demanded, my eyes narrowed, searching the room for anything that could be out of place.

My brother cocked his head, "What?"

"Just do it, now, please." I met my brother's eyes, and they looked so similar. They were a lighter shade than mine, a ring of dark red around them. They looked real, and they probably were, but now...now I needed to be sure because everything changed.

"Uh, okay, you..." He searched the air for what to say. "When you were eleven you decided it would be a good idea to disguise yourself as a human girl, so you found a spell, in a book discovered in the oldest part of the library, to change your appearance, so you did. And you sneaked out, and for two days we couldn't find you, and to avoid a national panic we didn't tell anyone. Then one day, you sneaked into my room, crying, begging me to change you back and I remember asking you the same thing. To tell me something only you could know, and you whispered in my ear, 'Daemon, I know you like to eat all the cookies the moment they come out of the oven, and you conjure up poorly made look-a-likes.' And then we searched the reverse spell which took us three days because you just had to go and choose the most difficult spell in the first place." He smiled, a tiny smile, at the memory. And I found myself mirroring him, walking towards him as my eyes brimmed with tears, and I pulled him into a tight hug.

"I've missed you, Dae," I whispered, sniffing, forcing the tears down.

"Me too, Siv, me too," He held me, for just a little longer, before we both broke free. "But what was that about? Did something happen?"

I sighed. "You trust me, right?"

"Foolishly, with my life," He scrunched his face, messing the top of my hair with his hand.

"Well, it's just that...we've discovered something, the location of the Neithisis for one, and something else. But I need to make sure it's real, that it's something worth worrying about and figuring out, before telling you. And I promise I will, I just, I want to make sure." My brother shifted, looking deep into my eyes.

"We've?"

I cocked my head to the side, "Sorry?"

"You said *we've*." The color drained from my face, my blood freezing.

Oh shit. Shit, fuck, how could I have been so stupid. He can't know about Ivar.

"Are you working with someone else?" He crossed his arms, and the worst part was he wasn't suspicious, the first thought that would cross his mind wasn't that I'd be working with our mortal enemy. He was just curious. There was no threat behind his words and yet I was sweating up an ocean.

If there was one person who could see through my lies it was Daemon, always. I didn't know how he did it, but he never needed magic. He could read between all the spoken lines of anyone and see the ones that weren't. I envied him for that.

"Junah," I blurted out. The panic brewing inside me slowly simmering.

"Junah?"

"Yes, Junah." I nodded, thanking Darkness that she existed and that she had helped us. "She's a student here that I met because she was extremely curious about me as everyone here was, hence the eyes." I motioned to my eyes; he nodded. "She mentioned she's studying mythical creatures, so I questioned her about the Neithisis. I said I was writing a story about it and I needed information, so she took me to the museum and then the library and after hours of searching I was able to uncover the location."

My brother nodded, uncrossing his arms. "That's great, where is it?"

"The Neithisis? Oh, in a cave, high up in the Raven Mountains." I offered him a smile, but my brother's face fell nonetheless.

"Sis, that's the biggest mountain range in Rodessa. How in the name of Darkness are you supposed to find this thing in less than four days?"

I hung my head, "I—I don't know. But I'll figure it out, I have to."

"Hey, Siv?"

I lifted my head, "Hm?"

"Why is there a protection symbol on your wall?" His eyes floated to the blood drawn on the wall across from the bed. I turned to look at the symbol, to avoid his eyes.

"Oh, for protection, can't ever be too careful." I laughed as my brother looked at me, one brow raised.

"No, you can't be." His voice was low, dark, as if alluding to something. "I smelled something, a scent, similar to our own, was that you?"

Darkness save me, freaking mages and our ability to sense magic.

I nodded again, running a hand through my hair, putting up a fatigued face. I hated lying to my brother, to anyone in my family. But the last thing I needed was for Daemon to stress over something that might be a result of an overactive imagination or to find out that I did something incredibly stupid that might be seen as treason. Saving the life of a mortal enemy. Stupid. Stupid. Killing him on the battlefield had better be worth it.

"Yes, it's me. I've noticed in a world filled with different magic, it's a bit stronger, I guess. I don't know." I shrugged, hanging my head, hoping he won't see past this lie this one time.

"Are you okay?"

No. I'm tired of all this, my mind hurts, I might be going insane because I was attacked by chaos mages, and that doesn't make sense, because they're gone. And I just saved Ivar's life when I should have dug the dagger deeper into him and left him for dead. My body aches, voices of dead people are clouding my thoughts, I want to scream, to sleep forever and wake up in a world where we aren't at war and that chaos mages are all gone. I just...I'm so tired.

But of course, I wouldn't say any of those words, not really. I'd let them swim around my mind. I'd keep them bottled up and hidden because that's what I've always done and always would do. Because not saying anything, not showing anything, was easier. Better. Pretending was better.

"I came here to tell you about the war, and Mother."

I stilled. *Mother. No, don't tell me something's happened to her, please, I don't, I can't take anymore...*

But all I could force out were two words. "What happened?"

"She's weakened, sick. Rhiannyn is now fully acting as queen in her place. I'm working on our army and training everyone to fight, everyone who wants to. The kingdom is a mess, Siv, there's fear everywhere. There's anger and hatred. There are those who want to fight the Lysmirans right now. There are those who propose sending assassins to finish the royals. And they all seem like incredibly enticing ideas. Yesterday a soldier was found dead, soul destroyed."

What?

I tensed in his embrace. Red emotions were swirling inside me, and slowly, I broke free from his embrace. "What did you say?"

"One of our soldiers was found dead, his soul destroyed, we've increased security, our men and women have eyes everywhere—"

"Who?" I almost cut him off.

"His name was Eiron, he was a villager who pledged to the war as a soldier. Fifteen years of age, his family, they pledged themselves the moment his murder was announced to the kingdom."

I knew Ivar wasn't at fault. He was here, had been in the Twin Cities the entire time, but I couldn't help but just allow the anger to bubble. A soul mage killed one of my people. Or maybe they didn't and another chaos mage was playing cruel tricks. I shook my head, shoving down the thoughts that threatened to rip my sanity apart.

"Listen, I need to go, I just thought you should know that the Meris you'll come back to will be different. It was never a perfect world, but it's darker now. Colder, if you can believe it."

I nodded, unable to form any words.

My brother lifted his wrist, the blood lifting, forming a symbol. From behind me he spoke softly, "Be safe."

"You too," I whispered, and he stepped forward, disappearing into the blood. In a flash of red, my room was once again dark and I was alone.

XXIX : IVAR THAEGAN

The Raven Mountains

The mountains loomed in front of us. The peaks were dotted with white snow, enhancing their naturally foreboding black color. Just ahead were trees, big, lush and green, looking perfectly innocent as if they came out of a children's book of happy fairytales. But the princess and I knew they were just as deceitful as those stories with happy endings.

I had heard tales, been told stories of heroes marching into the Raven Mountains, into the trees, up to where the snow was so cold it could turn anything it touched to ice. But they were all made up, and you could tell that by the way the story ended. Did the hero come back? Did he slay some mysterious thing? If they had, it was fake. No hero, real or made up, ever made it out alive. They went into the Raven Mountains not knowing anything about them, what laid within their picturesque trees and heavenly-looking snowy peaks. They went in knowing they wouldn't come back.

I knew we were potentially signing away our lives by stepping into these mountains. I knew if we made it out alive it would be a miracle, and if we also happened to find the Neithisis, that would be because the Darkness and the world and absolutely everything had been on our side.

I sighed, turning to face the princess, whose own eyes scanned the looming horizon.

"So, this is where the Darkness first came to be. This is where it originated, this is where it was destroyed by the Shadowbenders all those years ago." She spoke quietly, as if afraid that someone was listening, watching us from just behind the trees.

I reflected on her words, narrowing my eyes, figuring it must be true. Why else would no one who stepped in ever walk back out?

"Do you think it's true?" I asked her, my left hand tightly wrapped around the hilt of my sword, and my right, touching my dagger's sheath lightly, just to make sure for the millionth time it was there.

This morning, my body had refused to move, as if not completely aware it had been healed the night before. It felt weird, the magic she used on me. It was warm, yet ice cold, and it felt as if I was being suffocated by something. And for the entire night, my body felt heavy, as if made entirely of rocks, and this morning was no different. I woke up to the princess pounding on my door at the crack of dawn, dressed in a dark red dress, a black cape, dagger strapped to her waist, her hair in a braided bun and her eyes once again the color of blood.

She told me she was leaving in ten minutes, with or without me. So, I had splashed ice cold water on my face in hopes it would revive me a bit. I put on the warmest clothes I could find, my two blades and a satchel with bread and two apples and whatever else I had left in it, and then we were out the door, through a blood portal of hers, and in front of the Raven Mountains.

"I have no reason to not believe it," she responded after some time. "I mean, the mountains are ink black, all the monstrous beasts are said to reign here and all the stories of all the people who went inside never ended happily...I guess it would make sense that this is the place where it all started."

I followed her gaze up, past the trees and above us, to where the peaks were in the distance. I gulped.

"About those monstrous beasts, the ones we read about in the history books, the ones that roamed the world before empires and kingdoms?" The ones the Darkness twisted until they became spawns of it and became living nightmares of shadows and death.

"The Darkness blessed ones?" she asked, her hands in fists, bunching the skirt of her dress.

"Yeah, those."

"What about them?"

I looked into the forest, making out as many details as I could before all the branches and trees meshed together to make darkness. I shook my head, sending away the paranoid thoughts running around in my mind.

"Nothing." I stopped, forgetting the thoughts and straightening my back. The princess said nothing, letting silence come between us.

I looked up at the sky. It was dark grey, slowly becoming covered in clouds. I cursed the world. Of course, it would rain, and storm today of all days. Of course.

"We should hurry," I said as I shattered the silence. "We don't have much time, and by the looks of the clouds over there," I pointed to the clouds, "there's going to be a storm very soon."

The princess looked up, following my gaze. "Well great." She huffed, looking around. "I could portal us somewhere, to make it faster, so we don't have to trek up and take hours."

"It won't take too much out of you?"

"Well," she seemed to consider her answer carefully, "No, not if I do it just a few times."

I looked at her suspiciously, "Fine then, let's do that, walk a bit and see where we'll be."

She nodded, taking the dagger from her sheathe and cutting a shallow wound into her palm. I watched as the blood followed her command, flowing from her hand in a thin uniform string, that slowly started forming into shape. I watched as the symbol came together, and I was mesmerized, hating myself for thinking it was almost beautiful.

The symbol that seemed impossibly hard to memorize stopped glowing and the princess turned to face me. "Since I can't imagine the place very well, considering I've never been here, I don't know where we'll end up."

"How so?"

"It's best to have a clear image of the place you want to portal to, to avoid ending up somewhere else. It's not a requirement when it comes to these types of spells, but it does make it more precise. Now, I can imagine what the top of black rock and now covered mountains will look like, and we'll just have to hope we don't end up in Pyatovan mountains." She flashed an innocent smile at my paling face.

"Are you serious?" Panic blossoming in me like flowers in spring. I gulped. "Is there really a chance you'll send us flying into mountains in an entirely different country?"

Sivrehya laughed, shaking her head. "No, we won't as long as I..." She walked over to a mountain, to where the raven black rock was already towering in front of us. She punched it, splitting cracks into it. And she picked up a tiny little fallen rock, throwing it into the portal. No...*mixing* it within the lines of blood floating in the air.

I watched, eyes wide, as she worked the magic before finally stepping back, wiping her dusty hands on the skirt.

"As long as you mix a rock with blood?" I raised a brow.

"Two general rules for portal spells. One, if you can imagine the place fine, then there's no problem. If you can't, then you take anything from that place and mix it in with the spell, to avoid mistakes."

"And if you don't," I asked, "have something from the place you want to go to?"

"Then you're on foot, or horse, or boat, or any other means of travel."

Well damn. Blood magic kept getting more and more complicated by the day.

"But we have a rock from the Raven Mountains. So no chance we'll end up anywhere else." She flashed me another smile, before stepping up to the floating blood. "I'll go first. Just walk through it, you'll be fine."

I scowled at her. "You know, the first and most recent time I was sent traveling through a portal I fell from the sky."

She raised a brow, barely hiding her growing smile of amusement. She burst out laughing. "How, what? Oh, my goodness, I would have *loved* to see that."

I rolled my eyes, "Yes, yes it was hilarious. Your brother must think he is so funny."

She became quiet. "My brother? I thought he had sent you to Meris..."

He never told her? Perhaps she had already left for the city when he had pulled off his magic trick.

"Yes, just a few days ago to show us your father's body. That's when I saw his eyes. That they weren't how they would be, when someone's soul is destroyed. But then, after, your brother pushed my father and me out, and we fell from the sky."

I looked at her, seeing sadness in eyes, quickly hidden away behind the other emotions swimming within them. She seemed to contemplate what I said, like she wanted to say something herself, but instead she just nodded.

"Don't wait too long," she finally said, and then she walked through the symbol and disappeared.

I followed her through, walking into a large clearing surrounded by trees, a large mountain right in front of us. I turned around, looking at the scenery that surrounded us. We were higher, that was for sure. The air was colder, and a chilling wind blew ever so slightly.

"It seems that you could touch the sky, or the sun, or even the moon if you were at the top of the mountain." The princess looked up, healing her hand as she did.

"Yeah, you probably could touch the moon—the moon! Moonroot, I forgot the moonroot!"

Sivrehya whipped around, facing me. Her eyes were alarmingly wide. "The *what*?"

"Moonroot, you know..." I smiled, nonchalantly.

"Yes, I know what moonroot is, but what the fuck do you need with moonroot? " Suddenly she paled, her face falling. "No, don't tell me you *use* it!"

Suddenly I panicked, raising my hands. "Ph, no! No, no, goodness no. It's for a..." *What word do I even use?* "It's for someone else."

She narrowed her eyes, "Who?" She eyed me suspiciously, crossing her arms.

"For the man who was already half high on it, I learned the location of that Khadir man from him after basically spending the entire day asking just about the entire population of the city for information. Someone led me to him, he led me to Khadir, and to get him to talk I promised him moonroot if he was telling the truth. Which he did, so now, I owe him moonroot."

The princess just stared at me, in utter disbelief. "Well then, have fun trying to get the most illegal and dangerous drug in the world and not dying."

I smiled, falsely, "Thank you so much for your concern."

Silence fell between us. I stepped back, looking at the mountain, suddenly feeling like the air became colder. Something wet fell on my face, and then something else. Rain. I looked down at the princess, whose own face held immense disapproval.

"You wouldn't be able by any chance, be able to, I don't know, conjure something up to cover us?" I asked, just as thunder struck in the distance and the sky began sobbing and wailing. I shut my eyes, slowly feeling as my clothes became soaked, drenched and plastered against my skin. I shivered, feeling the wind that suddenly came to life. I looked around to the trees, debating if we should run underneath for some protection.

"Um, Ivar?" Sivrehya whispered, her voice shaking. She tugged lightly on my sleeve.

"What?" I turned around, facing her, but her eyes didn't meet mine.

"I might just be crazy, and hallucinating things because of all the horror stories we were told as children, but um..." She paused, never meeting my eyes. I furrowed my brows.

"But um what?" I pushed, impatient.

"I think I just saw something that highly resembles the rendering in the museum of a monster."

A small flicker of hope lit inside me. I forced myself to not smile, "A Neithisis! Already? And out of a cave?" I couldn't believe it, "This is ama—"

"Not a Neithisis." She cut me off, meeting my eyes for the first time. I looked deep inside them, searching for something. Within them, I saw a sliver of panic, or fear, or something between the two.

"Then what?"

"An...an Obscurae," she finished, looking back behind me, seemingly relaxing just a tiny bit.

I almost laughed, out of sheer agony.

"An Obscurae? An *Obscurae*?" She simply nodded, slowly. "You mean those wolf creatures that eat magic and fear fire or heat or light or something like that?"

She nodded again.

"Impossible," I said, as I shook my head, stepping back. "When the Darkness was destroyed, they withered away with it. They're gone, only alive in the horror tales told to chil...dren..." My eyes caught something behind the princess. They snapped up, glazing over the blurred trees. I blinked, cursing the rain. In the greying air, I could see something black, large and moving. I narrowed my eyes, taking back the step I took back. And my heart dropped, and my body stilled.

It suddenly smelled different, stale and dark. The figure morphed, becoming two and suddenly three. I craned my head to see, to watch as they moved slowly in our direction and saw that they were wolves. Large and covered in pitch-black fur with spikes running down their spines. Their lifeless hateful eyes were on us.

"Sivrehya..." I whispered, the air catching in my lungs.

"I'm not crazy right?" She asked, voice quivering.

"No," I told her, as I watched the beasts slowly stalk out of the forest. Their beady lifeless eyes were trained on us, their mouths, open, fangs sharp and ready to dig into flesh. They seemed to smile as they bared their hideous teeth, smiled at the fact that right in front of them were two mages, teeming with magic. What a lucky day it must be for them.

"How many are there?" She demanded.

"Three," I whispered as if afraid they might hear us and become more aggressive. "That I can see," I added, my eyes on the center beast. It was larger than the two behind it. It seemed older, having seen much more death in its days. One eye had a gruesome scar slashed through it, cutting its black fur, almost dividing its hideous face in half.

All three moved in unison as if they were one beast. They made their way towards us, closing in, letting us suffer in the knowledge of our near demise.

"There's four behind you."

I blinked, my hand instinctively reaching for the sword at my waist. My eyes still glued to the approaching creatures. Impossible. *Impossible.*

"How can we be so sure that these are Obscurae? I mean, no one has seen them in so long, they could very well be all dead like we've always thought they were."

"Yes, perhaps, but right now once believed dead things are actually *alive*," She responded, her red eyes still glaring into the lifeless eyes of the beasts behind me. "So honestly, I can't be surprised."

"Fair enough," I slowly unsheathed the sword, "I've read in books that they're afraid of fire, right? Or light? Conjure something up, anything, and we can figure out what to do from there."

"They also say they devour magic, Ivar." The princess jabbed at me, giving up only a second of eye contact with the beasts to meet my eye, and gave me a look of annoyed disappointment. "They might have a profound fear for anything that produces light, but when one wants something bad enough not even their deepest fear will stop them."

Oh. Fuck.

The realization dawned on me, shattering every hope I had of living through this adventure. Some part of me convinced myself that I would live, that Sivrehya and I would find the stupid Neithisis, get whatever answer we needed and we would be back in our kingdoms figuring this war out. But now the knowledge of an

Obscurae's terrifying ability to sniff out magic and its primal desire to consume it shattered any hope.

"We led them straight to us with that portal spell, didn't we?" I asked, dreading the answer.

"Yes, and if that weren't bad enough, we reek of magic anyway." The princess huffed, her body shaking, and I couldn't tell if it was from the cold rain pelting down on us, or fear, or both. "We have to fight, right? We could take them...I think."

"We could, but they're probably not the only ones in existence." I dreaded my answer as I said it. I hated hearing it, realizing it was right. "Our magic will no doubt attract a million others, and we're cold and tired. We won't last long. And we can't not use magic to fight them. These blades are barely enough to fight one."

She sighed, forcing her eyes on the beasts, but I could tell she wanted to close them for a minute and just think. But she couldn't; neither of us could. The monsters stepped closer, closer, close enough to where we could hear their growls. Their primal desire for our magic lingered in their lifeless white eyes.

"Another portal, can you make another one? To the top of the mountains, or anywhere but here at this point?"

"I could," She started, taking a step closer to me. "But not fast enough, the portal symbols are complicated on their own, I'd need another piece of the mountains, but there's—"

One of them growled, low and deep and full of threat.

"They'd be on us, fangs inside our flesh before I'm even halfway done with it." The princess finished, wincing from the powerful growl.

Shit. Shit. Shit.

I tore my gaze from the beasts, who must have sensed that we knew they were there, but remained ever so slow with their approach. I turned my head and looked to the left, where the ground ended abruptly. A cliff.

"Then we run."

The princess looked at me, "Run *where*?"

I nodded my head in the direction of the cliff, and slowly,

almost painfully she took her eyes off the beasts lurking behind me and glanced in the direction of the cliff.

"Are you mad?" She scolded, shaking her head, "We don't know what's down there. There could be rocks as sharp as daggers, or a huge slab of stone that our insides will paint red, or better yet, a group of Obscurae."

"Or there could be water?" I offered, but the only thing she gave me back was a raised brow.

"Someone must have traded our souls because I'm here doubting we'll make it out alive, and you're suggesting running off a cliff at the slight chance that there's water down there." She shook her head in disbelief, and I realized the meaning of her words.

Oh shit, she's right. Ew.

"We'll make sure to switch back, I don't need *any* of your positivity."

She rolled her eyes, her pale face suddenly shifting to a sickly grey. I narrowed my eyes.

"Wha—" But I had no time to finish. She grabbed my arm, bolting in the direction of the cliff.

"*Run!*" She screamed, her voice cut off by a powerful strike of lightning and thunder just above us. Our shoes sank ever so slightly in the mud beneath us, the growls and pounding of the claws of the monsters gaining on behind us.

We raced, as everything around us was becoming a grey blur. The air smelled of ice and death. As the ground squished beneath us, I could feel the proximity of the creatures behind us; I could almost hear them *breathing*. But I forced myself to ignore it, to plaster down the fear that sang through me and focused instead on the nearing cliff. My eyes were slits, blinking constantly, ignoring the pangs of the fat raindrops that collided with my face.

The moment the edge came, I heard a gasp of air. Sivrehya faltered, almost falling. There was a blur of black behind us, and I felt my bare hand touch crusty fur. My eyes widened, barely registering a beast's mouth alarmingly close to my face. There was a pungent odor of something sour, something like rotting flesh and years-old food.

I kicked my foot at anything, hearing a grunt. I looked behind us, and we were so close to the cliff that I yanked my sword from my waist and swung it blindly in the rain. My heart was pounding against my chest, one arm around the princess, the other one plunging my blade inside something, before someone screamed a word. Perhaps it had been "now," or "jump," or my name.

And we were falling into the unknown. I pulled the princess close, smelling metal. Blood. I couldn't feel pain; no part of me felt warm as it did when I bled. I looked up, ignoring the rain falling into my eyes. The cliff was already fading into the grey air, the fog, and the beasts hollered, though none followed.

And then, we hit something frigid, like ice. And it enveloped us in its cold embrace. I opened my eyes, only for a burning sensation to take over. I shut them tightly, my hair floating around me, my body convulsing in the water. Water. We were in water. I pushed up, feeling suddenly alone. The princess.

I opened my eyes, seeing the faded surface of the lake. I kicked my tired legs, until I pushed through and could breathe. I whipped the hair from my face, pushing it out of my eyes with my hands. I huffed, spitting out the water in my mouth, blinking, twisting around. Everything smelled like wet mud and frost. Around me the storm raged on, wind howling, lightning cracking like a whip in the sky, setting it alight for a split second before plunging the world back into dark grey.

"Sivrehya!" I screamed out against the raging storm. It felt like being out at sea in the middle of a tempest. I strained my eyes, searching for her, reaching out my arms in the water. I shivered, my body screaming for me to leave the water. I could slowly feel myself freezing to death, my body became heavy, my movements slow.

"Sivrehya!" I shouted again, seeing the edge of the lake nearby. I swam for it, raising my tired arms and pushing myself despite the pain to just continue.

I flailed my arms out in front of me, grabbing onto the nearest rock, and pulling myself up. I felt seaweed, kelp, some plant, wrap around my left leg. I kicked it off, my heart rate rising with every second that passed. I begged the Darkness that the thing had been a plant, some form of aquatic vegetation that I just happened to swim past, and nothing else.

A cold wet hand wrapped around my wrist. I tensed, looking up, ready to fall back in the water to avoid another monster. But it was the princess, drenched and shivering, pulling me out.

"Give me your other hand!" She screamed and I reached for her. She grasped my other hand, pulling me, using the last of the strength either of us had left.

I gasped for air, falling onto mud, grateful for land. I pushed myself up, my weak arms barely strong enough to lift me up. I twisted, turning around and laying down on my back.

Sivrehya sat beside me, pushing me. "Get up, we need to move, at least to the cave." She coughed, her head hanging.

I closed my eyes tight, shivering, forcing myself to sit up. My body refused to move, except to shiver, my teeth chattering so much they could break.

Suddenly the princess screamed, her arms flailing wildly in the air.

"Holy Darkness, holy *mother* of shit!" She kicked her legs, thrashing. I sat up, alarmed; my body was again rushing with panic and alertness. I searched through the rain, into the lake, only to see her in the water. I shook my head, blinking, wiping the hair from my eyes.

"Get off me!" I could hear her scream.

I stared at her, leaning forward. Her bright red eyes looked into mine, her pale arm wrapped around something, tightly, as if she was holding on for dear life. "Why the hell are you in the water?" I yelled at her, starting to reach my hand out for her to grab.

"What the fuck are you talking about!" She seemed to scream from beside me. I turned around, seeing her, wet and muddy, kicking her legs, a dagger in hand. Around the princess's leg was a bony hand with fingers that were too long to be anything natural. I blinked, turning back to the lake. And there, instead of the princess, was a figure, a woman of sorts, with grey-blue skin, and decayed scales. Her eyes were the color of her sagging skin, her hair was black and thin as sewing thread. She opened her mouth, as if to smile, showing her sharpened teeth that were stained brown.

What just...

My mind began spinning, questions unfurling in my head one by one.

"What, what the fuck is that!" I yelled out, scrambling back, away from the water.

"Who the hell cares! Hit it!" Sivrehya screamed through the storm, as the thunder crashed above us, as the rain pelted down and the lightning flashed in the distance. The princess lifted her arm and plunged the dagger in the creature's hand. It shrilled, screaming, groaning, yelping like a dying animal. It reached back and over its other arm and wrapped it around Sivrehya's leg.

The princess kicked at it, ferociously, as if she wasn't cold and shivering and on the brink of freezing to death. Adrenaline rushed through me as I reached for my own sword, but the sheath was empty.

"Fuck," I cursed beneath my breath. I had stabbed something and fallen off a cliff without taking my sword with me. My chest heaved, my heart pounding against my rib cage. I pushed the hair from my face, and blinked, feeling the ground, half-blinded by the rain. My hand touched a cold surface, hard like a rock. I picked it up and hurled at the creature's head. It collided. Through the storm I heard a crack, and thick liquid oozed out. Another ear-splitting shrill from the creature. I ignored the wail, and snatched a fallen branch, swinging it at the creature, screaming at it just as the princess was.

And then it fell back into the murky green water of the lake. The princess stopped thrashing her legs, ripping her blade from the severed hand of the woman that laid on the ground. She immediately stood up, her body waving from side to side. Her chest heaved, as did mine. I threw the stick aside, standing, bending over, holding myself steady, or at least trying to. I searched the lake, the water, for any sign of the decaying lady who came out of it. I stepped back, like a drunk.

"The cave," Sivrehya heaved, coughing. She pointed weakly to a cave opening just a little ways away. I nodded, making my way slowly to the protection of the cave.

Inside it was darker than night, but at least dry. I collided with a wall, sliding down it, sitting down. Catching my breath, I watched as the princess slumped down, a hand around her shoulder, shivering.

"Can you—magic to dry us?" I asked through chattering teeth.

Sivrehya shook her head weakly. I nodded, understanding that the risk was too great. This time we wouldn't have an escape plan if more Obscurae found us.

"*What* was that?"

"I—I don't want to know," she replied, sitting against the wall across from me. Her eyes met mine, half covered in wet black hair that stuck to her face. Our eyes lingered in each other's before I noticed her hand on her shoulder. It was red. She was bleeding.

"What happened to you?" I demanded, forcing myself to stand, my body screaming with every move.

"Nothing," she replied weakly, coughing.

I crouched in front of her, pushing her hand away. She didn't bother resisting; perhaps she was too tired, too weak to try. She let her arms fall on her stomach, revealing the large tear in her sleeve and the hole gushing out blood.

"You need to heal that right now."

"At what cost?" she shot back. "Our lives? We did *not* just jump off a fucking cliff and get attacked by whatever the bloody hell that was, to just *die* from the very Obscurae we managed to escape in the first place."

I ignored her logic, hating that I agreed with it. "You're bleeding a lot. Darkness knows how much blood you've lost already."

"I'll be fine." She waved a hand dismissively in the air, before reaching for her dagger.

"Sivre—"

"I said I'll be fine." She cut me off, her voice cold. Her eyes shifted from mine, and with her dagger in hand she began to tear at the skirt of her dress. Slowly, she ripped a piece of thick fabric, setting aside the blade, lifting her good shoulder and arm, and draping the fabric over her wound. I shifted, leaning forward.

"Let me." I reached out; she tensed.

"*I* can do it."

I ignored her and took her hand, moving it aside. I looked straight into her eyes, searching them. "I know, but you're going to take more time than we have. So, I'm going to do it, so we can go back out there and find this fucking Neithisis."

I saw a war in her eyes, but she let her arms fall in defeat. She moved her head to the side, letting me wrap the fabric tightly around her wound.

"I'm not going back out there." She coughed again, her body convulsing.

"We have to. How else will we find the beast?" I tied a knot, doubling and tripling it to make sure the makeshift bandage would stay in place.

"The cave, we could search the cave."

I leaned back, glancing into the darkness that loomed before us. It seemed like the secret passages all over the castle in Lysmir, shrouded in black. I looked back at the princess. She blinked, shaking her head yes.

"The caves it is, but if we get lost?"

"We're already lost," she huffed, shifting, forcing herself to stand. "The bigger problem is that we have no light. I'm saving my diminishing energy to talk to an ancient creature and to make a portal out of this place, but I can't make a light or a fire. We're going in completely blind."

I smiled, suddenly remembering that in my satchel there was the small light orb that woman had given me when I was searching for an inn to stay. I stood up, slowly, stepping back and opening up the drenched bag. I threw out the soaked bread wrapped in the cloth and the apples that had taken too many hits. At the bottom was the clear ball. I smiled, pulling it out.

I held it out for her to see, "No, we have light."

Her eyes lit up, just a little bit. "She gave you one too?" She almost laughed. I looked at her, confused.

"How did you know?"

"I went to the same place it seems, and this lady practically shoved it into my hands, along with a million apologies. Although I never did figure out how to use it." She lifted her good arm, pushing the stray hairs from her face and back. Her bun had fallen out, leaving her hair in a soaked braid falling down her shoulder.

I looked down at the orb, cocking my head to the side. "We have to spin it," I explained. I placed it on the uneven ground, holding it lightly with one hand, twisting my wrist to spin the orb but it rolled off.

I chased after it, snatching it from the ground. I looked up in front of me, coming face to face with darkness. It seemed so real, so alive, like it could have been the actual Darkness itself. I shivered at the thought. I knew that inside of me, there was a piece of it. After all, as a descendent of Luthyn Thaegan, the man thought to be the first soul mage, it was a given, as he was a direct spawn of the Darkness. And yet, the sheer thought of coming face to face with the cruel wicked thing that lived inside me, scared me more than a lot of things.

I shook my head, pulling myself back to reality. This was just the lack of light, not the Darkness. I looked down at the orb in my hand, lifeless and empty.

Beside me, the princess appeared.

"I feel like I'm looking at myself right now, and I hate it, so spin it now." She sounded scared; her voice was small. I understood her perfectly, shifting to face her instead of the darkness looming in front of us.

I opened my palm, placing it in the middle, spinning it. Slowly, in the center, there was a dim golden orb. And slowly as the orb started spinning it began to float above my hand, higher and higher, getting brighter and brighter until the cave was filled with a golden light and the darkness was no more.

Now we could see a series of caverns ahead of us, stalactites hanging from them, water dripping from them. Rocks were sticking out at awkward angles, bones were scattered and scurrying creatures skulked who hated the light.

"And voilà, there we are. Light!" I beamed, seeing the cave around us becoming illuminated. I began to walk slowly forward, the little orb of light following me. The princess mirrored my pace, walking beside me, wavering just a bit.

"You seriously need to heal yourself. I can't have you slowing us down."

"I will not slow us down, thank you. And if you must know, I plan to heal myself...just after we find the Neithisis and get the information we need," she replied back, crossing her arms. Ancient bones of some sort were crunching beneath her weight and pulverizing.

"Ugh," I groaned, "You're impossible."

Sivrehya scoffed, feigning offense, putting a hand to her chest. "I'm impossible? *You're* impossible," she spat.

I crossed my arms, a smirk twisting itself on my face, "Well, you're infuriating."

"And *you're* horrible." She countered, scrunching up her face.

"*You're* terrible," I clapped back, totally, one hundred percent meaning it.

"You are utterly despicable."

"And *you* are completely maddening."

"Abominable," she countered, standing, not even wincing as she made her way towards me slowly.

"Detestable." A smile edged itself on my face; I crossed my arms.

"Heinous."

"Wicked."

"Loathsome."

"Vile."

"You're a black-hearted jerk."

Oh Fuck...what else?

My mind was scavenging, looking for words as I shifted my position in hopes to distract her from the fact that I was at a loss for new insults. But it proved useless as I saw a smirk slowly growing on her face, her red eyes sparkling with contempt. Seeing my silence as defeat, she began walking past me, into the cave and all its terrible secrets. But I stopped her, grabbing her arm with my hand. She froze and then lifted her head to meet my gaze. Red eyes boring into my silver ones.

"You're a villainous demon," I whispered; my mouth opened with a devious grin.

She smiled, innocently, all the while mischief raged in her scarlet eyes. And then the princess raised her feet to whisper something back in my ear, "And you are a bastardous imbecile." Her voice held amusement, from perhaps knowing deep down that no other would jump into my head. I clamped my mouth shut.

Dammit, I thought. Because no words came to me. *She won.*

I let her go, accepting I had lost. As she walked away, deeper into the cave, her muddy dress bright against the golden light all around us, I could sense her smirk growing.

Curse you, Sivrehya Rithloren. Curse you and all you stand for.

XXX : SIVREHYA RITHLOREN

The Raven Mountains

"Hurry up, charming, we don't have all day!" I shouted to the prince, my words bouncing off the walls, filling the world of caves within the mountains. We had been walking for what seemed like forever and what was probably in reality just ten minutes. "Here I am walking ahead of you and you were the one who complained I would slow us down."

He scoffed, "Forgive me, I'm tired."

"*I* can't have you slowing us down." I turned around, relaying his exact words to him. He rolled his eyes.

"Funny." He gave me a fake smile before running up to match my pace.

I turned around. In the light I could see his body tense, walking stiffly through the cave, eyeing every little detail.

"Are you afraid of being in tight spaces?"

The prince looked down at me, shaking his head. "No, I've been in tight spaces all my life. In the castle, we have these series of ancient passageways in the walls and underground. My sisters and I would always chase each other down, use them to spy on people. Back when we were younger." His eyes shifted down to the ground as he came up beside me. His voice sounded almost pained, as if it hurt remembering his childhood, his sisters.

I knew he was my enemy, a monster like me, but he lost people he loved. As did I, and despite my mind fighting to hate him, to find every little piece of him revolting, I couldn't. He hid a sadness in his eyes, in himself, and I knew it all too well.

"This cave," he spoke more quietly this time, as we began

walking again. "It looks too much like one of those illusions they made, it's incredibly unsettling. That, and I'm freezing to the bones. I don't know how long I'm going to last."

I glanced down at my own attire. A once perfectly fine dress now had a giant rip at the top of the skirt, mud and little tears at its hemming, and it was drenched in green water. I felt disgusting and probably smelled ten times worse than what I looked like.

I couldn't make a fire. Well, I could make a fire, but for the sake of the Obscurae who could be in these very caves right now and my rapidly diminishing strength, it was best not to. Even though I yearned to make it, it wouldn't take much. Just a bit of concentration, a bit of blood. I could even draw it on the wall, I wouldn't even need to bend the blood...

No. No fire, Sivrehya. I told myself, over and over, like a command. I could barely feel my body. It had gotten so cold I was barely even shivering. My skin, in this light, was an eerie yellow shade, but if I focused hard enough, I could see the lilac. Or maybe it was my own mind playing tricks on me, my own fear of not making it out alive from these caves and never getting the answer, never seeing my brother and my sister and my mother.

No. Stop it. You're going to live. You'll survive. That's what you do Sivrehya. You get up, you keep fighting. Always keep fighting. I ran the words through my mind like a prayer, until it seemed to be the only thing I could think of.

I broke the silence between us, unable to withstand listening to the water drops falling in the distance. I reached through my mind, trying to think of something other than what just happened.

"Was walking through the portal, before, as terrible as the first time?"

Ivar stifled a laugh. "If I must be honest, this time was better. Simply walking into it and out is nicer than plummeting through the sky."

I hid my smile, "You know, in one of the illusions, I fell out of the sky too, into an ocean made of blood and there were voices laughing at me, claiming to be the dead that we killed."

The prince almost laughed but held it back. "What the hell? For real, you seemed to have gotten the illusion of a different world, dreamlike almost."

I smiled, "Yeah, but it sucked, it felt so terribly real. There was a part where I was on a pile of bones and I was being pulled under." I turned to look back behind us, where the cave's entrance had been long left behind. "The thing, the dead fish woman thing from the lake. When she grabbed me and tried to pull me into the water," I said as I shivered at the memory. "It gave me flashbacks of that illusion. It felt exactly the same, the fear, it just eats away at you, and you can't even scream or think, you're just paralyzed with panic."

The prince was silent for a bit, but then he cleared his throat. Bone was shattering to dust beneath him. "I got less imaginative scenery. I got one that actually happened. And I don't know how they knew, I can't, I have...maybe that's another question I can ask the beast."

"What did you see?" My curiosity got the best of me.

"Something I've been trying very hard to forget, something that's made up half my nightmares for the past several years." He seemed to want to leave it at that, and I opened my mouth to say something, but I closed it. What he saw scared him all over again, badly.

I reached for my necklace, pulling it out from under my dress. I touched the shard of red stone. It glowed faintly, in the middle, like someone stuck a small piece of light inside. I played with it, twisting the golden chain it was attached to.

"You never take it off," the prince suddenly said. I turned my head to face him, our eyes meeting for just a second before his floated down to look at the necklace in my hands.

I followed his gaze, eyeing the shard of glowing red in my hand, before letting it fall loose against my chest. "No, I never do," I confirmed, feeling for the chain, wrapping it around my finger.

"Must be something special."

I considered his words, thinking about the necklace, how it came to be, what it was and what it meant. "I guess, yeah, you could say that. It's a long story, pretty complicated," I started, letting the chain go and wrapping another finger around it. The memories, faint as they were, rushed back.

The prince said nothing, perhaps because he didn't know what to say.

"I guess we have the time, and nothing better to do," I laughed lightly. "You probably know about my older brother."

"Prince Daemon?" he asked. I turned away from the prince, shaking my head, looking at the little orb of light and then in front of us, where the cave's passageway continued on.

"No, not him. The other one, Laidon." I paused.

Ivar nodded, "Yes, yeah, I—I know about him."

"And you probably know what happened, or a version of what happened to him. I remember hearing so many I never knew which one *actually* happened. As a royal you always hear every version of every story, it's hard to keep track. And I think, I think maybe my family never told me what really happened to him, to spare me some of the world's evil. Maybe they thought I would be too young, that I was too young to understand, to be exposed to."

Around us, water fell, in drops, in the distance, but it seemed as if it was happening right beside us. I stared forward, grabbing for the shard of red rock again.

"I never bothered to ask the real story, even years later. I think it was because there was this invisible shift that happened after he died. I was just seven, and I barely remember him, but I remember something changed. In all of us, I saw there was a difference, a coldness came in and stayed. We were a lot less, I don't know how to put it, a lot less closed off and stiff before. I remember that. And then Laidon died...my family changed, in an instant." I paused, thinking on the memory, diving deep into it. "Yeah, that's probably why I never asked."

The prince cleared his throat, coughing. "I—I heard he was forced to fall into a pit of spikes after he forced someone else to do that."

I turned to face the prince; a brow raised. "Really? You seem to have different theories than us. I've heard many, one I remember the most is one that was popular on the streets. That he was lovesick, but the girl forced him with a curse to swim in boiling water after she saw him with another girl."

Ivar laughed, "My god, a young ladies man."

"Ha, yeah, seems so, with that story at least. But I don't know, I heard another where he went mad after accidentally drawing a symbol wrong, and he threw himself into a pit of fire." I smiled, shaking my head at the memory of the letter coming to our family with a variation of those words from a "concerned villager".

"I don't even *know* where the pit of fire would even be," I continued, "As far as I know, we don't have one. We just have fireplaces. But anyway, apparently there was some sort of curse involved, so my family, being the one to take every measurement of safety, took out this insanely large spell book, from the darkest part of the library. And inside it, there's this extremely complicated spell, that requires a lot of blood, and concentration and energy." I paused, wrapping my hand tightly around the stone. "A protection spell, against all curses, from any blood mage. But it has to be linked to an object that then must be bonded to you. So, there are a million steps and a lot of blood involved. And the catch is, you must be the one to do it, no one else can do it for you."

Ivar sighed, running a hand through his wet hair. "My goodness, blood magic is complicated."

"It's fucking *impossible*, I swear. You don't know how many hours of the day I spent training and memorizing all these spells. Some are easier to remember, like healing, and the portal spell. But some are actually hell, and the worst part is the stronger, more complicated the effect is, the worse the symbol will be. The more lines, the more twists and turns you have to make." I sighed. "I missed being a child because I was so focused on learning new spells, keeping old ones, training with blood bending. All my siblings, we were never really children. We barely played. When we did, it was always disguised as training. We play fought each other with real spells and real spears made of our blood. It was never really pretend."

Ivar's voice was rough when he spoke. As if he had been crying, "You're not the only one who never had a childhood. It seems as if the royals never get one. We're born and immediately thrown into the world of magic, and training, and learning and fighting, and more fighting."

I flung my hands up in the air. "Yes, exactly. I mean, I can't say I'm complaining. Being a child, not preparing for what the world is, for what it can do, would probably have killed me before I reached the age of sixteen. But I don't know, sometimes I see children in the markets, the streets, and they're being children. And sometimes I wonder what it would have been like..."

"But?" The prince continued, sensing I wasn't finished.

"But," I repeated, "If I could go back in time and choose to either have a childhood or to not change a thing. I wouldn't change a thing."

"Neither would I," Ivar said, softly, after a small length of silence.

I sighed, once again reaching for the chain and wrapping yet another figure around it. "The necklace is protection."

The prince shifted to face me, stepping over a small pile of rocks. "Protection?"

"Yeah, against curses, any curse, complicated as it might be, powerful as it might be. It's a protection against all of them. And that's not even what makes it nearly impossible to cast."

The prince raised a brow, "Oh?"

"Yeah, because not only does it require an obscene amount of your own blood, you have to be the one casting it. Then, this spell can only be placed on an object, not you. So, you have to enchant an object, in my case this necklace. My sister and mother chose a bracelet, my father and brother, rings."

We kept walking deeper into the cave, the ground becoming less and less flat. The walls seemed to start closing in on us, and more and more bones were littering the floors. And when I looked down at my feet, I swore I saw a hand before I crushed it beneath my weight.

"After all that," I continued, "you have to bond the object to you. You have to make sure it protects only you. And bonding spells are pretty difficult. Then, on top of that, you have to make sure you don't lose it. You have to make sure someone doesn't just yank it off you or steal it. So, you have to place a protection spell *on* the object."

"So," the prince elongated the word, "to put it simply, blood magic takes forever and I probably shouldn't touch the necklace, like ever."

I laughed, nodding at his words. My magic was frustrating, but if one was patient enough, they could do amazing and terrible things that made the impossibility worth it.

"And I mean," I shrugged, "you *could* try if you really wanted to. But, unless you want to be burned so severely that your skin starts to melt off, I wouldn't suggest doing so."

"It does that!" His eyes widened with bewilderment, looking down at the stone in my hands.

I grinned at his shock, "Yeah. It's harmless to me, but to anyone else, and I mean *anyone* else, it burns like hell."

"I'll keep that in mind," he said, tearing eyes off of my necklace wearily. "So, three spells then, for it to do its job?"

I nodded. "Yeah, three spells. A protection spell for us, a bonding spell and then a protection spell for the item we're bonded to." I paused, my hand still encasing the glowing stone. "It was complicated, impossible, and it should have killed me. I'm not sure why it didn't. I remember being told by my mother that I couldn't risk casting the spell, that I was too young and they would figure out something in the meantime when I got older. But I'm curious and defiant and I didn't accept the risk as anything actually horrible. So, I watched my family do it, and then in the night, I stole the book, grabbed my favorite necklace and did it."

"And?" The prince leaned towards me as if completely invested in the story. I smiled.

"And then I died," I responded bluntly. He stopped mid-step; a brow raised. I threw my hands up in defeat. "Kidding, I lived. I remember waking up, and my family was all around, and the maids kept asking how I felt, and I was so confused. And I was told that they found me, bleeding to death on the floor, this necklace around me and when they touched it, the poor maid...she, um, she died from the wounds it gave her. And they told me, I had been like this for a month. Just lying here, unconscious, for a *month*. My skin was paler than what it was usually, and I was dying, slowly. But I woke up, I lived, and no one knew how. My mom said it was because Rithlorens always get up, we always keep fighting." I smiled at the memory of my mother's hands through my hair, caressing me, smiling and telling me those words for the first time. "I think it was then that she started saying that. To me, to everyone. We get up, we keep fighting. Always."

I drew in a breath, letting it out, sighing. I hadn't told anyone this story. Not that I communicated with people outside of the castle that didn't already know all about it. But all the same, it felt weird. The first person I told the story to was my mortal enemy. I couldn't seem to wrap my head around it. But if there was something I was sure of, it was that these past few days had tested my sanity and patience more times than I could count.

"It's interesting isn't it?" He asked, his eyes in front of him, towards the darkness ahead of us.

"What is?"

"How you, how the blood mages are able to do all that they do. I mean, if you think about it, chaos mages and soul mages are almost similar. And blood magic is nothing like ours, not really. Your power, if anything, resembles that of the solar and lunar mages more than ours."

"Yeah, I know..."

"Why is that?" He turned to me, nearly tripping on the bony remains of an arm. "Do you know?"

I shook my head, "I don't know really. None of us do."

"So, the symbols, how they came to be...that's all a mystery, to even you?"

I looked up at him, his eyes once again ahead of us, his silver hair turning gold in the light.

"Yeah." I placed my hand over my aching shoulder, wishing I could just heal it already. "I mean, there are theories of how it came to be. That old blood mages fused their magic with solar and lunar magic and created the symbols. Others believe that it was the Darkness itself, that spoke to Maehra and gave her the symbols. Though I doubt the Darkness would do that."

He laughed, shaking his head. "Yeah, it doesn't seem like something the Darkness would do."

"There are some," I continued, "that think the symbols came from a time long before the Dark Crowns. That the three of them were never the first ones, but simply the most famous blood, soul and chaos mages."

"Interesting..." He trailed off, as we trekked on in the golden lit caves.

I nodded. It was interesting and entirely bothersome if I had to be honest. Not knowing truly where my magic came from, from what it was created had been something that itched away at me since I was small. But there were no books on blood magic history, not here, and not in the library in the Twin Cities. At least according to the man who had helped me before. It seemed as if the true origins of blood magic were long lost history.

"I always wear this." The prince shattered the silence, save for the drops of water. I turned to look at him, seeing him pull out the silver chain I had always seen around his neck. At its end was a small clear ball, inside a silvery thread, that almost seemed to glow in the light.

"It's beautiful," I said. The moment I did, he tensed, putting it back beneath his shirt.

"I hate it, I hate that I have to wear it, that it even exists." His voice shifted, becoming cold and harsh, almost pained.

"Why?" I asked, our eyes meeting for a split of a second before he turned and looked ahead into the winding passage.

"It's part of my sister's soul, what I could salvage before my father buried her."

"Verena's soul?" I regretted asking, as the wound of her death was probably still open and bleeding and I just made it worse.

"No, not Verena's." He spoke, softly, like a child, afraid of their own answer, of what it could bring. "Avilyn's."

I almost stopped, stumbling over what could have been a skull-shaped rock or an actual skull.

Avilyn. Avilyn Thaegan. I hadn't heard that name in years. No one spoke of it anymore. There was a time when the names of all the Thaegans were spoken, each with hate and disgust.

I had heard of the things that happened to her; I never knew which story was real. No one in Meris did, because as usual, there were a million versions of the truths, a million lies.

"I'm sure you heard things about what happened." He seemed distant, lost in the memory of it all, as I had been.

"I heard a lot of things," I whispered, remembering the stories that plagued the streets of my kingdom for weeks, months.

"No one really knows what actually happened, save for her." He stopped suddenly, the words stuck in his throat, as if they were too unbearable to speak. "My father and—and me, and well, the whole kingdom knows a vague version of it all when I made the drunken mistake of trusting a fucking stranger."

I remembered that. Faint word of it had made its way to Meris, but by then, most of the streets had already been saturated with countless theories, countless stories of how Avilyn met her tragic end. And no one had known that version of the tale had come from the prince himself.

Our pace slowed; the orb floating above us shining a little brighter than before.

"She was eleven, I was sixteen. All three of us were close, but since Verena was crown princess, she had her duties that some-times, most times, kept her away from us. So, when we weren't training, fighting, doing what we *had* to do, Avilyn and I would chase each other down in the passages of the castle, sneak out into the forests, even try climbing the mountains. But we were always discovered by our guards. And one day, we sneaked out, got caught by guards and they told us to wait until a carriage arrived. It was sometime in winter, six years ago. And Avilyn pulls me aside and tells me to race her to the castle. Naturally, I do, but she trips on something, and she falls. She yells at me to help her, but I was laughing, telling her I'd win and she'd better hurry up. I leave her, I don't stop running, and when I reach the castle, I assume she's right behind me. So, I go in, and after some time, I look for her, ask for her, but no one has seen her since this morning before we snuck out. And," he paused, and I saw him fighting back some sort of emotion. His body was stiff, his hands clenched. "And for one entire week no one can find her. We trail her soul but it leads to a different place every time. And one day, I found her, because in that week I avoided everyone in order to find her. I search my entire damn kingdom and I find her. But she's different, she's changed. I take her back to the castle. Everyone is rejoicing but she's acting differently. One night, three maids are found dead and tortured, our treasury was broken into, assassins found a way inside, my little sister, the angel of the family begins torturing people, commanding them."

We continued down the path, searching for any clue of the beast, but none so far. Around us water continued to drop, the air became colder, our bodies, slower, heavier, more pained than before. I yawned, closing my eyes just a bit before shaking my head quickly. I needed to rest; my legs burned with each step I took. One of my shoulders was currently spilling far too much blood and I was enveloped in a drenched dress.

"She changed, a lot," the prince continued, "in the most terrible way. And none of us knew why. Until I figured out why her soul was always leading us in different ways. Someone switched hers out for another and ripped hers apart." He paused, our heads turning, eyes meeting.

"Switched them out? How does that—that's actually a thing? You—you can do that? You can switch people's souls?" My eyes widened, my mind once again spinning. I had believed it was just a high tale, a lie that they told to make their power seem worse.

Ivar nodded, slowly, painfully. His eyes filled with hurt. "Yeah, but you have to be very good, powerful, it's incredibly difficult. But someone had done it to her, and they tore her soul apart, leaving it in jars, in different places to confuse us, and then they put the soul of a murderer, a Lysmiran rebel in her body and they gave her back to us. But it was all a part of their master plan to destroy our family. And the only reason they didn't succeed was because my father found out, collected all the pieces of her soul, destroyed the one inside her, killed everyone involved and threatened the entire kingdom with their rotting bodies left on the streets."

That, *that* I had heard about. The story of the decaying bodies of all the Lysmiran rebels killed by the king had made its way to Meris all those years ago. My parents had been shocked at the way the king of Lysmir threatened his people. In all my years, I had never seen my parents do anything of the sort. Sure, they had their fair share of torturing and killing rebels, but never once had they left their bodies out on the streets for all the world to see.

I shivered at Ivar's story, at the darkness of his father, how it seemed almost darker than my parents, my siblings, me.

"He stitched my sister's soul back together as soon as he could," the prince rubbed his eyes as he continued talking, "but she was always in pain. From what the people thought of her, of the atrocities she committed, despite it not really being her who had done them. It was her face, her name, attached to all the heinous crimes. And a soul being torn apart is hell. Even if it's stitched back together, it's not the same. She hurt, always, so much. So, one day, she came to me, begging me to destroy her soul, and I refused. Two days later, she was dead, covered in blood, cuts all over her. My father buried her the following afternoon, and I took a piece of her soul before he did. For memory, for, I don't really remember. To have her with me, I guess."

The prince stopped talking, sniffling, as we passed a series of jagged stones. Part of me wanted to comfort him, tell him that even though it was six years ago that slowly the pain would lessen. But it was clear for him that it never did.

"Verena looked like her, Sivrehya. She looked like Avilyn, only Avilyn didn't have a symbol drawn above her. But both of them were in their beds, lying so peacefully you'd think they were sleeping, if it wasn't for the red that soaked their clothes and the bed." He rubbed his eyes and sighed, long and heavy, "When I saw Verena, it seemed like looking, like reliving, Avi's death all over again. For a second, I thought I was dreaming, that it wasn't Verena, that my mind was playing tricks on me. Only it hadn't been."

Deep inside, swirling, was an unnamed, unknown feeling. A terrible one, that ate at me slowly, I could feel it growing in me, setting a fire of panic blazing. But I didn't know why, only that there was something that bothered me, something that didn't feel entirely right. But I pushed it down as we continued in silence, listening to the water fall. This time it was sort of peaceful, a sort of calming presence. With the light I could see the frost on the rocks, on the ceiling of the cave. I could almost see our breaths as we breathed.

"But all those years ago, I left her, I left Avi there in the snow, when she tripped, and *because* I left her someone found her and..." His voice cracked, and died inside his throat. I looked at him, half expecting him to be crying, but he wasn't. He was simply tense, one hand on the hilt of his dagger, gripping it tightly, the other in a fist at his side. "My father blamed me, I blamed me, and he never, ever let me forget what I did to her. What I let happen to her, to us."

I knew the king of Lysmir was cruel, that he had no remorse for killing, that he even enjoyed it. And I never blamed him. After all my parents were the same; however, they were never cruel to me. I never imagined the king of Lysmir being cruel to his own children, but now, hearing his story, I could imagine it. I remembered the king in our throne room just days ago, declaring war, and there was a coldness to him. His own personal block of ice that he sculpted into a warrior, a ruler for not only his kingdom but his children.

"And in the illusion, they showed me Avilyn's body, in her room, covered in blood. In the *exact* way it was. Which, I can't—I don't know how they knew. How they knew what happened to her, how they knew who I was and who she was to me. I just—reliving that, even if it wasn't real..." He opened his mouth, but nothing came out, the words lost inside him, or perhaps too painful to speak. He closed his mouth, staring off into the distance, shaking his head. He hadn't shed a single tear, but inside him was a raging storm of emotions. Emotions he kept hidden, for reasons I knew all too well.

"You were just playing," I told him finally after the silence that spread around us had been too much for me to bear. But I didn't know why I had said those words. After all he blamed himself so fiercely, and I was certain people had told him the same sentence I just had a million times over with no reaction, no change from his end. "But..." I spoke with ease, afraid to add air to the fire that burned so violently inside him, "I'm really sorry you had to relive that."

I dared to look at him, hoping for the love of Darkness he would look anywhere but me. Only our eyes met. And he gave me the faintest of smiles, a ghost of one, half there, half not. And his eyes went from mine to the ground, glancing at the bones and shattered rocks beneath us, "This little string of soul was the only thing I have left of her. And this dagger, she gave it to me when I was ten. She said she stole it from a market stand, and I told her not to tell anyone else, *especially* our father."

"Wow," I raked a hand through my soaked hair, "we have incredibly fucked up lives, don't we? And *very* tragic, complicated family histories."

He almost laughed, "We do, all the wonderful side effects of being a royal in this shitty world."

I mirrored his smile, "Yeah, you know, sometimes I wish I was a—"

A deep, threatening growl, in the distance, something of a beast, came roaring towards us. Both of us stopped, the orb floating above us freezing in the air. We turned to face each other, and then back at the cave, and the passage that seemed to never end.

"You heard that, right?" he asked, narrowing his eyes, trying to make anything out without having to move.

I nodded, gulping, "I did."

"You don't suppose it's the Neithisis, right?" He leaned back, taking a small step in the same direction.

"I mean," I shrugged, my hand wrapped around my dagger as if that would do anything against a gigantic monster. "It *could* be. I'd like to think it might be, so, you know, we can ask it and then get the hell out of here."

"Did we keep in mind it's a *monster* with eleven heads, and magical eyes that if opened might rip us apart or burn us or do whatever magical properties it has?" He asked, the words mushed together out of slight panic.

"You know," I shifted, running a hand through the mess that was my hair again, "I think we sort of did, but that was when we weren't half-dead, and drenched and completely out of energy."

Ivar ran a hand across his face, "We're fucked, aren't we?"

Oh yeah, definitely.

"Well," I ignored that voice in my head that seemed to think our demise was close, "you never know, it might not be as mean as the other monsters, beasts we've encountered."

Ivar turned to face me, a dark brow raised. "For some reason, I seriously doubt that."

I shifted away, pursing my lips together, nodding against my will. "Yeah, yeah, you're probably right."

"It might not be the Neithisis," he said as he took a step forward. "It might be an Obscurae's growl that is echoing from outside into here, or it might be our mind playing tricks on us, it might be nothing at all."

We slowly, warily, began walking again, making our way towards the noise, down the passage. Turning left, our ears perked, our eyes wide and darting in different directions.

"You're right, it might not be nothing," I whispered. "The sound came from not far off, but we haven't heard it since, so it might have just—"

"Holy Dark Father." His arm flew in front of me, stopping me in my tracks. I stopped, looking at him in confusion, and then I glanced past him. Just to our side was an opening, into a room of some sort.

"Mother of Darkness," I muttered under my breath, my heart pounding against my chest so hard it could escape if it wanted to. I stilled, and Ivar mirrored me. We both stood there in silence, staring into the opening, unsure of what to do or say.

We had been looking, searching tirelessly, and gotten attacked by potential chaos mages that might be back to destroy us all. We jumped off a cliff to avoid being eaten alive by Obscurae, I was almost dragged into the lake by a woman-looking creature with extremely boney fingers, and now we were here. In an endless cave, looking into a room that held our answers, or our demise. Or both.

Because there, in the dimmed light, all eleven heads bunched close, steam coming from the nostrils and each eye closed, was the Neithisis.

XXXI : IVAR THAEGAN

The Raven Mountains

We found it. The Neithisis. The creature with eternal life and endless knowledge that couldn't lie. The beast that had eleven heads, eleven mouths filled with sword-sized fangs, and eyes that, if opened, signified our demise. The monster whose necks were so thick that each one could swallow us whole, and whose claws were big enough to grab us both.

And now, the princess and I stood like stone figures, hiding our panic and fear the best we could. We had yearned for this moment, we wanted it, and it was here. We were face to face with the one thing we would get answers from. But we never thought of what we would say, how it would react.

Far too late for that now, Ivar.

"Do not bother hiding."

Both of us stilled, our eyes wide. In the light spilling over us, we saw the beast shift on the floor, its various heads moving in unison to the side, slowly making their way towards us. I stepped back, its deep, scratchy yet hollow voice imprinted forever in my mind. It held no emotion, nothing indicating its intentions. One could tell in one's voice what they truly wanted, but the Neithisis's voice was a void, an empty never-ending oblivion.

"I know you are there."

It almost sounded like a bored threat, as if the beast was a predator, we were the prey and it knew we were powerless to defeat it. I looked at the princess, whose eyes remained fixed on the beast, her tired face pulled into a fierce expression.

We let silence take over, and in it the beast once again moved, stretching its enormous eleven necks all the way up, like a charmed snake. I lifted my head, watching as the light travelled higher with the heads of the Neithisis. Its massive body turned, its claws digging into the ground, the floor cracking and splitting beneath it.

"Are you afraid I will eat you?" The monster taunted, from up above. Its hollow voice bounced off the walls, surrounding us like a lethal embrace. "You should at least speak, no? Out of courtesy. After all, you are royals. It is expected of you, is it not? Prince Ivar Thaegan of Lysmir, Princess Sivrehya Rithloren of Meris."

I should have expected it to know, should have seen it coming, and yet, my heart lurched and my body tensed, taken aback by its nonchalant character. One head came swooping down, and then the other. One in front of us, mouth open, fangs bared. I fought the urge to gag; its breath was enough to kill me. In the golden light, I could make out the dried blood crusting on the side of one mouth, and on the teeth.

A thought struck me. What *did* it eat? If it lived in caves, in the darkness, in a mountain range where only monsters seemed to reside, what did it eat? And then another thought crossed my mind, sending chills down my spine, into my entire body.

What if it didn't *need* to eat anything...and the blood on its fangs, around its mouth, was blood from something, or someone, it had eaten. Out of pure enjoyment.

I shook the thoughts away, just as something bumped into me from behind. I jerked around, the air half stuck in my lungs when I saw another head, another set of terribly sharp fangs smiling at me with evil written all over them.

"If you know who we are, you know why we're here," the princess said, her voice unwavering. I turned around, the head behind me having swooped, moving away after getting a good scare out of me. In front of us, the heads grouped together, entangling within themselves, swooping down. Half the mouths were closed, half open. I kept a wary eye on the Neithisis's eyes, the very things that if opened could kill us.

I hated not knowing what they held behind closed eyelids. My father, mother, the entire royal court and even the kitchen staff would always whisper in our ears that knowledge was power, and what we didn't know might just kill us.

Their words flooded my mind now, slowly filling it with the dread of not knowing what the beast was hiding, what it could do. For all I knew, the magical properties of the eyes were all a lie, but deep down, where my stomach twisted with rising fear, I knew it was far from that.

"And if I do?" It seemed as if it was enjoying this, giving us bored threats that were real, giving us questions as responses and not answers. It was another thing that reminded me of myself, of what I could become, what I was like.

I watched its mouth, as only one of them moved at a time when it spoke. The beast already sounded like a million voices speaking at once from the echoes of the cave. I could only imagine how fearful it sounded if more than one mouth spoke.

"If—" I started, half regretting it. "If we ask you a question, would you answer it?" My eyes darted all over, trying to focus on all the heads at once. But the monster seemed to know I was attempting at that, and moved them quickly, in a taunting motion, as if to give us another proof of our certain death.

The Neithisis was silent for a moment, reflecting its answer, as it moved its heads around us, surrounding us in a circle of bloodied fangs.

"I like to think, to believe," it started. This time, its voice sent shivers throughout me, chilling me to the bones. For all of its mouths moved at once, filling the cave, the passages, the entire mountain with its hollow voice. "That even if I can do something, it does not mean I have to."

And then silence and pure angst flooded through me as I understood what the monster's words could mean. All the mouths remained around us, ever so slowly moving closer. The princess and I faced them, walking in a circle, our backs to each other, our daggers in hand.

There was something in the air, in me, this dreadful heavy feeling. I closed my eyes, shaking my head, shaking the feeling away. I blinked, pushing the hair from my face. I gasped, looking up, only to see all eleven mouths opened to reveal sinister smiles, a laugh bellowing in the distance and one eye, opening. And seconds later, there was a clatter, and the light, the only thing on our side, was gone.

Fuck.

I cursed the world, and the light that seemed unbreakable from the moment it had rolled on the sharp rocks. It hadn't even cracked, and now, it was gone. Plunging us into darkness, blind.

I felt Sivrehya tense behind me, her arm brushing against mine.

"Can you," I whispered, so low, I was afraid she wouldn't hear it. "conjure a light?"

"No," she whispered back.

I furrowed my brows. "Why not?" I snapped. Our lives depended on it. Both of us were weak, half-dead, and light could be the difference between living through this and actually dying.

"Because I actually *can't.*"

I groaned. She survived making an extremely dangerous, difficult curse when she was a child. But making a little light was too much for her now?

"Well try," I pushed her, our backs no longer touching. Around us, I could sense the monster quietly laughing at us. It gave no sign of aggression, not yet at least. But the air was heavy, and filled with the primal desire to kill.

"I said, I *can't* Ivar. Get that through your thick skull," Sivrehya seethed, her cold body softly hitting mine. I turned around, trying to make out her figure, but it was useless. There was no way my eyes could ever get adjusted to this amount of darkness.

"Why the hell can't you?" I forced myself to not scream, to keep my voice down. But the Neithisis would know anyway. Our efforts were useless against a monster that knew everything about the present.

"How the fuck am I supposed to know? The moment the light

disappears, I become powerless. I'm not *trying* to sabotage us, thank you very much."

Oh. The eye. Oh, Darkness save us, the eye.

The realization hit me like a boulder. I hung my head, my hands tightly wrapped around the dagger's hilt, ready to strike.

"Father of Darkness, the eye, an eye opened, Sivrehya." I breathed out, twisting around the moment I felt something hot behind me. In an instant, my nose screamed. I pinched it shut, praying for the pungent odor of something worse than rotted death, to disperse. I waved my hand out, blindly cutting at the air.

"Oh fuck," the princess muttered, "that must have been something against magic, because I can't—I can't do anything."

I delved deep within me, where my power resided, where now, no matter how much I willed it to waken, it remained dormant. I closed my eyes, centering myself, focusing on hearing the beast rather than seeing it.

And my mind spun until I drowned in a memory.

I was standing in a room, blindfolded, but even so, I could tell there was no light. I had been in this room countless times, and yet, every time it was different. Today, I was given no weapons but my dagger. And today, they had been told to make me bleed. I might be their prince, but that meant nothing to my father, to them.

"To bleed is to become stronger. The more you bleed, the stronger you become." Another string of words my father spat out and never made us forget. He never seemed to see the obvious untruth behind his phrases.

The first blade cut me above my left knee. The second, a stab at my shoulder, came after a blow to the stomach. I coughed, ignoring the blood spilling, the immense pain that sprouted at my wounds. I began to feel for my power, immediately shutting the will down. I couldn't. Not today.

Instead, I opened my ears, hearing their steps, their breaths. These were not trained assassins, they were soldiers. They would be loud.

I pulled the dagger from its sheathe at my waist, and readied my hand. Let them wound me, let them come to me, and I would know where they were.

The third blade cut my other shoulder. In a flash I twisted, grasping at the air until my free hand wrapped around a wrist. I pulled at it, hearing the first blade clatter on the stone floor. I didn't waste time trying to find the best place to stab. I just plunged my dagger into flesh. I heard a sputter, warm blood falling onto me. I let the person fall, and the fourth blade found me.

But it didn't cut. I did, deep, twice, into the stomach, for the flesh was softer. I heard groans of pain. I smiled.

The fifth cut came quickly, a messy stab into the same wound at my shoulder. I turned around, lunging, falling on top of someone. I took my dagger, flipping around so the person was on top of me, and I dug my blade into the back of the person's neck.

I pushed them off, flipping onto my feet, my blindfold coming loose, falling. My eyes met pitch black, all around me. My ears, meeting silence. I stood, impossibly still, concentrating on hearing the next soldier. But there was nothing.

There is not *"nothing"* now, I thought. There were the loud breaths of the monster. And at least one eye open. I had nothing, my dagger, and the princess with hers behind me.

In the darkness, there were eleven heads, eleven eyes, eleven mouths. And not to mention the teeth and claws.

"Let them come," I whispered.

"*What?*" She spat out, in utter disbelief. I stifled back a laugh at the scene playing in my head. I imagined the princess turning around to glare at me like I was stupid.

"Do you trust me?" I muttered, our backs hitting once again.

"To be honest, *not* really."

Okay fair, I'll give her that.

"Well...trust me on this. Let it come to you, and then, you know where to aim your blade."

"And if the—" Sivrehya screamed, as something behind me knocked me to the ground, forcing the air out of my lungs. I coughed, gasping for air.

Beneath me, the ground began to move and rise. But it wasn't the ground, the material beneath me was rough, and scarred. It seemed like chipped scales of an ancient—

My thought shattered in half as I was flung into the darkness, colliding with an ice-cold solid object. My head exploded with pain, my ears hearing one too many cracks that couldn't have been the rock I hit.

Falling, I turned around, straining at once, seeing only pure black all around me. And then, there was a light, bright and glowing, orange. I narrowed my eyes, my blood freezing as it got brighter and hotter and I could see the monster mouth opening and the fire coming from it. Right above it, another eye, this one the same hue as the flame I was falling straight into.

I closed my eyes, bracing myself for the impact. But it never came, at least not from the flame. To my side, something pushed me out of the way, and we hit another wall, and onto the floor. I grunted, tasting blood between my teeth.

"Sivrehya?" I said weakly into the darkness, the fire gone from the room, leaving behind the smell of smoke.

"Yes, me," she said. "We can't let this thing kill us. We need to get those answers."

"I think that—" I coughed up more blood, my head splitting. "That it will be hard," Another cough, "Impossible." I wiped the blood from my mouth.

Beside me, I heard her getting up, probably pushing the hair from her face, that held an impossibly fierce look on it.

"You said it, let it come to us, so let's play bait." In the darkness, I imagined her wicked smile.

I forced myself to stand, ignoring my body screaming for water, for warmth, for rest. "What do you plan to do?"

"Well," she started, the Neithisis laughing around us in its hauntingly hollow voice. "We have two blades, small but sharp. There are eleven heads, one eye that's open. No way of knowing which one it is unless it opens all of them at once."

The meaning of her words dawns on me.

"You *can't* be serious?"

"Unfortunately. You take the left, I take the right. We wound its body, make it angry, provoke it."

"And how do we destroy the eyes?" I asked, but the princess remained silent, perhaps already making her way to the beast. I gulped. It was a rough plan, with little chance of success, but it was something.

I turned around, blindly. I collided with a softer surface than the stone around us, but all the same it was rough and brutally ancient. I plunged my dagger into it, hearing a soft groan. I spared a smile for the minuscule success.

Another little whine. I yanked out the dagger, grabbing onto the scales, the spikes, and hoisting myself up, onto the body, feeling for the neck. The Neithisis hollered, thrashing. Above me, I saw a flame, and the neck it was attached to, the neck I was currently climbing.

I filed the dagger back in its sheath and held tightly on the spikes, beginning the climb, fighting against the monster waving its neck around in a violent manner, as if to shake me off.

In the near distance, there was a blast of white ice, illuminating the cave with the bright white of its newly opened eye. Slowly the cave began to chill, and warm, as the fire and ice began a war of their own.

I reached the top, feeling for the eyes. My hands touched something slimy. I yanked my hand away in disgust, quickly grounding my feet between scales for support, and then I pulled out my dagger, praying for a clean stab. And I brought the blade down.

This time the Neithisis screamed, shattering the ice that began to crawl all over the cave. Huge chunks fell, one by one, spilling onto the monster.

"Fools!" it seemed to sing, and then it screamed.

I fell from the head, rolling down the falling neck and onto the body once more. And then, my body paralyzed, unable to move. And in the distance, there was a light, white and hot. I closed my eyes, the only part of me that seemed to be cooperating. I cursed the world.

Two other eyes. If the princess successfully disarmed the one with ice, that meant there were nine left. From what I could tell, the head that was the farthest to the left was the one with the light, and above, before the light had blinded me, there was a green eye staring straight at me.

"Fools, fools, fools." This time the monster laughed. The pain from its injured eyes was seemingly gone. Perhaps this beast could heal. Though from the lack of incoming fire and ice, I reasoned that it couldn't. At least, I hoped.

I racked my brain. One eye made light, and the green one paralyzed us. Suddenly it was dark again, I fluttered my eyes open, slowly, just a bit, to see if it was safe. I was once again greeted by pitch black, but my body remained still, in place, like a marble statue.

It was possible to overcome magic done on you. When mages fought each other, and one had the other's life in their hands, the other, if willed enough, if strong enough, could reverse the roles. I had done it before, my father had, plenty of our soldiers had. I didn't know if it was the same for blood magic, for chaos or this type of magic. But it was worth a try. We were impossibly close, and we didn't survive two beasts just to be bested by the third.

I blinked, focusing not on my power, but on the magic rendering me immobile. I imagined, with all my remaining strength, what it was like to move my fingers, and my hands, and my feet. I imagined what it was like to control my body and just simply move.

Slowly, my fingers felt light, and they twitched. And then the feeling in my feet slowly came back, painstakingly slow. I shut my eyes tightly, continuing, even as the beast hollered and lurched up, sending me falling to the ground.

I backed myself up against the wall, dragging my body with my one good hand. My legs began to slowly crack from their magical shell. I moved them carefully, until they were fully free and I jumped up, slightly hunched and crouching. The left half of my upper body was still stiff and unwavering to the magic. But having two legs and one arm back was better than nothing.

I faced the darkness ahead, feeling the air around me shift and from three sides came three heads, mouths open. As one spat out water, I fell back against the wall, the rush of water missing me. The second, to my left, simply roared, coming so close it could have easily grabbed me whole and swallowed me. I raised my good arm with the dagger and threw it into the eye, not knowing whether it was open. The monster let out another terrifyingly high-pitched shriek, and its massive boney head knocked me to the ground. The Neithisis swooped its head back and forth, trying to get free from the dagger lodged in its head.

A warmth washed over my dying body. There was a spark that came back to life, a spark that woke up from being dormant. A flash of hope threatened to overcome me, so I pushed it deep down and tried, almost afraid to reach for my powers.

And they came to life, raging inside me as they always did. I blinked, almost frozen in shock. My ears drowned out the screams, the shattering and cracking of the cave walls around us.

I had my magic back. We both did.

"Sivrehya!" I screamed, not waiting for her response, "Powers!"

And then I lifted my half-broken arms and squeezed both my hands into tight fists, the magic inside me swirling and in an instant, the beast froze. And beside me, a few feet away, there was a small light floating, blinking off and on, but behind it I could see the princess, bleeding and smiling, sweat trickling down her angelically glowing face, a dagger in her free hand.

There was an unspoken understanding between us as she made her way beside me, and then the light was out, plunging us both back into darkness.

"Our turn to play monster," I said as I smiled wickedly, holding the monster under my grasp, feeling for its soul and its various magics that lay within it. I prayed for the magic behind its eyes to be linked to its soul as all other magic, save for blood magic, was. I searched for them, and felt all eleven powers meshed with a black soul.

So, I grinned, *your magic is in your soul. Better for me.*

It was a terribly frightening ability that we soul mages had. The one to take control of someone's powers just as easily as their soul, because all magic originated somewhere. Unless one was a blood mage, that "somewhere" was their grey-colored life source.

I felt for them and clenched my hands into fists, taking a hold of the beast's dark soul, of its dark magics, painfully aware that I was decaying from the action. Nonetheless, I stood firm and licked the blood from my lips.

"Should I hurt it a little more?" the princess spoke softly beside me. Even though she couldn't see me, I shook my head.

"You need to get us home. I'll keep this monster in check."

"Monster?" the Neithisis seemed to scoff. "I am offended."

"I don't care," I spat back, tightening my grasp. If it hurt the Neithisis more, it made no sign of it.

"Fine," Sivrehya sighed. I sensed disappointment in her voice. I was, after all, keeping her away from a good torture. "Then let's get this over with quickly." She took in a deep breath, "Are the chaos mages back? Did they kill Florek and Sierah? All those years ago? What is their plan, what are they trying to do if they are back? And if they aren't, if this was never the doing of chaos mages, then who killed my father and the crown princess of Lysmir?" Sivrehya gasped for air at the end of her string of questions. Given the gravity of the situation and our quickly depleting energy, I bit back a laugh. How we were still standing surprised even me. I wagered it was sheer will at this point.

"I do recall the prince saying 'if we asked you *a* question.' Not *questions*," the Neithisis spoke, its voice once again filling the room. Only this time it was disguised to sound strong.

"That's great, you have an incredible memory," the princess responded bluntly. "Now answer the damn questions."

I felt a smile forming on my face, my eyes rolling.

"You have no manners," the Neithisis huffed, judgmentally.

"When manners are needed, I can have them. Now. Answer. The. Questions." She was impatient; I could hear the looming threat, the anger in her voice. I almost felt bad for the beast, and if we weren't half-dead, I could be afraid for it.

"If I don't, will you kill me?"

"You know who we are, you probably have an idea of what we'll do."

"But you are both so weak. Even now, princeling, I can feel your magical grasp on me withering and fadin—"

"For the love of Darkness," Sivrehya bellowed, "answer the goddamn questions and do *not* test me. I may be half-dead, about to fall from exhaustion and succumb to the numerous wounds inflicted by mother fucking Obscurae, a fish woman thing and *you*, but if need be, I *will* turn you to bloody *ribbons*."

This time the cave shook with the princess's voice, the remaining ice shattered, falling and the beast seemed to retreat. I tightened my grasp once more, and when I did, I felt my head spin, becoming heavy. My body swayed and a trickle of blood from my nose itched the skin above my lips as it slowly fell, plopping on the ground beneath me.

"Before I do," the beast responded dully, "answer mine. What do you fear the most? The questions themselves, or the answers."

It didn't need to hear our answer to know. And even in the lack of light, I could see all its mouths opening, baring its fangs in eleven wicked smiles. And finally, in the darkness of the cave, the silence of the mountains, the Neithisis gave us our answers.

XXXII : SOMEONE TOUCHED BY DARKNESS

The Twin Cities
Moonsier, Inner City

The woman does not see us. We do not let her see us. Instead, we show her something else, something she would have expected. We show her herself, in the mirror, and behind her, closed double doors. She sees her long brown hair, spilling onto the floor. Her brown skin, glowing in the golden light, the powder in her hands disappearing onto her face, making it sparkle. She is getting ready for the first night of the festival, as they all have been. She wears a beautiful yellow dress with golden accents. The sheer sleeves show off the designs drawn on her arms. The suns, the stars, and nature etched into her skin, alive with magic. The gold sun medallion hanging from her neck gives away her power, the position she has in the city. It too glows, perhaps from the light, or perhaps from magic.

She does not see us in the reflection. None of them do.

She is the last one here. After her, there will be others to fall in other cities. Others who will also be blinded, and not see us. They will only think they are safe because we let them think that. Because we want them to.

Because when we drop poison into their cups of wine that will decorate their skin with a rich green like the forests of our kingdom, we do not want them seeing, we do not want them knowing.

We only want them to fall, and their cities to fall with them and our kingdom to rise from their destruction.

∽

The night is alive with magic, with people from the cities, from all over. Ancient traditional costumes are worn and on display, tattoos of suns and moons that glow with power decorate the skin of so many.

It is the first night of the Midnight Sun festival, the largest annual festival in all the lands of Rodessa.

We turn to face each other, as we blend in the crowd, wearing these despicable clothes, boasting shimmering designs on our pale arms and hiding our amber eyes with cleverly placed illusions.

"It is a shame it will be their last, no?" One of us says, dark desires in their eyes.

All of us nod, in unison, as one. "Yes," We reply, "A shame indeed."

And then, we laugh, dispersing into the crowd, taking our leave from the Twin Cities. *For now.*

XXXIII : SIVREHYA RITHLOREN

The Twin Cities
Moonsier, Inner City

The last thing I remembered seeing after the prince and I tumbled through the portal that was barely big enough for the both of us was Junah's face. Her eyes wider than the moon, her voice morphing into a high-pitched scream that yelled for help. And then, I fell into darkness.

"Tess?" Someone spoke out, their voice filled with uncertainty and worry, was faded and distant.

Who the hell is Tess, but the thought remained in my head, my mouth unable to open and function.

"Tesseria?" The voice asked again.

Tesseria? Who—oh...right.

I felt a soft nudge at my shoulder. I lolled my head to the side. Something fluffy beneath me was strangely comfortable. "You must get up, the first night of the festival is almost over, the sun is almost fully up and you do not want to miss it."

But I stayed put, the voice finally clear. I recognized it as Junah's calming voice. My eyes remained closed as I slowly became aware of the pain that once plagued me to near death was no longer there.

"Come now, you have been healed. You and your friend, both in terrible condition, what in the name of the Sun Goddess have you two been doing? I mean, honestly, I do not think I have ever seen anyone in such a condition. You can imagine the panic that went through me when you two appeared from nowhere. How did you manage that? You honestly ju—"

"Junah," I rasped out, coughing slightly.

"Yes, Tesseria?"

"Not Tesseria," I mumbled, forcing myself up.

"Sorry?" Junah's voice turned high pitch with her question. I shook my head, stretching my arms and legs in front of me like a cat. Slowly, I flickered my eyes open, yawning, getting used to not being filled with near unbearable pain.

"What day is it? What happened? How long have I been asleep?" I turned to face her, and the moment our eyes met she screamed, jumping back, the chair falling to the floor with her in it. She scampered away, backing herself up against the wall, though the door was next to her.

She mumbled a string of foreign words; she looked at the ceiling for a split second then back at me. All the while I was incredibly confused until it dawned on me.

Crap.

The eyes. *My* eyes. They were back to their natural bright red shade; she had only ever seen me with brown eyes. And she was smart, she would have no trouble deducing what red eyes meant.

"Are y—you a b—blood m—m..." She couldn't seem to bring herself to say the words.

I nodded, slowly, looking down.

"I am," I said, too tired to think of an excuse.

She looked around the room, processing the information, "Could I know your name?"

"*That*, that will make this a lot worse." I really didn't want to do this now, or at all.

She laughed nervously, "Why? It is not like you're a princess of Meris or anything."

I didn't say anything, I didn't even know what to say. But in my silence, Junah found her answer. Her brown skin paled to a sickly shade of cappuccino.

"Oh, *oh*, oh...oh," she said, as if she was about to faint. I jumped out of bed, catching her before she fell. She writhed out of my grasp in fear and disgust. "Stay away, oh gods, oh *gods!*" She fanned herself, grasping onto anything with a white grip to help her from falling. She moved away, making her way to the bed, before slumping on it, her head surely spinning.

"Are you okay?" It was an incredibly stupid question. I didn't even know why I thought asking it would do anything to make this terrible situation any better.

She glared at me, but her golden yellow eyes were too soft, she was too good to cause any fear with her stares.

"You—you are evil," she spat out, voice shaking along with her body.

I raised my hands, pushing my hair back and sighing, taking a deep breath in and out. "I'm *cruel*, but I'm not completely evil. There is a difference between being cruel and being evil. I prefer to have a motive for torturing and murdering; evil people don't. They do it purely for fun because they feel like it."

"*That* does *not* make it better." She almost scolded me, like my mother, when I've come up with a terrible excuse for doing something equally terrible.

I looked her in the eyes, then down to the ground, "No, I suppose not."

Silence fell between us, and I scanned the room. No sign of another bed. It was simple with a million books piled on the floor and on shelves, a glass orb of light floating about the desk, a mountain of parchment and quills, a window displaying a slowly pinking sky and a bed.

"Where am I?"

"Y—you are in my dorm room," she replied in a small voice. I turned to face her again. This time in her trembling hands was a protection spell, shining gold.

I sighed. "I won't hurt you."

"You *honestly* expect me to trust you?"

"No, I don't. But I'm not saying this to scare you, even though I might, but if I wanted to hurt you, I would have already."

She almost laughed in disbelief, but she let the protection spell fade away. I cocked my head.

"It's not fully day right, how are you able to perform magic?"

She looked at me, fear still shrouding over her like a storm cloud on a rainy day. "It's the festival of the midnight sun, half-sun, half-moon, it's the one week of the year when solar mages can use their powers during the night."

Oh! I almost jumped, sending panic through poor Junah. My heart, if I even had one, went out to her. She didn't deserve to be shaking in fear of me. But I knew there was little I could do to calm her.

"Ivar. Where is he?" I looked around the room, then back at Junah. She looked at me in confusion.

"Ivar?"

Oh shit. I hung my hand, running a hand down it. I scrunched my face, my hand on my forehead as I painfully said, "Sovan?"

At that Junah's eyes lit up in recognition. "Oh, Sovan he—" She paused, eyes once again impossibly wide. Her hand flew to cover her mouth. "*No*, do not tell me. Sovan is Ivar. Ivar is Sovan." She gasped, the pieces falling into place in her mind. She pointed out the window, "He is a soul ma—and you are the princes—and he is the prin—oh *gods*." She ran her hands through her hair, looking at me, at the ground, at everything in the room and back at me. "How in the name of the Sun Goddess have you two not *killed* each other?" She screamed, wildly, her arms flung out in the air.

"You know, that is a fabulous question!" I almost laughed, my voice raised in exhaustion. "I'd like to know that too, because I do *not* know how we're both alive right now."

Junah gave me a weak smile.

"But that aside, I need to know where he is." I softened my voice, "I need to go home, quickly."

She stood up, hurriedly making her way past me and to the door. She opened it with a shaking hand and beckoned me to follow. "Come, I will take you to him."

~

Moonsier, Outer City

We reached the center of the Outer City. I once thought it couldn't fit any more people. I was wrong. If I thought it was busy on a regular afternoon or night when the markets were booming, this was a mile above busy. I could barely move; everywhere we went we touched at least five people at once. The noise was to a volume where I could hear everyone else *but* myself.

Junah turned around, her mouth moving to form words I couldn't make out.

"What?" I screamed at her, with no avail. She had already turned around, softly pushing her way through the cluster of people.

After what seemed like a lifetime of being nearly suffocated with so many bodies, we arrived at the Stone's End Inn. Even here, where it was usually quiet, deserted, there was life. There were so many people we almost had to climb over them and wage a war just to get to the front door. Junah pushed it open, slamming it behind when I walked through. The man who was usually behind the counter was gone. In fact, so was the fire that always seemed to burn in the fireplace. This place seemed like a ghost town.

"He said he would come here to pick up your things, saying the same thing, that you two needed to leave."

I nodded, shaking the spices and flower petals that somehow found their way onto my clothes. My clothes. I looked down, finally taking notice of what I was wearing. It was a plain muslin dress, lightly embroidered with suns and flowers.

"Who put this on me?" I demanded, distinctly remembering that I had been wearing a dark red dress.

"I did, after I healed you." Junah replied, trying to not put emotion into her words. "You were in no condition to continue wearing that entirely soaked dress that smelled awful."

"I—" I didn't know what to say. "Thank you, really, thank you."

She offered a small smile, distant and feigned. I looked down, knowing she would now forever see me as the person the tales depicted me as. But for the first time in forever, I wasn't sure I wanted it.

"Ivar!" I yelled out into the silence, my voice echoing slightly.

"Sivrehya?" A faint answer from upstairs sounded. I could hear heavy footsteps and the floor creaking.

Minutes later the prince came down, carrying his bag and my own in both his hands. He was clean of all the mud and dirt that had stained his silver hair and pale skin. I had forgotten how uselessly pretty he was, and how much I had hated him for being quite possibly the most handsome male I've seen. He wore a shirt matching mine and white pants. His single dagger that remained was placed neatly in its sheathe at his waist.

I almost ran towards him, a smile edged on my face like it was on his, but just feet away I stopped. I was not just about to hug him. I was not happy to see him, just pleased he wasn't half-dead like before and ready for the trip home.

My eyes flickered down to the part of his chest that showed; it was bare. It shouldn't be.

"Your amulet," I stated, too bluntly for my liking.

He looked down. If it made him sad, which it naturally would have, he gave no show of it. "I lost it when fighting the Neithisis I assume."

There was no way it didn't faze him not having the silver chain hanging around his neck. And I knew we had to leave at all costs as soon as possible. But...

"Wait," I motioned, pulling out my dagger and slicing my palm. The blood floated out of me in the same fashion as it always did and this time it formed a common yet pesky symbol.

Summoning.

I closed my eyes, trying my best to remember its shape, its

meaning and the story behind it. The color of the chain, the small clear ball containing a single strand of a soul once bright and shining. I opened my eyes; the symbol having ceased glowing. I held my hand out.

"Give me something, anything, that is yours."

The prince looked at me, pure confusion in features. "Why d—"

"Hurry, we don't have much time to waste."

He dropped the bags, kneeling down over his and opening it, rummaging through some items. He looked up at me and tossed something in my direction. I caught it with my free hand. It was a shirt, balled up and bloodied. I wagered it was the one he had been wearing when we had fought the Neithisis.

I took the balled-up shirt in my hand and threw it into the symbol. A flash of red blinded the room and then there, in my still bleeding palm, was his amulet. I let it fall in between two fingers and I let it hang there. Ivar looked at it, barely believing it. I tossed it to him. In a blur, his arms moved to catch it.

"Sorry for the blood," I nodded at the amulet, but he just stared at me, blankly, as he put it around his neck. I healed my hand and reached for my bag, turning around to face Junah.

"It's time we leave," I told her, and she nodded.

"You will be better off following me through the lesser known streets to get to the main gates, otherwise you will reach them by sundown tomorrow, and only then." Her voice was almost cruel. With no emotion in either her eyes or face, she turned around, opening the door and walking through it.

"Thank you," Ivar said behind me. This time the words flowed out of him, unlike when he struggled to say it after I had healed him.

"You're welcome," I responded, smiling softly, and following Junah out the door, left the Stone's End Inn behind.

We reached the gates within minutes using the smaller, more quiet alleyways that Junah had taken us through. I looked up at the looming gates, wide open for the entire world to walk through. Just mere days ago I walked through these gates, thinking my life had changed and with one goal in mind. And now, I was leaving, walking through them once again, my life having fallen apart and the answers from an ancient beast spinning inside my head, weaving nothing but dread.

Ivar walked ahead, after saying his thanks and goodbyes to Junah. They didn't hug, or shake hands, or even touch. Not that I blamed her. She just came face to face with two monsters she only ever heard horror stories about.

I walked up to her, "I—"

"There is no chance in which you would tell me why you were looking for the Neithisis, right?" She cut me off, slightly hopeful. I could see it in her eyes, the flaming curiosity that everyone in this city held.

I shook my head, "It's best if you don't know."

"Will we ever see each other again?"

I remained silent, trying to choose my words carefully, but Junah beat me to it.

"It is probably best if we do not," her voice was almost sad. My heart clenched. I nodded, confirming her answer.

"Yeah, it's probably best if we don't. But *thank you* for everything, you've been a great help, truly."

She offered me a small smile; her eyes sparkled with content. "Of course, yes, yeah."

I pulled her into a hug, her body stiff from surprise at first, but slowly she let her guard down and wrapped her arms around me tightly. I pulled back, and she mirrored me, smiling and turning around. I watched her walk away.

"Junah," I called out, suddenly. She stopped, turning, our eyes meeting. "Talk to her," I didn't need to say her name; she would know who I meant. "And this time more than just 'hi'."

She laughed a little bit, nodding, "I will try Sivrehya, I will try."

And then, she disappeared into the sea of people. I stepped back, turning, feeling a sort of sadness that washed over me.

Ivar looked at me, "Are you ready?"

I nodded, and once again, I pulled out my dagger and ran a clean cut across my palm.

XXXIV : SIVREHYA RITHLOREN

Border between Meris and Lysmir,
Historic Battlegrounds of the Rodessian Kingdomlands

Grass spanned around us, and only in the far distance could the mountains in Ivar's homeland be seen. The wind swept around us, but it was almost calming. I closed my eyes, letting it caress my face.

"Now we know." Ivar's voice was crisp as the air.

I turned around, my hair whipping around my face wildly, "Now we know." I nodded, looking at him and then down at the grass beneath us. It was a faded green now, but so long ago, when the war between the three kingdoms reigned, I imagined it turned red for some time. And soon, it would once again be stained with scarlet. I wanted to believe that what the Neithisis said would change things for the better. I wanted to think there was a chance that now, Meris and Lysmir would not shed each other's blood, but the blood of our age-old enemy that ripped us apart. But, I knew, we both did, deep down, that this would only make things a lot worse.

Ivar looked up, into the sky, his silver hair flying around his face. He sighed, his hands in his pockets. The sun, slowly hiding behind thick grey clouds, shined weakly on his skin. I looked at him, seeing him for the first time, without blood in his hair or clothing, or a look of pure murder on his features.

He turned to face me, "I don't think..." He started, running a hand through his hair, "I mean, it's going to be hard to tell my father. To convince him that the chaos mages were never truly destroyed and that they were the ones who started all of this hatred between the kingdoms by killing Florek and Sierah. And that," he said as he turned his back towards me, his eyes towards his kingdom. "That Verena and your father were victims of their twisted scheme. He'll never believe it. He'll never *want* to believe it."

"None of us do," I told him, offering him a weak smile.

"Do you think your family will?"

"Honestly," I looked up at the sky, narrowing my eyes to block out the last rays of the sun, "I don't know, but we *have* to try to make them believe."

He sighed, nodding, stuffing his hands back in his pockets. "We should go."

Our eyes met. And for once, there was no hatred, no worry, no hurt. There was almost nothing. As if we were staring into a mirror, ourselves being the reflection of each other.

"Yeah, we should." I looked down at my still bleeding hand, "Where do you want to end up?"

Ivar searched the air, "Picture a room, with white walls and white curtains and a silver bed. There are two ceremonial swords with opal hilts and white blades in the shape of an 'x' hanging above it."

I nodded, wondering as I raised the blood, if it was his room he had described to me. The blood moved, twisting and turning, following my command, to form two portals. Behind me, and in front of me, red light stopped glowing. I turned my head, seeing past the red lines, and imagining my home, there, waiting to be burdened with what I held inside my mind.

"I tried my best," I told him, motioning to the portal behind him.

"I know, thank you." He said, looking back, no doubt imagining his home as I was mine. He turned back to face me, "Be careful."

I offered him a smile, "You too." We maintained our eye contact for just a few seconds longer and then I broke it, knowing it was time. I turned around, facing the portal that stood in front of me, the one that would lead me home. I sighed.

"Goodbye Ivar Thaegan," I turned my head to see him one last time. Darkness knows when we'd see cross paths again, if it would be going to war with one another on this very battlefield or in a civil meeting between our kingdoms, or never again. I didn't think about it too deeply; the thoughts would drive me mad.

"Goodbye, Sivrehya Rithloren." He didn't wave, nor smile, and he turned around as I did, stepping through the portal to his castle, as I stepped into mine.

∼

Kingdom of Meris,
Royal Palace, City of Maeh

There was barely any light in the biggest of our drawing rooms in the castle. This one was part of the library, and it gave view to the gardens through the windows that made up an entire wall. I smelled the familiar scent of the room, the warmth of it, feeling calmer despite the hell that reigned over us.

I set down my bag of things and walked deeper into the room, looking out the window, seeing the garden, slowly dying. The summer months were passing, and ever so slowly would come the fall.

"Siv," I turned around, to see my sister, her pale face paler than usual.

I ran towards her, burying my face into her rose-scented hair. She wrapped her arms around me, caressing my hair. "Sivrehya, are you okay, did you just get back?" She leaned back, her hands still on my shoulders. Her eyes moved down, and up, one brow raising. "What the hell are you wearing?"

I stepped back, looking down at the colorful clothing Junah had given me and back up into my sister's light red eyes that were filled with worry. "It's a long story that I—I need to tell you, all of you, about."

She wiped the hair from my face, tucking it behind my ears. She offered me a small smile, holding me close once more.

"Mother is too unwell to move at the moment, but I will get Dae, General Silian, and Jace. In the red room, ten minutes." She kissed my forehead, walking me to the door before making her way to the left, and I, the right. My hands shook; my whole body did.

~

I looked them all in the eye, one by one, as they filed through the double doors of the red room. The tea the maid had brought was in the middle of the table, steam coming from the pot. My sister, brother, the General and his son, Jace, stood at the other end of the table.

"You—you're all going to want to sit down for this." I told them. They looked at each other in the silence, and each, as if controlled, took their seats at the table.

"Sivrehya, are you—are you alright?" my brother asked, looking at me, as I slid into my own seat, pouring a cup of tea with a shaky hand. I put the pot down, sliding it to the General. I brought the cup to my lips, taking in the smell of roses and lavender.

"No, I'm not." I set the cup down, letting the steam from it caress my chin and neck.

"What happened, Your Highness, what did you learn?" the General asked as he passed the pot to his son.

"This past week has, to say the least, tested my sanity in various ways." I leaned back in the chair, a hand to my forehead. They all stayed silent, passing the tea amongst them. From all of them spilled worry and curiosity. "Since I am telling you this, I might as well tell you everything."

And I did, and time seemed to stop as I did. As I told them of Ivar, and Junah. Of the museum that held the exact same symbol that was drawn on Princess Verena's wall. Of the mysterious mages that attacked us at night, of their curiously chaotic magic. And of the Obscurae and the half-dead fish woman. And finally, of the Neithisis. Of its hideous breath and even more horrendous eyes. But mostly, of its hollow voice and what it spoke of.

And by the end of it, they were silent. Each of them, still, like statues. Until my sister dropped her tea cup on the wooden table, shattering it.

"I—" she started, "How dare you! That soul-sucking bastard is our mortal enemy, and you just mean to tell us you—"

"Rhiannyn, that's enough." My brother stood up, silencing her.

"You *cannot* be serious, he is o—"

"Yes, I know! I know who and what he is. I know. But Sivrehya is fine, and right now, by the looks of it, we have much bigger issues."

Rhiannyn looked down, sighing. I couldn't blame her outburst. She glanced up at me, all the while blood floated around her and the tea cup she shattered fell back into perfect condition.

"I'm sorry sister, I—you, it's," She stumbled, finally sighing, "... I'm sorry."

"No, don't apologize. I hated myself for it too, but without him, as much as I would like to *not* say it, I wouldn't have gotten the answers. I might even be dead."

"What do we do now?" The General also stood, followed by Jace, who remained quiet, his eyes darting between my brother and the table.

"How do we know the Neithisis cannot lie?" It was my sister who spoke this time, "How can we be so sure that the chaos mages still exist? As far as we know they are *dead*."

"Do you not trust me, Rhi?" I tried to not be mad, to not be hurt, but I was. And no part of me could blame her.

"Of course, I do, with all our lives if need be, but I don't know, sis. I just, the chaos mages *can't* be back. They—" She fell back into her seat, shaking her head viciously, "We *destroyed* them, we killed them all."

"Princess Rhiannyn is right," General Silian stated, putting his hands behind him, "Though I trust your word, Princess Sivrehya, more than that of most, we cannot be sure, as we did not see."

"But they're real!" My voice cracked, "I promise, please, you have to believe me." I stood, frantic, looking at each of them, almost pleadingly.

"I—I need to show you all something. That might make you believe." My brother spoke quietly, slowly walking out of the room. I looked at Jace, and Rhiannyn, even the General, but none spoke. They all, slowly, followed my brother from the red room to the basement, where on a slate of stone lay the black coffin of my father.

"What are we doing here, Dae?" My sister asked, looking around the room. Daemon reached for the coffin, opening it. I gasped, the air suddenly a thousand degrees colder. Inside was my father, but not as he was before. Before he was a pale-dry husk of a man, with colorless white eyes and decaying skin.

But now, he was different. He was pale, yes, but there was still color in his skin where there once was none. His skin was firm, but not at all decayed. I staggered back, from the shock. I shook my head, my mouth covered with shaking hands. I looked at my brother.

"What—what is this?" My sister asked, her eyes painfully wide.

"When we," he said, his eyes locked with Jace's, "were preparing the coffin, I sensed there was something unnatural. So out of a whim, I made a simple spell, to take away whatever magic might have been done to him. And..." His eyes floated down to our father's corpse.

"This what we found; he was poisoned. Here," Jace leaned over, reaching for the right sleeve of his red suit jacket and pushing it up just a bit, for all of us to see the thick green veins that travelled from his palm up his arm. "We asked the nurses. They recognized it as green ivy root."

My head snapped up to meet Jace's gaze. "Green ivy root. But that only grows in..."

"In the Sourielian forest of Vylara, deep inside, where their royal city once stood." Jace finished for me, and silence creeped in, as the five of us looked at each other in horror.

No one ever dared enter the ruins of the Fallen Kingdom. Those who did, never came back. It was like the Raven Mountains, because in its shadows, the Fallen Kingdom also held secrets that would kill. And though no one outside knew it, no one stepped foot in the overgrown forests. The terrifying realization hit me like a boulder. If no one walked into the kingdom to get this specific poisonous plant and survived, then it must have been someone from the inside. A chaos mage.

"There's one more thing." My brother pushed the sleeve back down, closing the coffin. "The boy I told you about, the one whose soul was destroyed, he has the same markings."

"But that, that doesn't *have* to mean that the chaos mages aren't all dead, it could just be a crazy person like you said when we found this." My sister was clinging onto the reality we were taught, the reality that we knew, the one that we wanted now, more than anything.

"Rhi, I know you don't want to believe it. I don't either, I don't think any of us want to. But the proof is here."

"That's a plant that *any* lunatic brave enough to walk into those forests could have gotten."

"I know, but Rhi, think about it. You might be right, it might have just been a lunatic mage who was brave enough to walk into those terrifying forests and walk back out with a bunch of poisonous green ivy root to kill Father. But we would have known from the *very* beginning, without ever even thinking his soul was destroyed, if that was just that. Someone made it *seem* like Father's soul was destroyed, someone *wanted* us to see what they wanted us to see. And only one type of mage has the power to do *just* that."

He didn't say the two words. We all knew them, and in the silence, in our minds, we could hear the words perfectly well.

"Okay fine! Fine, let's play along. They're back, they never left. If this Neithisis says they want to destroy our kingdom and Lysmir, why did you encounter them in the Twin Cities? Why would they bother with a Free City all the way across Rodessa? That makes no sense." My sister played nervously with her hair, wary to not let the carefully placed pearls that hung in her hair fall.

"I'm sure there's an explanation for that, the city is home to the most knowledgeable people in the world, or maybe they were also after the Neithisis. But whatever it was, it no longer matters." Daemon brushed his hair with his hands, "One thing is clear; our enemy is no longer just the soul mages. The king of Lysmir is not a believing man. I think once he believes in one thing, his mind cannot be changed. We cannot rely on the prince to sway him. We cannot begin to trust every soul mage. We trust *only* ourselves."

The words struck me, as I looked at my brother. No part of me could be sure that Ivar would be able to convince his father, but it was his father. And surely a father would listen to his son, especially if our world and existence was gravely threatened.

But I kept the thoughts to myself, not daring to shatter the already delicate situation. I would trust the prince. I had to, because it was the only way I could see this ending in our favor.

"When do we tell the soldiers, the army, the people?" the General asked, his hands tightly around the hilt of his enchanted sword, his body positioned for battle.

My brother looked at me, then at our sister and then Jace. Then his red eyes met those of General Silian. "Now."

XXXV : SIVREHYA RITHLOREN

Kingdom of Meris
Royal Palace, City of Maeh

Our army knew, our soldiers, guards, and servers knew. The cooks knew, the handmaidens and stable boys knew. And so did our people. The word had spread like a wildfire, and though there was no wind plaguing the kingdom, the fire spread faster than ever, until in just mere hours, the entirety of Meris knew the terrible truth.

And just as fast the rumors washed over the cities and the people. Some started to think it was just a story fashioned by the soul mages to scare us. That one particularly irked me, and my brother had to stop me three times from storming out the castle and letting everyone know how wrong they were.

Some didn't believe it. Not that any of us blamed them. And some, some had fear in their eyes, fear like I've never seen before. And slowly we felt as if a shadowy demise swept over our land.

For the past days, the kingdom was preparing itself for an enemy it knew well. And now, it was forced to prepare for an enemy that was once thought gone, an enemy no one had fought in centuries but the prince and me.

The five of us had retired to bed in the early morning after our revelation, only to awaken a few hours later to inform everyone of the sudden change in reality. But that was yesterday, and now, the kingdom was no longer in shock. It had put that behind it and now once again trained tirelessly for a war that might come between us and Lysmir, and the threat of the chaos mages. Yesterday, after my siblings and I relayed the news to the kingdom, the castle became a bustling mess of newly recruited soldiers, new nurses, and enough food being cooked for years as if a never-ending winter was coming, not chaos mages.

Today, I had spent the entire morning and a majority of the afternoon surrounded by armored men and women, the General and my brother, telling them all I knew about how chaos mages fought. That my encounter with the mages was brief, and though it involved no use of blades, I told them that didn't mean the chaos mages weren't proficient with swords. I told them of the visions, of how real they were, how real they felt.

"It feels like you are losing your mind," I told them. I also told them that I had to tell myself it was fake, and that took more energy out of me than I thought I had. "We are in a very dangerous game now. These mages do not fear us. Perhaps they once did, but now, no longer."

If they did not fear us, it made them more powerful than we hoped. And it made us weaker, for we very much feared them.

But now, I sat in my room, the window open, to circulate the fresh air. I had promised my family to rest. My sister, acting as the mother to all of us, had practically ordered me to bed. But I didn't rest, I couldn't sleep. My head was too heavy for that. So, for the two hours that I had been in my room, I attempted to read a part of the history book I never finished and I had downed five cups of pomegranate tea, gone to the bathroom only to come back and drink two more.

The empty cups sat on a silver platter on the table by the opened window. The three pots, still warm to the touch, were right beside them. I stared at them, losing the sense of time, before picking them up one by one to see if there was any more tea left.

"Do I need more tea; do I *want* more tea?"

I did, but I didn't. I hated being forced to be here, even though I had done nothing wrong. I hated needing to rest while the world fell apart around me, while my kingdom had to prepare for two threats, and I had lingering wonders that plagued me about Ivar being able to convince his father.

I felt utterly useless sitting here, drinking tea, but I knew my sister meant well. She knew I needed to rest. Darkness knows, I hadn't slept or rested well in the past several days. But the feeling that I could be, should be, doing something to help was eating away at me.

There was a knock at my door.

"Who is it?"

"Your worst nightmare," my brother teasingly said. I laughed.

"Do come in then," I opted for a haughty accent. It was like the old days, when we pretended we were blood mages from the ancient days, having no idea if they talked with fancy accents or not.

My brother, who carried another silver tray with another teapot and a plate of cookies, walked in, setting them on the table. He pulled out a chair, sitting down, sighing.

"You're supposed to be resting."

"I'm *supposed* to be helping you and Rhi, anyone at this point."

"I agree," I'm almost about to thank him for liberating me from this forced resting time, but he held his hand up, silencing me. "After you've rested."

I groaned, falling onto my bed, laying out like a starfish, my legs dangling from the edge. "I don't want to rest, I can't. Not when the world is crashing down around us."

"I understand, trust me. But you said it yourself, these past days have tested your sanity—"

I leaned forward, sitting up. "My sanity has fully recovered thank you." I stuck my tongue out at him; he scrunched his face and made a baby face.

"Congratulations, sis. That isn't going to change the situation though."

"But...but what if General Silian and our soldiers have more questions for me, about how to fight the chaos mages?"

He gave me a face, an "oh-please" kind of face. "We both heard you saying you had nothing else to say, that you said it all, regarding that night."

I sighed, letting my head fall into my hands. I rubbed my forehead, the headache of yesterday and this morning weakening slowly. My brother walked towards me, sat down and wrapped his arms around me. He leaned over, kissing my forehead.

"Siv, I know you want to help. I know, but I need you to know that you have already helped in ways we couldn't imagine. And what you've been through, what you've seen, what you've learned merits rest. I know you don't want it, but please, rest. You're strong, but even the strong need to take care of themselves. You are of no use to any of us if you've over-exerted yourself."

I leaned back, offering him a small smile. "I know, I just..." I looked down, playing with the folds of my skirt. I threw my arms up in the air, "Ugh! I don't know!"

Daemon smiled and said, "None of us do." He stood, making his way to the door, but not before snagging three of the cookies.

"Hey!" I called after him, running to the door, but I stopped to see him laughing, running down the hall. I smiled. This, this was my brother, who despite having the world on his shoulders, still managed to find ways to laugh.

I had been circling my room for what seemed like forever when someone knocked at the door. I watched as the knob twisted, the door opening slowly, revealing my maid since childhood, my second mother, Lissa.

I smiled as she came fully into view, holding a basket full of blood red bed sheets.

"Hi Lissa," I sighed, finally sitting down in my desk chair.

"Hello Sivrehya darling, how are you?" She set the basket down, her pale red eyes meeting mine, her grey hair framing her gentle face.

"I'm—I don't entirely know."

She offered me a kind smile, like she always did.

"I feel useless."

"I doubt me saying this will bring you comfort, but you are not useless," she said as she started stripping my bed of its old sheets.

"I know, I know, I just feel like it." I swiveled around, staring out the window, my eyes catching something small and dark flying towards it.

A bird. A *raven*. It came flying in, screeching and gawking. I stared at it, its presence startling.

I reached for the dagger hidden in the pockets of my skirt and quickly ran a line across my wrist, bidding the blood forward. This might very well be just a simple bird, with no malicious means but to bring news in the form of a scroll attached to its thin legs.

Or it could be something else.

The symbol floating in the air stopped glowing and the bird cawed, as if in pain, and then flopped to the ground, wings fluttering. The blood flowed back inside me.

I put the dagger back in my pocket, picking up the little bird in my hands. "So, little one, you're nothing chaotically magical. Good." I set it on the table. It cocked its head, seemingly glaring at me.

"What? You can't blame me for being cautious."

I glanced down at the small scroll attached around his leg with a brown string, and carefully yanked it off. The moment the bird was free of it, it cawed once again and took flight, out of the window. I watched it disappear into the distance before turning my attention to the small scroll rolled up in my hands. I had no idea who could have sent it and why. If it was someone from the castle, they had no reason to use a raven. If it was someone from one of our cities, why would they have addressed the raven to only me? I took the string off, slowly unraveling the little scroll.

It looked so much like the last scroll brought by the raven I had seen. The one that we received less than a week ago detailing the unexpected arrival of the king of Lysmir and his entourage of the prince, his guards and several members of the royal court. And this one looked no different, though this time, there was no silver seal with the crest of House Thaegan.

I unfurled it, stretching it to its maximum until the paper lay flat in between my hands, and the words written in the blackest ink were clear.

Your Highness, as you might have guessed, my father is difficult to convince. I have spent the past hours both today and yesterday trying to make him believe. But he will not. Please, I ask for your help. I understand the loathe and hatred between us is not at all gone, but this is a matter of both our kingdoms and all our lives.

- I. Thaegan

I almost laughed at the formality of his letter. The only time either one of us bothered being our royal selves to each other was when we were fighting, and even then, it was entirely sarcastic. Why was he so formal now?

Perhaps he was being watched, or perhaps he had been taking measures of safety. Surely a prince would have no business writing an informal letter to anyone, not at a grave time like this. And certainly not one asking for help. I set the scroll on the table, watching as it curled in on itself like it was protecting itself from something.

I groaned, leaning into the chair. Of course the king of Lysmir was being an unmoving rock, of *course* he was being difficult. I should have expected it. I did, but maybe I was too wound up in my own kingdom's problems and the hope that he might listen to his son this one time to realize he never would. That man never listened to reason, not from my unpleasant experience.

I turned around, seeing Lissa come out of my bathroom, carrying towels in her hands. She looked at me, and then out the window.

"Was that a raven?" she asked, tossing the dirty towels in the basket along with the sheets she had taken off the bed.

I nodded, "yes it was."

Suddenly, a thought crossed my mind. A wild and mad one.

"Lissa?"

"Yes?" She lifted the fresh blood red sheets and placed them on the chaise lounge chair behind her.

"This might sound strange, but I have to go somewhere, and obviously seeing how my entire family is forcing me to rest, they won't approve of me going anywhere. So, could you tell them I'm taking an incredibly long bath, and sleeping or simply resting? Could you tell them I wish to not be disturbed?"

She considered me, raising a brow. This hadn't been the first time I asked her to cover for me. I had done it once when I was younger, when there was a food festival in one of our cities I had wanted to attend but couldn't.

"Where are you going?" she asked.

I smiled, "Nowhere dangerous, I'll be back soon," I reassured her.

She nodded after a while, continuing with the bed sheets. "Fine then, but don't be gone for too long. I can only imagine they'll truly believe you've decided to finally rest for a day or two."

I ran up to her, kissing her cheek. "Thank you!"

"Of course, miss," Lissa smiled back at me, patting my head before returning to her work.

I walked back to my desk and picked up the small scroll and then my eyes shifted to my still bleeding wrist. I closed my eyes, taking in a deep breath, and in a bright flash of intricately woven lines fashioned by blood, I disappeared.

～

Kingdom of Lysmir,
Royal Palace, City of Lorys

Darkness was the first thing I saw. And silence was the first thing I heard, but not the silence that meant peace, or the tranquil kind; this silence hurt, it was filled with the agonizing feeling of terror. I looked around me, my eyes darting everywhere, taking everything in. I was in a hallway, made entirely of stone. The air was fresh and cold, as if nearby there was a window open.

I looked down at the scroll, then down the hall, where one end led to a metal door, and the other to a stairwell. I tapped the rolled up parchment on my hand, debating what to do.

The door or the stairwell. My feet carried me to the door. After all, I was closer to it than the stairs. I looked down at the scroll, cursing it for having led me here. I had used the tracking symbol hundreds of times, I knew how to draw it without mistake, so why had the letter not led me to the prince and instead to an empty hallway?

My hand lay gently on the handle of the door, my heart pounding. I gripped it tightly, and lowered it, letting the door slowly open in front of me. The light inside the room spilled over me, as I walked in.

On the floor, kneeling, head hanging, was the prince. I ran to him.

"Ivar!" His eyes met mine, big and afraid.

"S—Sivrehya?"

"Yeah, me. I got your message—" I looked up from the scroll in my hands. Ivar didn't move. I leaned back, seeing his hands bound behind him with thick ugly silver bracelets.

"Why—why are you in chains?"

"What are you doing here?" Panic shot through his voice, his eyes painfully wide. I gulped the moment his eyes flickered from me to something, or someone, behind me. I stilled, hearing the footsteps behind me stop, the low chuckle.

"Hello, Sivrehya Rithloren."

That voice. I knew it, all too well. I turned around, slowly, and my eyes met his.

I almost swayed with shock, as it hit me square in the chest. I watched him walk over, unable to breathe. This man was *dead*. He had been exiled from the kingdom years ago, after his treasons against us were uncovered and word got back to the kingdom that he was found *dead*, near Lysmir of all places, but dead all the same.

And here he stood, very much breathing, color to his skin, red eyes glowing, a vicious smile on his harsh yet thinned face. He had the same scars running down the left side face as always, but he wore a newer one now, running down his jaw to his neck. I always found it strange that he never healed them.

His clothing fit him oddly. No longer was he dressed in Merisan red and black but instead in grey and silver. His skin was paler than usual, and his dull red eyes had dark bags underneath them. His dark brown hair, once always braided with golden accents to his waist, was now close to being fully shaved off.

Standing there, hands clasped behind his back, looking famished and older by at least fifty years, he looked like a glorified prisoner.

I almost laughed. Of course, he was alive. Everything dead seemed to have come back to life, all at the same time. As if the world was playing a cruel joke on all of us.

Of all of the traitors, I thought, fighting back tears as old wounds threatened to tear themselves open. An acidic feeling, rotten and hot, grew inside me, as my heart beat inside my chest at an alarming rate. I felt sick. *Out of all the goddamned fucking traitors it had to be him. He had to be the one that lived.*

"Darholm," I grimaced, trying my best to keep my voice flat and unbothered. But my body had already betrayed me the moment our eyes met. I tensed, taking a step back, blinking as he made his way over me quickly. The train of his faded silver robes trailed behind him. My mind was spinning, trying to figure out how he was even alive, how he had survived what my father had done to him, what *I* had done to him.

"You're supposed to be dead," I growled, fisting my hands.

He let out a small laugh nonchalantly. "That makes two of us, Rithloren."

"What do—"

But my words were lost inside me the moment he grabbed me. I gasped, my instincts kicking in. None of this made sense. Darholm was alive and here of all fucking places, and the prince was in chains. The scroll in my hand fell to the ground. I spared seconds to watch it fall, suddenly remembering it was there.

It seemed to me that Ivar never wrote that message. He couldn't have, *wouldn't* have. I cursed myself, the realization hitting like a cold wind.

It had been a trap. My brother had done a similar trick just a few days ago. He had told me he sent a raven with a scroll that could transport the Lysmiran royals to Meris.

I tried to push away from Darholm, but his grip was like stone.

"Did *you* write the bloody message?" I demanded, staring into his eyes with hate, rage, with all the ugly emotions that weren't fear.

"No," he shrugged, "He did." He turned me, grabbing my face with his cold, wrinkled hands. I struggled in his grasp, but my eyes met another pair of silver ones. The king of Lysmir.

Suddenly, I was painfully aware of my heart beating in my chest. The blood was rushing through me as the world around me seemed to slow down. My head spun, the world spinning with it, as my breaths became short, labored, staggered. I tried calming down, I tried breathing, tried telling myself I was hallucinating, that this nightmare wasn't real.

"Father, let her go," Ivar demanded behind me, his voice scratchy. I heard the clash of chains. "This is betw—"

"Enough!" The king bellowed with such force that the walls of stone seemed to split. I watched, doing my best to mask the rising panic inside me, as the king walked over.

"Not so high and mighty now, are we, Your Highness?" His eyes glimmered with Darkness, like a black wave of evil had washed over them for just a split second to hide their silver glow.

I lifted my head against Darholm's grip, staring into the king's eyes with no intention of letting him or anyone else know that I was fearful. King Alaeric smiled, baring his stark white teeth as he came closer. I wished I could pinch my nose to save myself from his hot smelly breath.

"You don't seem like the one to break easily." The king leaned dangerously close to me, his eyes looking me up and down before finding their way to my eyes once more. "This is going to be fun."

I held back the urge to spit in his face. And when he was out of range, I regretted it immediately. Behind me, Darholm jerked me around and I almost tripped on the skirt of my long dress.

"Don't *fucking* touch me, you piece of shit."

"No." He spoke, his voice like hard steel, cold death. Soulless, heartless.

"The *hell* are you doing here anyway?" I seethed, thrashing in his strong, unrelenting grip.

"I think you can figure that one out, Your Highness," Darholm's chilling voice rang through the suddenly silent room. I looked into his eyes, and then I saw in their depths my answer.

I turned to face the king, who stood where he was, one hand on his sword, another hanging at his side. And then I looked back at Darholm, glaring death and infinite curses on him.

"You *traitor*," I seethed through gritted teeth. I raised my left leg to stomp on his toes with the heel of my shoe, but a sudden white-hot burst of pain rang through my body.

I opened my mouth but nothing came out, the scream stuck in my throat. My eyes landed on those of the prince, and they were wide, with shock, with fear, perhaps like mine. He screamed my name, chains crashing against each other, filling the room with metallic music.

I doubled over, onto Darholm, and when he moved, I fell. My hand flew to my waist to cover the wound. I closed my eyes, willing my blood to form into a healing spell. But my hand only quivered, and my blood kept spilling from me, trickling down my skirt, pooling onto the floor.

Jorus Darholm, once a confidant of the Merisan crown, to me, now twice a traitor, laughed his wicked laugh. He looked up at the ceiling, and though pained and suddenly weak, I followed it. My heart dropped at the sight of the bloody symbol against magic painted on the ceiling.

"Sivrehya!" The prince yelled amid the desperate clanking of chains.

I looked down, coughing, falling to the floor. My head hit the stone beneath me, tears falling from my eyes. The voices around me meshed together, faded. I could hear a laugh, and then another. I could see, through the tears, two silver figures standing tall in front of me.

Screaming, laughter blurred together. And the pain stood out because Dark Mother save me, there was so *much* pain. It was hot and sudden, like a flash of lightning across a night sky. Bright and scorching.

There were shadows in my vision, clouding it, obscuring it until there was only darkness. First a little, then it became a cocoon of black void, and then the cold crept up, and both weaved within each other creating the tapestry of my demise, the unforgiving blanket that enveloped me whole until I heard nothing, until I felt nothing.

Until there was simply nothing at all.

XXXVI : AMARIANNA WYSTERIAN

Kingdom of Vylara
Royal Palace, City of Vhis

– TWO DAYS BEFORE –

A small breeze whipped the front of Amarianna's bright and fiery orange hair all around. She had the rest of her lengthy hair tied back in a thick braid with lush green vines from a poisonous plant grown in her beautiful kingdom. Just minutes ago, a man had come to her, a loyal soldier, to tell her that the last of the suns and moons fell last night. Along with the displeasing news that she had lost two of her people, to a blood mage and soul mage.

Rage filled her tainted veins, fury climbing her like ivy did on ancient castle walls.

She would find those mages and destroy them herself. There was still a chance they would not know she and all chaos mages were very much alive. But Amarianna was not the one to leave anything to chance, and there was a sliver of a chance that the two mages might have figured out what their victims were.

And for her master plan to unfold perfectly, they would need to die. But she needed to remain in the shadows for just a bit longer. As she looked at the golden orange color of the sunrise, she decided she would later write a letter to her silver friend and request a small favor.

Yes, she thought, a terrifying smile curving into her features. *That will do just fine.*

Her eyes flickered from the sunrise and back down to the beauty below her.

Yes, her homeland had been destroyed almost five hundred years ago. But beauty is in the eye of the beholder, because after all, her kingdom to a stranger's eye might be nothing but ruined stone buildings with ivy vines and overgrown grass riding up its walls. But Amarianna Wysterian, princess of the Fallen Kingdom, princess of Vylara, a once proud empire, chose not to see her kingdom for what it was now. But instead for what it could be.

A place of beautiful chaos. With buildings that marked their power. With dark magic teeming in the air. With people under their rule, their crown, their reign. With her, sitting on the gold and forest green thrones, or perhaps standing on the balcony she was on now, gazing down at what they had created. A world of beautiful chaos. And Amarianna smiled wickedly, because she knew that one day, Vylara would rise again. *They* would rise again, and would take the world with them.

All she and Arkos had to do first was to destroy what stood in their way.

Which, of course, was *everything*.

TIMELINE OF RODESSIAN HISTORY

The timeline of Rodessian history is marked by the conquest of Empress Tesseria Aslaria Solavon of Otrina, as it was the first event that truly shaped the world. Because of that, the dates shall be written with BTC or ATC to indicate the years before or after the conquest of Empress Tesseria.

(This is an abridged version of Rodessian history. Only the most important dates and events are recorded.)

THE DARK AGES – 6,000 BTC to 1,000 BTC
When the Darkness flourished and was first thought to have come into existence. There are no traces of life in those dark times; however it is widely thought that there were in fact Shadowbenders. The Dark Ages were said to have lasted five thousand years.

AGE OF KINGDOMS – 1,000 BTC to 78 BTC
The first kingdoms rose and fell in this millennium; their names have been lost to history. And in the end, only the Kingdom of Otrina, which was then named an Empire when it overtook the fallen kingdoms, survived.

CREATION OF THE EMPIRE OF OTRINA – 78 BTC
The Kingdom of Otrina was named an Empire in 78 BTC when then King Mianos Solavon and Queen Liana Ilias completed their conquest of the smaller kingdoms who were weakened by the growing Darkness. Their children were: Princess Kallina (who would inherit the throne after her brother Crown Prince Liandor's death in 56 BTC due to an illness), and Princess Alis.

EMPRESS TESSERIA'S BIRTH – 23 BTC
The young empress was born on a sunny day in 23 BTC to Empress Kallina and King Jaeris Aslaria. Soon after her birth, at age five, she contracted a deadly disease called Decay Disease that was rumored to be

another product of the Darkness. It plagued Otrina and surrounding areas for decades and most who were touched by the disease died soon after. Tesseria Aslaria Solavon, however, did not, though she remained forever weakened because of it.

EMPRESS TESSERIA'S (FALSE) DEATH – 5 BTC

Tesseria Aslaria Solavon was thrown to the Darkness in the middle of the night by cloaked figures, said to be the guard of the family, as instructed by her younger brother, Prince Cassian and their mother, Empress Kallina. It is also said that Tesseria's lover, a stable boy whose name was lost to history, was killed on the same night that Tesseria was left to die.

THE REIGN OF EMPEROR CASSIAN – 5 BTC to 0

Emperor Cassian Aslaria Solavon was known to be a terrible ruler, who was cruel and unable to keep stability in the empire. Many wondered in those times what became of his mother. It is rumored he kept her in a cage at the top of the highest tower. During his reign, they were many rising rebel groups, each destroyed by the Emperor and his soldiers.

EMPRESS TESSERIA'S CONQUEST – 0 BTC

No one knows for certain how long the conquest took, but it lasted almost a year. After five years of growing her skills in Shadowbending, Tesseria Aslaria Solavon and her new-found allies stormed the palace of Otrina where she slayed her brother, slayed her mother and all those who had conspired in her demise. She was crowned Empress soon afterwards by an empire glad to see the reign of her brother over and their missing princess returned.

THE REIGN OF EMPRESS TESSERIA – 0 BTC to 52 ATC

The reign of Empress Tesseria Aslaria Solavon was the longest reign of any Otrinan monarch, before or after her. In her days, she was able to restore peace and the people in her empire were at ease and happy. She ruled with an iron fist but was known to be gentle and understanding. It is said she was the greatest ruler in the history of Rodessa, rivaled by the

Dark Siblings of their kingdoms who were also known as great rulers for their respective kingdoms.

FOR MORE INFORMATION ON THE OTRINAN RULERS BETWEEN EMPRESS TESSERIA AND EMPRESS FIONA, SEE THE ARCHIVES IN HISTORY SECTION OF ANY RODESSIAN LIBRARY.

BIRTH OF THE DARK CROWNS – 300 ATC

In the middle of the night, Empress Fiona gave birth to three children: Maehra, Luthyn and Vaehlys. They were said to be born as shadows, straight from her womb, who then turned to flesh with terrifying features. Red, silver, copper eyes. Black veins covered their bodies. And magic hummed beneath them, magic that was there and then hidden from the Otrinan empire for the safety of the imperial family. Empress Fiona died in childbirth. Her husband, Ezian Kolmire, became the new ruler of the Empire of Otrina.

THE DESTRUCTION OF RODESSA – 321 ATC to 322 ATC

In just one year, the Dark Crowns, using their powers, called forth the Darkness and destroyed Rodessa. (Let it be reminded that the Darkness was destroyed during the Age of Shadowbenders, which marks the beginning of Empress Tesseria's reign.) They first took Otrina, and in the present there is nothing left of the great empire that reigned for so many years. The Dark Siblings then took the world, the small villages and cities that grew at the borders of the kingdoms. There are those that followed them, that also showed the same powers as them. In little time, the Siblings created armies of blood, soul and chaos mages, and soon Rodessa was theirs.

THE SURVIVAL OF THE TWIN CITIES – 321 ATC

The Twin Cities, established in the years before the birth of the Dark Siblings, was able to survive the destruction of Rodessa thanks to the magic that it possessed. Lunar and solar was said to have come into existence in a similar way as the Shadowbenders had. While weakened, they survived and so lived on in the great city that became a harbor of knowledge throughout the entire world.

THE CREATION OF THE DARK KINGDOMS – 322 BTC

Soon after Rodessa was theirs, the Siblings decreed to make kingdoms of their own, for each of their kind. Taking words from their ancient language to create the names of cities and kingdoms, Maehra, Luthyn and Vaehlys created the three Dark Kingdoms: Meris, Lysmir and Vylara.

THE CREATION OF THE FREE CITIES – 290ish ATC to 325 ATC

The first of the Free Cities is the Twin Cities, said to have been established in 290 ATC or some years after. Soon after the creation of the Dark Kingdoms, the Siblings became less aware, or perhaps they did not care of the growing cities in the land that would then become known as The Land of the Free Cities. The second city was the fire mages, Ashmoor, 323 ATC. The fire mages of Otrina that survived created their own city. The third was the city of the surviving water mages, Rinelle, established in 324 ATC. The last of the Free Cities, Ferreow, was established in 325 ATC.

THE WAR OF THE DARK KINGDOMS – 705 ATC to 706 ATC

This was the bloodiest, deadliest war in the entire history of Rodessa, that lasted only half a year, but spanned between two. It was said that half of Lysmir and Meris lost their lives along with the entirety of the kingdom of Vylara. It started one fateful night, when King Harren and Queen Nessamira Wysterian of Vylara's forces fell upon the other two kingdoms. The two monarchs and their people (who were said to be convinced to conquer Meris and Lysmir by the royal family), wished to not only have Vylara but the land and power of the two kingdoms. But Meris and Lysmir allied soon after the first attack, and the forces of blood and soul mages rained on those of the chaos mages.

FALL OF THE KINGDOM OF VYLARA – 706 ATC

Vylara was not destroyed in one night, nor two. But three. Or so history says. The blood and soul mages ruthlessly tore apart each Vylaran city and killed all the chaos mages and all the members of the royal family, *the king, queen and their four children. The Fallen Kingdom was left to history and to the forest, and in the years since, no one has stepped foot in it and the kingdom was left to be a tale in the stories told to children and the books of history. Since the war, Meris and Lysmir remained allies, until mysterious deaths drove them apart as well.*

DEATH OF PRINCESS SIERAH RITHLOREN OF MERIS AND PRINCE FLOREK THAEGAN OF LYSMIR – 829 ATC

Princess Sierah Rithloren of Meris was the darling of her kingdom, and the first-born daughter to King Maximus and Queen Isilla. She was betrothed to the first-born child and son of King Orael and Queen Sylina of Lysmir. Both were said to be very much in love; however, before their marriage they disappeared and many suspected foul play. They were proven correct when three days before the young royals were meant to be married, their bodies appeared in their kingdoms. Sierah's soul had been destroyed, and Florek's body had been bled dry by a blood curse. The two kingdoms, despite being allies and friends, quickly blamed each other for the deaths, and thus started the ever-growing tension and animosity between Meris and Lysmir. The deaths of Princess Sierah and Prince Florek were never solved, and their murderers, never captured.

DEATH OF CROWN PRINCE LAIDON RITHLOREN OF MERIS – 922 ATC

Whether the crown prince was murdered or whether he was simply killed by an accident of his own making is something that has plagued the Merisans and history for years. Though, what is certain, is that one tragic spring morning Laidon Rithloren was found dead, his body broken and very bloody. Rumors would fill the streets of both Meris and Lysmir for months before quieting down. Though it should be known that soul mages were not known to express any sort of condolences.

DEATH OF PRINCESS AVILYN THAEGAN OF LYSMIR – 928 ATC

From the words of the Prince Ivar Thaegan himself, Princess Avilyn was first kidnapped and tortured before her untimely death. Those responsible for the former, were caught and killed by King Alaeric and Prince Ivar himself. The one who murdered the young princess in her room, however, was not. It was an unfortunate day for the entire kingdom, though one can imagine the Merisans did not care in the slightest. The unfortunate event would also spark Queen Soriel Thaegan's death some time later, another tragedy for the Lysmirans.

DEATH OF KING ROLAN RITHLOREN OF MERIS AND CROWN PRINCESS VERENA THAEGAN OF LYSMIR – 934 ATC

King Rolan of Meris and the Crown Princess Verena of Lysmir were found murdered in their respective beds on the morning of fateful spring day in 934 BTC. King Rolan's soul had been destroyed and Crown Princess Verena's body had been bled dry by a blood curse. The two kingdoms once again blamed each other for the deaths and King Alaeric Thaegan of Lysmir, on an afternoon in 934 BTC declared war on the Kingdom of Meris.

But what was to become of the two powerful monarchies and the blood and soul mages alike would be left for the future to decide.

PRONUNCIATION GUIDE

THE MERISANS (MARE-is-ans)

Maehra Rithloren – MAY-ruh RITH-loren
Isilla Rithloren – ISS-illah
Maximus Rithloren – MAX-e-mus
Sierah Rithloren – SEE-air-ah
Valoria Rithloren – Va-LOR-ia
Rolan Rithloren – RO-lan
Laidon Rithloren – LAY-don
Daemon Rithloren – DAY-mon
Rhiannyn Rithloren – Ria-NIN
Sivrehya Rithloren – Siv-RAY-ah
Silian Faraday – SIL-e-an FAIR-ah-day
Visiria Faraday – Vi-SEE-re-ah
Jace Faraday – Jace
Jorus Darholm – JOR-us DAR-holme
Ivanov – IVE-in-off
Killian –KILL-ian
Lissa – LISS-ah
Ophelia – Oh-FEEL-e- ah

THE LYSMIRANS (Lis-MEER-ee-ans)

Torin Elfaed – TORR-in ELF-aid
Sylina Thaegan – Sill-INA THAY-gin ("g" like "gorge")
Orael Thaegan – Or-AYE-ill
Florek Thaegan – FLOOR-ik
Alaeric Thaegan – Uhl-AIR-ic
Soriel Thaegan – SORE-e-elle
Verena Thaegan – Ver-ENNA
Ivar Thaegan – AYE-var
Avilyn Thaegan – AV-uh-lin
Dorian Salvaen – DOOR-e-an SAL-vain
Alanna Salvaen – Ah-LAN-ah

Maeghalin Salvaen – MEG-a-lin
Avran Salvaen – Ahv-RIN

THE VYLARANS (Vill-ARE-ans)
(See timeline)
Harren Wysterian – HAIR-in Wis-TEAR-e-an
Nessamira Wysterian – Ness-AH-meer-ah
Lorelei Wysterian – LORE-el-i
Arkos Wysterian – ARC-os
Amarianna Wysterian – Ah-MAR-e-anna
Sylaria Aolaine – Sil-AR-ia A-o-laine
Abriel Vasstrid – Ab-REE-elle VAS-trid

THE SUNSIERANS AND MOONSIERANS
Sabah Malan – SAH-bah MAH-lan
Junah Malan – JUNE-ah
Kason Rajmani – KAY-sun Raj-MAH-nee
Soha – SO-ha
Feba – Feh-BAH
Mahin – MAW-hin
Nooran – New-RON
Suran – Sur-ON
Ishan – EEE-shan
Khadir – Kah-DEER
Fardin – FAR-din
Cyra – SEE-rah
Biva – BEE-vah
Fara – FAR-ah

THE OTRINANS (AW-tree-nans)
(See timeline)
Mianos Solavon – ME-an-os Soul-AH-vaughn
Liana Ilias – Lie-ANNA Ill-EE-is
Liandor Ilias Solavon – Lie-ANNE-door
Kallina Ilias Solavon – Call-INA

Alis Ilias Solavon – Alice
Jaeris Aslaria – JER-is As-LAR-ia
Tesseria Aslaria Solavon – Tess-EAR-ia
Cassian Aslaria Solavon – CAS-ee-an
Fiona Salvaen – Fee-ONA
Ezian Kolmire – Ez-EE-an Coal-my-ER

CREATURES IN RODESSA
Neithisis – NYE-thuh-sis
Obscurae – Ob-SCURE-a
Taenebris – Ten-UH-bris
Peryton – PAIR-uh-ton

KINGDOMS / EMPIRES OF RODESSA
Otrina – AW-tree-nah
Meris – MARE-is
Lysmir – Lis-MEER
Vylara – VILL-are-ah

KINGDOM CITIES
Maeh – May
Risno – RIZ-no
Lorys – LOR-is
Vhis – Vis

FREE CITIES
Moonsier – MOON-seer
Sunsier – SUN-seer
Ashmoor – ASH-more
Rinelle – Rin-ELLE
Ferreow – FARE-uh-OH

PLACES IN RODESSA
Palace Iishraq – Palace EESH-rack
Nivrashmo Street – Neev-RASH-mo Street

Sourielian Forest – Sore-EEL-ian Forest
Raven Mountains – Raven Mountains

COUNTRIES OF THE WORLD

Pyatov – PIA-tov
Soteros – Su-TARE-us
Shao Yun – SHAY yoon
Azaneh – Az-an-NAY
Navias – NAW-vee-us

ACKNOWLEDGEMENTS

~

One doesn't usually think, as I did before writing this book, about all that's behind the book, the story, the words. When one reads a book, one reads of the world being built, the characters who belong to it, but they might not really realize the blood, sweat, tears and stress that imagined the world and the story and the people.

I knew writing a book would be no easy task, however, I never in a million years thought it would be this hard. But as hard as it was, it was so rewarding as well. And though, while writing I was alone, in my own little world imagining wonderful and dark things with my earbuds in, throughout the entire process of writing this book, I was grateful enough to be surrounded by people who believed in this story as much as me.

I'd like the start by thanking all my friends. Also, Teah, Emily, for being there when I had questions, for answering them. Thank you for the simple things like telling me through the stress rushes that it'd be okay, that it'd be worth it, and also thank you for being there when I had to gush about something because I was too excited to keep them inside.

Next, I'd like to thank my parents. For being there, for believing in me, for helping me. You've both supported every one of my strange dreams, especially this one. For that, I will be forever grateful, so thank you a million times. Mamma, thank you for pushing me to pursue this story. Without that, without you, this story might have not even existed. I love you both very much.

Thank you to my editor, coach and the answerer to all my countless questions, Kim. You have loved the idea from the beginning, you adored Sivrehya and Ivar (despite him being slightly a jerk at times) just as much as I did and because of you I was able to share their magical, dark (and dangerous) story. Thank you for answering all my questions, for helping me share this book, the beginning of Siv and Ivar's and everybody else's story with the world.

And finally, I want to thank all of you. Thank you for picking this book up, for reading it, for experiencing Siv and Ivar's journey. This may have just started as a project simply because I wanted to read this book, but it's become so much more now. So, thank you.

CPSIA information can be obtained
at www.ICGtesting.com
Printed in the USA
LVHW080415160122
708507LV00010B/478/J